Fiona McCallum has enjoyed a life of contrasts. She was raised on a cereal and wool farm in rural South Australia and then moved to inner-city Melbourne to study at university as a mature-age student. Accidentally starting a writing and editing consultancy saw her mixing in corporate circles in Melbourne and then Sydney. She returned to Adelaide for a slower paced life and to chase her dream of becoming an author – which took nearly a decade full of rejections from agents and publishers to achieve. Fiona now works as a full-time novelist and really is proof dreams can come true. Fiona writes heartwarming stories of self-discovery that draw on her life experiences, love of animals and fascination with the human condition. She is the author of ten Australian bestsellers: *Paycheque*, *Nowhere Else*, *Wattle Creek*, *Saving Grace*, *Time Will Tell*, *Meant To Be*, *Leap of Faith*, *Standing Strong*, *Finding Hannah* and *Making Peace*. *A Life of Her Own* is Fiona's eleventh novel.

More information about Fiona and her books can be found on her website, www.fionamccallum.com. Fiona can also be followed on Facebook at www.facebook.com/Fiona McCallum-author.

T0363143

Also by Fiona McCallum

Paycheque
Nowhere Else
Leap of Faith

The Wattle Creek series
Wattle Creek
Standing Strong

The Button Jar series
Saving Grace
Time Will Tell
Meant To Be

Finding Hannah
Making Peace

FIONA McCALLUM

A Life of Her Own

First Published 2019
Second Australian Paperback Edition 2020
ISBN 9781489287250

A LIFE OF HER OWN
© 2019 by Fiona McCallum
Australian Copyright 2019
New Zealand Copyright 2019

Published by
HQ Fiction
An imprint of Harlequin Enterprises (Australia) Pty Limited (ABN 47 001 180 918), a subsidiary of HarperCollins Publishers Australia Pty Limited (ABN 36 009 913 517)
Level 13, 201 Elizabeth St
SYDNEY NSW 2000
AUSTRALIA

® and TM (apart from those relating to FSC®) are trademarks of Harlequin Enterprises (Australia) Pty Limited or its corporate affiliates. Trademarks indicated with ® are registered in Australia, New Zealand and in other countries.

A catalogue record for this book is available from the National Library of Australia
www.librariesaustralia.nla.gov.au

Printed and bound in Australia by McPherson's Printing Group

To all who have been preyed upon by bullies and manipulators: May you find your strength, freedom and peace.

Chapter One

Alice heard David's key in the front door. She raced up the hall and waited until he'd put his bags down and closed the door behind him before throwing her arms around his neck.

'Welcome home – to your new home!' she cried, determined to treat it as a celebration. He travelled so much she usually didn't bother to make a fuss on his return – for David, coming back from Europe or Asia was pretty much the same as coming in from the Melbourne office half an hour away – but as it was the first time he'd come home to their new abode, she thought it warranted a bit of extra fuss.

'Thanks,' he said, grinning. 'Hooray, all the boxes have gone. Well done, you.' He pecked her on the lips before easing her away from him.

Alice didn't feel as if she'd been dismissed – they weren't a very touchy-feely couple. She'd been a little disappointed in the beginning, nearly four years ago, but she had become accustomed to his lack of romance and displays of affection. David had plenty of other fine qualities.

'I'm a bit manky,' he said. 'I didn't get to have a shower in Singapore.' He left his bags where they were and strode down the hall, into their spacious open-plan living and dining area. 'Oh, wow, how much better does this place look with everything unpacked?' He folded his arms across his chest and slowly did a three-sixty degree turn, taking in the space, a smug, satisfied expression plastered across his face. 'Yum, something smells good.'

'I've got a lasagne in the oven. I thought you might be craving something home cooked.'

'Sounds perfect,' he said with a contented sigh. 'Do I have time for a quick shower?'

'Yep. No problem.'

*

Alice was just putting their plates heaped with lasagne and green salad on the table when David walked back in. She smiled at seeing his tousled dark hair and casual attire – loose track pants and t-shirt. She loved him in a suit too, but to Alice this was more her man, and a side no one at his work ever saw. David Green was the epitome of cool, calm, collected, controlled, and driven – and he dressed accordingly. Sometimes it seemed to Alice as if by putting on his suit David was putting on a costume and getting into character. She had always kept this thought to herself. David didn't like being made fun of, no matter how innocuous. Not that he didn't have a sense of humour. He did. But he was very ambitious and took his career, money and success very seriously. He'd worked hard to be able to afford this house – well, for the deposit, anyway.

They were staring down the barrel of thirty years of being tethered to the bank. Of course Alice had helped a little with the hefty deposit. She would have been happy with a small fixer-upper, but that didn't suit the image David was keen to project. Anyway, with him travelling all the time, when would it ever get done up? No, this place might not exactly be to her taste, but it was a sensible plan for their future. And oh how she loved no longer having to traipse from property to property all weekend, every weekend, and stand around at auctions being beaten by wealthy, cashed-up investors who were simply adding to their portfolios.

A little over a month ago, she'd been stunned when she realised they were the successful bidders for this place, so much so she'd stood there in silence for a moment wondering what had happened after the hammer had gone down. And then, instead of jumping up and down, Alice and David had stared at each other with their mouths open and eyes wide until real estate agents flanked them and clasped them each by an elbow and urged them towards the house to sign the papers.

Now, here they were, in for just over a week and boxes and all signs of moving out of sight. They were now able to properly breathe and settle into their new home. Alice was sure she'd grow to love it, find character in its new construction and clean, sharp lines, and bright white walls.

'So, tell me about your trip,' Alice said after they'd clinked glasses of wine and each taken a long, satisfied sip.

'Same old. Planes, meetings, hotel rooms, lunches, dinners, and not much else. How was your week? Hopefully more interesting than mine, though unpacking probably isn't so much fun. I hope you managed to rake up some hours for Todd.'

'I have some news on that front, actually. Look what Todd gave me today,' she said, taking a large envelope from the chair beside her and handing it to David. Todd was a friend of David's from uni – a few months ago he had given her a casual job doing some market research and cold-calling for the packaging firm where he was business development manager.

'What's this?' David asked, opening it up.

Alice didn't say a word while he extracted two A4 pages and slowly read them. After she and Todd had talked about the offer, Alice had left the CEO's office feeling as if she'd been given the opportunity of a lifetime, even if she wasn't all that excited about it. She'd felt flattered, which was a pleasant change after all the fruitless job hunting she'd done. But the more she thought about it, the less excited she became. Marketing for packaging? She'd rolled it around on her tongue several times, trying to muster some enthusiasm, and failed. If it were not for the fact Todd was a friend and would mention it to David in due course, if he hadn't already, she might have torn the offer up and pretended it had never existed. Anyway, what successful company took a risk on an unknown like Alice with such an important position as marketing?

'Oh wow. A permanent job. That's great,' David said, leaning over and kissing her. 'Phew, well, we certainly need this,' he added.

'Yeah,' Alice said, digging her fork into her meal.

'So why haven't you signed it yet? Or is this a copy?'

'No, that's the one I have to sign.'

David looked up at her over the document, clearly waiting for an explanation. She hated the way he could reduce her to feeling inadequate, even child-like with just that one look.

'Sorry, David, but I don't want to do it. I'm just not excited about it.' She shrugged.

'It's an amazing opportunity. Look at this, they're going to train you up in marketing and you could be national marketing manager in a year. Wow, Alice, that's huge!'

Yes, I have actually read it, Alice thought.

Why wasn't he getting it, hearing her? She wanted to scream with frustration. Instead she tried a different tack. 'It is a bit strange. I mean, I don't even have any marketing qualifications. That's a whole degree right there.' She really didn't want to disappoint him, but ...

'So? If they didn't think you were capable they wouldn't be making the offer. And we really do need the extra money. How do you know you won't grow to love it if you don't give it a chance?'

How else do I say it just doesn't float my boat?

'A challenge is a good thing,' he said, misreading her silence. 'Look how well you did at uni when to start with you didn't think you could do it. You've got to believe in yourself, Alice.'

'It's not that I don't think I could do it – with the appropriate training ...'

'So, what, then?'

'I've told you, it just doesn't interest me.' She hated how petty and ungrateful she sounded. But it was the truth. And why shouldn't she be honest with her partner, the man she loved?

'You can't keep waiting for a museum job, or whatever, to come up. It might never happen.'

He was right about that. And that it was an opportunity when she hadn't found anything else promising.

'And you can't stay at uni. We've discussed this,' he said, reading her mind, and let out a tired, exasperated sigh. He was right – again. What Alice really wanted to do was stay at university and do honours in History, despite not having settled on an area she really wanted to delve into in depth. She'd just loved university life, full stop. Being surrounded by books and knowledge and people passionate about learning, being encouraged to think for herself, and be analytical had really stretched Alice intellectually for the first time in her life. She'd realised she had an insatiable thirst for knowledge. She hadn't always found her studies easy, but she'd enjoyed being challenged and had discovered an energy and sense of determination she never knew she had. The three years at uni had been filled with moments of joy and excitement as well as hard work. Now it was over, and she was scared – well, terrified, actually. She really didn't want to disappoint David. But if she had to get a full-time job, she wanted one she was truly excited about – otherwise she figured she might as well go back to admin temping. Her eyes had been opened, her soul fired up, now she wanted more, to keep moving forward. In that sense, university had proven to be a double-edged sword.

David should understand that – after all, it was because of him that she'd embarked on her studies in the first place. He'd seen her change, watched as her wings had unfurled, all the time telling her how proud he was of her progress and achievements. Gradually Alice had begun to believe she could be more than a wife and mother in a small town in country South Australia, contrary to her mother's indoctrination.

Alice had met David in Adelaide, at a party held by a friend of a friend. Only a few weeks before, her marriage to farmer Rick had imploded. She'd fled Hope Springs, Rick, and her unsupportive mother, Dawn, and her sister, Olivia. Without her dear friend Ruth she might never have had the courage to leave the district. Ruth was a warm, loving mother figure to her, the opposite to Alice's own mother. She had organised for Alice to stay with her daughter Tracy in Adelaide while Alice tried to pull herself together and deal with two-fold heartbreak – the end of her marriage and losing her best friend of twenty-five years, Shannon, who'd let slip she'd slept with Alice's husband. Only the once, mind! And it really didn't mean anything – according to both Shannon and Rick. As if that made a difference!

In the days and weeks after finding out about the betrayal, Alice struggled with her anger and disappointment. She didn't know who had hurt her the most, then concluded that Shannon's actions were the more painful and their friendship was actually the bigger loss. Shannon and Alice had been best friends since meeting on their first day at kindergarten and were the last of their school group still living in the district. One by one their friends had left for a job, a relationship, to study or travel, or just to have a better or different life. Once a close group, these days their interactions were mainly confined to Facebook, email, or the odd text message.

After the experience with Shannon and Rick, Alice vowed never to let anyone get so close again. Ruth told her the pain would ease and to not let it change her generosity of spirit. Unfortunately Alice thought it probably already had. She came to understand first-hand the meaning of the saying 'Once bitten, twice shy'.

Alice hadn't planned to stay in Adelaide permanently – Hope Springs and its surrounds were all she'd ever known and thought she wanted.

The last thing on her mind when she met the alluring, friendly, confident and sophisticated David had been finding a new love interest, so instead of being coy or mysterious or flirty, she'd confided in him about what a mess her life had become.

When David suggested that going to university might be the answer, Alice had been taken aback. She'd never considered it before – she had only been an average student at school and had no burning career desires. She'd always thought she'd work alongside her dad in the family's corner shop and, being the elder sibling, eventually take over when the time was right. But soon after her father died, her mother had dropped a bombshell – the shop would go to the younger daughter. Olivia was always the golden child, and the chosen one now too. Alice had sought solace in an admin job at the largest business in town – an insurance brokerage. She loved her job, but was shocked when four years in she was let go in favour of the boss's teenage daughter, who had just returned from secretarial school in Adelaide.

David pointed out that a few years at university would give Alice time to sort herself out while having a focus, and she could see it made sense. When he added that she could afford to live in the city by working part-time in admin or temping, it became possible, and exciting. Over the weeks and months Alice slowly began to believe him and, more importantly, to believe in herself.

They were meant to just be friends, but it soon became physical, and gradually they seemed to form a stronger bond. When David announced he was moving to Melbourne, Alice was devastated. He'd become her rock. But then he suggested she could come too, if she wanted to. It wasn't a marriage proposal or declaration of together forever, or even love. He wasn't gushy or very emotive, but Alice didn't mind. David was dependable and supportive and was offering something completely different from her old life, and that was what mattered and appealed. She wasn't even sure she believed in true love anymore, certainly not happily ever after. Maybe she just needed time.

Alice made the big move to Melbourne with not much more than a few suitcases and a ten-year-old hatchback car, which she'd sold soon after. Now, nearly four years on, she felt so much bigger than Hope Springs – not better, but that she'd outgrown it – and only went back for significant events such as Christmas, weddings, funerals and milestone birthdays.

Having found her feet and discovering that she really loved to study, Alice had well and truly left behind her average student status and excelled academically. Being realistic, she knew she had to find a full-time job, and she wasn't sure she wanted to become an academic, but the extra year of study would surely help her prospects. Four months on from uni – not to mention just turning thirty – she still hadn't sorted out a proper career. She'd volunteered for a day a week at the National Trust head office in various departments and enjoyed every minute of it, but unfortunately there weren't any paid jobs going, especially for someone who didn't have a specialist area of expertise or post-graduate qualifications. She'd love to be in archiving, doing research, helping others with their research, or involved in writing policy, but she hadn't found any vacancies for jobs that came even remotely close to what interested her.

At her graduation a few weeks ago she'd felt quite sad when she realised that her university days were behind her and it was unlikely she'd ever be able to go back to study. She was almost on the verge of tears – not at all triumphant and excited like everyone else. It hadn't helped that none of her family had been prepared to make the trip from South Australia, especially as she was the first in her entire family – cousins included – to go to university, let alone graduate. Alice suspected her mother and sister's disinterest had more to do with jealousy or tall poppy syndrome than the inconvenience of travelling to Melbourne. It wasn't a secret that they thought Alice saw herself as high and mighty for leaving Hope Springs, and completely above herself for daring to study at university.

'Alice?' David prompted, his eyebrows raised.

'I know,' she said, her thoughts turning back to the offer letter on the table in front of her. Yes, she was being picky. But why shouldn't she want to do something she was at least a little excited about? *And what sort of a name for a business is Outercover? Even if it is packaging.*

'Well, you've got the weekend to think about it. But we can't afford for you to be too choosy. The salary is good. It's a good job.'

Alice stared down at her plate of food, her appetite having left her. David was right. He usually was. She needed to forget uni, and start being a proper adult and an active contributor to society, and their bank balance. Not that she hadn't been, but she thought she'd never have an income that would equal David's – even this 'good' salary was only around a third what he earned.

Okay, so come on, get excited about it. It's a great job. Be grateful, she told herself as she forcibly chewed a mouthful of pasta.

'Todd's nice and you said everyone else there seems nice too,' David added.

'Yes, they are.' And wasn't that a good enough reason on its own?

'Half of any job is the people,' David pointed out.

'You're right. I'll accept it on Monday,' she said, smiling as she stood up and started to load the dishwasher.

David smiled. 'All change is scary. You'll be right. You just have to push through it,' he said, drawing her to him and kissing her.

'I know,' she said quietly.

'I've got an idea. We should celebrate – the new job and the house – and I know exactly how.'

'How?' Alice said, brightening and looking up at him.

'Let's go to the pet store and get a dog. Now we don't have a landlord who doesn't like pets. And it'll be good training for us ...'

'Oh, wow. Really? You mean it?' Alice nearly skipped in excitement, but restrained herself.

'I don't say things I don't mean, Alice.'

Well, you do, actually. Quite often, Alice thought, but let it go.

'Can we go to one of the shelters instead?'

'Sure. Whatever you want,' he said, yawning. 'I'm knackered. I'm just going to check my emails and then have an early night.'

'Okay, I'll be in soon.' Alice smiled, properly this time. She was going to get her tablet out and look at what dogs were available for adoption. Something small but not one of the shrill, yappy breeds. They didn't want to bother their new neighbours with a barking dog when they were both at work all day. They didn't have much of a backyard but thankfully the park was only a few streets away.

Chapter Two

Alice sat at reception to do an hour-long stint filling in while Chelsea, the usual receptionist, went out to run a few errands. She hated doing reception duties, but as the casual, Alice didn't feel she could refuse when asked. It didn't help that she was tired after a couple of sleepless nights, thanks to their new Jack Russell terrier.

She couldn't believe such a beautiful dog was at the RSPCA shelter. Her heart ached to think of what the story of Bill's first two years of life might contain. She and David had walked along the rows of cages, keeping their distance, before Alice had led the way back to Bill's. He appealed to her because he was unlikely to be as raucous as a puppy and as he was an adult they might have a better chance of knowing his true personality from the outset. She was also drawn to him because he appeared smart and curious, and a little sad but not frightened.

Bill sat back against the wall and observed Alice as she was observing him. This went on for a few minutes until he came over, sniffed the hand she offered through the wire and then sat and gave her fingers a lick before sitting back on his haunches just out of reach. When Alice went into the cage to sit with him, Bill greeted her like a long-lost friend, circling her while wagging his tail so fast that his whole body gyrated. He then threw himself into Alice's lap and stood up with his paws on her chest, trying to deposit slobbery wet kisses on her neck. After his brief burst of exuberance, Bill curled up in her lap and settled for a nap. Looking down at him, Alice knew the deal was sealed – well, from her end, anyway. David approved because he was a handsome looking dog and not 'one of those dangerous breeds the Bogans have'. Alice couldn't be bothered pointing out that the RSPCA had a duty of care and wouldn't offer dangerous or untested dogs for rehoming. She didn't like the look of the thickset, bullish type of dogs anyway. She loved German Shepherds and Kelpies and Border Collies, but would never want to keep one cooped up in a small yard. Alice thought those breeds needed to run for miles, chase and round things up, to be truly happy.

They purchased Bill along with all the bedding, toys, food, treats and assorted stuff that would be needed to ensure his comfort, and made their way home with Alice talking non-stop to the dog, reassuring him. David remained silent – most likely too busy holding his breath in the hope the dog wouldn't soil the Beemer, Alice thought.

They spent the rest of Saturday showing Bill around the house and settling him in. While cooking dinner that night, Alice had looked out the kitchen window and smiled when she saw David on the small patch of lawn in the backyard, testing Bill's obedience with treats and tossing him a tennis ball. She laughed out loud when she noticed that it was David doing the fetching.

'He's got you sussed,' she said when she went outside to join them.

'I know. Call me a sucker,' David said, laughing. 'Mate, I'm taking it easy on you today because you're new,' he told Bill, who was sitting with what looked like a big grin on his face, his tail wagging.

When they called Bill for dinner he trotted in carrying his tennis ball. He gently deposited it between David and Alice and sat to attention, looking from one to the other as if waiting for it to be tossed. David and Alice laughed.

'Aww, who's a clever boy?' Alice said, leaning down and patting the dog.

'Later, Bill, not in the house,' David said firmly.

'Go and lie down on your bed,' Alice commanded, and was actually a little surprised when Bill obeyed, taking his ball with him.

'That's one smart dog,' David said with obvious satisfaction as he set the table.

'But he looks so sad.'

'Better get used to it. I wouldn't be surprised if that's his signature move. We're going to have to learn to ignore him a bit.'

'Hmm, yes, we don't want him spoilt and naughty.'

'Or fat – I might have given him too many treats before.'

'Yep, I think saying no is definitely going to be the hardest thing,' Alice said, and turned her attention back to dishing up their meals.

All had been well until it was time for bed and Bill was left on the other side of the closed bedroom door. After he'd whined for seemingly hours, Alice wanted to relent and bring his bed in and let him sleep on the floor. But David reminded her that they'd agreed the dog needed discipline, boundaries and consistent routine, and insisted Bill stay where he was while grumbling that he hoped the dog wasn't doing any damage. Reluctantly

Alice agreed, briefly wondering how they would be when it came to agreeing on how to raise a child. She pushed the thought aside. It was not something to dwell on at three o'clock in the morning.

When the alarm went off on Monday they both dragged themselves through the shower and off to work, after too little sleep thanks to their naughty but loveable new dog. The second night had been a little better, with Bill settling down at around two, when Alice and David could finally get some sleep. At least he hadn't shown any inclination towards chewing anything he shouldn't, and there hadn't been any toileting accidents, Alice thought with huge relief as she reluctantly got ready for work.

She blocked open the sliding glass door just enough so Bill could squeeze through to get outside if he needed to and not so much that anyone could get inside. She really hadn't wanted to leave and had hovered in the hall patting the dog for ages. Being a casual employee, she didn't get paid if she didn't turn up and calling in sick wouldn't be a good look, especially when Todd would have seen her and David's Facebook posts announcing the new arrival. He would know the real reason why she didn't come in. Anyway, she was going to accept the permanent position today, even though she still hadn't signed the contract.

At the reception desk, Alice wished the phone would ring or someone would walk in and she'd have something to do. Sitting around with nothing going on wasn't helping her state of tiredness at all. She'd give her left pinkie to curl up under the desk and take a nap. She was afraid of getting caught with her eyes closed, but she was losing the fight to keep them open. Her phone pinged, but checking messages or talking on her mobile while on reception was an absolute no-no.

She looked up on hearing quick, heavy footsteps on the polished floorboards. Someone was walking towards her from down the hall where all the offices were located. *Please don't be Todd or Aaron wanting the signed contract.* It was Aaron. She heard his voice before she saw him stride past without looking at her, heading to the photocopier at the far side of the room. He held his mobile up to his ear and he was now shouting to whoever was on the other end – something about a fucking debacle and heads rolling. He was beyond red – more a purplish colour. *Careful, you'll have a heart attack.* Alice looked down so she wasn't in his line of sight if he turned around.

The next moment she heard the distinctive sound of the photocopier's lid being raised, none too gently – the creak of the hinges straining – and then a crash of plastic as it was closed again, hard. She could hear buttons being stabbed at with fingers, over and over, and Aaron growling. Alice slowly raised her gaze. He was ending the call. She half expected to see the phone flying towards her, but watched as he roughly shoved it into his trouser pocket. Then he started shouting at the machine in front of him. Someone should point out that he needed to – gently – press the button to take it off standby before it would be any use to him, but Alice wasn't about to be the one breaking that particular news.

Her eyes bugged when in the next second Aaron ripped the lid up and shouted, 'Oh for fuck's sake! Fucking work, you stupid fucking thing!' Then he slammed his clenched fist onto the glass bed holding the sheet of paper he was presumably trying to scan or copy. There was an almighty crash and the unmistakable crack and splintering of glass. Alice ducked her head down behind the panel in front of the reception desk. Her heart was racing. She didn't have a problem with swearing, could let out a few choice words of her own when the need and feeling arose, and she hadn't exactly been raised in a gentle household, but she did have a problem with aggression and violence.

What should I do? Her flight instinct was kicking in, but she was trapped behind the desk. There was no getting out without passing within striking distance of Aaron. Alice began to feel queasy.

Suddenly the front door opened. On shaking legs, Alice pushed back into her chair and sat up straight, willing the heavy thumping in her chest to ease as she took in a deep breath. A man in taxi company livery walked in.

'Taxi for Aaron Troubridge?' he said, beaming at Alice.

'About fucking time! You're late!' Aaron shouted, striding across the room before Alice had a chance to say anything. 'And get that fucking thing fixed!' he said, pointing back towards the photocopier as he passed by.

Alice's heart was beating wildly. She ventured over to check the damage – yes, there was indeed a big crack diagonally across the glass. Back at the desk she retrieved the number of the copier repair business the company used and wrote it on a sticky note. Her fingers and voice were still a little too shaky to call yet. Thankfully the phone hadn't rung. And so far no one else had needed to use the copier.

'Are you okay? What the hell was all that commotion?' Steve from sales appeared at the end of the hallway.

'Um, Aaron just tried to put his hand through the photocopier in a fit of rage.'

'Shit. Are you all right?'

Um, no, not really. 'I'm fine. But I'd better get someone to come around and fix it.'

Steve went over to the copier and lifted the lid. 'Christ, I thought you were exaggerating.' He looked back to Alice with wide eyes. 'He really did a number on it.'

'Yup. He certainly did.'

'You sure you're okay? You look a little pale. Can I get you a cup of tea, glass of water, or something?'

'I am a little shaken up, to be honest. Thanks, but I'll be okay.' *Can I go home and be with Bill?*

Actually, Alice did need a cup of tea, which she realised as soon as she'd taken the first sip of the sweet milky tea Steve had delivered to her desk without another word – simply a sympathetic smile – a few minutes later. One by one staff members filed past and expressed their disappointment in the situation and what Alice had had to witness. Gradually she came to realise no one was actually expressing any surprise. She was relieved when Chelsea came bouncing back in and walked around behind the reception desk to unload some bags of stationery supplies.

'What?' she said, looking at Alice who was trying to find the right words to say, the right questions to ask. 'Yeah, I heard about Aaron's hissy fit,' she said. 'Paula in accounts texted me.' She waved a dismissive hand. 'Don't worry about it. He gets over things pretty quick. I'm sure he'll be fine by the time he gets back.'

Alice had to stop her mouth from dropping open. There was nothing fine about what happened, and certainly nothing to be flippant or dismissive about. Oh well, it doesn't really matter, she wouldn't be here much longer. It was a small company and she knew that since the marketing manager had left, all marketing for the company was under Aaron's control. There was no way she was taking a job that would mean working closely with such a man, regardless of how good the salary was and the great opportunities down the track. He was the founding owner of the business, so Alice was sure there would be no repercussions, no change of behaviour.

'I've called the photocopier people. They'll have someone here as soon as they can,' Alice said, picking up her handbag and coffee mug.

'We're probably keeping their service department going. No, it's not the first time,' Chelsea said, rolling her eyes.

'Right,' was all Alice could manage in reply. 'Well, have a great day,' she said as she left with a wave.

'Thanks for filling in. Sorry you had to … you know.'

Alice offered a weak smile in response before hurrying along the hall and then up the three flights of squeaky stairs to her office at the top of the ancient building. The term 'office' was being far too generous – it was barely more than a cupboard, and didn't even have an air-conditioning duct. It had been as hot as a furnace during the middle of summer. Thankfully it had a small sash window that opened just enough to let out some of the stifling air. She squeezed her long legs behind the small but sturdy desk that took up nearly all the space, feeling pleased that she was tucked away from the action in the offices below. The solid old stone walls and heavy desk for protection in front of her had never felt so comforting. She reached into her bag and drew out the envelope containing the offer letter and the contract, opened it up and took out the documents, and then tore them in two. And two again. And again. The job offer had felt wrong all along, otherwise she'd have signed up and been on the permanent payroll as of last Friday. She raised her eyes to the peeling paint and stained patches on the ceiling. *Thank you*, she said silently to whomever, whatever, had been looking after her and, with a satisfied smile, she placed the pile of torn paper on the corner of her desk. She really hoped David would understand.

The disappointing thing about this was she now had to head back into the horrible, murky pool that was job hunting – not that she'd ever actually left. Oh well, she consoled herself, she'd thought the house hunt would go on forever and it hadn't, so she'd find a job. Soon. She had to. She really didn't want to go back to temping. She wanted to belong somewhere, feel connected. Sighing, she put her thoughts aside and turned on the computer to get to work securing more leads for Business Development Manager Todd.

An hour or so later Alice looked up at hearing a gentle tap on her door. 'Oh, hi,' she said to the tall man filling up most of the doorway.

'Can I come in?' Todd said.

'Sure, it's more your office than mine,' she said. She waved a hand to indicate the space in an effort to welcome him in, though there was nowhere for him to sit. So he leant against the wall.

'I heard about this morning. Sorry you had to witness that.'

'Thanks. It wasn't pleasant. Todd,' she said, 'I'm really sorry, but I can't take the job. I appreciate the offer, but ...' She suddenly was lost for words.

'Not because of this morning?' he said, staring at the torn-up paper on her desk.

'Yes, because of this morning. Well, that sealed it.' Alice was incredulous. Why was Aaron's behaviour okay? 'I'm not spending my days wondering if I'm going to have a laptop or lever-arch folder or something thrown at me from across the room.'

'He's not that bad.'

'Well, I can't know that, can I? Todd, this is not okay. It's not appropriate behaviour anywhere, let alone a workplace – and for the CEO. This is supposed to be a successful national company, for Christ's sake. Can't you see that?'

'But I thought you liked working here – liked working for me.'

'I did. I do. It's not about you, Todd. The man needs help.'

'But it's such a great opportunity.' *So everyone keeps saying.* 'You can get trained up and then leave if you want. You'll be set up and

Fiona McCallum

well on your way after a year or two here. I'd give you a brilliant reference.'

'Sorry, Todd. You know I think the world of you and I've been so grateful for the work these last few months, but I just can't do it. I've been a nervous wreck since it happened. I can't work like that. And I'm not over-reacting. It might not affect you, but it's not something I'm prepared to put up with.'

'So, where does it leave me, and Outercover?'

'If you want me to go now, I will. Aaron will be back and wanting my answer on the job soon anyway. I got the sense offering me the position was as much about quickly plugging a gap for you guys as me being the right person for the job. So, he'll probably be pissed.' At that moment Alice's flight response started to fire up again. The last thing she wanted was a confrontation with Aaron.

He'd seemed so nice when they'd sat down together to discuss the role and when he'd made the offer. She had heard a rumour that the marketing manager had left suddenly under a cloud – she'd had an affair with one of the board members. Alice hadn't asked Todd about the story. It was none of her business and she tried not to get involved with gossip. She'd had enough of that in Hope Springs. But if it were true then Aaron was under considerable pressure to get the marketing department back in order quickly. Combine that stress with his unpredictable behaviour and Alice was sure that things would only get worse before they got better, and she didn't want any part of it.

She wouldn't have minded staying on as Todd's assistant while she looked for something more to her liking – she'd enjoyed doing the research. But she'd only been filling in while someone was away. Why did she need a career as opposed to a job, anyway? To pay their whopping big Melbourne mortgage. That was why. Also, Alice felt a certain pressure to show she was worthy of a place beside David. She knew she was her own person and shouldn't buy into such a shallow view, but she also knew all too well David's high standards and the vision he had for his life, and theirs together. His determination and ambition had initially drawn her to him. He was everything her previous partner, her husband, hadn't been. So she couldn't complain because it was pretty much what she'd signed up for.

Todd's phone in his hand pinged with a message. 'Sorry, I'd better check this,' he said.

Alice looked back at her screen and as she did was notified of a new email too. She glanced at it while Todd was distracted.

'Oh!' she said at seeing it was from Aaron and 'Many Apologies!!' was in the subject line. She read the message where he apologised for his behaviour that morning and acknowledged how unprofessional it was. 'Pah!' Alice said aloud at him blaming it on being under too much pressure. She shook her head. There was no excuse for his behaviour. He closed with saying he really looked forward to her joining the company and being part of the team. *You've got to be joking!* Alice thought.

'So, I take it that's still a no, then?' Todd asked.

Alice looked up, frowning.

'I was blind copied in,' he explained.

'Oh. Right.'

'So, I can't print out another copy of this?' he said, picking up scraps of the torn-up offer letter.

Hell no! 'No, thanks.' Alice began to fume as she re-read Aaron's email. What a cop-out to not apologise in person – although maybe Aaron realised she didn't want to be in the same room as him again. He could have called her. *Email, for god's sake.* It was probably best for her, too, she thought, and she started to simmer down. Alice didn't do confrontation of any sort very well, and tended to get embarrassed, awkward and tongue-tied when put on the spot or verbally backed into a corner. But she was still angry, which was helpful right now, she thought, as she pressed *Reply*.

'Don't go saying something you'll regret, Alice,' Todd warned, clearly sensing what she was doing.

Dear Aaron,

   Thank you for your message. Your apology is accepted. However, I have decided not to accept the position in the marketing department.
   I wish you and Outercover all the very best.
   Alice

She re-read her message. She longed to give Aaron a decent lecture about his deplorable behaviour and tell him what a childish prat he was, but refrained. If she started, she'd probably end up with a two thousand-word essay. Best to stay professional and on point. So, instead, she copied in Todd, as he was the one who'd brought her into the company, and quickly pressed *Send*.

'Damn. I've gotta run. I'll talk to you later. Again, Alice, I'm really sorry about this morning. Keep doing what you're doing for me here – work from home if you'd prefer until the dust settles. Just let me know where you are.'

Chapter Three

Alice couldn't concentrate and found herself stiffening and holding her breath whenever she heard anyone on the stairs. Finally, she decided she'd finish off the last of the research at home, as Todd had suggested. If he caught up with Aaron, no doubt Alice would be banished from the building anyway. Now that she was seeing Aaron in this new light, she realised he might have the capacity to get quite nasty. Anyway, she was pleased to use any excuse to go home to Bill. Hopefully he would be happy to see her and hadn't spent the morning pulling the house apart in distress because he was on his own. Once she'd finished her work, she'd take him for his first decent walk.

Alice had just sent Todd a text letting him know her movements, said goodbye to Chelsea at reception, and left the building when her phone began to ring in her hand. She got such a shock she almost dropped it. Actual phone calls were a rarity when everyone tended to communicate online via social media and send text messages and emails. The number was marked private. She hesitated as she had a policy of not answering unknown numbers, but then reminded herself she was still on the books at plenty of job agencies and was now officially back on the hunt.

'Hello, Alice speaking.'

'Alice Hamilton?'

'Speaking.' She sounded a bit abrupt and unfriendly, but Alice was cautious of those scams that tricked you into saying yes and then drained your bank account because you'd apparently given verbal permission, or however it worked.

'This is Brenda Andrews from Gold, Taylor and Murphy Real Estate. Do you have a moment to speak?'

'I do, but my partner and I are no longer in the market. We've recently settled on a property – moved in, actually,' Alice said while trying to remember which house the woman might be calling about.

'Congratulations, that's great, but this call is not about a property. You put in an application for a job in administration a month or so ago.'

'Oh. Yes, yes, I did. But I received a letter saying I was unsuccessful.'

'Yes. We kept your CV on file, as promised, and a similar position has come up. If you're still looking for work, that is?'

'I am, yes.'

'I'm terribly sorry about the short notice, but would you be able to come in for an interview this afternoon at four o'clock?'

'I could make four today. Do I need to bring anything with me?'

'No, just yourself. I think we have everything. You'll be meeting with Carmel Gold. I'll text you a confirmation with our address so it's all clear.'

'Great. Thanks very much for the call.'

'My pleasure. Well, I look forward to meeting you in person should you be successful. Good luck.'

'Thank you.'

Alice checked the time. If she got a wriggle on, she could make it home, give Bill a quick walk or have a play in the yard, shower and dress more appropriately. She hurried to the train station.

*

Alice smiled at hearing claws clicking on the hallway floorboards, getting louder. She bent down, ready to catch the dog before he raced outside.

'Sit, Bill,' she commanded loudly, and was surprised and impressed to find him sitting just beyond the door when she opened it. 'Stay,' she said, and edged inside and closed the door behind her. 'Oh, what a good, good dog you are.' She squatted down and made a fuss of him. 'I hope your day has been less eventful than mine,' she said, giving Bill's ears a final ruffle before standing up again. 'Do you fancy a walk? Then I have to go and try to get myself a new job.'

Alice changed her heeled shoes to runners and attached the lead to Bill's collar. 'Now, let's see if you really are as well behaved as they said you are.' She was half expecting a sudden show of wilful exuberance as she got out onto the footpath, but Bill trotted along beside her perfectly, and stopped and sat every time she asked him to when crossing the streets on the way to the park. It made her wonder how he'd come to be available for adoption. The shelter hadn't told them anything about him beyond his name, age, suspected breed, and health and vaccination and de-sexed status.

As they walked, Alice alternated between talking to Bill and running through imaginary interview scenarios and questions in her head. Before she knew it, they'd done a whole lap of the park. She was feeling calm and okay about the interview, although she wished she didn't have to go back into the city and face an interrogation.

'Shall we go home, Bill?' she asked, leaning down to give the dog a pat. Bill stretched out on the grass, his tongue hanging out. Oh dear, had she overdone it? She'd walked briskly, not thinking about the dog's short legs. He didn't strain at the lead, so she hadn't given her pace any consideration. She stood up straight. 'Come on then, off we go,' she said, and gave a gentle tug on the lead. But Bill stayed where he was. 'You poor thing,' she said, scooping the dog up. She was fully aware she might be creating a problem by giving in to him so easily, but she didn't have time for life lessons right now. *Thank goodness we didn't end up with a larger or heavier breed, like a Golden Retriever or something*, she thought, tucking the solid little dog under her arm. She laughed when Bill licked her ear.

'Okay, you're welcome, but don't get used to it!'

*

'Now, wish me luck, Bill,' she said as she prepared to leave the house again, having showered and put on her best navy skirt suit. 'You stay. I'll be back later. Hopefully David will be here before too long.' Her heart strained as she backed out the door and closed it on Bill, who was lying on his tummy with his head on his outstretched front paws. *Oh, that look*, Alice thought, feeling decidedly sad and guilty to be leaving him.

Right, interview mode, she told herself as she found a seat on the train. It had arrived on time and the carriage was almost empty, which she took as good signs the interview would go well. Then the butterflies started to flutter inside her. *Oh god, I hate interviews.* And she was feeling so much pressure now that she had no alternative employment or other options to fall back on.

Chapter Four

Alice's finger shook as she pressed the button for floor twenty-four in the shiny elevator. Stepping out, she took in her surroundings. Very nice, she thought. All around her was chrome, black marble and glass. On the marble reception desk was a tall, colourful floral arrangement of green foliage and orange blooms, which had a spiky and architectural look to it. She gave her name and Carmel's and went across to sit on one of the chairs arranged around a marble-slab coffee table with a smaller, matching floral arrangement in its centre. Alice stared at the arrangement, trying to decide if she liked it or not. Probably a strategic choice for such an office, she thought – friendly enough but also spiky, so you never forgot who had the upper hand. Though, this was not where real estate clients came, was it? She realised what was missing and looked around to double-check. No, there was no display of photos of properties for sale or rent. There was probably a window at ground level full of advertising she hadn't noticed, and perhaps the agents only met clients out at properties or in cafés. In that case, the flowers definitely were spiky to remind visitors who was in charge, she decided.

Alice reminded herself to breathe, while her insides were clenching and quivering. She wiped her clammy hands down the sides of her skirt. God, how awful if Carmel were to arrive now and be greeted with a wet handshake. Urgh. She checked, for about the fifth time, that her phone was on silent and then frantically tried to remember the interview questions and answers she'd been running through over and over in her head. But her mind was blank. *Oh no. Why this job? What are my three proudest moments? Where do I want to be in five years' time? Oh god. I don't know.* Alice pulled out a plastic bottle from her bag and took a sip of water, and then struggled to get the top back on. She was still fumbling when her name was called. She looked up, cursing the flush creeping up her neck, signalling she'd got caught out doing something she shouldn't. Had she? No, she was just stressed all round. She leapt up quickly, tried to pick up her handbag and compendium, dropped them, caught them, and got up. *God, pull yourself together, Alice!*

'Alice, I'm Carmel Gold, lovely to meet you,' the woman said, smiling and offering her hand. She was impeccably groomed in a grey pinstripe suit with the firm's black and gold logo on the pocket. Alice took a deep breath while trying not to look too obvious, ran her fingers quickly down her thick dark brown hair to smooth it, and then clasped the hand. Carmel placed her left hand over Alice's.

'Just a friendly chat, no need to be nervous,' she said, looking Alice up and down.

'Thanks,' Alice said, a little breathlessly. She smiled back and felt herself relaxing ever so slightly.

'Through here.' Carmel led the way into a small room with a round table and three chairs around it and several more pushed back against the wall. The room was sparse and basic, done out in pale timber and navy carpet with nothing of the opulence of the reception area. A jug of water and five glasses sat in the centre of the table.

'Take a seat,' Carmel said, picking up the jug and pouring water into two glasses. Alice sat with her back to the window so as not to get distracted by the view, which she was dying to inspect. Whenever she was in a high-rise she loved looking down onto the city, figuring out which direction she was facing and then trying to pick out favourite landmarks. Carmel placed a glass in front of her.

'Thank you.'

'You're welcome,' Carmel said and sat down opposite Alice. 'So how do you feel about being trained to become an agent yourself, Alice? Are you a self-starter? I need someone with great initiative who can think quickly on their feet. Is real estate for you, do you think?'

Alice was a little taken by surprise at the lack of preamble. 'Oh. Yes. That sounds great. Yes, I think I'd be good at real estate,' she said, recovering.

'I'm looking for more than a PA – I'm looking for a protégé. It's a great opportunity for the right candidate, and I think that might be you, Alice. You're intelligent, you're adaptable, you clearly work hard and you're impeccably groomed,' she said, 'which is a must in our industry.'

Wow, you got all that from my CV, application letter and two minutes face-to-face with me? Alice thought.

Being tall and lean with big hazelnut-coloured eyes, long lashes and masses of naturally wavy hair, she had received compliments about her looks before, but it was rare for anyone other than her uni friends to comment on her intelligence.

'So, what do you say?'

It felt like something out of a team-bonding session or get-rich-quick seminar. Maybe Carmel had attended a few of those in her career. But Alice did like her direct approach, which left no room for ambiguity. And she did seem friendly enough, despite her slightly abrupt style of asking questions.

'Absolutely, count me in!' Alice said, instantly regretting her level of enthusiasm. She sounded like the schmuck who'd just signed up their life savings to a dodgy investment scheme.

'I thought heading out for a coffee might be nicer than a stuffy conference room,' Carmel said. 'There's a lovely café downstairs. What do you think?'

'Sounds great.'

'Come on then.'

In the confined space as the lift doors closed on them, Alice caught a whiff of Carmel's perfume – it was bold and deep, bordering on the masculine more than the feminine. If not actually a man's aftershave, it was definitely an oriental, sandal-wood type of scent, unlike the delicate rose-based perfume Alice wore. She only knew these things because soon after she'd arrived in Melbourne, David had taken her into Myer and David Jones to test every perfume in order to choose her a 'signature scent' for when he next went through Duty Free and could buy it cheaply. After much discussion with the shop assistants and learning more about perfume than she ever thought there was to learn, Alice had ended up deciding on one that smelt like roses. Well, David probably made the decision in the end, really. She liked it, but she wasn't a scent-wearing kind of person. A small part of her had secretly hoped he'd have forgotten all about it when next he went overseas. But he hadn't. Alice still had to be occasionally reminded to put on perfume when they went out together. She actually thought she preferred men's scent generally.

'So, how has your day been?' Carmel asked, breaking the silence.

'Interesting,' Alice said with a laugh.

'Ooh, I'm intrigued. Tell me more.'

'The boss where I've been working had some sort of meltdown this morning and cracked the glass on the photocopier – right in front of me while I was filling in on reception. I got quite a fright.'

'Oh, my goodness. That sounds very unnerving. Well, I can assure you no one at Gold, Taylor and Murphy is prone to such violent outbursts!'

'I was meant to sign a contract to work for him, too. That certainly changed my mind.'

'I'm not surprised.'

'So, how was your day?' Alice asked, suddenly feeling that she'd said too much.

'Great. Successful,' Carmel said, beaming.

'Brilliant,' Alice said.

'Yes, even after all these years I still get a buzz out of a sale.'

'That's great. My partner and I have just bought our first home together.'

'Congratulations.'

'Thanks.'

'So you know the excitement, but from the other side of the fence, so to speak.'

'Yes. Though, to be perfectly honest, I think I was more relieved there'd be no more weekends full of house hunting and disappointment.'

'I'm sure. It doesn't pay to get too emotionally involved. Here we are. After you. Just around to your left.'

'Is here okay?' Alice asked, standing next to a small table tucked into a corner.

'Perfect. You take a seat and I'll order the coffees. Or would you prefer something else?'

'No, a latte would be lovely, thank you.'

Alice watched as Carmel raised a hand and waggled her fingers when she was halfway to the counter. Two waiters scurried forward to help her, either sensing she was important or in a hurry, or both. Perhaps they knew her well.

Carmel had barely sat down when their drinks arrived – espresso for her and a creamy latte for Alice. Alice took note that Carmel drank her coffee exactly as it came, figuring it might be useful to know later on.

'So, you've just finished an Arts degree. And almost all History subjects I see.'

'Yes. I chose subjects that interested me – since Arts isn't really vocational anyway.'

'Right. What made you go back as a mature-age student? That must have been hard,' Carmel said, picking up her tiny cup and taking an equally delicate sip.

'My marriage ended. I felt the need to get out of the small country town I was born in and do something for myself while I decided what I wanted to do with my life.' *Well, David played a big part in it, but I don't think that's what you want to hear … And, anyway, I'm a different, stronger person now.*

'And what did you discover?'

'Sorry?'

'About yourself, the direction you want to take. Did you find the answers?'

Alice was about to laugh and say no, not all of them – especially about her dream job – but reminded herself just in time that this was a job interview and she needed to sell herself, not indulge in idle chit chat.

'Let's see. I did well at university and I discovered I was smarter than I thought. In my second year my results put me in the top fifteen percent of the year across the entire university, and I was invited to join an international honour society. I thought the membership was a bit of a gimmick, but I was still pretty chuffed,' Alice said, then realised she should stop talking about how much she loved uni and start talking about work.

'Also, I like to help people. In my last full-time job they actually nicknamed me "Little Miss Helpful",' Alice said, grinning.

'Little Miss Helpful. How sweet,' Carmel said, and took a sip of her coffee.

Shit, stop being so open, Alice told herself sharply. *Professional. Be professional.* But Carmel was so disarming and easy to talk to that conversation – even personal stuff – seemed to flow almost too easily. Alice wasn't sure if Carmel was being genuine and charming, or condescending.

'I'm organised. I learnt I can do anything I put my mind to, and I'm driven to succeed,' Alice said, pulling herself together.

'In what? Driven to succeed in what, exactly?'

'Oh, well, I just meant driven to be my best in whatever I'm doing – my uni results, for example, as I mentioned.'

'Yes, they are very impressive.'

'Thank you.' Alice was proud of her results. Not long after starting at university she'd begun to feel her whole being physically shifting. Awakening. It was as if she had wings and they were slowly unfurling for the first time, stretching to test what span and strength they had. Discovering that she was much smarter than she'd been led to believe and actually really quite intelligent had initially given her a slightly strange, uneasy feeling – a bit like the sand shifting under her feet at the beach when a wave retreated, or discovering Santa wasn't real after all. She realised there was so much more to life than marriage and babies, which is what her mother had in mind for her.

'So, what's next for Alice Hamilton?'

'Well, I'm hoping real estate now that I've met you ...' Oh dear, too gushy, judging by Carmel's raised eyebrows. Alice became flustered. 'Unfortunately I don't have a dream job or career in mind. Well, I didn't. What I mean is, I think perhaps I'm a toiler. I'm a hard worker, but I don't feel the need to be at the top of management or the centre of attention. I think I'm happy providing support from behind, below,' she said, hearing herself starting to ramble. 'It's not that I'm not ambitious, it's just that my ambition lies more in being comfortable and happy than really rich,' Alice added, thinking aloud. She cursed the straight up honesty that was such a big part of her character. *Oh shit! Just shut up!*

'Why can't you have both? I do,' Carmel said, waving a hand – a little theatrically, Alice thought.

'Oh. Well. Perhaps I just haven't found my groove yet.'

'Alice, you're thirty, you'd better get your act together.'

Alice was a little taken aback. *God, you sound like my mother! It's not my fault there aren't any jobs going that use my passion for history. I'm doing my best.* When she enrolled in Arts, she'd chosen to study modern history because it captured her interest and she'd shared a love of the subject with her dad. It had been one of their 'things', and theirs alone. As a child she'd sit on his lap, he in his big reclining faux leather chair, their heads close together, flicking through books about the olden days, people they'd never meet and places they'd most likely never go to. When she thought about it, Alice realised she had found her groove in her studies. Now she needed to find it in a job.

'I'm probably too driven,' said Carmel. 'And I knew I wanted to be in real estate when I was ten.'

'I envy people who know exactly what they want from an early age.' Alice might have seriously considered modelling as a career, if she didn't enjoy food quite so much and hated the idea of starving herself, and her mother hadn't said over and over that being vain and drawing attention to oneself was vulgar. Strange coming from a woman who couldn't walk past a mirror without stopping to inspect her reflection and adjust her hair or apply more lipstick …

'Yes, it certainly makes it easier for planning one's life. But don't underestimate what you've gained through trying different things and keeping an open mind,' Carmel said, smiling warmly again, all hint of the criticism from seconds ago gone. She turned her phone over and checked the time on the display. 'Right, so what do you think about being my PA? A three-month probation will ensure we're the right fit and then if you're interested we'll see if maybe your groove is real estate.'

Oh really? Wow. Alice was suddenly excited about the prospect of becoming an agent. It was something she'd never thought about, but the more she considered it now, the more she thought she'd be great at it. She could see that helping people to find and purchase their dream property, or sell and achieve their dream price might be right up her alley.

'I think I'd love to be your PA, with the view to becoming an agent, Carmel. Thank you so much.'

'I like your enthusiasm, Alice. Now, I warn you, I can be a hard taskmaster at times. I'm always fair, but I am firm. I have strict ways I like things done, but I can promise there'll be no smashing of photocopiers.'

Alice cringed. She really wished she hadn't shot her mouth off like that.

'I look forward to living up to your high standards, Carmel.'

'Great. Now, I need to cut this short; I have another appointment and you're expected back up in reception,' she said, standing up.

Alice leapt to attention, leaving behind the coffee she'd only taken two sips from, and hurrying to catch up to Carmel.

Carmel spent the lift ride back up to the twenty-fourth floor in silence, focussed on her phone. Alice found the atmosphere considerably colder than when they'd been going down, but shook the feeling aside. The woman was successful. Being busy and remaining focussed on the tasks at hand was no doubt how she came to be one of Melbourne's leading real estate sales people, which is what a quick Google of the company had told Alice.

'It was lovely to meet you, Alice. I look forward to you being my new protégé, should you accept the position,' she said as they stepped out of the lift. 'And now I'll leave you with the management team to discuss things further and for them to consider your suitability.'

'Oh, right. Okay. Thanks, Carmel,' Alice said. She was starting to feel a little dazed at Carmel's intensity. *Did she just offer me a job or not?* She began to hold out her hand, but Carmel was already striding away, giving a wave to the man and two women standing near the reception desk – all dressed in company livery. Still none the wiser, Alice turned towards them.

'Alice, great to meet you,' the man said. 'I'm Paul Taylor, Chief Executive Officer, and this is Mary Murphy and Rose Sharp from our management team.' They all shook hands and Alice tried to remember which woman was which. Did Rose have the red hair or was she the blonde? She was a little surprised the HR manager, Brenda Andrews, wasn't there. Why wouldn't HR be involved? Oh well, she wasn't about to question how they ran their very successful business.

'Come through here,' Paul said, ushering her into the same room Alice had been in earlier with Carmel.

'So, what were your impressions of Carmel?' he asked when they were settled.

'Lovely. Really lovely,' Alice said. *Was that an odd question? No, probably not when they're interviewing for a personal assistant role.*

'She is very exacting and can come across as a little forceful,' Rose said. 'Do you think you'd be okay with that?'

'Oh, yes, no problem at all. Of course there'll be a learning curve and it'll take a little time to understand her nuances, but I'm really excited about the chance to be working with – er, for – someone of her calibre.'

'Fantastic, that's what we like to hear,' Mary said, seemingly with a hint of relief.

'I can get along well with most people,' Alice said cheerfully. 'And I'm organised, efficient and pretty exacting myself.'

'Okay then,' Paul said, opening his black leather compendium and taking out a document. 'Here's a job description and what we're offering, should you choose to accept.' He pushed the paper towards Alice and said, 'Three-month probation, after which time you can decide if you want to do some study. If you do, you'll be given a paid day of study leave per month, plus of course time off for lectures and tutorials.'

'That's very generous,' Alice said.

'It's not a day off – we'd expect you to be working. And we'd be expecting exceptional results, which I'm sure, given your recent studies, you'd have no problem achieving. We're a success because we have the brightest and best people. We understand that requires some investment. Then we hope they'll stay with us long term and repay that investment. But we're getting ahead of ourselves. You might find real estate is not for you. Anyway, over the page is the salary we're offering,' he said.

Alice turned the page. She had to stop her mouth opening at seeing the very large number printed in bold black type. It was ten thousand dollars a year higher than what Outercover had been offering. And she'd thought *that* was a good starting salary. As she stared, pretending to read, she told herself to put her game face back on. She wasn't greedy, but she hadn't lived with David's influence for this long to not at least attempt a negotiation.

'I see that includes superannuation. I'd be looking for that salary plus super. At a minimum,' she said, putting on her boldest, most professional sounding voice. She met Paul's gaze and held it in an attempt to tell him she was serious, and then looked to Mary and then Rose. It was worth a shot. Alice didn't want them thinking she was a pushover – great offer or not.

'I think we can stretch to adding super and another five thousand,' Paul said and looked to Mary and Rose. They both nodded. 'Alice?'

'That's great. Thank you. I accept.'

'Brilliant.' He made a note in his compendium and leant over and made the changes to the paper in front of Alice. 'I'll get it amended and emailed to you tomorrow,' he said, 'but in the meantime, take this so you have everything to hand. If you have any questions, contact Brenda Andrews in HR – her details are at the bottom. Does the start date, next Monday, work for you?'

'Yes, that works perfectly,' Alice said. She watched, almost mesmerised, as he put his pen back into the loop in his compendium and zipped it closed.

'Right, then, great. Welcome aboard, Alice,' Paul said, standing up and holding out his hand.

'Thank you,' Alice said, leaping to her feet and grasping his hand. She then exchanged handshakes with Rose and Mary, who were standing beside Paul.

'May it be a long and rewarding experience for you,' Mary said.

'I'm sure it will. Thank you for the opportunity,' Alice said, beaming, her thudding heart finally beginning to slow.

'All the best,' Rose said, smiling warmly.

Alice was ushered back out to reception.

'Thanks, Alice. The updated document will be forwarded to you by the end of business tomorrow. Hand it back, signed, to Bianca here at reception when you arrive. We look forward to seeing you around the office from Monday.'

And then they were gone, leaving Alice to feel a little like she'd been through a cycle in the tumble dryer for the past hour.

'Thank you. See you Monday, Bianca,' Alice said to the receptionist, and walked towards the lift on legs that didn't quite feel connected. She nodded in greeting to the young man and woman already in the lift and rode silently with them to the ground, the whole time thinking, *Golly, I've just got myself a damned fine job with a damned fine salary – woo-hoo!* So excited, she wanted to pump her fist in the air or tap-dance. Instead she smiled and clutched her two bags so tightly to her chest.

Outside on the footpath she looked around. *What now?* It seemed so ordinary to simply go home, such an anticlimax. Oh well, that was life, wasn't it? Ordinary punctuated by less ordinary. One couldn't celebrate every exciting event. And, she'd only got a job – hundreds of thousands of people around the planet did just this very thing every day. But she knew that David would be pleased. She took out her phone. There were two missed calls from him, but no notifications of any messages. She tried his number, but it went straight to voicemail so she hung up.

Everyone else would be in lectures or at work and out of contact too, she realised, running quickly through her list of nearest and dearest friends. *Welcome to the real world*, she thought, and put her phone back in her bag with a slightly disappointed sigh. At least Bill would look like he was pleased to hear her news, even if he didn't understand it. She brightened a little and then began to smile again as she headed back to the train station. *I'm going to love being in real estate, and be really good at it*, she told herself.

Chapter Five

As Alice unlocked the front door she listened for signs David was already home. You couldn't tell with this house. With the apartment there had been a glow around the front window shutters if the light was on, which it usually was when they were in. She'd only have to look up and feel a sense of comfort when she saw the gentle light. It happened so rarely that she arrived home after David and it was a feeling she loved. She'd never told him, though, as she didn't want him to feel guilty about the long hours he worked. Her husband had been lazy and always there and she'd never felt she could have any time on her own. But with David she didn't crave having time alone.

Perhaps after her marriage ended she'd called out her frustration to the universe loudly enough and she'd been given what she'd asked for – an energetic go-getter. She was determined not to complain about David's absences and long hours. She did her best to be home waiting for him when he came back from a work trip because she knew the comfort of entering a warm, inhabited space. She could see why keeping the home fires burning had been so important during wartime, which she'd studied at university. She wondered if David appreciated the simple things she did for him, though she doubted it. She was more the romantic at heart.

With this house, even once she'd walked in it was impossible to tell if anyone was there or not, because the open kitchen and living area was behind the bedrooms, at the end of a long hallway. She shook aside the thought that she missed the old apartment and reminded herself how cramped they'd been. And there'd been no Bill, she thought, feeling a wave of warmth instantly flow through her. She'd carefully opened the door in case the dog happened to make a run for it. She hadn't heard his claws on the floorboards.

Her heart swelled as she saw him sitting to attention a metre or so back out of the way.

'How good are you? What a beautiful, clever boy,' she said, putting her bags on the floor and kneeling down to give the dog the attention he deserved. 'Are you all alone or is David here?' she asked, ruffling Bill's ears.

'Alice, is that you?' came David's voice.

'Yes. Hi.'

'I'm in the kitchen.'

At that moment Alice detected cooking smells and her heart swelled even further. *Could this evening get any better?*

'Come on, Bill, let's see what's for dinner.' Alice scooped up her handbag and tote bag – David didn't like mess or items out of place – and with Bill trotting alongside she made her way through to the kitchen.

'You didn't happen to bring zucchini, did you?'

'Um, no.' *Why would I have stopped and got zucchini? How random.* 'Did you leave a message about it? Sorry.' He'd called but hadn't left a message, so she hadn't rung him back. She'd assumed he had just wanted to say hi or more likely tell her about his latest work triumph, or debrief or rant about what some idiot had or hadn't done at work.

He was frowning as he stood there in his navy and white striped apron. Damn. Clearly not in the best mood. He claimed he loved cooking, but got quite frustrated when things didn't go perfectly to plan or he didn't achieve exactly what he'd set out to. He followed recipes to the letter. Alice didn't. She felt cooking came from the heart, not the head. This was a source of consternation for David and was sometimes a real bugbear between them, but Alice did her best not to play the game. When David wanted to cook, she let him, even though preparing their evening meal was one of her favourite things to do each day. She'd learnt early on in their relationship that for David, wanting to cook was more about competing, winning and one-upping her than any desire to actually prepare meals for them to enjoy together. He needed to be the best at everything. Alice just wanted to love and be loved in return – she was a born nurturer. At times cooking seemed positively torturous for David and it took all Alice's strength not to step in and try to take over. As the more easy-going of the two, she was happy just to enjoy the fruits of his labour and lavish an appropriate amount of praise when required – whether the food deserved it or not.

'I rang. I didn't leave a message,' he said.

And you thought I'd know to pick up zucchini, like a psychic? Seriously? 'Sorry,' she said.

'Doesn't matter,' he said, with an exasperated sigh. It clearly did matter.

'I can go and get some. The store on the corner will still be open. I can take Bill for a walk while I'm at it.'

'No, this will be ready in five minutes.'

Alice doubted that. Where David's abilities in the kitchen often fell short, his timing in the kitchen was absolutely appalling.

They had been known to have main course split into two, twenty minutes apart – meat for one course and then the vegetables – because David could never get the cooking times right.

'Okay.' She settled on a stool at the bench to watch him, which he loved her doing, though she couldn't understand why when he was so inept. 'How was your day?' she asked.

'Pretty good. There's talk of a reshuffle of the team.'

'Oh, right. Is that good?'

'Could be. Bit early to tell.'

'How was Bill when you got home?'

'Okay. Sitting on his bed.'

'I came home earlier and took him for a walk.'

'Yes, Todd rang me. He's really disappointed you didn't take the job.' *And so am I*, were the unspoken words his demeanour told her.

'Did he tell you what happened?' she said, trying to keep the rising note of defensiveness from her voice.

'Yes, he did.' Though clearly it didn't mean anything to David.

'I'm not working for an unpredictable git like that.'

'It was a good opportunity, Alice.'

'So you've said. Please don't scold me like I'm a child, David. You weren't there. Hell, Todd wasn't even there! So don't tell me what's fine and what's not.'

'I didn't.'

'It's written all over your face. You're disappointed in me.' David might not raise his voice, but that look of disappointment could wound like a knife. Alice felt its cut now. 'Well, be disappointed in Aaron bloody Troubridge – he's the fool who can't keep his temper in check!'

'Alice, calm down. I only said …'

Yes, but it's what you're not saying, she thought.

'Right, here we are. Dinner is served,' he said placing two plates on the stone bench top. 'Steak and green peppercorn sauce,' he added proudly.

'This looks great. Thank you,' Alice said, truthfully. David's plating was perfect – neat and beautiful – though Alice's appetite was waning.

'So, are you going to go back to temping full-time now? We can't afford for you to be ...'

'Be what? Slacking off? Not pulling my weight?' Alice was annoyed.

'It's tight, Alice, that's all I'm saying,' he said, as he attacked his meal.

Alice cut a square of steak, speared it with her fork, added a scoop of mashed potato and pushed a piece of almost raw carrot onto the pile before putting it into her mouth. They ate in silence. Out of the corner of her eye Alice noticed Bill nearby watching them intently.

'Did you feed Bill?' she asked between mouthfuls.

'Why would I have fed him?'

Why wouldn't you?

Alice got up without a word. After pouring the right amount of food into his bowl, she spent a moment ruffling the dog's ears before returning to her own meal.

'I got a new job today, actually,' she said nonchalantly, as she settled back onto her stool.

'A temp assignment?' David said, not looking up.

'No, a proper job. PA to Carmel Gold, lead partner at Gold, Taylor and Murphy Real Estate.'

'Really?' He shot her a little sideways glance as if disbelieving.

'Yes. They rang me to come in for an interview and offered me the job on the spot,' she said, allowing herself to sound a little haughty. *So there!*

'How much?'

She stood up and retrieved the document from her compendium in her tote bag and handed it to him.

'They're adding super and five thousand and will email an updated version – hence the handwritten note. I start Monday.' David ignored the two pages of terms and conditions and went straight to the salary.

'Not bad,' he said, with a lot less awe than his expression revealed.

'Yes. I negotiated the additions.'

'Well done, you,' he said. 'Oh, Alice, that's great. I'm proud of you.' He gathered her to him.

Proud maybe, she thought, *but more like relieved your freeloading partner is finally going to be contributing properly.*

'Thanks,' she said. Alice knew she should be thrilled, but she wasn't quite. A small part of her yearned for a job in the field of history and historical research, or to still be enjoying university life. She could continue studying online in her own time if she really wanted, but it wouldn't be the same. She missed the student lifestyle – the coming and going to uni, and not being answerable to a boss. And the challenge of striving for and getting great grades. Though she was excited about her goal of being the best damned PA Carmel Gold had ever had, and then a fine real estate agent when the time came.

'They're actually going to train me to sell real estate, too,' Alice added.

'Now you're talking!' David said, not hiding any of his awe. They'd both commented on the prestige cars parked outside all the properties they'd visited over the past months. It was clear people selling property in Melbourne made money – serious money.

Chapter Six

On Monday morning Alice was already exhausted when she arrived in the city for her first day at Gold, Taylor and Murphy Real Estate. She'd been unable to sleep and had got up extra early to see David off on an overseas trip. She liked that her train was a comfortable five-minute walk away from the office, though.

She reached the large Bourke Street tower block ten minutes early, so she took a stroll around to get her bearings and see what amenities were close to her new workplace. She discovered that everything she would need seemed to be within a one-block radius of her office – dentist, pharmacy, supermarket, chiropractor, physio, and a multitude of restaurants and cafés of varying degrees of quality and presence. She paused at the window of a doctor's surgery. She wondered if that was the place where Steph from uni was working. She'd said she was a part-time receptionist and admin assistant at a doctor's surgery in the north-west corner of the city. It would be nice to have someone she knew nearby. Though she'd meet plenty of nice people soon, she thought as she arrived at reception right on the dot of nine o'clock. She'd been surprised to find she was the only person in the lift coming up.

'Hi, Bianca,' Alice said brightly to the receptionist. 'Good weekend?'

'Hi, Alice. Yes, thanks, nice and relaxing.'

'Lovely.'

'So you didn't change your mind about working here, then?'

'No. Here I am. Now, I have the signed employment contract and the banking details form. And here are the details for my super fund,' Alice said, handing the documents over to Bianca. 'I think that's all. Let me know if I've missed anything.' Alice cursed her clammy hands and just hoped the pages didn't show signs of damp fingerprints. Damn being so nervous!

'Great. I think you've got everything. I'll do you a copy to keep for your records,' Bianca said, turning around and lifting the lid of a small photocopier beside her. 'There you go. I'm sure it's all in order. Now, sign here for your pass,' she said, giving Alice a lanyard and pushing a clipboard towards her. 'And just wait over there. Jen's going to give you your orientation and get you settled. She should be here any second.'

'Brilliant. Thanks. Thanks for everything.'

God, how many times was she going to use the word 'thanks', Alice thought. But what could one say instead? And manners were important to her. As she settled into the chair, she took several deep breaths. Her heart had been thudding hard but was finally started to slow. She watched as the doors to the three lifts opened and closed and throngs of noisy people flooded into reception – some in company livery, plenty not – and then filed through the frosted-glass doors, chatting as they went. Alice hoped before too long that would be her – catching up with her workmates on a Monday morning, and perhaps some becoming friends.

Having been bullied right through high school for being quiet and studious, the thought of making new friends was always a source of anxiety for Alice. She'd felt that way when she'd started at Outercover and also on her first day at uni. She'd stood there just to the side of the imposing quadrangle, a smile on her face to hide the jangle of nerves and uncertainty eating her up. She'd felt so old as she'd cringed while watching the drunken antics of the students enjoying O Week – the 'kids' sculling beer and doing silly things to earn themselves more freebies. She'd sipped on an iced coffee while she tried not to look as lost or out of place as she felt. And then she'd heard a thick English accent right beside her.

'I'm too old for that shit.'

Alice turned, already grinning. 'I was just thinking the same thing. Makes me ill just thinking about a hangover,' she said.

'Who even drinks alcohol at ten in the morning? I'm Lauren, by the way,' said the woman, who was a few years younger than Alice. She thrust her hand out to Alice. They were both tall and stood out above the throngs of other students.

Lauren and Alice had talked for the next hour or so and gradually three other women and two men of around their age and older joined them, each making comments about being too old or declaring knowledge about how the young things would suffer later. They laughed about being sensible, mature-age students. And just like that a little group with Alice and Lauren at the centre had been formed. Eventually someone said they were too old to be standing up for hours and too wise to sit down on cold concrete, and the group meandered towards the nearest café. It turned out they were all taking different courses and so for the next three years Alice always had at least one friend on campus to catch up with when she wanted to, as well as the other students in her Arts subjects.

The group grew to around fifteen and had a dedicated Facebook page. Apart from an annual Christmas get-together, which included partners, they tended to keep their socialising confined to campus, with a regular Friday lunch catch-up. Being mature age there seemed to be a collective understanding that they were there to study more than to build a social life or really close friendships – they each had a separate life outside of university. Also, they were all living in different directions and varying distances away from campus. Oh how she missed them.

Other than her studies, Alice's world centred on David because she still felt like a newcomer to Melbourne, and after the experience with Shannon, she was wary of forming really deep friendships. But Alice and Lauren kept finding themselves catching the same tram, and over conversations to and from university a close bond had formed. Alice hadn't seen a lot of her in the last few weeks as her time had been taken up with moving house, so she made a vow to remedy that by inviting Lauren around to her new home soon. There had been an off-campus catch-up lunch for the group at a city pub a few weeks ago, but Alice had been working at Outercover and couldn't go along. It was the end of an era. *But it doesn't have to be sad or bad. Change is good*, Alice thought. *Why not set up a weekend catch-up and see who wants to come?* Maybe she wasn't the only one who was missing the camaraderie.

Yes, I'll do it, she decided, just as she heard her name called.

She looked up to find a beaming young woman with bright red hair and matching red glasses frames standing nearby.

'Hi, yes,' Alice said, leaping up.

'I'm Jen.'

'Jen, lovely to meet you,' Alice said, pumping the offered hand enthusiastically.

'Welcome to Gold, Taylor and Murphy,' she said in an English accent Lauren would have described as 'well posh'.

'Thanks.'

'I'm to show you the ropes.'

'Great.' Alice felt herself relax.

She took several more deep breaths and then blushed when Jen said, 'Yeah, terrifying being the newbie, huh? But you'll be fine.' She had clearly noticed Alice's anxiety.

'We don't bite. Well, most of us don't,' she added with a laugh. 'Right. I need to put my lunch in the fridge, so we may as well start with the kitchen. Word to the wise, the food court down-stairs is a rip-off and had a health department issue of some sort last year. I always bring my own.'

'Me too,' Alice said. 'My partner and I have just bought our first house so we're counting the pennies.'

'My partner and I are counting ours too, but for a different reason. We're pommy backpackers – hence the accent. We're working our way around this fine country of yours. Off up north on Saturday before the cold weather comes in.'

'Oh, that's great. How exciting,' Alice said as her heart sank.

'Oops, hang on. Almost forgot,' Jen said, with her hand on one of the glass doors Alice had noticed earlier. 'Toilets are out here,' she said, turning back and pointing. Then she pushed the door open. It closed with a whoosh and then a thump after them. 'Now, take note. It's easy to get disoriented. We've come in from the door to the left as you leave the lifts. The lifts and reception are in the centre and us worker bees are around the outside. At least we get a window, huh? Anyway, if you're anything like me you'll take a wrong turn or go too far and regularly end up doing a full loop. Take note of the view out the window as a way of getting your bearings because all the desks look the same and people change the stuff on their desks all the time, so that's a useless point of reference. You'll see.

'There's only one kitchen. Label your lunch and put it into the fridge early and then hope for the best.' Jen extracted a lunchbox from her oversized handbag and opened the fridge.

Alice followed suit.

'Oh, you're organised,' she said, looking approvingly at Alice's labelled container filled with cheese, crackers, celery, carrots, nuts and sultanas. 'Not your first rodeo, huh, isn't that what you Aussies say?'

'Something like that, yes,' Alice said with a laugh.

'We'll come back for a coffee in a bit. Give the rush a chance to die down. First I want to show you right around so hopefully you won't get as lost as I did the first few days I was here. Maybe you're better than me with direction, but it can't hurt to be sure.'

'No, good idea. I appreciate it.' Alice followed Jen along the corridor, stopping every few steps to be introduced, losing count of the times Jen said, 'Hi, ya' or 'This is Alice, Carmel's new PA – you're going to have to look after her when I'm gone,' and high-fived people. A part of Alice missed her already.

'God, I wish everyone wore name tags,' Alice whispered when they paused to check the view and get their bearings.

'Don't worry, they'll understand. We've all been a newbie at some point. Now,' Jen said, opening another set of glass doors. 'Here we are back at reception, only the opposite side to where we went in. Got it?'

'Yep. Got it.' Alice felt as if she'd walked miles of corridor.

'So, we're halfway – kitchen is right across there, through that door.'

'This place is huge.'

'Yeah. We've got the whole floor – two actually, but marketing and advertising are down one. You'll cover that another day. Oh, and management don't like us walking across reception. Apparently it's not a good look in front of clients.'

Perhaps they shouldn't have toilets in reception, then, Alice thought, but kept it to herself.

'Okay, so now to where you'll be spending most of your time,' Jen said, closing the glass door and heading further along the corridor. 'And here we are,' she finally said after many more stops to greet people and introduce Alice.

'Nice,' Alice said, walking over to check the view out the window. She reckoned they were overlooking Flagstaff Gardens and in the distance she could see the Queen Victoria Markets.

'Yes,' Jen said, 'it's quite something. But don't get caught looking at it for long. There's a reason we're positioned with our backs to it – and it's not so the light's over your shoulder, if you know what I mean. Okay, so dump your stuff,' Jen continued without giving Alice a chance to answer. 'Now we'll get coffee. I'm not trying to teach you anything without caffeine,' she said, picking up a mug from her desk. She reached into the top drawer of the filing cabinet under the desk and took out another mug. 'Lose sight of your mug and it's gone,' she warned. 'I'll be taking mine with me but this one will be yours,' she said, holding up the one with the company logo. 'Whatever you do, don't put it in the dishwasher if you ever want another coffee again. They disappear like socks in the wash.'

'Got it,' Alice said, smiling. *How much fun is Jen?*

'You might have guessed, coffee's a wee bit important to me,' she said with a laugh. 'I can get quite ferocious without my fix, can't I, Pip?' she said to a young blonde woman who had just arrived on the other side of the partition. *Is everyone around here twelve and glamorous?* Alice suddenly felt very old, and frumpy. They were all so well dressed. Alice was neat and tidy, and her height helped, but these girls looked like they'd strayed in from the Myer Fashion Week catwalk.

'It doesn't bear thinking about,' Pip agreed, grinning.

'Good weekend?' Jen asked.

'Yep, but too short as usual.'

'Pip, this is Alice,' Jen said.

'Hi, Pip,' Alice said, stretching her hand over the partition.

'Great to meet you, Alice. Welcome aboard. Are you Carmel's latest PA?'

'She surely is. So she's going to need all the love you can muster when I'm gone.'

'Don't remind me. I'm nearly in tears at the thought. Please don't go,' Pip said, putting on a whiny voice.

'You can always come with.'

Their voices faded as Alice wondered why Pip had called her the 'latest' PA, and what did Jen mean about her needing all the love Pip could muster? Most likely because of Carmel's very exacting nature, she figured, pushing it aside. You didn't get to the top of your career without stepping on a few toes along the way. Well, that's what seemed to be the general consensus. And it was so much harder for women, so no doubt Carmel had put her stilettoes into plenty of people as she built up her career.

'Come on, coffee and then the rest of the tour. And then into it. Catch you later, Pip.'

'Righteo.'

'Even though Pip's right here, we won't really speak to her again until lunch. We usually eat our lunch together – you're welcome to join us – but chatting is frowned upon in the office. It all seems easy-going now, but after nine-thirty Monday morning we're expected to knuckle down and be busy little worker bees. Luckily for you Carmel is out and about most of the time. But when she's here you'll know about it.'

'Oh?'

'She's nice enough, but she can just get a bit bossy and full on. And everything has to be done this quickly,' Jen said, snapping her fingers, 'and perfect. One thing – don't start coming in earlier than nine or staying after five, or she will expect it for ever more, and they don't pay overtime. I'm sure you'll have noticed there was no mention of penalty rates on your contract.' Jen looked at her with raised eyebrows and Alice nodded. 'If you get on the treadmill of doing extra hours you'll never get off. Given half a chance, Carmel will suck you dry,' she whispered, 'but you didn't hear that from me.'

'Right. Got it.'

Chapter Seven

Alice was completely drained by the time she said goodbye to Jen, Pip and a few others she'd met in her area of the office, and left for the day. As she caught the train with seconds to spare, she made a mental note that the walk to the station without the adrenalin and first-day nerves propelling her took close to eight minutes. Unable to find a seat for most of her half-hour ride, she was looking forward to flopping down on the couch and turning on the TV. But as soon as she saw Bill's gleeful little face she knew she simply had to take him for a walk. At least his short legs meant it didn't need to be too far – another reason to be grateful for a small dog.

While she walked she thought about what she'd learnt that day and pictured the processes and notes Jen had taken her through. So far they all seemed to be pretty much stock-standard admin tasks – typing, filing, answering phones and emails. Carmel might not have been in the office much – had breezed in with a flash of pearly whites, and heavy gold jewellery and Louis Vuitton her only touches of individuality to the company uniform – but Alice certainly felt her presence via the almost constant stream of text messages and emails sent from her smartphone. So many times near the end of the day Alice found herself rolling her eyes. *Seriously, she wants me to find out how many cafés and restaurants are in the vicinity of one of her properties?* But as tedious as she thought it, Alice, keen to make a good impression, quickly did her Googling and sent the information.

Sometimes it felt as if Carmel was testing her – like people tested Suri on their iPhones. Oh well, she'd play along and hope the novelty would wear off sooner rather than later.

By Tuesday afternoon Alice was starting to feel a little more in control, with some things coming together in her mind, and she was feeling more at ease in the office generally. She was even beginning to see some areas where she could improve efficiency, and was starting to look forward to being left to her own devices and to make her own mark once Jen had gone and she was alone. She'd miss Jen's vibrancy and company, but without her there, Alice would be more focussed and could concentrate better. She could see Jen wasn't quite as organised as she was, but she did appreciate all the notes and cheat sheets she'd typed up for Alice.

On Wednesday morning, Jen stressed that the most important aspect of Alice's job, apart from keeping Carmel happy, though it went part and parcel really, was staying on top of the ads for listings. She had to make sure they were correct and get the online ones up straight away and those for newspapers and magazines in on time. Wednesdays were the biggest day of Alice's week, and every second one – which was today – when they had to get the ads in for the company's fortnightly glossy advertising magazine, was huge! Alice thought Jen was exaggerating – she'd seen she was a little prone in that direction, but when they pressed the button on the last submission at two minutes to five, Alice was exhausted. They made the deadline by the skin of their teeth. She was also exhilarated by the pace and the feeling that she'd achieved something major – not worthwhile in the league of brain surgery, perhaps, but worthwhile to the company. As she sat back in her chair to take a moment to savour the day before leaving, she realised she hadn't drunk any water for several hours, nor been to the loo. And suddenly she urgently felt the need for both. But as she was about to stand up a gaggle of people swarmed a nearby cubicle. And then a champagne cork was popped and glasses of bubbles were handed around. Within seconds paper plates began appearing with cheese and crackers haphazardly piled on them. Alice pushed her chair back out of the way as people came by to hug Jen, say their goodbyes and wish her luck. Voices were choked and eyes brimming. Alice looked up and caught the eye of CEO Paul and smiled. He raised his glass to her, which she took as a gesture of welcome and hi and cheers – all of the above.

Suddenly Carmel was there, her presence seemingly brought forth by some powerful force, like a whirlwind. Alice thought she saw Carmel take the glass from someone who'd just taken a sip from it, but decided she must be mistaken – her tiredness was playing tricks on her.

'Jennifer, darling,' Carmel cooed. 'Thank you for taking such good care of me this past month and training Alice to take over. We wish you well with your new adventures, wherever they may take you.'

Alice was sure she felt the mood in the area shift ever so slightly – and not in a good way. Perhaps that was to be expected when management arrived and was like a cat amongst the pigeons. And sure enough, minutes later everyone scattered, including Carmel, leaving Alice and Jen and Pip standing there.

'Jen, thank you so much for everything,' Alice said, hugging Jen tightly. She was surprised to find tears filling her eyes. She barely knew the girl.

'Go forth and be wonderful,' Jen said, a little theatrically. 'Just remember, you're an executive personal assistant, not a slave, Alice. Don't take too much crap,' she added with her hands on Alice's shoulders and looking into her eyes with a serious expression. Alice nodded and tried not to cry. She felt a little overwhelmed at the thought of suddenly being cast adrift.

'I'll leave you to say your goodbyes,' she told Jen and Pip. 'I so badly need to pee,' she said, and bolted.

At home Alice felt a little guilty at thinking she was relieved David wasn't there asking questions and expecting her to debrief with him about her day. With the time difference between Melbourne and London, they'd played phone tag for the past few days. Alice had enjoyed her walk in the park chatting with the non-judgemental and silent Bill, who had trotted along beside her. Later, she'd flopped down on the couch to watch something trashy on TV that didn't need any thought – no plot to follow. For the third night in a row she decided she might make another toasted cheese and onion sandwich for dinner, and enjoy no one being there to complain that her meal didn't contain all the colours and food groups. Alice was a little shocked by the thought that she was not only not missing David's presence, she was actually glad he wasn't there. He'd travelled regularly since they'd met around four years ago, but she'd never felt like this. She was over-tired and emotional, she told herself and tried to shake it off.

★

By the time five o'clock came around on Friday Alice couldn't wait to leave the office. She actually watched the hands on the clock on the wall tick over and grabbed her bags from under her desk right on the dot.

'Where do you think you're going?' Pip asked, popping her head over the partition.

Um, home, Alice was about to say. *Oh, please don't be about to suggest hitting a bar.* At that moment the office suddenly became noisy and Alice detected the distinct sound of bottles and glasses clinking.

'Friday night drinks – yay!' she heard someone exclaim. And, 'Finally,' from someone else.

'What's going on? Another farewell?' Alice asked Pip.

'Friday night drinks – didn't Jen tell you?'

'No.'

'Don't worry, only for half an hour or so. Or several hours – whatever you choose,' she added cheerfully, holding out a paper plate of cheese and crackers, just like the other day.

This must be management's answer to the responsible service of alcohol, Alice thought.

'Oh. Okay.' She tried not to sigh. It wasn't that she was anti-social, but she'd had a big, tiring week. But she also knew the right thing to do was to make an effort to fit in and that it would be good for her long-term future there.

'Good girl,' Pip said as she noticed Alice put her things back under her desk. 'Red, white or beer?'

'Actually, a beer would hit the spot, but only a light, thanks,' Alice said.

'Righteo then, coming up. Jared, a light beer for the young lady over here in the corner,' Pip said.

Alice joined Pip and Jared. 'Cheers,' she said, raising her bottle. After taking a sip and having accepted she was doing the right thing in staying, Alice started to relax. God it felt good to have the first week under her belt and start to feel a little more in the loop.

She heard her phone in her bag ping with a message, and almost groaned when she saw there was a text from Carmel.

A. On Brunswick Street just north of Alexander Parade Fitzroy. What is the closest and best restaurant to me? C.

Alice blinked and then did sigh aloud.

'What?' Pip and Jared said at once.

Alice pointed the phone towards them so they could read the message.

'Ignore it,' they both said in unison.

Alice almost did, but then reminded herself they weren't new here like she was and they weren't Carmel's assistants. Alice Googled the 'Good Food Guide', wondering as she did why Carmel couldn't have done that herself. She'd seen her phone, it was the latest Samsung, and she'd also seen that Carmel was very adept at using it. Alice found the most expensive, most awarded restaurant in the area and sent the link. She also included the link to the 'Good Food Guide' home page as a hint. As she pressed *Send* she knew in two seconds she'd receive a text asking – or rather telling her – to book. Sure enough: *A. Book me a table for two for six-thirty. C.*

Thankfully they had an online booking service and by some incredible stroke of luck a spot for two at six-thirty. *Thank you*, she said silently to the booking gods, or whoever took care of these things. She sent a text to Carmel advising of the booking and couldn't refrain from closing her eyes and shaking her head in frustration.

'Now, turn the bloody thing off and tell us all about yourself,' Jared said, and snatched the phone from her hand and turned it off himself. Alice thought that if she hadn't still been in the office she wouldn't have responded – next time she wouldn't – and she cursed Friday night drinks.

*

Instead of her walk with Bill helping her to calm down after her first week of work, Alice became more confused and frustrated with each step. She had a feeling there was something not quite right about the job, but she couldn't put her finger on it. Was it her? Was it Carmel? Or perhaps they just weren't a good fit together. But Alice didn't see why they needed to be a good fit. They didn't need to be friends. She respected Carmel – idolised her a little actually, if she were being completely honest – and as far as she'd been able to see from their meeting, Carmel felt some respect for Alice too. Otherwise, why would she have given her the job? So what was the bloody problem? *Why do I feel so useless when I know I'm good at my job? And I have great references to prove it. So why can't I seem to do anything right or quickly enough?*

'Oh, Bill, being a human is complicated,' she said when they walked back inside the house. She unclipped his lead and set him free. A moment later her mobile rang with David's name on the screen.

'Hi, there. How's things?' Alice said.

'Okay. Good, actually. I've been invited to play a round of golf tomorrow with the unit head here. Fingers crossed the weather is kind.'

'Nice to be some,' Alice said, trying to sound light and enthusiastic, but failing.

'Are you okay? You sound grumpy.'

'Just tired. It felt like a very long week.'

'Working full-time takes some getting used to. And you're probably on a pretty steep learning curve,' David offered.

'But I'm not,' Alice said. 'I'm not doing anything I haven't done before and that I'm not already good at.' *Though, the pace is pretty hectic at times.*

'Well, you are in a different industry, remember.'

'I know, but it's still admin – filing documents, phone calls in and out and emails. It's not difficult, David.'

'What, so it's boring, is that it?'

'No. I'm frustrated.'

'Why. Isn't Carmel nice?'

'No. Yes. She's nice enough, but … Oh, I don't know. Something just feels a bit off. I don't know what it is.'

'Sounds like someone's overthinking again.'

'Yeah, probably.' It was easier just to agree. Alice realised that what she'd just said made her sound petty and whiny. She couldn't pinpoint what was really bothering her so she couldn't put it into words.

'If you've got an issue, maybe go to HR?'

'Yeah. Maybe.' *And say what? Admit I'm not up for the challenge after all?*

'It's early days, Alice, hang in there. You just need to nut Carmel out and get in sync. You'll be right.'

'Let's hope. She said she likes things done just so, well that was the understatement of the year. She's only one notch off crazy, from where I'm sitting.'

'I guess you don't get your name on the door of one of the largest real estate firms in the city without being pretty clear about how you want things done.'

'I suppose. She could at least say "please" and "thank you" occasionally.'

'Well, you are her PA. I guess it's expected you do as you're told without any palaver.'

'But …'

'Now you're just sounding over-sensitive.'

Am I, though? How hard is it to show some appreciation or even basic manners?

'You're probably right.' Again, it was easier just to agree. But Alice was beginning to fume. Would a man ever be told he was being overly sensitive or overthinking, or some other such patronising tripe? Oh well, no doubt David was trying to help, in his own way. He was not the most sensitive, emotionally in-touch or romantic person. But he was solid and dependable.

Anyway, it was a lot bigger than Carmel not saying 'please' or 'thank you'. Alice's head began to ache when she pictured an incident that had happened the day before, and tried to figure it out. Carmel had accused her of not getting the approval for a client's ad budget in time, but Alice had put the printout on Carmel's desk an hour before. And then when Carmel had found it – right in plain sight on the immaculately tidy desk, where Alice said it was – she had got shitty about Alice having gone behind her back and contacting the client direct. Of course she hadn't raised her voice – Carmel didn't need to in order to be terrifying. That low hiss right by Alice's ear literally made her quiver with fear and begin to sweat.

Alice had left her cubicle feeling disappointed with herself, but with no idea why, and confused about what had actually gone on. More than a day later she still didn't understand what Carmel thought she'd done wrong. Carmel had said from the outset she wanted a self-starter, someone who showed initiative and didn't need constant supervision. So why then was what Alice did apparently wrong? Why was she not supposed to contact clients directly when she was Carmel's assistant and Carmel's phone was regularly diverted to Alice's anyway? Why the bloody hell Carmel couldn't use voicemail like a normal person was beyond Alice, as was most of what Carmel did and expected, as it turned out.

And then there was the barrage of emails – it sometimes seemed as if there was one for each thought Carmel had – coming in throughout the night as well as the working day. Didn't the woman ever sleep? They were mainly messages checking up on things they'd discussed and cleared away the day before. By the time Alice had answered them she was way behind getting started on her work for the day. Was the woman suffering dementia, or something, or just being overly pernickety?

Alice was exhausted, confused and demoralised. *Perhaps I'm not as good as I thought I was. Perhaps this step up from general admin to executive personal assistant* is *too much for me.* She couldn't go to HR when she couldn't work out exactly what the problem was, and because she desperately needed this job. She was on probation. Carmel could terminate her employment immediately and without explanation if she chose to.

'Just think of the great money,' David said cheerfully, breaking into her thoughts and the silence that was starting to feel awkward.

'Yeah.' Alice found herself thinking she wished she'd asked for more. Danger money for losing her mind, because that's how she was beginning to feel.

'Seriously, though, go to HR if you're having a major issue. They might have some advice or strategies for how to cope.'

That stung. *How to cope? It's not me!* Alice wanted to shout. But what was the point? She couldn't really put her feelings into words that wouldn't sound petty, and she ran the risk of being told she was sounding hysterical. It didn't help that David was so far away when probably all she needed was a hug and his strong arms around her. Then she'd feel much better. Their phone calls often left her feeling down, even though she always looked forward to hearing his voice. *Speaking of being out of sync*, she thought.

'Why don't you go and get a massage or your nails or hair done as a treat over the weekend? You deserve it.'

'You know, I think I might. Thanks.' *Hm, I probably should tell you Bill is sleeping in our room now …*

'How's the house?'

'Good, same as when you left. Bill's missing you.'

'I doubt that,' David said with a laugh.

'Well, I am,' Alice said, and was surprised to find tears springing into her eyes. 'Speaking of which, I've just come in. I'm starving and need to feed Bill. I can't stand the way he's looking at me,' she said, trying to sound light and keep the choke out of her voice.

'Okay, I'll let you go.'

'Enjoy your golf tomorrow.'

'I will. Thanks. And you enjoy your weekend. Relax and rest up. Next week is a new one. It'll get easier.'

Alice smiled at David's final little pep talk as she put the phone down. He always concluded a conversation by reiterating the main points he'd made – just like a university essay, really. Or one of his meetings, most likely. That was upper-middle management for you. Alice wished Carmel would be clearer like that and stop communicating in riddles and making Alice guess and second-guess herself while trying to figure out what her boss wanted. And while she was at it, Carmel should stop with the snide, sarcastic comments. At least she spent much of her time out of the office. Alice might be a nervous wreck by now if Carmel were nearby all day, peering over her shoulder, listening in to her phone calls and then commenting on what Alice had said and correcting how she'd said it for next time.

Though, perhaps then there wouldn't be so many apparent misunderstandings, and Alice wouldn't feel like an incompetent fool.

Gah! I don't know!

'Come on, Bill, let's go and get some takeaway.' Alice knew she was probably about to self-medicate with food, but she didn't care. At least she wasn't ordering in. More fresh air would be good, and having a mission instead of walking aimlessly around the park with Bill might help her clear her head and form some coherent conclusions about everything. A sudden craving for rich, juicy garlic bread took over her thoughts.

Chapter Eight

Saturday morning Alice opened her eyes with a start. She sat up and looked around, trying to figure out what had woken her. She rubbed her eyes. *Oh god, that's right, it was a dream.* But what had she been dreaming about? Alice rarely remembered her dreams, rarely dreamt at all, actually. Now her eyes had adjusted to the dark, she could make out Bill on his bed beside hers sitting to attention. She must have been tossing and turning. Alice leant over to check the time. Six-thirty – her usual time to wake. She felt a little groggy – like she needed another hour's worth of sleep. But she'd never go back to sleep, she never did. Lying here would be relaxing but a complete waste of time.

'Do you fancy a walk, Bill?' she said, throwing back the covers.

The dog wagged his little tail and turned around and around in his bed, apparently very excited. Alice smiled as she got dressed, her tiredness evaporating thanks to Bill's glee at the prospect of being taken out.

In the kitchen, she put her travel mug under their hideously expensive but very cool looking automatic coffee machine. It was an example of David's skewed economics. He thought that if they bought this machine they wouldn't need to buy coffee out again, which would save them money in the long run. Alice wasn't sure how many cups the machine would have to make in order to pay for itself, but estimated it had some way to go. Oh well, it did make great coffee.

As she took her phone from the charger, she noticed there were about twenty-five emails from Carmel. She rolled her eyes as she scrolled through the first few. They were essentially 'notes-to-self' more than messages to her. As a very tidy, organised individual, Alice hated an overloaded email inbox, and items that hadn't been dealt with tended to make her feel a little anxious. One thing she was quickly realising was she was now accessible to Carmel 24/7 via her smartphone. She felt a whole new wave of respect for Todd's sparse communication, and was also beginning to understand why David spent so much time with his eyes practically glued to his phone. Dare she delete her Gold, Taylor and Murphy email account? They weren't paying for her phone. She could have what she wanted on her own device, couldn't she? Her heart rate spiked slightly. No, the IT department had set it up, so that kind of made it don't-touch company property, didn't it? Even though it was her phone? Probably. Anyway, it was useful to have everything right at hand all the time. She'd just have to learn to not give a toss about the volume and steadily work her way through all the emails and messages. Otherwise she might go completely mad.

She tucked the phone and keys into the pocket of her running leggings and left the house with mug in one hand and Bill's lead in the other. She'd never been one for headphones when she was walking – she didn't like not knowing what was going on around her. And now she had Bill to take care of, she wanted to give him her full attention.

It was a cool, brisk morning but even when Alice got back to the house with a panting Bill, she still didn't feel wide-awake and invigorated. She was usually energetic, especially after some fresh air and exercise, but thanks to Carmel and Gold, Taylor and Murphy Real Estate plaguing her thoughts she just felt drained. She really needed to do something to take her mind off it all. *But what?* she wondered as she headed into the shower. She'd do the weekly shopping at the local fresh food market as she and David always did. But then what? Often when she was alone or wanted to let off some steam she went to the pool and swam laps. Today she didn't have the energy. She could go clothes shopping and get some retail therapy or other therapy, as David had suggested. Her favourite shopping buddies were Liz, Sarah and Claire – wives of some of David's colleagues who had warmly and generously welcomed Alice into their tightknit group when she'd first arrived in Melbourne. She always had a great time out with them, except for the slightly insecure, deflating feeling of having to be careful with her money while they loved buying designer clothes and barely even checked the prices before handing over their credit cards.

The thought of going shopping with them and treating herself with David's blessing should have filled her with happiness. But as Alice rinsed the conditioner from her hair an image of what the day would look like formed in her mind. They'd each chatter about what they'd been up to since they'd last caught up. And they would ask Alice about her new job, which she'd excitedly announced to all of her friends via text message. It had been so lovely to receive their enthusiastic responses, but now Alice wished she hadn't been so hasty. Not that she could have held back such news for long when her job hunt had been her main topic of conversation for months. The thought of talking about it with anyone – even Lauren or Ruth who were her dearest and wisest friends, and would probably have some good advice or at least make her feel better – suddenly made Alice feel exhausted. No, what she really wanted and needed was a quiet day by herself to recharge. She'd do the market shopping and then head to South-bank for a wander through the National Gallery, but she wouldn't visit the impressionist exhibition that had just opened because David would want to go to it with her. Visiting art galleries was one of the few things they regularly did together.

Out of the shower, sitting in her robe while trying to decide what to wear, Alice picked up her phone. She couldn't resist trying to reduce the email inbox a little. Perhaps she could delete some of Carmel's more trivial communications. But did she dare? Sometimes she'd noticed Carmel didn't seem to recall sending something or mentioning something, but then other times she would make a big deal about something that, to Alice, seemed a complete no-brainer or not even worth a breath or key-stroke to mention. At least Carmel seemed to get over things quickly. Though how quickly was a little disconcerting.

Alice gasped aloud when the phone began to vibrate in her hand and then started to ring. Her eyes bugged as she saw Carmel Gold's name on the screen. Her heart raced and she began to quiver all over – as if she'd been caught doing something she oughtn't. Jen's words, 'She will suck you dry', came to her. For a split second Alice thought about hitting the red spot on the phone and sending the call to voicemail, but stopped herself in time. Then Carmel would know she was ignoring the call. Instead she sat and listened through the six rings – which seemed to take forever – her heart hammering more and more. She really felt watched, as if Carmel could actually see her sitting there not answering the call. She looked around. Her face was burning. She took several deep breaths while she waited to see if Carmel would leave a message. Perhaps it wasn't important enough to leave a voicemail.

Oh, but apparently it was, Alice realised with a sigh, when a text came informing her she had a message. Should she ignore that? But curiosity got the better of her. She didn't have to respond … She dialled the number and put it on speaker.

'I'll be there in ten minutes,' Carmel said in the message.

Alice frowned. What? No, she must have dialled the wrong number. Not for the first time Alice cursed Carmel's brevity and lax use of manners and salutations. Hang on. Did she say 'Alice' right at the end just before it cut off? Alice played the message again. And again it was hard to tell. She couldn't rule it in or out. What to do about it? She didn't want to phone Carmel and check. It was her day off – one of two, in fact. No, she'd get dressed. And she'd get dressed nicely so as to be feeling bold and confident just in case Carmel did turn up. Then she'd be ready to have a firm, rational conversation and set some boundaries.

As she put on her favourite dressy black jeans and electric blue and black top Alice started to feel calmer. Carmel wouldn't know where she lived, anyway. *No, that message wasn't for me.* Most likely Carmel has a friend called Alison and it was a message meant for her. *Oh, but should I phone her back and let her know I got the message instead? Oh god.* Damn it, why did all thoughts of Carmel tie her up in knots? Alice had always suffered episodes of mild anxiety – usually brought on by her mother – but nothing like this. She was being ridiculous.

I don't have to do anything, it's my life. But so much rests on Carmel liking me, Alice reminded herself. No, she didn't need to do anything except find something interesting to do with her day. If Carmel had dialled the wrong number, it wasn't Alice's fault. She'd turn up at Alison's and maybe have to wait while her friend got organised – poor Alison, Carmel hated being kept waiting – and then in the car they'd laugh at the confusion and Carmel would say how Alice must have wondered what that message was all about. Or maybe not. Alice hadn't seen any sign of a genuine sense of humour in Carmel. But she'd seen plenty of examples of sarcasm and little digs. Yes, they'd probably take great joy in Alice being disturbed by a weird message on a Saturday morning.

Listen to me, Bill, I'm going completely nuts. As if Carmel will give it a second thought if it doesn't directly have an impact on her right at that moment. Alice zipped on her boots and went to the kitchen for more coffee. Suddenly she was hungry and microwaved pizza left over from the night before seemed the perfect breakfast and antidote to all her mental toing-and-froing and anguish. *Yep, overthinking!*

Alice paused in her chewing of her slightly rubbery but delicious breakfast when her phone pinged with a text message. She tilted the device towards her to check it. It was from Carmel.

Out the front. Car is running! Hurry up!

Telling herself it wasn't meant for her, she resumed eating.

When the doorbell rang Alice cocked her head. Was her hearing playing tricks on her? But there it was again – twice. Her heart stopped and she froze. No, surely not. She made her way gingerly on tip-toes to the door and looked through the peephole. And saw Carmel with her back to Alice. *Oh my god. It is her. But thank god, she's leaving. Giving up. Yay for no patience!*

Uh-oh. Spoke too soon, Alice thought as the horn of the black, two-door Mercedes honked. *Jesus, it's eight o'clock on a Saturday. Stop it!* Alice cringed. The last thing she needed were cranky neighbours when she'd only just moved in.

A second – longer – honk made Alice tear open the door and run the few steps down the path to the kerb. The dark window slid down.

'Carmel,' she said, but that was all she managed to get out.

'Come on,' Carmel said. 'We're running late.'

'I'm not, um … I …' Alice stammered.

'Alice, do you want to become an agent or not?'

'Well, I … I.'

'Where's your handbag, your phone? You'll need to take notes,' Carmel said. And then it dawned on Alice and she wondered how she could have been so thick. Saturday is one of the biggest days in real estate. *Der!*

'Hang on.' And before Alice knew what she was doing, she'd ducked back inside the house, grabbed her handbag, thrown her phone into it, called goodbye to Bill – she could hear his metal name tag jangling against his food bowl – locked the door and was folding herself into the passenger seat of Carmel's car.

Alice looked around her in awe at all the leather and opulence while cursing her lack of backbone and inability to say no. What was it about this woman? What had she done to Alice? *For goodness sake*, she thought, putting on her seatbelt.

'Right, here's our work for today,' Carmel said, handing Alice her black leather folder. *The day? Work? Oh well*, Alice thought settling back into her plush seat. *It will be good to see how it all works from the other side. And maybe Carmel might start to like me more.* Perhaps the fact that she was taking her along today was a good sign and the start of a better working relationship.

★

Alice stood for a moment watching Carmel's car drive away, unable to move. God, what a day. She was exhausted from hurrying to keep up with Carmel. She couldn't believe the energy of the woman, who had consumed nothing all day, except what appeared to be some kind of green smoothie and a large coffee – the containers of which were stacked in the Merc's cup holders. Alice's stomach had given up protesting over an hour ago. It was nearly four-thirty and she usually ate lunch as close to noon as possible. Her feet had stopped protesting, too, having been numb for the past half hour since she'd sat down in the car. But now she was back standing up she wasn't sure they'd get her to the front door and inside. And these were her most comfortable boots, or so she'd thought. How the hell did Carmel totter about on stilettoes all day – and get around so quickly? Alice had struggled to keep up, even with her long legs. It had been an interesting day, but not exactly educational. All she'd done was stand and hold stuff for Carmel and scurry about after her.

The most disappointing thing about her giving up her day was that she didn't think she'd made any headway with getting to know Carmel better or endearing herself to her. As per usual, Carmel hadn't given her any encouragement or wasted her breath with any pleasantries. Alice felt a wave of anger and disappointment that Carmel hadn't even thanked her for giving up her day. Unpaid. Suddenly Alice's stomach began groaning loudly. And then she started to feel headachy and a little dizzy. Thank god for the leftover pizza, she thought, dashing inside as fast as her tired feet would take her.

*

After a brief conversation with David where she didn't get a chance to express her dismay about all things Carmel Gold because he was too busy giving a hole-by-hole description of his round of golf, Alice turned her phone off. She knew it would take all her will-power not to turn it back on and check it – something she did at least every five minutes – but she was determined that tomorrow there would not be a repeat of today. No siree!

'We're going to have a quiet day alone tomorrow, Bill,' she declared, plopping down on the sofa with the remote. She felt completely drained and needed to recharge – and it wasn't just physical. Carmel really did seem to somehow suck the life out of her.

Chapter Nine

Alice started the working week with a serious case of Monday-itis. It was lucky she had Bill to get up to, otherwise she might have considered calling in sick despite not having accumulated any sick leave yet. But when she'd taken Bill for a walk she convinced herself to suck it up and get ready. As David had said, a new full-time job took some getting used to – physically, mentally and emotionally. It didn't help that she'd only had a one-day weekend. The more she thought about working, unpaid, on Saturday the more annoyed she was that it hadn't been a useful experience. Instead of helping her to figure Carmel out, spending the day with her had only made Alice less sure about the woman. Apart from her lack of pleasantries and occasional terse expressions of frustration, Carmel had smiled and sometimes even seemed pleasant enough and bubbly, but there was something about her that bothered Alice, something she just couldn't put her finger on.

On Sunday night, sitting with a big bowl of popcorn binge-watching *The Good Wife*, Alice had remembered how Carmel had snapped at the auctioneer at the auction of a house in

Hawthorn – a snap that was only audible to Alice because she was standing so close. If she hadn't heard the hiss of words, she would have thought they were having a friendly conversation because Carmel had had a smile plastered on her face the whole time. At one point Alice remembered wondering if Carmel's face was full of Botox because her expression seemed so fixed. Oh well, whatever she did and however she was seemed to work. She was hugely successful, by all accounts, and the Hawthorn property had sold at a price two hundred thousand dollars over the reserve – when bidding had seemed to be well and truly stalled just below the reserve. Carmel was clearly very persuasive as she moved between bidders. Initially some had shaken their heads, seeming to indicate they were at their limit. But after Carmel talked to them they went on to hold their paddles up several more times, finally making the successful bid. Oh how Alice's heart had sunk as the young couple with a baby in a pram and another child on the woman's hip had left looking so dejected.

*

Alice let out a deep breath as she sat down at her desk and began going through her emails before tackling the necessary Monday morning routine of updating the results from the weekend on the database and various websites. She had to get this done as quickly as possible, in between dealing with the calls diverted from Carmel's phone from people wanting to book in a time to see a property they hadn't got to on the weekend. All the while she was trying to outrun the new instructions coming in thick and fast from Carmel and not give in to the feeling of being completely overwhelmed. She was only just holding it together, furiously blinking back tears of frustration. She wasn't even hormonal. God, how would she be then? Trying not to sigh out loud, she glanced up to see a small, friendly looking, middle-aged woman standing beside her cubicle.

'Knock, knock,' the woman said, and smiled warmly. 'Alice? I'm Brenda Andrews, the HR Manager. We spoke that day to tee up your interview with Carmel.'

'Oh, yes, hello,' Alice said, getting out of her chair and extending her hand.

'Can we organise a time to chat?'

No. 'Sure.' *God, what have I done wrong?*

'I just want to see how you're settling in,' she said. Alice thought she must have detected her pessimism.

'Oh. Okay. When?'

'How about four pm? We can get a coffee and go to a conference room?'

'Um, er, I'm not sure. I've got heaps to do,' Alice said, already feeling queasy at the thought of leaving her desk and then getting told off by Carmel for whatever she missed doing.

'Okay, so I'll see you at reception at four? We won't be long. Just half an hour. It's okay, put your phone through to reception.'

God, Alice thought, groaning to herself, *half an hour here is like a whole day everywhere else.* She regularly had to remind herself to pee and now filled up several water bottles at the start of the day so she didn't have to leave her desk so often to walk to the tap in the kitchen. As she was quickly realising, every minute counted here at Gold, Taylor and Murphy Real Estate.

'Okay. See you then,' Alice said, with what little enthusiasm she could muster. *But I'll be blaming you when I get in trouble. Although, you're probably going to tell me off about something anyway.*

Chapter Ten

Alice stood in line at the shoe repair place trying hard not to tap her feet and appear as impatient as she felt. In ten minutes she had to be back upstairs meeting with Brenda from HR. She'd thought she'd easily get this errand of Carmel's done first, but she'd been standing here for more than five minutes. And she didn't want to give up now. Also, Carmel's text had said to collect her shoes before four pm. Alice wasn't sure why when they closed at five-thirty, which was clearly stated on the door. Once she might have thought Carmel's message was a personal reminder accidentally sent as a text to Alice – it was more like what you'd write on a post-it note for yourself than an instruction to someone else. But she'd become used to the abrupt style. She was more annoyed that Carmel hadn't sent the text before lunch so she could have done it then and not compromised the real work she had to do, not that she ever took her full lunch-hour. She just didn't have time. It wouldn't be so bad if she didn't have to meet with Brenda.

At last it was her turn to be served. Alice gave Carmel's name and mobile number and apologised for not having the ticket, and then flamed bright red when she had to confess she had no idea what the shoes looked like.

'Sorry, they're for my boss, that's Carmel. I just got a text message telling me to collect them,' she said, offering an apologetic cringe and holding up her phone as if in explanation. Oh god, it was five to four. Brenda would be waiting for her soon. It took everything Alice had not to say, 'Please hurry up, I'm in a rush.' If the errand wasn't for Carmel she'd just leave and do it another time.

'That will be thirty dollars, thank you,' the woman said, placing a pair of red high-heeled shoes in their open box on the counter.

'Oh. Right. Oh.' *Jesus, Carmel*, Alice thought, dragging out her own bank key card and tapping it.

'Receipt?'

'Yes, please,' Alice said, hoping it was the matter of pressing a button and waiting another second for a printout. She was dismayed when the woman proceeded to write in a small docket book – the sort with carbon paper between the top sheet and a copy underneath. Damn it. But she needed the receipt if she were to get Carmel to reimburse her. Thirty dollars probably wasn't much in the scheme of things, but it was to Alice. And, anyway, it was the principle. Alice didn't like loose ends of any sort.

'Thank you,' she said, as she took the piece of paper while trying not to look like she was snatching. She tucked the shoebox under her arm and rushed out, almost collecting two people entering.

'Sorry,' she called. 'I'm so sorry.'

In the lift she pressed the button over and over in a frenzy, despite knowing full well it wouldn't help to get her upstairs any quicker.

'Brenda, hi,' she said, breathlessly as she stepped into reception and rushed towards the HR Manager. 'I'm so, so sorry. I …'

'Oh, what gorgeous shoes,' Brenda said, peering into the box that Alice had forgotten to put the lid on.

'Yes, they are. They're Carmel's. I just had to pick them up. Before four. And then there was a line up. And …'

'Alice,' Brenda said gently. 'Breathe. It's all right.' She smiled. 'Really. It doesn't matter. You're here now.'

'Thanks,' Alice said, taking a few deep breaths. 'I'm normally very punctual. Never late. I hate being late,' she babbled.

'And that's one of the reasons you're so good at your job. It's okay, Alice, what's a minute or two between friends?'

Or four or five, Alice thought, cringing while sneaking a peek at her watch.

'Would you like a coffee or water or anything?'

'Just water would be good, thanks.' Alice would have given her right pinkie for a silky, milky latte right then, but she was already a little jittery.

'There should be a water jug in the room. This way,' Brenda said, opening the door to the same room where Alice had met Paul, Rose and Mary what seemed like months ago, but was in fact less than two weeks. Alice was a little stunned at the thought.

'So, tell me, how are you finding it here?'

'Well, everyone I meet seems lovely and friendly. It's full on and, to be honest, I'm still getting used to juggling everything. I think being my first full-time role after a few years is taking a little getting used to as well.'

'Alice, you don't need to tiptoe around on eggshells with me. I'm here to make sure you're happy and, if there are any areas you're having difficulty with, I will try to provide you with whatever support you need. I'm fully aware that Carmel can be very demanding and difficult, and even a little intimidating at times,' she said, with a sympathetic smile. 'So, please, be honest with me and together we can iron out any teething issues. Because, frankly, and I hope you don't mind me saying, you seem a bit stressed. If that's just down to adjusting, fine, if not, let me help. We're on the same team, Alice.'

Alice felt a weight leave her shoulders. She wanted to leap across the table and throw her arms around this wonderful, understanding woman with the big brown friendly eyes and sympathetic gaze. She took a deep breath as she felt the beginnings of tears forming behind her eyes and blinked furiously a few times while she thought of how to start and what to say.

'I am a bit overwhelmed, to be honest. I think I'd be fine if it were just the office tasks, but, Brenda, I don't think I quite realised the extent of personal attention I'd need to give Carmel herself. I know the job title means that. I wouldn't mind, only if I don't put the admin stuff first I know I'll get told off from down the line. And, also, there are other people, other departments relying on me to get work to them – I don't want to let anyone down and add to their stress levels. I really need this job. I'm really good at admin – well I thought I was. I'm organised and a self-starter and all I promised in my application and CV and interview, but I feel like I'm doing a really bad job here. I don't know what's wrong with me, but I just can't seem to get it all together. I don't like letting anyone down, but I'm afraid I am.' Her throat was tightening, and Alice was dangerously close to releasing her tears now.

'Alice, I think perhaps you're being too hard on yourself. Have you missed any deadlines or are you behind on putting everything onto the database or the websites?'

'No, but it's always so frantic and I know I'm not doing my best work. I'm trying to do my best, I really am, but it's not enough. Perhaps this just isn't the job for me after all,' she said with a sigh.

'It's still early days, Alice, don't give up too soon.'

The last thing Alice wanted to do was admit defeat, especially with a role like this, which she'd really thought she could practically do with her eyes closed. It's a job in admin, for god's sake, not bloody rocket science!

'Is it a time issue or do you feel you're not adequately trained?'

'No, definitely time. Jen was fantastic. Honestly, I think I'd be fine if it weren't for the constant orders flooding in from Carmel. Even if perhaps she put together a to-do list at the start of the day or at the end. And maybe even an update at lunchtime, because we all remember stuff along the way. It's just the barrage. And the abruptness. I guess because I'm so desperate to please and prove myself I let it get to me. I need to be better at prioritising. That's all. I thought I was good at that, but I'm beginning to wonder if perhaps that's where I'm failing.'

'So what you're saying is Carmel is asking too much of you, personally, aside from the work tasks?' Brenda said.

'Yes, but, well I *am* her personal assistant, so …'

'Can you give me an example?'

Just one? 'Well, these shoes. I got a text message at three-forty saying they needed to be collected by four. I'm not sure why because they're open until five-thirty, and she would know that. I'm not expecting Carmel back in today. But I guess she'll pick them up from her desk after hours or something. I initially wondered if the message was sent to me by mistake – that's something that's taking me a bit to get used to …'

'Sorry, what is?'

'Her manner. A lot of her messages read like notes-to-self or what you'd put in a memo on your phone or a post-it. I know she's very busy and we're all different in our manner,' Alice added, suddenly feeling she had overstepped the mark. She could practically hear 'Dibber dobber' being chanted at her, like what used to go on in the schoolyard all those years ago.

'Can you show me, please?' Brenda said, nodding towards Alice's phone.

Alice brought up the line of text messages.

'Oh. I see what you mean,' Brenda said, blinking, which Alice took as slight surprise.

'It's the same via email, too,' Alice said, and leant over and brought up the email, which just so happened to show that over a dozen messages from Carmel had come in during the last half hour.

'I have to ignore some of them because I just don't have the time, but it's hard to know which ones are important to her. We don't seem to be on the same page with that.'

'Hang on,' Brenda said, scrolling back.

'Honestly, Brenda, I'm struggling to keep up.'

'I'm not surprised.'

'Do you have any advice? Other than quitting. Unless you're going to recommend firing me. I feel like I need my own assistant just to do all those bits and pieces,' Alice said with a laugh, pointing at her phone.

'Well, you must be doing okay because Carmel hasn't made a complaint or said anything to me.'

'Sadly, I think it's only a matter of time,' Alice said.

'Thank you for being honest with me, Alice. I think the best course of action would be for the three of us – you, Carmel and me – to sit down and nut out a productive way forward, together.'

Alice felt a jolt of fear run through her. *God, she'll know I've complained.*

'Just a friendly chat. Carmel wants to get the best out of you just as much as you want to do your best work for her. And for the company as a whole. It's a much better outcome if we can achieve harmony. I'll tee up a time. Meanwhile, Alice, I suggest focussing on the admin side of things first and foremost – if we let that slide it has repercussions down the line, as you've pointed out, and upper management would need to get involved. And then it can get messy. Also, you're doing well. You have to believe that. If you weren't I'm sure I'd have heard from Carmel – or someone else – by now.' Brenda stood up and Alice followed suit.

'Thank you for confiding in me and trusting me with this, Alice. Hang in there. You're not alone,' she said, looking up into Alice's eyes.

'You've no idea how much that means. Thank you. I really appreciate it.' *Appreciate* you.

'I'll be in touch soon.'

As Brenda was walking away, Alice realised she hadn't mentioned working on Saturday. Damn. What if Carmel did the same thing this week? She almost called Brenda back, but figured she'd probably given her enough to deal with.

She felt much better when she returned to her desk, placing the shoes along with the receipt on top of Carmel's desk on her way.

Back in her chair she took a moment to send David a quick text: *Met with HR. Feeling much better. A good idea of yours. Thank you. Xx*

It wasn't really his idea, considering Brenda had come of her own accord, but David would appreciate feeling a part of things and being right. She didn't expect an answer straight away – he'd most likely be in a meeting of his own over in London, depending on the time, or dinner or lunch or some other schmoozey, boozy affair.

Alice put her phone aside, turned to her computer screen, took a deep breath and started going through the new emails to sort

Carmel's personal instructions from the professional requests. She felt a little uneasy about taking Brenda's advice and ignoring some of Carmel's directives, but also knew more strongly now that she couldn't go on the way she had been. Something had to give and the way she was heading it would be her mental state.

Chapter Eleven

Alice was apprehensive about the meeting, but relieved to be getting it over with and having her concerns and frustrations all out in the open, and hopefully finding a solution. The job was interesting, the industry intrigued her, and she really liked most of the people she'd met at Gold, Taylor and Murphy. And of course she loved the salary – so leaving was not an option at this point. *Please let Carmel be calm and understanding*, she silently prayed to no one in particular as she entered the conference room. That was her greatest fear about this meeting – not that Carmel would rant and rave and scream at her. She couldn't picture Carmel doing that. She was always so measured and in control. But her way of calmly scolding while smiling at you was terrifying and unsettling. The smile and softly spoken words, 'Alice, can I just have a quick word please,' made Alice feel as if she was being lured into the web of a venomous spider. She'd come up close so no one else could hear, tell Alice off – in the nicest possible way – and then dismiss her with a wave. Free again, Alice was left feeling discombobulated, wondering if what she'd thought had happened had happened – had the spider bitten or just played with her? The clincher was how quickly Carmel seemed to get over things. All was well the next moment, as if there had been no reprimand, and the incident was never mentioned again. Alice supposed that was better than open hostility but, still, it was disconcerting.

'Hi,' she said to Brenda who was seated at the head of the table.

At three minutes past their appointed time – six minutes after Alice's arrival, when she and Brenda had passed the time discussing the weather and what they'd had for lunch – Carmel breezed in, followed by Paul, Mary and Rose. Alice's mouth fell open, her heart began to race and her armpits became damp. *Uh-oh.* Carmel seated herself opposite Alice and the others to her right, with Paul taking the foot of the table or second head, depending how you looked at things. Carmel appeared calm, although Carmel Gold always appeared calm. She folded her hands and placed them slowly on the table in front of her, giving Alice a glacial stare as she did – or had Alice imagined that. She then looked expectantly at Brenda. Alice turned to look at Brenda too, who seemed to have paled in the past ten seconds. She swallowed and moistened her lips and began to speak.

'Carmel, this was to be an informal meeting between the three of us. There was no need to bring anyone else in.'

'I'm entitled to have whomever I wish beside me, as is Alice. Perhaps you'll be so good as to get started, Brenda. I have a lot on and really don't have time for trivial meetings about whining subordinates. No offence, Alice,' she added, flashing a wide, sugary smile.

Alice felt sick to the stomach. *Oh god, what have I done? No, I'm not doing anything wrong in raising something that's causing me issues. And it might be trivial to you, Carmel, but it isn't to me.* Alice wished she had the courage to say this aloud, but Carmel was frightening. Part of her wanted to get up and run from the room, the building, and never come back. But she didn't think her quivering legs would hold her up if she attempted to stand right now, let alone move. *Stay strong*, Alice told herself and forced herself to calmly take a sip from the glass of water she'd poured when she came in, while staring down Carmel with the most challenging, steely look she could muster. She probably just appeared to all like a terrified rabbit caught in car headlights.

'Right, Alice, Carmel,' Brenda said, 'we're meeting to ensure all is working as well as it can be.'

'Well, clearly it's not, is it? Because I've been summoned here away from work that *actually* matters, to be criticised for goodness knows *what*,' Carmel said.

'Carmel, there's no need to get defensive,' Brenda said.

'Really?'

Alice noticed the cold glare Carmel directed at Brenda, the intensity of which told her there was some history to Carmel's hostility towards the HR Manager. Suddenly she found herself wondering how many of Carmel's PAs had sat here before her, how many meetings like this had been called. Alice straightened her back and became determined not to be the next one to leave.

'I suggest you just get on with it. What petty complaint has been made about me this time? Let me guess, Alice is complaining about being too busy, unable to cope with the fast pace of this office, my exacting manner. We've had words along these lines already, which doesn't bode well for long-term employment, does it, really? Alice, didn't you tell me in the interview you were known as "Little Miss Helpful"?' Carmel said sweetly, her head cocked to the side and smile firmly in place.

'Carmel, I'd be fine if you didn't have me running all over the city for you on personal errands,' Alice said, unable to remain silent another moment.

'You're my personal assistant, Alice, it's what you signed up for,' Carmel said with a sneer.

At that moment Alice thought her the ugliest woman she'd ever seen – how could she have thought Carmel beautiful, been in awe of her? Alice had no response that wouldn't sound petty. Thankfully Brenda took control again.

'We're here to find harmony, not attack anyone, Carmel. If Alice can't get all her important work done, then we have a problem.'

'No, we find someone who works quicker and smarter,' Carmel said. 'And I thought you held such promise, Alice.'

And I you, Carmel, Alice thought, too bewildered and scared to speak. This wasn't what she'd been expecting at all.

'She's under probation, just get rid of her,' Carmel said. 'Why is she still here if she isn't happy, anyway?'

'She has impeccable credentials and comes highly recommended, Carmel,' Paul said.

'Well, someone or several somebodies lied,' Carmel said.

'She really was the best candidate,' Mary said.

'Yes,' Rose said, nodding.

Hey, I'm right here, Alice wanted to say.

'Look, can we please just stick to the facts and find a satisfactory way forward,' said Brenda. 'Carmel, I've seen the volume of, um, personal texts and emails you've bombarded Alice with and ...'

'Oh dear, it's like being in high school all over again,' Carmel said, with a brittle laugh.

'No one should be expected to respond to them all and fulfil their other obligations,' Brenda continued, ignoring Carmel. 'And, bombarded is not an understatement,' she said, looking at Paul. 'Frankly, I'm surprised Alice has done as well as she has so far.'

'Oh, come on, Brenda, what would you know about anything? You're HR, for goodness sake.'

Again Brenda ignored the barb directed at her. 'For the record, Carmel, Alice didn't come to me. I asked her to meet with me to check how she was settling in, which is actually an important part of my job. Alice is too much of a professional to …'

'But you're not, Brenda. I know you've got it in for me. Just remember whose name is on the door.'

'I'm fully aware, Carmel, you don't need to threaten me,' Brenda said patiently, keeping her tone neutral. Alice was impressed at her fortitude and restraint.

'Ladies,' Paul said, 'we don't have time for squabbling. I want to see these text messages and emails. Or have you deleted them, Alice?'

'No, they're pretty much all there,' Alice said and passed her phone over. There was silence while he scrolled and read, his eyes opening up wide as he went.

Alice looked down, feeling Carmel's gaze burning into her. Her head pulsed with the intensity of a hammer hitting her temple over and over.

'What's this about Saturday?' Paul asked, looking at Alice. 'We haven't approved overtime for Alice yet,' he said, now looking at Carmel.

'How's the girl going to get a grasp of the industry without attending auctions and opens? I was doing her a favour, for goodness sake. What is wrong with you people?'

Girl? Excuse me, I'm a thirty-year-old woman!

'It's too soon – let her get a handle on how things work back here first,' Paul said.

'She should be able to handle both, otherwise she'll never get anywhere.'

'Carmel, you need to keep it work-related – her job description might be personal assistant, but … We've been through this before,' he added with a tired, exasperated sigh.

Uh-huh, Alice thought.

'Well, thanks a lot for your support, Paul,' Carmel practically spat.

'Seriously, Carmel, just leave Alice alone to do her job,' he said.

'I might if I thought she had enough initiative, enough smarts.'

'Perhaps you need to trust her. We won't know what she's capable of if you keep hovering and overloading her unnecessarily, Carmel,' Brenda said.

'Carmel, I really want to learn from you,' Alice said, looking up pleadingly at Carmel. *I need this job.*

'Well, lesson number one. Don't be a tattle tale,' Carmel said, rising, flashing Alice and then Brenda sickly smiles, and striding across the room. Mary and Rose grimaced apologetically at Alice before getting up and following her out.

'I'm sorry, Alice, Brenda,' Paul said, nodding to them both. And suddenly Brenda and Alice were alone.

'Well, that was fun,' Alice said in an attempt to lighten the mood.

'I'm really sorry, Alice. Some people just can't take constructive criticism of any sort.'

That's the understatement of the year, Alice thought, but kept the comment to herself. 'Where to from here?'

'Carmel might have seemed unwilling to listen, but Paul's words might have hit home.'

'Hmm. I'm not the first, am I, Brenda?'

'Unfortunately not. But I can't say any more than that. I hope you'll understand.'

'I really need this job.'

'I know. And Carmel really needs a decent PA, so let's hope something good has come out of today's meeting, even if it doesn't look like it right now. I'm sorry about how uncomfortable it was for you, especially with her bringing an entourage. I had no idea she'd do that.'

'Thanks for standing up for me, Brenda. I really appreciate it.'

'There's no need to thank me, Alice, I'm doing my job. I'm just sorry it didn't go better. I'll keep in touch, but remember, you're not alone. I'm just a phone call away if you need to talk. Any time.'

'Thanks.'

Alice returned to her chair feeling dejected. Thankfully Carmel had left the building.

'How did it go?' Pip asked, her head appearing over the partition.

'Terrible. I don't think we achieved anything except piss Carmel off.'

'Oh dear. Well, that's not hard. Hang in there. Please don't think it's you.'

'Thanks. I'll try. Um, Pip?'

'What?'

'What happened to her last PA?'

'Carmel happened,' Pip whispered. 'And to the one before and the one before that.'

'How many?'

'Something like six in the last two years.'

'Wow.' Alice's eyes were wide. 'Seriously?'

'Yup,' Jared said, popping up beside Pip.

'Why didn't you tell me?' Alice said.

'I really wanted it to work out with you,' Pip said. 'It didn't feel right to taint your experience.'

'Yeah. Jobs are hard enough to get at the moment as it is,' Jared said. 'When you said you were talking with HR, we really wanted to share some home truths, we really did. But we're not allowed to talk about it – under threat of being fired.'

'Mmm, that's right,' Pip said.

'Really?' Alice said, her eyes now even wider with slight disbelief. 'God.'

'Yes. Seriously. It's like the company's dirty little secret. But you didn't hear that from us,' Pip said.

'No, you most certainly did not. Please don't be mad at us,' Jared implored, tilting his head and putting on puppy-dog eyes and a pout.

'Of course I'm not mad with you guys. It's not your fault this place is strange and secretive. And I do get that rules are rules. I really appreciate you taking the risk now. It's a bit of a relief to know it might not be just me, so thanks for that.'

'If only there was something we could do to actually help,' Pip said, offering a grim, sympathetic smile.

'Well, it means a lot to know you care.'

'Oh we so do,' Pip said. 'We're here for you, Alice.'

'Yes, chin up. You're too beautiful to be sad,' Jared said, pouting again. 'Chin up.'

'Yes, hang in there, Alice,' Pip whispered, putting her hand over Alice's and giving it a quick squeeze. 'Come on, Jared, we'd better get back to it. I'm not entirely sure this place isn't bugged,' she said. Their heads disappeared and the next moment they could be heard tapping on their keyboards.

Alice didn't think the office really was bugged but found herself shuddering nonetheless. After today, she'd put nothing past Carmel.

Chapter Twelve

Alice was pleased she'd already told Pip and Jared that morning that she had to get home early and wouldn't be staying for Friday after-work drinks. As she made her way down Bourke Street to the train station, her head was still spinning from the meeting and the brief conversation afterwards over the partition. *Wow, what an exasperating but eye-opening day!* She wasn't mad with her work friends for not saying something before. She'd probably have taken the same approach if she were in their position. And really, knowing the truth didn't change anything, except perhaps make her more determined to succeed. She still needed the job.

Alice was looking forward to David arriving home in a few hours; that's what she needed to focus on. Boy did she need a hug and his calm, solid, sensible presence. She was cooking a lamb roast with all the trimmings to celebrate. It would be a late meal, but one worth waiting for. She was also making a sticky date pudding from scratch, knowing that cooking always eased her tension and tonight it would take her mind away from work. She really hoped David's plane would be on time and he'd be home at a reasonable hour. At this point she was aiming to eat at eight o'clock.

At least I don't have to worry about being summoned by Carmel tomorrow, Alice thought as she settled into a seat and the train took off smoothly. She wouldn't dare now. Though Alice did feel a slight pang of regret. It hadn't been such a bad day and she was keen to learn all the inside tricks from someone so successful.

On the way home, Alice noticed that her anxiety levels had gone down a notch, now that the barrage of requests of a personal nature had ceased – suddenly and completely, as if a tap had been turned off. Actually, there hadn't been a single text or email from Carmel since the meeting. Like Brenda said, she'd be off process-ing what had gone on and deciding how to proceed. Alice really hoped it would be a better, more realistic and productive relation-ship going forward. But the knot still tied in her stomach told her Carmel's reaction had been quite benign and that she was kidding herself if she thought the woman would change her ways because some newly appointed PA happened to call out her behaviour.

Oh well, at least it was all in the open now and Alice seemed to have the support from Paul higher up. And of course she had Brenda on her side. It felt good to have aired it – she didn't feel quite so alone – but being a 'dobber' didn't sit well with her. It was such a no-no at high school and she'd carried that attitude with her into her adult life. But she really hadn't been left with any alternative, had she? Perhaps she should have told Carmel she was struggling and asked if she could tone down the personal requests. *Yeah, right*, Alice scoffed. She actually shuddered at picturing herself approaching Carmel direct. She wished she could put her finger on what it was about Carmel that so intimidated her. It wasn't just that she was her boss and one of the heads of the organ-isation. Alice had never had a problem with authority. And she certainly didn't with Paul. She really liked him. And it wasn't because Carmel was extremely wealthy. Rich or poor, people were just people to Alice.

She opened the front door and looked around to see where Bill was. As usual he was well back out of the way, sitting like a good boy.

'Darling Bill, god, you're a sight for sore eyes,' she said, picking him up. She was so tired and over-wrought from the meeting and the subsequent toing-and-froing in her head she almost wept. She knew that owning a pet was good for one's mental and emotional wellbeing. She'd read plenty about it in the press recently. But she never would have thought that the effect of just seeing Bill's wagging tail and non-judgemental face greeting her at the door would be so dramatic and immediate. She didn't even care that her clothes got covered in a fine layer of white and brown fur.

'You've no idea how much joy you bring, Billy boy. If only you could come to work with me. You'd have Carmel wrapped around your little paw and the ice in her veins would melt and flow warm in no time.' Alice reluctantly put the dog down. She didn't want to stop feeling his warm little body and heart beating against her.

'You deserve a walk before we start on dinner,' she said as she went through to the bedroom and got changed. 'A walk, what do you think?'

'Woof,' was the response.

Alice laughed. 'Good boy. Come on then.' She did her shoes up and grabbed his lead and clipped it on. 'Your dad's going to be home later and we're cooking him a yummy dinner.'

Alice heard the key in the front door just as she put the pudding into the oven. She slid her hands out of the oven mitts, placed them on the bench, and raced down the hall to greet him, Bill trotting ahead of her.

'Welcome home, darling,' Alice said. 'Ooh, that's nice, you don't smell like an icky traveller at all.'

'No, I managed to get a shower in Sydney on my way through. God, it makes such a difference,' he said. But still he didn't embrace her.

'How are you feeling, how was the flight?'

'Okay. It's nice to have a welcoming committee,' he said, reaching down to pat Bill. 'Something smells good,' he said with a smile.

'Roast lamb and then sticky date pudding,' Alice said proudly. 'Thank goodness you've already showered, because it's ready right now. If you're okay to eat?'

'I certainly am! The trip was good, thanks. Everything is coming together.'

Alice wasn't sure what David did on these trips or what the meetings or social functions entailed or what was discussed, and she didn't care to know. A few years ago she'd given up really listening to his work chatter after she'd realised it was more about him venting, debriefing, and getting stuff off his chest than helping her to understand what he did in his job, or encouraging her to have an opinion. She'd learnt the hard way that he thought it would all go over her head. These days she nodded with interest and made soothing, encouraging noises and shows of sympathy when appropriate.

'How did your meeting go with HR and Carmel?' he said a few mouthfuls into his plate of roast meat and vegetables swimming in gravy, just the way he liked it.

'Terrible. But it feels good to have been heard and I'm not so alone. But she turned up with Paul, Rose and Mary. And there I was with Brenda. Talk about mortifying and intimidating!'

'I guess that was rather the point. I don't blame her, though. I probably would have done the same.'

'But why? It was just meant to be a meeting between Carmel and me, facilitated by Brenda.'

'I guess she felt threatened. It's unlikely a meeting like that would be called to give someone a pat on the back for a job well done. Of course you're going to get straight on the defensive, if you're smart.'

'Right. Well, anyway, she threw a hissy fit – well, a Carmel-completely-measured-and-composed-hissy-fit. She got snarky, wouldn't really listen and sort anything out. Defensive, really, and then she walked out.'

'And you're surprised, why?'

'I don't know, I suppose I thought she'd be more interested in working through things and sorting out a satisfactory way forward.'

'You dragged her into a meeting with HR because you complained about her, Alice, of course she's going to be pissed.'

'What else was I meant to do? Anyway, you suggested it!' Shock mixed with Alice's rising frustration.

'I know, but I didn't think you'd take that option quite so quickly. It's been less than a month. There are always going to be a few teething issues and settling in time needed. I've told you all this. And don't forget, as far as she's concerned she's done nothing wrong – you're the newcomer who's meant to be working for her.'

'So, you think I'm being a petty dobber? Well, thanks a lot!'

'Come on. I just think you're taking longer to get into the swing of things than you'd hoped and you're letting the frustration get to you.'

'You don't know what it's like. It's horrible,' Alice said, picking up her empty plate and taking it to the sink.

'It's a pity you turned down the Outercover job then, isn't it?'

Alice blinked back tears. Where was David's love and support? She wasn't being melodramatic or overly sensitive. Working for Carmel *was* horrible.

'Just leave, then, if it's so bad,' David said.

'I can't without a reference and three weeks wouldn't look good on my CV, would it?'

'So, stay and work it out. But you can't keep complaining about it.'

'For fuck's sake, David, discussing it with my partner – who's supposed to be supportive and who I've had maybe one ten-minute conversation with in the past two weeks, which was nine minutes about him, as usual – is hardly someone who, *quote*, keeps complaining about it,' she cried.

'Alice. God, where did that come from? Calm down, now you're sounding hysterical. And you hardly ever swear!' He looked genuinely stunned. Alice was glad she'd shocked the composure from his face.

'Come on, Bill, we're going for a walk.'

'But what about sticky date pudding for dessert?'

'It's in the oven, get it yourself!'

Alice's cheeks were flaming and she was glad to step out into the chilly evening air. David was right about one thing: she rarely swore out loud – well, not the 'f' word, anyway. But she'd also never felt so frustrated, lost and unsupported. Maybe if she'd told Carmel to shove her restaurant bookings, shoe repairs, et cetera, up her arse and let her do some real work all would be well. Perhaps the problem was Carmel thought her too weak. She wasn't weak; she was kind and caring by nature and gentle. *And there's nothing wrong with that!*

By the time Alice reached the road going around the park, she was starting to feel a lot calmer. 'Thank goodness for you, Bill,' she said, giving the dog a pat while they waited for a decent break in the traffic. 'You're a good, good boy.'

And what difference did her having been out of the workforce make, anyway? She went back over the conversation while she and Bill traipsed their way around the park on the concrete path under the lights. 'I can do the technical aspects of the job. I've mastered all the new computer programs and database and office processes. The problem I'm having is with people. People don't change and I've been interacting with humans all my life. Fuck you and your patronising comments, David! You don't know what the hell you're talking about!' Alice said aloud.

She took a deep breath. It was her experience and hers alone. Of course he didn't know. He was only commenting on what she was saying, which she could see probably did sound like a whinge. Feelings were very individual things. And from her four years with David she knew he didn't have a whole lot in the emotional vault. He tended to be very black and white. So why the hell was she so surprised?

Alice felt a little sheepish as she made her way inside the house. She unclipped Bill and deliberated over going to bed instead of facing David.

'Amazing sticky date pudding,' he called and she sighed and went through to the kitchen. 'Best one ever,' he said, looking up at her and smiling weakly.

'Thanks,' she said. And that would be that. The argument was over. This was always the way it worked with them. 'Sorry, I'm just really frustrated,' she said, going over and wrapping her arms around his neck. She was still annoyed, but needed to swallow it down. Staying angry wouldn't help. David just didn't understand.

'If it's really that bad, leave,' he said. But while Alice welcomed his comment, which might have seemed supportive to anyone looking in from outside, she knew that from David it was barbed. It was a challenge. He knew Alice possessed a stubborn streak and didn't give up easily, especially when challenged. His tone held the unspoken words, *If it's too much for you to handle.* Alice hated to disappoint anyone, and David would be very disappointed in her if she gave up so easily.

'Maybe it'll get better,' she said, tucking into the bowl of pudding, cream and ice-cream he'd dished up for her. 'She already seems to have stopped with the stream of trivial messages.'

'Well, there you go. Maybe it was the jolt she needed.'

'Apparently it's not just me,' Alice said. 'Pip from work said I'm the latest in a long line of PAs who've left.'

'Another reason why you don't want to just leave – you'll be another number, a statistic.' David said these words in the sort of tone that suggested he'd not told her to leave, but encouraged her to stay. Alice stopped herself from pointing out his hypocrisy.

'Apparently the staff is sworn to secrecy about the other PAs leaving – under threat of dismissal. Isn't that a bit extreme?'

'No. Loose lips sink ships, Alice. They're protecting their brand. Loyalty within is really important.'

'I guess. It's nice to know Jared and Pip are looking out for me,' Alice said, not sure what else to say.

'The sooner you realise most people who pretend to be your friend, aren't, and that most people can't be trusted, Alice, the better off you'll be.'

'God, David, when did you become so cold and cynical?'

He shrugged. 'It's the truth, backed up by experience. People are usually only nice because they want something in return.'

Alice felt a painful surge of disappointment. How sad to be so negative. She was a little shocked. She stared at David, wondering who this man was who she was planning on marrying and spending the rest of her life with – if he ever proposed. *Is nothing real or genuine anymore?* She had the uneasy feeling that her whole life was imploding. Thankfully David had got up and was too busy rinsing his plate to see her stunned, sad expression as she continued to stare at him.

'I reckon we should go and look at some open houses or auctions for fun tomorrow, since you're now in real estate. What do you say?' David said, turning around from the sink.

'Okay. Thanks. Sounds like fun.'

Poor David, he probably thought this was just the sort of support she was wanting from him. He didn't have a clue. Alice forced herself not to shake her head at his ignorance. Thank goodness she had lunch on Sunday with her uni mates to look forward to.

Chapter Thirteen

Alice was the first to arrive and take a seat in their usual spot in the corner of the pub with a glass of white wine. Within a minute or two Lauren arrived and waved her leather-bound journal in greeting as she made her way over with a glass of wine, picking her way around the other tables and chairs. Alice smiled and waved back.

'Hey, how's things?' Lauren asked as they had a quick hug before she sat down.

'Good. And you?' Alice suddenly realised how much she'd missed Lauren and felt a pang of disappointment in herself. She'd been neglecting their friendship since she'd started working at Gold, Taylor and Murphy. 'It's really good to see you. I'm so sorry I've been such a crap friend lately.'

'You haven't. Never. We've been texting regularly. I get that you need time and space to find your feet and adjust to life in the real estate business. You know you can always call if you need a decent chat. And I know if I need you, you'll be there for me. Seriously, don't think anything of it,' Lauren said.

'Thanks. You're too kind.'

'How's it going, anyway – Ms Budding-real-estate-tycoon?'

'Oh ha-ha. I'm not taking on the world just yet. In fact, I'm barely keeping my head above water at this point,' Alice said, attempting to sound light.

'I gather from your texts that it's a really big learning curve.'

'Well, it is that! I'll get there.'

'Yes, I know you will.'

'How's the writing going?' Alice said.

Lauren was determined to forge a career as a novelist, and writing was pretty much the sole focus of her existence, other than being a good friend to a lot of people.

'It's not. Well, I'm still not writing the Great Australian Novel, anyway,' Lauren said.

'Oh, dear. I'm sorry to hear that. It'll come,' Alice said.

'Yeah, maybe when I've finished my masters. One can only hope, and there's no point worrying about it. Meanwhile, it's short stories for me,' she said, raising her glass. 'Cheers.'

'Cheers,' Alice said, raising her own glass.

'Hello, ladies.' Brett appeared with a beer in his hand.

Alice and Lauren both leapt up and gave him a quick hug.

'So, what have I missed?' he said after taking a long sip from his glass.

'Nothing at all. I've just this minute arrived,' Lauren said.

'And I've only been here long enough to get a drink,' Alice said.

'So, Alice, how's it going out in the big wide world?' Brett asked.

'Great,' Alice said with all the enthusiasm she could muster. 'It's nice to have some decent money come in.'

'And I saw on Facebook you and David got yourselves a child substitute,' Brett said.

'We did. A rescue dog – Bill. He's a Jack Russell, two years old and absolutely the dearest thing. He's settled in really well.'

'Well, come on, I know you're dying to show us a thousand photos,' he said.

'Careful what you ask for,' Alice said with a laugh. She beamed as she got her phone out, brought up the photos, and held the device out for them to see.

'He's so gorgeous. I can't wait to have a cuddle,' Lauren said, leaning in to look at the screen.

'A handsome fellow, indeed,' Brett said.

'Do you know what his story is? How he ended up at the shelter?' Lauren asked.

'No. They didn't tell us anything. I don't want to know, anyway. Just knowing someone might have given him up makes me really sad.'

'I hate hearing how old people going into nursing homes have to give up their pets. Imagine being utterly broken about losing your independence and the home you love and then having the extra heartbreak of needing to give up your pet. It's just awful,' Lauren said.

'There are actually some places that allow pets to go with you now,' Brett said. 'The Animal Welfare League has a great website where you can search for pet friendly nursing homes. A friend's gran is in one.'

'Oh, thank god for that,' Lauren said with a visible sigh. 'It makes the thought of getting old less terrible.'

'Lauren, you're not even thirty!' Alice said.

'I know, but I'm always thinking.'

'Maybe that's what you can write about,' Alice said, 'a woman who causes trouble for her family because she won't give up her pet to go into a nursing home.'

'Ah, still looking for that elusive seed eh, Lauren?' Brett said.

'Yup. I think I need to travel,' she said wistfully. 'Maybe I won't find the story I'm looking for in Melbourne. Mum and Dad are having the best time on their cruise.'

'Floating retirement homes, my gran used to call them,' Brett said.

'Yeah, you're probably right. I know I'm trying too hard, but I can't seem to help it. I want to write something great.'

'You'll figure it out,' Alice said. 'But I still don't get what's wrong with writing short stories.'

'I love doing them, and they've all got good grades so far, but there isn't the market for them that there is for a novel. I could never make a living by writing them. And if I'm being really honest, I'm probably snobby about novels being the be all and end all.'

'There's nothing wrong with knowing what you want to do and sticking to your guns,' Alice said.

'Yes. And inspiration will strike when you least expect it,' Brett said. 'Isn't that what they always say?'

'Who?'

'Oh, I don't know, all the old literary masters. What would I know? I'm an engineer. We deal in certainty and *make* things happen.'

'Speaking of masters. How's yours going?' Lauren asked.

'It's bloody hard,' Brett said. 'Can we not talk about it – I need a day of not thinking about it or work. That's hard at the moment, too. Thank goodness I'm only there three days a week. Let's order food. Do you think anyone else is coming?'

'No, I suppose it's just us,' Alice said. She found herself feeling a little relieved that Helen was a no-show. Or perhaps she was just running late – she hadn't sent a message to say one way or the other. The older woman was pleasant enough, but she tended to rub Alice up the wrong way sometimes because she was so forth-right. She reminded Alice a little too much of her mother. Helen had done Marketing and English Literature and Alice thought she was now doing Women's Studies, but couldn't remember for sure. Alice also didn't like that Helen had declared a few times that she didn't care what size student loan debt she ended up with because she wasn't planning on earning enough to pay it back – she was going to stay studying until she retired. Alice didn't think that was quite fair or the right thing to do.

'Yes, I'm starving,' Lauren said, picking up the menu despite most likely knowing it by heart. 'Did you check the specials? I completely forgot.'

'I did, as it happens,' Brett said. 'Pie of the day is beef and mushroom, soup is pumpkin, pasta is spag bol, and roast of the day is chicken.'

'Thanks for that. Glad someone was taking notice,' Alice said. 'My brain's a bit fuzzy at the moment.'

They took turns going up and ordering so they didn't lose their spot.

'So why is your brain fuzzy?' Brett said when they were all seated again after ordering. 'Is the new job a bit too full on?'

'Something like that,' Alice said.

'Alice, is something else wrong?' Brett said after she didn't go on to say anything more. 'If you don't mind me mentioning it, you're not your usual jovial self,' he said. 'Aren't you enjoying the job?'

'No. I'm not, actually. It's hard. Well, no, it's not that *it's* hard. My boss is hard.'

'As in not nice hard or piles on too much work hard?' Brett asked.

'Bit of both, maybe. I'm not sure. I can't put my finger on it. Perhaps it's just too early to tell.'

'I reckon you'd know within a day or so if someone's not nice,' Lauren said.

'Yes, but it takes time to know if you can or want to work with someone who isn't nice,' Brett said.

'So, what's going on?' Lauren said.

'I think it'll be fine now, I met with HR to try to sort it out.'

'Wow. Three weeks in, is it? I hope HR didn't tell your boss you were complaining,' Brett said.

'Why?' Alice asked.

'How would you feel if a subordinate complained about you – because, let's face it, a meeting with HR is never going to be about good news,' he said.

'God, you sound like David,' Alice said, her cheeks colouring.

'Ignore him, it's the pragmatic engineer in him,' Lauren said.

'Thanks a lot,' Brett said.

'It's really getting to you, isn't it?' Lauren said, scrutinising Alice more closely.

'Yes. I think I'm a complete failure. And I feel like I'm losing my mind,' Alice said, her throat constricting. It was a huge relief to finally talk openly about it to someone other than Bill. She'd known from the start that she would have to be careful when discussing it with David. She had to sanitise her experiences to a certain extent, so she didn't come across as a moaner. Now she wished she'd called Lauren to talk about it earlier.

'Why? What do you mean?' Lauren asked.

'I'm second-guessing myself about stuff I've been able to do for years. I'm losing my initiative – because I'm supposedly not allowed to have any. Though, in the interview, that's apparently what she wanted in a PA. So I'm stuffed if I know. I was also going mad with her bombarding me with all these silly personal things to do, like booking restaurants and running errands all over the place. I know I'm a personal assistant, but it was getting beyond ridiculous. That's why I went to HR. Well, the HR lady came to me first to see how I was settling in and it all just sort of came out. I couldn't help it. There're all these things I have to do for the company and if I don't I'll get yelled at from other departments. You'd think as one of the heads – with her name on the door – she would get that. She might now. She seems to have stopped with the excessive messages. We'll see tomorrow – the meeting was on Friday.'

'Is she mean to you, is that it?' Lauren asked.

'I honestly don't know.'

'How can you not know if she's being mean to you or not?' Brett said.

'I did say I felt like I was losing my mind. It's a feeling, like she's being nice but there's something not nice behind it. It's really subtle. Oh, I don't know, it's like she's putting on an act. And she loves a snide comment and a sneer. I hate that. It's so rude. And she's abrupt, and I know it's a bit petty, but she never says "please" or "thank you". Or "sorry". She was so affronted she stormed out of the meeting. No, not stormed, Carmel only ever acts with composure and decorum, but I would have expected her to say sorry or at least appear a little remorseful. Someone doesn't go to HR without having good reason, no matter what you say, Brett,' Alice said.

'Hey, don't attack me. Why don't you leave if you're not happy? And clearly you're not, because you're all over the place. Sorry, just calling it as it is,' he said, raising his hands, palms out.

'He's right about that, Alice,' Lauren said gently. 'You're practically a nervous wreck. Your hands are even shaking. And since when do you have so much trouble deciding on what to eat?'

Alice hid her hands in her lap out of sight.

'I didn't sleep well last night. Actually I haven't slept well for a while now. I keep having bad dreams about it all.'

'That's not good. So why aren't you leaving?' Lauren asked.

'I'm not a quitter. I, we, need the money – having just bought the house. The usual boring reasons,' Alice said with a wan smile. 'I'm beginning to wish I'd taken the other job I was offered – with the man who put his fist through the photocopier. There just aren't many jobs around. Well, either that or no one wants me. And the job I have is great money.'

'Money isn't everything, Alice,' Lauren said. 'I know I'm in no position to comment on that and I'm not in your situation but, seriously, your health has to come first.'

'I was so thrilled when they rang me, said flattering things in the interviews and then offered me the job. I was on top of the world. I really thought it was the perfect job,' Alice said sadly.

'Flattery will get most people,' Brett said.

'Well, you're only human,' Lauren said.

'You know, I don't think real estate is about helping people at all,' Alice said.

Brett almost spat out his mouthful of beer. 'That can't be what you thought going in. Surely not. Come on, you're smarter than that. It's never been about that, Alice.'

'Brett, don't be cruel,' Lauren said. 'I can see where Alice gets that idea – you'd be helping people find their perfect home and other people the right price.'

'Exactly what I thought. Thanks, Lauren. I feel like such a fool.'

'Don't. I'm sure there are plenty of people in real estate who feel that to some extent. Perhaps you're just with the wrong company.'

'Again, I pose the question,' Brett said, 'why are you still there? Other than the money.'

'It wouldn't look good on her CV to leave so quickly,' Lauren said.

'Leave it off, then. What's a few weeks?' Brett said.

'Oh, but then I wouldn't be being honest,' Alice said.

'Argh,' Brett said, waving his hand dismissively before taking a slug of beer.

'And she can't leave without a reference, and if she's struggling, then …' Lauren said as if thinking aloud.

'Exactly,' Alice said.

'But you've got a reference from the previous place, right – the one that offered you the marketing job?' Brett said.

'Yes, but I think they're shirty I didn't take it, so if anyone rang I don't think the comments would be quite so glowing now. And, anyway, they might let slip that I took another job. Todd's a friend of ours, so he knows.'

'And then they'll wonder why that job isn't being offered as a reference,' Brett thought aloud.

'That's right,' Alice said. 'Also, I really don't want to give up. I want to conquer it, prove I can do it – even if it's just to myself. I've never backed away from anything hard in my life.' *Not even my awful marriage*, Alice thought. It was her ex-husband who had called it quits. She'd been miserable, but like the good, loyal woman she'd been raised to be – and one who would not bring shame on the family by getting divorced – she'd been committed to staying, no matter how intolerable. *Pride, stupid pride!*

'Don't let pride get in the way of your real best interests and health, Alice,' Lauren warned. Alice was a little startled at having her thoughts read so accurately.

'I also don't want to become a statistic,' she said absently, still a little shaken by Lauren's perception.

'A what?' Lauren and Brett said at the same time.

'Huh?' Lauren added.

'What on earth do you mean?' Brett said. 'Please explain, as Pauline Hanson would say.'

Lauren and Alice laughed at his impersonation of the colourful rogue political figure.

'I found out on Friday. I'm not meant to know, but I'm about her seventh PA in around two years.'

'Woah! That's a lot,' Lauren said. 'Seriously?'

'Yep.'

'It sounds like the problem is not with you, then,' Brett said. 'Sounds like you're not the one who should be quitting.'

'She brings in too much money for anyone to pull her into line,' Alice said.

'Hmm,' Lauren said.

'I really think you need to start from the beginning and tell us the whole story,' said Brett.

'Oh. No, I don't want to monopolise the day with my problems. I was just venting. I'm sure it'll get better. I'll shut up now.'

'No, this is interesting,' Lauren said, leaning forward on her chair.

Alice rolled her eyes at Lauren.

'What? I'm a writer. And that means I'm a student of the human condition, remember?'

'Seriously, Alice,' Brett said. 'I'm happy to hear it if it will help. You've always been the calm one cheering us all up over the past few years with barely a blip or complaint. But if you've discussed it at length with David and want to just leave it, that's up to you. It might help to have a different perspective, or two. Even if you did say I sounded like David,' he added a little indignantly.

Just then their meals were delivered. Alice wasn't sure she wanted the spaghetti bolognaise after all, but started to dig at it anyway.

'God, I love the food here,' Lauren said.

'Yes,' Brett agreed.

Alice stayed silent. It wasn't the food – it was her mood that wasn't letting her enjoy her meal.

'So, Alice, you were about to tell us the full story,' Lauren urged after she'd made her way well into her burger, chips and salad.

'If you're sure you don't mind. You can tell me to shut up if …'

'Just tell us, Alice,' Lauren said.

'I'm all ears,' Brett said.

'Right. Well …'

'And that's everything,' Alice finally said. 'Well, what I can remember, anyway. And don't forget my brain has turned to mush, so you're probably thinking I'm completely insane. I'm starting to wonder myself, actually. How nuts does some of that sound? And it really does sound petty and that I'm just being a whinger, doesn't it?' she said when no one had spoken. 'I need to just suck it up, right?' Her heart sank. *Why aren't they saying anything?*

'What?' she said a few moments later, looking at Lauren and then Brett. 'You think I'm making it all up, don't you, or I really am nuts? I knew it,' she said when they had still not spoken. She sighed, feeling sad and defeated.

'Oh god, Alice, I'm so sorry. That's a horrible experience. What a bitch,' Lauren said.

'Please don't pity me. I couldn't bear it.'

'Oh. I'm sorry. I'm not. I'm just very upset for you – that what you thought was a dream opportunity has turned out to be such a rotten experience. I think anyone would be feeling off kilter after all that. What does David say?' Lauren said.

'That it's early days.'

'I doubt it's ever going to get any better,' Brett said thoughtfully. Lauren and Alice turned to him.

'Alice, I think what you're dealing with is someone with a serious personality disorder – a narcissist, psychopath, or sociopath, or combination,' he said.

'Aren't serial killers psychopaths and sociopaths, and aren't narcissists what they call people who are obsessed with sharing selfies on social media? I haven't been asked to bury a body yet and I'm pretty sure Carmel isn't into taking selfies.' Alice tried to laugh it off.

'Yes, that's a bit dramatic, isn't it, Brett?' Lauren said.

'No. I'm being serious. Sociopaths and psychopaths are predators. I don't know as much about them as I do narcissists – and, as I said, someone can have multiple conditions. And there are scales – yes, simply being attention-seeking is at the low end of narcissism. But a full-blown narcissist is so obsessed with themselves and achieving gratitude, dominance and ambition that they disregard everyone else as they ruthlessly pursue their goals. They lie, cheat and manipulate in order to achieve the adoration they crave. And because they're not capable of having empathy they don't care who they hurt or destroy along the way. Obviously I'm no psychiatrist or psychologist, and I'm trying to simplify a complex subject here, but I'm pretty sure that's what you've described, Alice. You need to get out. These people can become physically dangerous, and in some cases they can completely ruin you mentally or emotionally – leaving you feeling a lot worse than out of kilter and doubting yourself.'

'Oh, I don't think …' Alice started and stopped.

'Alice, you're already displaying symptoms of mental abuse – you're doubting yourself, you're confused, you think you're going crazy. And I hate to tell you, but if I'm right, you going to HR will have made things a whole lot worse. Her laying off you might be the calm before the storm,' Brett said.

Alice's head was swimming.

'I'm pretty sure what your boss is doing is gaslighting you. It's when someone uses subtle psychological tactics that undermine your reality, make you doubt your sanity – basically portray you as the crazy one. It all feels off, but you're not sure why. Just what you've described. Here, read this,' he said, bringing up a website on his phone and handing it to her.

Alice scrolled through the article in silence while Lauren read it over her shoulder. The further Alice went, the slower her heart rate became. And then she began to feel queasy. The article put into words a lot of what she'd been feeling and experiencing.

'Wow,' Lauren and Alice said in unison when they'd got to the end of the piece.

'Exactly,' Brett said, as Alice handed back his phone.

Would it really only get worse? Could Carmel really be that dangerous? Perhaps it wasn't as bad as she had made it out to be. Perhaps it really was all just a series of misunderstandings. But, no doubt about it, she did feel like she was seriously losing her mind.

'So what do I do?' Alice said, despite already knowing the answer in her heart. There was only one option.

'I told you. Get out,' Brett said, a little exasperated.

'But as she said, she can't without a reference,' Lauren said.

'I get all that but, Alice, your health, your mental wellbeing, is more important than anything. I could be wrong. I hope I am, but ...'

'How do you know so much about this stuff, anyway?' Lauren asked.

'Personal experience, unfortunately.'

'In a workplace?' Alice asked.

'No, my father. It's a long, unhappy tale but, suffice to say, I'm estranged from him.'

'Oh,' Alice said.

'As in not speaking to him?' Lauren asked.

Alice tried to stop her mouth from dropping open. Her father had been gone for several years and her mother and sister regularly drove her mad – to the point she dreaded the obligatory Sunday phone calls, when they focussed on themselves and showed little to no interest in her life. However, she couldn't imagine not speaking to them.

'Yes. I've had to cut them out of my life – my father and my sister. My mother died years ago.'

'Can you do that?' Alice asked, the words out of her mouth before she could stop them.

'Of course. You're the owner of you. Why should you put up with being treated badly just because you're related?' Brett said. A little defensively, perhaps, Alice thought.

'Wow, you're blowing my mind,' Lauren said.

Mine too, Alice thought.

'Don't judge until you've walked in my shoes, lived my life. I can assure you, it wasn't a decision I made lightly.'

'How long have you been estranged?'

'About five years. And I can tell you, my only regret is that I didn't do it ten years earlier. Sadly, I discovered the hard way that this notion that family is everything is absolute bullshit.'

'Is it hard? Do they contact *you*?' Alice asked.

'They finally stopped trying to communicate with me a few years ago. Thank goodness for caller ID. And, yes, it's hard – you have to deal with a lot of guilt, mainly because of society's expectation. This family-is-everything rubbish. Look, it's not about punishing anyone or giving them the silent treatment or anything like that, and expecting things to change,' he said, looking at the bewildered faces of the two women. 'It's about putting myself first – my emotional and mental needs. You didn't know me before I figured out what was wrong with me. I was a mess. It was having a narcissistic father and a sister who's the same. It's sadly very isolating because no one else in my extended family gets it. They think I'm just being up myself or too good for them. The thing with a narcissist is they're fakes with a façade, so only the victims see the truth – not that I want to be known as a victim, I'm using that word in an academic sense,' Brett said.

'So how come you're not like them?' Lauren asked.

'That's thanks to my relationship with my mum and my gran. Having good, normal people in your life can have a neutralising effect, apparently. That's what my research tells me, anyway. But enough about me. Seriously, Alice, if you don't get away from it, it could destroy you. That takes years to recover from, believe me,' Brett said.

'I don't think it's really that bad with Carmel,' Alice said. *How much damage can she do in eight hours a day, five days a week?* It wasn't as if Carmel was one of her parents who'd had a strong influence on raising her, Alice thought as their plates were collected.

They thanked the waiter and said how much they'd enjoyed their meals.

'Do some research of your own if you don't believe me,' Brett said when they had all been silent for a few moments.

'It's not that I don't believe you, I just think my situation isn't that serious,' Alice said.

'It's your life. Only you know what you're living, experiencing. But please don't bury your head in the sand and be in denial just for a job and money.'

'I'm sorry you haven't had a supportive family, Brett. That's sad,' Lauren said, laying her hand on his arm and looking up at him.

'Thanks, but don't pity me, Lauren. It is what it is. I've dealt with it – well, I'm dealing with it, probably will be for as long as I live. That's how it feels, anyway.'

Chapter Fourteen

Monday morning Alice reluctantly said goodbye to Bill. She was finding it increasingly difficult to muster enough energy to head off to work. She'd never had this problem with uni, even the tutorials with old Dr Bragg – the lecturer from hell. She was tired from lack of sleep thanks to the constant churning of work-related thoughts that kept turning over in her mind, and bad dreams that saw her wake with fright several times a night. Thankfully David was a reasonably deep sleeper and didn't tell her off for disturbing him.

She was annoyed with herself for letting Carmel get to her. *Just ignore them and they'll go away,* her mother had said on the few occasions Alice had told her about the bullying at school. She couldn't exactly ignore Carmel, now could she? Or what Brett had said and what she'd read about narcissists and gaslighting, et cetera. It was seriously scary stuff. But did it really apply to her, to such a dangerous extent? Perhaps she could keep a lower profile at work, and if Carmel's limited contact continued, it would help.

Alice scowled at David's back, insanely jealous that he was taking the day off in lieu of his recent travel. She was also trying really hard not to be annoyed at him for his latest 'pep talk' last night, when he'd as good as told her that what she was experiencing was her own fault.

'Just do everything right and she won't have any cause to pick on you, will she?' he'd said. Alice had been stunned at his comment. Had he not listened to her at all or did he not care? It was clear he cared about her ability to contribute to the mortgage ...

After he'd said it, she'd turned from the kitchen bench where she was cutting up some fresh fruit for their dessert, ready to retaliate. But David had walked away and was standing with his back to her, practising his golf swing minus the club. Alice was beginning to see David was often in a world of his own. She'd always known he was quite self-obsessed – his confidence, decisiveness and snappy dressing were things she'd originally been attracted to – but was he getting worse? She'd barely spoken to him for the rest of the evening and this morning, but again, he didn't seem to notice. Suddenly the alarm Alice set on her phone to get her to the train on time, since her mushy brain could no longer be trusted, went off and she snapped to attention.

'Bye. Have a good day,' she said, in truth more to Bill than David.

'You too. Just remember who the boss is. You need this job,' David called cheerfully as she made her way up the hall. Alice hadn't told David about what Brett had said and what else she'd read because she couldn't bear a further show of his lack of support. If she heard the words 'Oh, Alice, don't be silly,' come out of his mouth one more time she might actually scream.

As she walked to the station, Alice thought about quitting, if only to piss David off. She sighed. Where was this coming from?

She wasn't vindictive. She didn't pick fights. This was her partner, the man she loved. It was just a rocky patch all round. Sometimes she wondered if David was really as composed as he appeared, or if it was something he worked hard at. Was there a volcano inside of him getting ready to explode at some point? What would it take? Alice shook it all aside to try to focus on getting into work mode.

God, I don't want to go, she thought as she climbed the stairs to the platform, each step feeling as if she were lifting concrete blocks attached to her feet.

As she walked from the station to work her heart began to race. She was actually feeling fearful. *Stop it!* she told herself, pausing and taking a few deep breaths. *You're being ridiculous. You can't let it, let Carmel, get to you. But how do I not?* was her next thought. *Why can't people just be nice? And genuine.*

'Hi, good weekend?' Alice said as she stepped into the lift with Pip and Jared. It was a relief to see their friendly faces.

'Yep,' Pip said. 'You?'

'Yes, thanks. Nice and relaxing,' she said, smiling through the lie.

Alice said goodbye and wished them both a good day and moved on to her cubicle in the corner. She sat down and took a moment to assess how she was feeling. Stressed. Damn it. *God, I hope Carmel's not in.* She went over to Carmel's area and glanced around to check for signs of her boss – recently used coffee mug on her desk, phone or handbag. Nothing. Usually this would see her relax. Today, however, it made Alice feel more anxious. Carmel had a scary knack of materialising silently beside her. The first few days it hadn't bothered Alice, but now just the thought of Carmel suddenly appearing, looking over her shoulder to her computer screen, made her feel jumpy. *Stop it, Alice. Get on with putting the weekend results into the database.* That was another thing

Alice realised she'd started doing sometime in the last few weeks –
talking to herself in her head, guiding herself through tasks gently
like Jen had. Thankfully she hadn't started speaking her thoughts
aloud, but with the uncertainty around everything she was feeling
lately who would know. Pip and Jared hadn't mentioned it, so
hopefully she'd done nothing more than mumble occasionally.
Alice felt she needed this constant mental dialogue with herself
to keep on top of things. *Okay*, she said silently, *let's get these done.
You've got this.*

Alice quite enjoyed this task, especially when Carmel wasn't
standing over her shoulder telling her she wasn't being quick
enough or constantly changing the wording she was trying to
type in. Each weekend Carmel wrote the details – auction results,
the number of serious bidders or visitors to inspections, and other
notes onto a brochure. Then she took a photo of it with her phone
and emailed it to Alice to add the information to the database. She
usually sent the emails straight after each auction or open house
inspection, and Alice would work her way through them first
thing Monday morning. She'd thought from the beginning there
must be a better, more efficient way – what did the company do
before smartphones with cameras? Perhaps this was another of
Carmel's idiosyncrasies. Jen hadn't known; it was just the way it
was done. And, as Alice now knew, you didn't question Carmel.

She turned her computer on and opened her email. She liked
that Monday morning started with an easy task, and she enjoyed
the routine of it. She hadn't received any emails over the weekend,
and now when she looked at her inbox she saw it was quite empty
compared to the past few weeks – disconcertingly so. It was good
that she didn't have a stack of unimportant messages to wade
through and prioritise, but where were the results she needed to
input right away? She pressed *Refresh*. Everything seemed to be

working, but there were still no new emails from Carmel. *Oh well, she was entitled to be a bit late occasionally, no matter how out of character that would be.*

By ten o'clock she still hadn't received the images from Carmel. She was trying not to worry, instead dealing with other, less important things on her list. Unable to concentrate, she found herself re-tidying her already impeccably tidy desk in an attempt to stall what was fast becoming inevitable – contacting Carmel. Dare she call her? The thought sent a shiver up her spine. And then she relaxed slightly. Carmel's phone was currently put through to hers, so dialling would be pointless. With shaking hands Alice constructed a quick email she hoped would appear breezy enough:

Hi Carmel,
   Good morning! I hope you had a lovely weekend.

Oh, shit – do you say that to someone who works most weekends? Oh well, what else did you say when you didn't like the person all that much but had to be polite? She swallowed back her anxiety and continued:

   I'm just wondering if you can please send the weekend's property details so I can update the database.
   Thanks,
   Alice.

She read it several times in an effort to delay sending it, hoping the information she needed would arrive first. From what she'd seen, Carmel would not take kindly to being prompted. *Oh god.* She pressed *Send.* At that moment her desk phone rang. *Maybe that's her now, apologising, providing an explanation.* But no. It was Matt from marketing demanding to know why the results hadn't been loaded, and ranting about needing to collate the details and get social media posts organised and loaded, or something. Alice stopped listening. She knew it was important, but didn't need to know why. She just had to do her part in the process.

'I'm so sorry,' she stammered, 'but I don't have them yet myself.' She cringed at knowing she was essentially putting the blame onto Carmel, who would be furious. 'I'll get onto it,' she added quickly in case Matt said he'd ring Carmel himself. Alice's heart was racing and she was beginning to sweat. There was no answer yet from her email.

'Yes, get onto it. We needed it half an hour ago,' Matt snapped and hung up. Alice sat staring at the phone for a moment. *Oh god.* She was feeling really shaky and had a headache, which she just hoped wouldn't turn into a migraine. But then she'd at least have an excuse to go home …

Okay, focus, Alice. You need to deal with this. She could text Carmel direct, couldn't she? Alice didn't know for sure, but thought text messages probably still went through when the phone was diverted. She'd never had the need to divert her own mobile phone, so couldn't be sure how it all worked. *I'll text her in ten minutes if I still haven't had a response from the email*, Alice decided.

She went and got a cup of tea and when she returned to her desk she quickly checked her email for a message. She even went all the way back through to Friday's messages in case she'd missed the information somehow – or anything else. Unfortunately she hadn't. Nothing. *Damn it. Damn you, Carmel!* She took a deep breath and dialled Carmel's number in case she was taking calls again – there was no way of knowing beyond Carmel telling her, which she never did – and held her breath. She let out a gasp of both relief and fury when her own voice came on the line asking the caller to leave a message. She was just putting the phone down again when it rang. God, what was it with shaking fingers these days?

'This is Carmel Gold's office, Alice speaking. How may I help you?'

'Hi, Alice. This is Catherine Watson. I'm not sure if you can help me. It's my settlement day and Carmel was meant to meet me here at the property on Malvern Road, Toorak, at nine o'clock this morning to hand over the keys, but she hasn't arrived. I'm here to move in. I've got two removal trucks waiting to unload and I can't even get in. I don't know what to do,' she said, sounding as stressed as Alice felt.

'Oh no,' Alice said. 'I'm so sorry. I'll just put you on hold and see what I can find out.'

'Thanks.'

Alice sat staring at the phone with the blinking light indicating the call was on hold while wondering what to do. Where the bloody hell was Carmel? God, I hope nothing has happened to her, she thought in the next breath. Perhaps she was sick or injured – too sick or injured to call, to get to her phone. Alice didn't have Carmel's home address – only knew which street and suburb she lived in. She pictured her own recent moving day. God, that had been stressful enough and everything had gone smoothly. *Poor Catherine. What can I do?* She nibbled on her bottom lip. She knew all the keys were kept at reception, with Bianca the custodian in charge of keeping them safe and handing them out when necessary. *Dare I leave the office?* Alice didn't have a car. Also, Carmel might have the keys with her and just be running a bit late. But it was ten-thirty – handovers were always right on nine, or, sometimes even eight-thirty.

Alice tried to walk quickly out to reception, but broke into a run. She was a little breathless and had to force herself not to drum her fingers on the desk while she waited for Bianca to finish her call.

'Alice, what's up?' Bianca said.

'Bianca, sorry to bother you, but do you have the keys to the Malvern Road property purchased by Catherine Watson?' She tried to sound authoritative instead of unsure and terrified. She'd never been asked to get keys before and didn't know if only the agents were allowed access to them.

'Sure. Hang on a sec. I'll check,' she said, tapping on her keyboard. 'Yep, it looks like they should still be here.' Alice almost let out a loud breath when Bianca said, 'I'll just get them.'

It was probably only a few seconds before Bianca returned from behind a partition to hand Alice a blue tag with three keys attached, but to Alice it felt like an hour had passed while her headache hammered painfully at her temples. She quickly checked the address, surname and date.

'That's the one, thanks.'

'Just sign this.' Bianca placed a clipboard on the counter and handed her a pen. 'You look like you're in a hurry. Run, I'll fill out the details.'

'Thank you so much, Bianca, you're a lifesaver,' Alice said, and bolted back to her desk, thinking as she went she needed to get a bit fitter.

She took back the call. 'Hi, Catherine? It's Alice back again. I'm so sorry to keep you waiting. I have the keys here in my hand and I'm going to bring them to you myself. Right now.'

'Oh, Alice, that would be fantastic. Thank you so much.'

Alice sensed the woman was almost in tears. 'I'm really sorry again for the delay. I'll be there as soon as I possibly can.' Alice shoved the keys in her trouser pocket, grabbed her phone and handbag and raced back out to reception.

'I'll be back soon,' Alice said to Bianca.

'Hey, Alice,' Bianca called while Alice was waiting impatiently for the lift. *Shit! What now? I'm in a huge rush.*

'Yes?' she said, turning back around.

'You're not doing a handover of keys to the homeowner, are you?' she asked.

Er, no. Shit. 'Um. Yes. Carmel didn't turn up and the poor woman is stuck there with removalists getting shirty,' Alice hurriedly explained.

'Well, you'll need one of these. It isn't cold, but it's better than nothing,' Bianca said, holding up a bottle of champagne – the standard company gift to new homeowners on their move-in day.

'You're awesome, Bianca. What would I do without you?' Alice said, striding across the space and grabbing the bottle just as the lift arrived.

On the ride down Alice hoped she'd find a cab at the taxi rank. *Please let there be one there – and available. Please let me be doing the right thing.*

She was in luck. A taxi was pulling in just as she got there. She quickly gave the address to the driver and sat back and quelled the urge to tell him to drive faster. Thankfully the morning peak had ended and the traffic was quite light. In twenty minutes she was asking the driver to wait while she leapt out of the car and ran up the path where she could see someone sitting on the step. The woman jumped up.

'Alice?' she asked.

'Yes. Catherine?'

'Yes. Oh, thank god.'

'Here are the keys,' Alice said, handing them over.

'Thanks, I'm just going to check they work while you're here,' she said, going and unlocking the door. 'Brilliant!'

'And this is to celebrate your new home,' Alice said, passing her the bottle of room-temperature champagne. 'Congratulations. May you spend many wonderful years here.'

'Thank you so much. You're an absolute lifesaver.' Suddenly Alice was being pulled into a hug.

'I really appreciate you doing this.'

'It's my pleasure,' Alice said brightly. 'And, again, I'm so, so sorry about the delay. I'm not sure what happened.'

'Well, no one died. I'm really sorry about my frantic call. I'm a bit stressed, as you can probably tell.'

'It's okay. I completely understand. I moved recently myself. Well, I'd better let you get on with it.'

'Thanks again so much,' Catherine said, giving Alice another quick hug.

Alice got back in the taxi and wondered how she'd get reimbursed. Who did she need to give her expenses claim to? She dreaded asking Carmel. Was this something covered in the company handbook and Jen's notes? Carmel still hadn't reimbursed her for the shoe repair. *Oh god.* Alice felt a wave of exhaustion mixed with nausea come over her. And her headache was starting to get really bad. She searched her handbag for paracetamol and found some, but then realised she'd come out without her bottle of water.

Walking back into the office, she felt good about having sorted out the keys. Catherine's reaction told her she'd definitely done the right thing. Keeping clients happy was what the company was all about, wasn't it?

'Okay?' Bianca mouthed from behind the reception desk where she was on the phone. Alice gave her a thumbs up and a smile and Bianca responded with a thumbs up of her own.

She sat back down at her desk and took a moment to congratulate herself. But then she saw her office phone message bank light was blinking. The first was a message from Matt demanding again to know where the data was. If he was offhand and rude last time, now he was positively filthy. *Shit!* She quickly checked her inbox. No answer from Carmel. God, she hadn't sent the text. Alice couldn't put it off any longer. But would she reply? Just then the phone rang in her hand again. She answered it and hadn't got through her spiel when Carmel's icy, sugary voice asked, 'Alice, why am I getting text messages from Matt in marketing telling me our figures are late?'

'Um. I'm really sorry, Carmel.' *Why am I apologising?* 'But I don't have the information to put into the database.' Her heart was threatening to burst through her ribs.

'Everything you need is on your desk, Alice. I suggest you open your eyes.'

'But, where? You always email ...'

'On the USB stick right in front of you. For god's sake, Alice.' And then Alice saw the USB stick. 'Okay, thanks, got it.'

'Next time open your bloody eyes, Alice. I shouldn't have to be doing your job for you.'

'Oh, Carmel, before you go, Catherine Watson called and ...'

But Carmel was gone. Alice's face was flaming and her eyes were prickling with the beginning of tears. She picked up the USB stick. How had she missed it sitting right there in front of her keyboard? *I'm losing my mind. I really am. God, Carmel's going to kill me next time she sees me.*

Chapter Fifteen

'Alice, a word please,' Carmel said, suddenly appearing beside Alice's work area. Alice tried not to look as startled as she felt. She was doing nothing wrong – just dealing with emails. 'Now, please.' Alice got up, finding as she did her legs felt like jelly. She tried not to sigh out loud. This was clearly not a conversation for the ears of the others working around her. Alice followed meekly behind Carmel, feeling like a naughty school child being walked down to see the principal. She wasn't as worried as she might have been. Carmel was probably about to thank her profusely for her quick thinking in dealing with the Catherine Watson keys situation two hours earlier. Of course Carmel wouldn't want to admit in public she'd stuffed up.

'Sit,' Carmel commanded as she closed the door to the small conference room with a solid metallic click. Alice sat with folded hands on the table in front of her and smiled at Carmel.

'What do you think you were doing undermining me in front of a client?'

Alice's smile faded away and her face fell.

Sorry? When? How? What have I done? She was genuinely baffled. Why couldn't the woman communicate clearly?

'The Watson woman,' Carmel continued. 'This morning. How dare you leave the office! What were you thinking?'

'Um, that I was taking her the keys to her house, which she was meant to receive over an hour and a half before then?' Alice said, haltingly. *Seriously, I'm in trouble for this?*

'Don't you talk down to me. How embarrassing do you think it was to hear you'd gone behind my back and welcomed someone to their new property – the property *I* sold them? Just who do you think you are? You're my assistant, Alice, you are not an agent with this firm. And at this rate you never will be!'

'But, I thought …' The fog was still not clearing for Alice.

'That's your problem. You don't think. Or when you do, you do the wrong thing. God, what is wrong with you? Little Miss *Un*helpful, more like it,' she added with a sneer.

Alice could see Carmel was in such a state there was no point defending herself. *Is the woman actually insane or are we talking about something else that I don't have a clue about? Oh god, I'm so confused.* She stayed silent in case she incurred more of Carmel's wrath and was fired on the spot.

'And how dare you drag Bianca in reception into it, place her job in jeopardy?'

Alice's face was bright red and her neck was now catching up. She bit her lip as she felt it begin to tremble. Her chin quivered.

'I'm really sorry, Carmel,' she muttered, her voice choking.

'Don't you dare cry, Alice!'

And then Alice was shocked and dismayed to feel, in one fluid movement, her throat tighten, her chin wobble and tears burst from her eyes and trickle down her face.

She couldn't stop the tears and anguish she'd been forcing back these past few weeks. Completely mortified, she sniffled and then openly sobbed. She just couldn't make herself stop. And then she became breathless and close to hyperventilating. She couldn't look at Carmel and tried desperately to get her breathing under control.

'Jesus, Alice! You're pathetic. Pull yourself together. And don't involve yourself in things above your pay grade or undermine me again. Got it?'

Alice could only nod.

'Now clean yourself up and get back to work.' And with a whoosh of air and waft of heavy perfume, the smell of which at that moment Alice positively loathed, Carmel left the room, closing the door with a much louder clunk behind her than when they'd come in.

Gradually Alice's tears stopped and her breathing steadied. *Oh my god, how embarrassing! But I didn't get fired, did I?* She sat there for a few moments trying to compose herself and figure out what had just happened. She went back over the conversation, well, rant, but was still none the wiser. Alice was genuinely mystified. Carmel had definitely been talking about Catherine Watson and Malvern Road because she'd said so. And she'd mentioned Alice leaving the office. *But what did I do wrong? Well, other than leaving the office.* She knew that had been a risk.

Jesus, you bitch. I bloody made you look good and spared you an irate client. What's your fucking problem? I showed some initiative — your favourite bloody word — and you put me down. Jesus. What do I have to do?

Alice remained confused. She could see what Carmel was upset about, but couldn't understand why. Wasn't a personal assistant meant to catch the ball if her boss dropped it? Wasn't the company all about looking after clients? And why have the phone put through to her if she was not meant to actually do anything about the calls she took on Carmel's behalf? Alice's temples were pulsing hard.

No matter how many times she shook her head – physically or mentally – Alice couldn't understand why what she'd done was wrong. One thing Carmel was right about, she thought, was she had to pull herself together, clean herself up, and get back to work. At least she hadn't been fired. She sighed, dried her eyes and blew her nose loudly before slipping out of the room and racing into the ladies bathroom, which was thankfully just next door. She stared into the mirror, wondering how to get her puffy eyes and red raw face back to normal without any makeup to hand. She couldn't stand there all day and wait for nature to take its course. Alice knew that in minutes Carmel would be on the warpath looking for her, or someone would come in wanting to use the facilities and ask her what was wrong. She didn't want to give Carmel any more ammunition or cause to look down at her with that demoralising sneer – it was perhaps even worse than her cutting words. That look of disgust mixed with satisfaction. That's what it seemed to Alice. *She's just a bully*, Alice silently and gently told her reflection, *rise above it*. She wet a wad of paper towels and held it to her face and eyes and then, when the heat had subsided, she patted herself dry.

Alice was glad Bianca wasn't at reception – it was the lunch fill-in, Amy, sitting there on the phone. Carmel didn't look up when Alice walked past her to resume her position behind her own desk. In fact Carmel didn't speak to her for the rest of the day, despite Alice asking her several questions in order to clarify things she was working on. Each time Carmel put on a very good show of not actually having heard her. Finally Alice twigged on the third occasion of being ignored. And was stunned. *You're seriously giving me the silent treatment. What are you, twelve?* Alice thought, shaking her head with disbelief as she returned to her desk. Carmel eventually answered each of her queries, but by email – snarly little one-liners.

Near the end of the day Alice was shocked to realise she'd been staring at her computer for several minutes daydreaming about sticking the sharp letter opener into the back of Carmel's neck. *Jesus, what am I becoming?* Shocked, Alice was beginning to see how murders were committed.

As she left the office, she briefly thought about trying to catch up with Brenda, but decided Carmel would love to have more ammunition to bully her about being a tattle tale, or the satisfaction of Alice giving in and quitting. Anyway, she'd already embarrassed herself enough for one day.

She was still running through the events in her head while cooking dinner – they just wouldn't leave her alone. And she was no less confused about her day by the time David walked in after having gone to the driving range to belt a bucket load of balls out into space. Perhaps that's what she should do to deal with the stress, she thought. Golf had never appealed to her, despite David initially wanting it to be their 'thing' to do together on weekends. Alice just didn't see the point. To her it was not only a waste of a nice walk, but an expensive waste. Sometimes she did go and walk around with him while he played.

She was still teary, and frustrated she couldn't pull herself together. She'd deliberately decided to cook with onions so she could blame them for her red eyes if David noticed and said something. And she'd chosen to make risotto so she could appear engrossed and not have to engage with him too much. She'd decided she was not going to tell him about her day.

'I'm loving the new driver,' he declared. 'And my slice is improving,' he said, sidling up to her while moving his arms in a swinging motion.

'That's great,' she said, managing a decent show of enthusiasm.

'How was your day? Better?'

'Yes, thanks, pretty good.'

'See, I told you, didn't I?' he said with pride. At that moment Alice thought she might actually hate David. Instead of being startled by the thought, she just felt sad and lonely.

Thank goodness for you, Bill. She looked across at the little dog curled up in the bed nearby. As if reading her thoughts, he opened his eyes, looked up at her over his paws, and flapped his tail. *Darling thing*, she thought, hoping he'd pick that up too. She'd be a complete wreck if she didn't have him. Tears pricked again at the idea of life without him in it.

'Hey, are you okay? Your eyes are red,' David said, peering at her, frowning.

'Onions,' she said. 'And allergies,' she added for reinforcement. Though, did anyone suffer hay fever this time of year?

'Ah. Yep, that'll do it,' he said cheerfully. 'Wine?'

'No, thanks. I've got a bit of a headache.'

Chapter Sixteen

On Friday morning Alice sat on the couch after her shower and taking Bill for his walk. She was in her robe and would be running late for work if she didn't get dressed and leave in the next seven minutes. But she could not make herself move. She stared into space, dazed, her brain empty. Alice thought she should be concerned that she felt so relaxed when ordinarily she'd be a ball of anxiety.

She searched her body for aches and pains – something she could use as a reason to call in sick. She was past caring that she wouldn't be paid if she didn't go in, having not accrued enough leave yet.

Thankfully David wasn't there trying to give one of his cajoling spiels, which she could only hope were well meaning. He'd gone to the office early to be in on a conference call with one of the overseas offices.

'Oh, Bill, what am I going to do?' she said to the dog sitting beside her with his head on her thigh. Bill snuggled closer, looked up adoringly at her and flapped his tail. Alice rubbed his soft silky ears. *I've got to get organised and go. Carmel will be furious if I'm late.*

At the thought of Carmel, a shiver made its way from the back of her skull right down her spine, leaving an icy feeling in its wake. Tears erupted. She hugged her robe tighter to her, not so much against the cold but to comfort her clenching insides. Her chest was so tight it hurt. Suddenly she couldn't breathe. If she didn't turn up, Carmel would have an absolute conniption. She really had better get going. But still Alice sat. She watched the digital clock on David's flash sound system in front of her click onto the time her last train left the station to get her to work by eight forty-five. She couldn't make herself care. Alice stared at her phone on the table in front of her. Dare she call in sick? Her pulse quickened as she picked the phone up. She turned it over in her hand. Who should she call? Other than Carmel. She couldn't bear to hear her scorn, her criticism. What had the handbook said? Alice didn't have a clue. She could call Bianca on reception when nine o'clock arrived. Brenda. She'd call Brenda from HR. Wasn't this within her job description? Probably not. Alice was a little ashamed at how gutless she was being. And then it dawned on her slowly, like a bank of beautiful thick black clouds rolling in over the ocean onto land ahead of a storm. *I never want to face Carmel again. Ever. And I don't have to. I'm going to quit. David, you can shove your patronising comments and disappointment up your arse – you don't know what it's like. Carmel, you won. Well done. Let me be a statistic. I no longer care.*

'Bill,' she said, causing the dog to look up at her and flap his tail, 'I quit. And I don't give a fuck what anyone thinks.' God, swearing felt good. Yep, sometimes there was no better word than 'fuck'. If only she'd told Carmel to fuck off. That might be her only regret about quitting like this.

Alice turned the phone over and began to search for *Brenda* – *HR*. Her insides quivered, but this time more from nervous excitement than fear. *God, am I really going to do this? Seriously? Yes!* She dragged her finger across the green spot to dial. She took several quiet, deep breaths while waiting. A part of her wanted it to go to voicemail. She'd give her name and say, *I quit, tell Carmel she won. I'm not coming back*, and then hang up. Her heart rate spiked as Brenda answered.

'Alice. Hi. Is everything okay?'

'Hi, Brenda. No. I can't do this for another day. I'm not coming in again – ever. I understand I don't have to give notice, since I'm on probation. Right?' Alice's heart was hammering so hard she could barely hear herself think.

'Yes, that's right. Alice, just slow down a second.'

'I've made up my mind. Thank you for all you've done for me, but I just can't do it anymore. Carmel is too much for me.' *There, I've said it!* Oh how Alice hated admitting that.

'I understand. I'm very sorry to see you leave, but you have to do what's right for you. Could I just ask a favour of you, though?'

'You can ask.' Alice felt a little sad to be letting Brenda down. She really liked the quietly spoken woman.

'Meet with me this morning for coffee.'

'Oh.' Alice looked down at herself. That would require getting out of her robe, into clothes, and leaving the house. She wasn't planning on doing that.

'Please. You need to return your security pass, and it would really mean a lot to me. I feel I've let you down.'

'Oh, Brenda, please don't feel that. Okay, sure, I'll have coffee with you. But not near the office.'

'Great. That's fine. How about nine forty-five?' Brenda said.

'That's fine.' *Oh, and I still need reimbursement of the taxi fare and shoe repair.*

'I'll text you the address of a little place out of the way.'

'Okay. I'll see you there.'

'Thanks, Alice, I'll see you soon. And, Alice?'

'Yes?'

'Thanks for agreeing to meet with me – I really appreciate it.'

Alice hung up the phone. She was still shaking slightly.

'I did it, Bill, I actually did it.' She sat back into the couch to gauge how she felt. Good? Not really. Relieved? Yes, definitely. Scared? Yep, kind of – of meeting with Brenda and of what David would say. *If he loves me he'll understand, or at least be okay with my decision.* Alice took several long, deep breaths. She'd better get cracking if she were to get into the city and to the café in time.

'Don't worry, Billy boy, I won't be long. I promise. Only a couple of hours, tops.'

Outside the world felt much brighter to Alice than it had just an hour or so before when she'd gone for her walk. She almost laughed at her thought and at how much better everything seemed this morning now she was free. She nearly broke into a skip on her way to the train station. She just hoped Brenda wouldn't try to change her mind. She'd hate to have to disappoint her further.

Alice found the café Brenda had chosen down an alley. It was a lovely place – grungy chic, she supposed the colourful, cluttered, slightly old-fashioned decor would be called. She stepped inside the dark space and looked around for Brenda, and saw her tucked away in the corner at a small table.

'Hi, Alice, thanks for coming,' Brenda said. They hugged, Alice thinking Brenda held on longer than was usual for two colleagues who barely knew each other.

'I'll just get us a coffee. What would you like?'

'A latte would be lovely, thank you.'

Alice waited for Brenda to return. It seemed to take forever and when she came back with their drinks Alice saw why – they didn't do table service.

'Ah, that's good coffee,' Brenda said after taking a sip. She closed her eyes briefly and the slack look on her face and the sigh she let out as she put her cup down suggested a moment of pure ecstasy. Alice smiled and found herself relaxing a little.

'Mmm. It certainly is.'

'Brenda.' 'Alice,' they said, speaking at once.

'Sorry. You go,' Brenda said quickly.

'I just want to say I'm really sorry for letting you down and leaving the company in the lurch by leaving so suddenly. It's not me. Actually, I have not liked the person I've become recently. Once, I would never have considered being so unprofessional, but I just can't spend another second with Carmel, as pathetic as that sounds.'

'It's okay, Alice. I agree, it's not ideal, but I do understand. You have to do what's right for you. At the end of the day it is only a job. And as you were on probation, Gold, Taylor and Murphy could terminate you at any moment if they chose. It cuts both ways. So don't feel bad. Some things just aren't meant to be.'

'Thanks for saying that. I'm disappointed though. I was so sure I'd … Oh it doesn't matter now. Here's my pass before I forget,' Alice said, handing over her security pass with the lanyard wrapped around it. 'I don't ever want to go into that building again.'

'It's no trouble for me to hand it in.'

'The other thing, and this is a little awkward, but I never got the thirty dollars reimbursed from the shoe repair I picked up for Carmel that day of the meeting. Unfortunately I don't have the receipt – I left it with the shoes on Carmel's desk at the time, so I now can't prove it. She denies she ever saw it.' Alice cringed. God she hated sounding like a dobber.

'Right. I'm sure I can get payment sorted. Thirty dollars?' Brenda said, making a note in her phone.

'Yes. Thanks. Also, I'm so sorry to be loading all this onto you, but I had a forty-eight dollar taxi fare too when I …'

'Ah, the keys, yes. I heard about that.'

Alice coloured and looked down at the table in an effort to hide her embarrassment.

'Oh, don't be embarrassed, Alice, management was very impressed.'

Alice looked up, frowning.

'Seriously. Well, not Carmel, probably. But, the woman, Catherine Watson, I think it was, rang Paul, insisted on speaking with him to say how you saved the day.'

'Oh, that was nice of her. I have the taxi receipt,' Alice said, opening her large wallet and fossicking through it. 'Here,' she said, handing it over. 'I just didn't know who to claim it from or how.'

'I'll take care of it – I'll have both payments included in your final pay. Leave it with me.'

'Right. Okay, I think that's all I needed to tell you about,' Alice said. She was relieved to have it all out of the way and out of her head. For the first time in days her brain was actually thinking clearly and logically. The fog was starting to lift. 'I'm sorry to unload that on you, but I've been so all over the place that I needed to deal with it before I forgot.' *Because after this I don't ever want to give Gold, Taylor and Murphy Real Estate another thought!* 'Now that's me sorted, what did you want to see me about?'

'I just wanted to check you were all right and apologise in person for not being around enough to give you the support you needed and deserved. I'm afraid I've been dealing with a few personal issues.'

'Oh, I'm so sorry. I hope everything is okay.'

'It will be. But it's meant I haven't been there for you as much as I've wanted to be, as much as I ordinarily would have been. I feel I've let you down, Alice. Please accept my apologies.' Brenda looked down at the table.

Alice felt sorry for her. She was probably very good at her job, but, like Alice, she had been hamstrung. And of course she had to toe the company line so she might not be able to be as honest as she wanted to be.

'It's not your fault, Brenda.' *Not your fault that Carmel's an evil, manipulative bitch.* 'And you did try to help. I know that.'

'That's very generous of you.'

'I know now it's not entirely me,' Alice said, suddenly feeling a little bolder. 'I was good at what I did before meeting Carmel and having her systematically break me down. Do you know, I could probably sue for the anguish, the mental torture? I won't, I'm just glad I've seen the light. I know you can't comment because of your loyalty and professionalism, but the way Carmel treats people is not okay, regardless of how much money she brings in.'

'I know it's not. And, you're right, I can't comment. Oh. I'd better get going,' Brenda said, checking her watch. 'Thank you so much for meeting with me, Alice.'

'Thank *you*, Brenda, for everything – for at least trying.'

'I will make sure the extra money for the shoes and taxi are added to your final pay,' she said, getting up.

Alice stood and the two women hugged again. This time it didn't feel weird that they lingered.

'Good luck, Alice. And remember, you have great skills and are a truly lovely human being.'

Alice felt a wave of sadness at watching Brenda leave. She sat back down to compose herself before heading off. *Wow, I'm free. I really am. Well, now what? I'm going to go home and spend a quiet day with Bill.* She would not think about what was next, beyond that. She needed to recover from Cyclone Carmel. Alice felt a lot stronger already.

Chapter Seventeen

Alice texted Lauren: *OMG I did it! I quit! Eek!*

She didn't really expect a response as Lauren was a morning person and she was probably in the throes of writing. Alice didn't want to be the one to stop whatever flow of words might be happening, which is why she'd sent a text instead of calling. Though, she realised, Lauren would surely have her phone turned off or on silent if she didn't want to be disturbed. She almost jumped with joy when her phone sounded with a response:

Well done YOU! Text me your address and I'll bring cake to celebrate. Xx
Seriously? Alice replied.
Absolutely! Xx

And then the phone actually rang. Lauren's name was on the screen.

'Hey,' Alice said.

'Unless you don't want the company,' Lauren said without preamble. 'Are you okay?'

'Yes. No. Honestly, I don't know now,' Alice said as a mixture of emotions started to swamp her.

'Where are you?'

'In a café near the office. I just met with HR. I'm heading home now.'

'Would you like to be left alone to process or have some company? And cake – I have chocolate cupcakes.'

'Yum. But I don't want to put you out.'

'You wouldn't be. Anyway, I'm the one offering.'

'Actually, Lauren, I'd love some company. Thanks.'

'No problem. Thought you might. Text me your address and I'll be there in around half an hour. Your new place isn't far from me.'

'You're a gem.'

'I can't wait to see your house and meet Bill.'

Alice hung up and sent the address to Lauren. She couldn't believe her closest friend in Melbourne, after David, hadn't already visited the house, and, worse, that she didn't even have Alice's address. What had happened to the last six or so weeks? Had she really become so withdrawn? God, and she hadn't even returned Ruth's cheery phone message from last week, either. Shit. She'd sent a text to say she'd get back to her and then she'd completely forgotten. How could she have forgotten her like that – Ruth of all people? Her dearest and oldest friend. Jesus, Gold, Taylor and Murphy Real Estate had completely sucked her dry. More than she'd even realised. Well, not anymore!

*

Through her bedroom window, having just changed into track pants and a t-shirt, Alice noticed Lauren out on the front looking around as if she wasn't sure if she had the right house.

'Lauren,' she said, throwing open the front door and making her way down the path. 'Thanks so much for coming.' She gave her friend a hug.

'You're doing me a favour, actually. I made these and you're saving me from eating them all. They're called Procrastination Cupcakes,' Lauren said with a cheeky grin as she lifted the lid on the Tupperware container she held to reveal rich chocolate cupcakes with little hats on top of mounds of cream.

'Oh, wow,' Alice said.

'Sorry, Bill, none for you, little man,' Lauren said. 'Hold this,' she said and put the lid back on before thrusting the container into Alice's chest. She then squatted down. 'Come here, you gorgeous thing.' She picked up the small dog that was wriggling all over with delight at the attention. 'Ooh, aren't you a handsome boy.'

Lauren put him down and looked around, taking everything in. 'It's lovely. Not what I was expecting, but lovely.'

'Thanks. Come on in, I'll give you the grand tour.'

'It's very white. And everything's so straight and neat. It'd last two minutes like this if I lived here,' Lauren said with a laugh. 'I didn't have you pegged as having OCD. Does David?'

Alice laughed. 'No. Probably not far off though. David, not me, that is. He does like everything in its place and clean and tidy. I like tidy, too, but …'

'In that case, I'm surprised he was okay with having a dog.'

'I think Bill was an appeasement present.'

'Sorry?'

'To soften the blow of him being away so much,' Alice explained.

'Oh. Right. God, I'm loving your stone bench tops,' Lauren said, sitting down on a stool in the kitchen area and running her hands across the grey stone.

'Tea or coffee?'

'Oh. My. God. That is one stunning coffee machine! Coffee, please. White with one,' Lauren said. 'So, what did David say about you quitting? Is he okay with it?'

'I haven't told him. I'll tell him tonight.'

A part of Alice wanted to send him a text or leave a voicemail – David rarely answered his phone while at work – so he'd have blown any anger out by the time he came home. Another part of her said that telling him in person was the only way. She was ignoring the little nagging voice in her head that told her she was being a coward in putting it off.

'One of the appealing things about being single is not having to tell anyone anything,' Lauren declared, taking the chocolate hat from a cupcake and placing it in her mouth.

'Hmm,' Alice mused.

'So, how are you feeling? Honestly.'

'Relieved. Disappointed. Scared. Like I'm a failure. Exhausted at the thought of looking for another job. All of the above,' Alice said sadly.

'It'll be okay. You found this one – you'll find another.'

'It just feels like I'm under so much more pressure now – because of, you know,' she said, indicating the space around her.

'Try not to be too hard on yourself. From the sounds of it, it was that Carmel woman, not you, who failed. Failed at being a decent human being. Bitch.'

'Four weeks. Can you believe I only lasted four weeks? That must be some sort of record.'

'So, what did they say when you quit?'

'Nothing really. I rang Brenda from HR. She's great. I didn't need to give notice because of still being on probation.'

'That's good. And what did she say?'

'Well, she wanted me to meet her for coffee – hence being in a café in the city when you called. I had to return my security pass anyway and god knows I never want to go into that building again, so killing two birds with one stone seemed a good idea. I think I was hoping for an apology, or at least some acknowledgement that Carmel is a nightmare and her behaviour is the reason why I've left. I told you I'm like the seventh PA of hers to leave in two years, didn't I?'

Lauren nodded. 'You'd think they'd start connecting the dots by now.'

'Well, if they are, they're not letting on. Brenda was clearly toeing the company line. It was as good as a shrug and *Sorry it didn't work out – all the best.*'

'Did you tell her you know about Carmel's track record with her PAs?'

'No. I didn't want to get anyone in trouble. It's so disappointing knowing that nothing will change.'

'Well, money has the power.'

'I really thought I'd found my place. I think I would have been good at real estate,' Alice said sadly.

'To be honest, Alice, I think you'd have been too nice.'

'Yeah. Maybe you're right. Thanks so much for coming around. It means a lot.'

'No worries. I just thought you might be feeling conflicted and lost. It's a big, brave thing you've done.'

'Yeah, right,' Alice scoffed. 'I ditched a job after only four weeks.'

'But you had the courage to put yourself, put your wellbeing first, to say, this is not okay, enough is enough. That takes some guts. You should give yourself some credit.'

'I don't think David's going to see it like that.'

'Well, sod him!'

'You know, I still can't quite put my finger on what the problem was.'

'Carmel was. You know that.'

'Yes, but she seemed so nice at first.'

'From what I've read about narcissists since Brett told us about them, that's the thing – they're charismatic. They mentally wear you down until you don't know what's up and what's down.'

'That's exactly how I felt,' Alice said. 'Like I spent my whole day – every day – not knowing which way was up. I've become so unsure about everything, and myself.'

'Thankfully you realised it isn't right to feel that way.'

'What I don't understand is why she would want to drive PAs away like that. What does she gain?'

'Power? Who would know? They're complicated people. I wouldn't waste too much time trying to analyse it – it'll do your head in even more. Just accept she's a sad, damaged individual who wouldn't know good help if it bit her on the arse, and be grateful you got out. I think the trouble is that PAs generally are kind and caring people who want to please. And that's what a narcissist is attracted to and then feeds on. Maybe? I don't know.'

'Yeah, I read that too. God, it's so bloody complicated. I didn't want it all to be true – to be a victim.' The truth was, Alice had been disturbed by what she'd read and had tried to forget it. It wasn't just Carmel who seemed to tick a lot of the boxes …

'Exactly! Which is why you need to stop thinking about it. Have another cupcake, I say!'

'Good idea. God, I'm glad you're here, Lauren. At the risk of sounding like a true millennial, real adult life away from uni is hard!'

'Oh yes it is. Well, I can't really talk; I'm fully aware, and very grateful, for my situation.'

'You'd make a good counsellor, you know,' Alice mused.

'Thanks, but I think I'd be too judgemental and far too blunt!'

Alice added sugar to their coffee cups and thought for a minute. 'What am I going to do without a reference?'

'I don't know. But worrying about it won't help. You could always explain the situation to the next prospective employer. If they won't give you a job without the reference from your last report, anyway, I don't see how being honest will hurt. They might even appreciate your openness.'

'Hmm.'

'Don't think about any of that now; at least take some time to recover your equilibrium. You've been hit for a six, Alice, don't forget.'

'I feel like I never want to step foot inside an office again – any office.'

'And that's okay.'

'Not when you don't have any other skills, it's not.'

'Go back and do your honours and masters.'

'David would have a fit if I even suggested that.'

'Please don't place your whole future and wellbeing in David's hands. I know, I know,' Lauren said, holding her hands up, 'what would I know, being single and all.'

They enjoyed their second cup of coffee and cupcake before Lauren said she'd leave Alice to enjoy some quality time with Bill.

'Good luck with telling David tonight,' she said when she hugged Alice at the gate. 'If he truly loves you, he'll understand. No one should want their significant other to be in a job that makes them miserable and messes with their whole psyche the way yours was. I'm only a phone call away if you need me. And, remember, no job hunting today or tomorrow. Better yet, for a week or so. You need time to get your mojo back, rebuild your confidence. Bye, Bill, it was lovely to meet you, you gorgeous thing.'

'Thanks so much for coming around, and for the cupcakes – and everything,' Alice said.

'My pleasure. I hope I helped. Just be kind to yourself, Alice, and don't over-analyse it all. Some things, like the behaviour of a person like Carmel Gold, can't be easily explained or understood. You just need to let it go.'

Alice was grateful for having Lauren as a friend. She felt they'd taken their friendship to another level today, and she was so appreciative.

Now if David was as supportive and understanding tonight, she might just be okay.

Chapter Eighteen

Alice had taken Bill for a walk and then enjoyed a long soak in the tub – and in doing so had gained a whole new appreciation for the new house. Oh how she'd missed having baths. The apartment hadn't had a tub, just a shower. Afterwards she'd curled up on the couch with Bill and watched a daytime movie on TV.

Now she stretched. It was four-thirty – she'd better start getting dinner organised. But she sighed heavily and stayed put. She didn't feel like doing anything. Maybe a particularly good dinner might make her news more palatable to David. Green chicken curry or stir fry?

Her mobile phone sounded with a text. It was from David: *Need a steak. Heading out for dinner …*

Even better. Have fun. I'll happily stay right where I am, she thought as she unlocked her phone to read the whole message. *Oh no!*

Need a steak. Heading out for dinner. Pick you up outside your office at 5.15.

Alice's pulse spiked. *Oh no. Do I tell him I'm not there? God no, then I'll have to explain why. More lies. Very bad idea.*

Suddenly her head was the clearest it had been in ages and after a few quick calculations and checking of time and train timetable knew what she needed to do.

Okay. But I'll be a bit late – 5:30ish.

No problem, was David's reply.

'Sorry, Bill, change of plans,' she said, and leapt off the couch. She could make it if she hurried. Breaking the news in a public place was a good idea. David didn't do scenes – ever. Maybe he was celebrating a promotion or a bonus, and she'd be able to feel less guilty about quitting.

In their bedroom Alice was just about to drag on her jeans when she realised her error. *I'm meant to be coming straight from work – I don't wear jeans to work.* At that moment she felt a new stab of guilt under her ribs.

White lies are okay if they're told to protect someone from pain, a wise person had once said. *So, this is okay, isn't it?* she told herself. Oh god. She was starting to break out in a nervous sweat.

'Stay. Good dog,' she said to Bill as she left with one minute up her sleeve. She only hoped the train was running on time.

Alice's knees were practically knocking when she sat down and the train doors clunked shut behind her. She fiddled with her handbag strap and tapped and shifted her feet. Thankfully the carriage was nearly empty and there weren't too many people to stare at her. *Should I tell him as soon as I get in the car or wait until dinner? And, if waiting until dinner, before ordering, or eating, or after? Shit.* Alice was beginning to regret not telling him straight away that morning.

Despite the crisp, cold evening, she was hot and a little clammy under her arms by the time she'd made her way to the building where Gold, Taylor and Murphy had their offices. Waiting at the lights with the imposing modern tower looming high above, the glass and steel glinting in the late afternoon sun, needles of nervous energy began to dart through her. Her breath kept catching. She didn't want to go anywhere near the place. Certainly didn't want to see anyone she knew. She almost didn't walk forward when the light for pedestrians went green, but a bump from people around her, expecting her to move, propelled her onwards and across the street.

Oh shit. She darted behind the little street vendor stall that sold magazines as a group of Gold, Taylor and Murphy employees spilled out onto the street. She stayed half-turned away and kept her head down while carefully examining the magazines as she prayed for the group to move away.

'Not a library. You buy,' the man behind the counter said. Alice cast a covert glance towards the building's main doors. Damn it. They were milling, not dispersing. Putting her head down again, she fished in her handbag for her wallet, opened it up and bought the nearest magazine with bold headlines about some scandal involving Tom Cruise. She stepped aside and opened it up. She just hoped David would pull up here, ahead of the taxi rank and not park illegally right in front of the building and her previous co-workers. Not that she knew any of them all that well. Uh-oh. She'd just spied Pip and Jared coming out and joining the throng.

She turned nervously at hearing a honk, but almost turned back when all she saw was a taxi pulling up. The back passenger door opened and she heard David call her name. She stuffed the magazine into her handbag as she leapt in beside him. She didn't know the two men who were with David in the car.

'Hey,' she said.

'Tom, William, this is Alice.'

'Hi,' Alice called as a general greeting and pulled her seatbelt on. Clearly David was planning a big night if he was leaving the car at work. Alice wasn't sure if this was better or worse for her situation. Ordinarily she hated drunkenness, but tonight it might actually help her.

'Good day?' David said as the cab pulled away from the kerb and Alice let out a slight sigh of relief that no one from the office seemed to have noticed her.

'Yep. You?'

'Not bad. The usual. You know. Tom and Will have flown in from Auckland.'

'Great. Welcome,' she said. She was beginning to feel desperate to unload her news – to get it, and whatever consequences came with it, out of the way. But now she'd have to be in hostess mode – charming, friendly. And definitely not on-edge like she currently was. Was it noticeable? Hopefully she just seemed a little tense after a big day, a big week.

They joined the peak-hour crawl through the city and then the amble along St Kilda Road. All the time David was pointing out things to the men – the National Gallery, places to visit and eat, landmarks of note. Were they clients or colleagues? Alice tried to remember if David had said. It didn't really matter, either way. She couldn't say anything now. He would be mortified to learn news like this in front of others. While he projected a very together, polished façade, she wondered if he was actually quite insecure and fragile inside. A couple of times she'd been stunned to find him practically reduced to a bumbling little boy – usually the result of a bad golf hole or round, or when a project he was managing wasn't quite going to plan.

'So, what do you do, Alice?' Will asked from the front seat, half turning around to look at her.

Well, funny you should mention my work, she thought to say. *Oh, the temptation …*

'There, look,' David cried, pointing, before Alice could answer. 'Alice is PA to her – there on the billboard. Carmel Gold, real estate agent extraordinaire!'

'Oh wow,' Will said.

'Cool,' Tom said.

Alice groaned inwardly. Oh if only she'd rung him that morning. Telling lies, by omission or in whatever form, was tying her in knots. She thought she might even be close to throwing up if she didn't keep her wits about her. She'd had two of Lauren's cupcakes for lunch and nothing else, and was now regretting it.

'She looks formidable,' Will said.

'Yeah, I bet she keeps you on your toes,' Tom said.

Oh you have no idea. 'Yes. I've only been there a few …' she said.

'And she's training Alice up to be an agent,' David said proudly.

'Well, down the track a bit. I'm still on probation,' Alice said, after swallowing down the rising bile.

Walking into their favourite St Kilda restaurant, they were shown to a great table, which Alice took as a good sign. Hopefully the churning in her stomach would stop after a hearty meal. Oh how she wished she were still home in her trackies on the couch with Bill.

When they ordered quickly Alice felt renewed hope that it wouldn't be a late night. But David had chosen to catch a cab, so no doubt he'd make the most of that decision. She was both relieved and disappointed to discover that Tom and Will were his colleagues. Relieved because it meant less pressure on her to impress them, and disappointed because David probably didn't need to either, and so he could let loose. Weighing it up, she decided it was probably better that they were his colleagues. Then she wouldn't be under the same scrutiny – from David as much as from the two men – that she would be if they were clients. Small mercies.

Unfortunately, towards the end of the meal, as they were considering the dessert menu someone suggested a round of shots. Alice cringed. She was already feeling queasy and tipsy thanks to her cupcake overdosing and the red wine during the main course.

After much goading from the men and much resistance from her, Alice agreed to one round, instantly cursing her weakness in submitting to peer pressure. But in some dark part of her brain, she was hoping that by appearing to have a great night and heartily joining in, David might be more receptive to her news later. Or was she just finally unwinding, letting go of all the tension that had been consuming her? Usually she hardly drank more than a glass or two of wine with a meal.

At least they didn't choose tequila – that would have seen Alice throw up for sure. She loved liquorice, so the black Sambuca went down well. And the second. Before she gave it too much thought, they'd all bought a round – well, each put a round on their table's tab, presumably for the company credit card – and they were laughing with more uproar than was necessary at how black their lips were. Suddenly the men were telling stories about colleagues in common and project stuff-ups, laughing like they were the funniest stories they'd heard in decades. Getting bolder and bolder about things they'd told their previous bosses, each man was bragging loudly, seemingly trying to outdo each other. Alice was happy to sit and listen. She was suddenly feeling very, very drunk.

'Come on, Alice, surely you've got a horrible previous boss story?' Tom said.

'Alice has been out of the workforce for a while at uni, so she doesn't have a bad boss story,' David said.

'Actually,' Alice said, and told them the story about the photocopier assault incident.

'Wow,' Tom said.

'That's crazy,' Will said. And the mood seemed to fall flat.

'You should have taken that job, you might have been happier,' David slurred.

'She seems happy enough to me,' Tom slurred and raised his glass to Alice with a wink and a smile.

Alice smiled back. 'Thanks, Tom.'

'Doesn't stop her complaining all the time, though, does it?' David said, and then rolled his head back.

'Ha-ha, David's the first one to go,' Tom said, and cheered, and Will joined in. Then they promptly ordered another round.

'Actually,' Alice said, breaking into the silence, 'you don't need to worry about me complaining anymore, David. I quit today.' *So there. How do you like that? That'll teach you for putting me down in front of your friends.* For a split second she felt victorious. But in the next she felt awful.

'Ooh,' Tom said. 'Um. Good for you?'

'Yeah. Go, Alice,' Will said with very little enthusiasm.

Suddenly everyone seemed completely sober. Except Alice. Her head was swimming. But perhaps that wasn't because of the alcohol.

'You did what?' David said, straightening up, glaring at her.

'Quit. I quit.'

'Fuck. Without discussing it with me?'

'Well, you did say if I was really not happy … And I wasn't. I was miserable. Carmel Gold is a bitch.'

'I think that's our cue to leave,' Will said, cringing. Out of the corner of her eye, Alice saw him signal a waiter.

'Yep,' Tom said. 'Can we get the bill, please,' he asked the waiter who had come over.

Jesus, David, say something. Alice wasn't sure if she'd said the words aloud or not. A part of her was glad her secret was out. Another part of her was alarmed by the look on David's face, which she couldn't quite read. White hot anger? Had she seen that expression before, she wondered as she searched her memory.

Before long they were outside shaking hands, exchanging grunting, slurred pleasantries and then piling into two taxis – one for her and David and one for Tom and Will.

Alice gave the driver their address. David remained silent, and stayed that way for the entire trip.

At home they stood side by side and cleaned their teeth without a word and then climbed into bed and rolled over with their backs to each other.

Alice's head was spinning and she didn't think she'd ever get to sleep. *God, what a day!* She felt awful about upsetting David, but also glad her news was out. Maybe David was just drunk. Maybe he wouldn't even remember. That thought almost made her laugh out loud. *One can hope!* Though, having to tell him again in the morning didn't bear thinking about …

*

Alice left David sleeping to take Bill for a walk. Her head was pounding with a massive hangover headache, but the dog had appeared beside the bed, scratching at her and she hadn't wanted to risk waking David by telling him no. She figured the longer they avoided talking about last night, the better.

When she returned, the paracetamol and water had taken effect and she was starting to feel less queasy. The fresh, crisp morning air, while an initial shock to her system, had helped too.

David was sitting at the kitchen bench, his hands wrapped around a steaming mug when she entered.

'What's this?' he said, pointing to the container of cupcakes on the bench. Alice cursed to herself – they had cream in them and she'd forgotten to put them in the fridge. Were they still edible?

'Lauren brought them over yesterday. To, um, commiserate with me about quitting.'

'I thought you'd have been celebrating,' David said icily.

Well, that too, she wanted to say, but didn't. David was angry. And clearly he hadn't forgotten the bombshell she'd dropped publicly the night before.

'So, hang on,' he said, 'you didn't quit yesterday afternoon, at the end of the day?'

'No. I couldn't make myself go at all. I'm sorry, David, I just couldn't.'

'So you had all day to tell me, but you didn't? You waited to blurt it out in front of strangers? How do you think that made me look, Alice?'

'David, they were fine.'

'That's not the point ... Wait a second. You were dressed for work when I picked you up from the office. Why would you ...?' His eyes were as big as saucers, suddenly full of comprehension.

Alice couldn't hold his stare. She went over and busied herself with the coffee machine, which thankfully required some attention before completing its task.

'Oh. My. God. Alice, I can't believe the level of your deception. I don't even know who you are anymore.'

'I ...' she began. But he held up his hand.

'I can't even look at you right now. I'm going to the office.'
But it's Saturday. Fine, just run away, David.

*

When Alice could ignore the itching guilt of quitting and upsetting David, she felt light and exhilarated with her decision. She
was determined not to let David's scolding ruin her day. He hadn't
been the one working for Carmel Gold. And if he'd been more
understanding maybe she wouldn't have blurted her news out like
that at dinner. No matter what he said, she still felt right about
leaving. Free. God, it felt good to be free. While she hadn't been
physically cooped up, she actually felt as if she had. It was like she
wanted to throw the doors and windows open after a long, cold,
damp winter and run out into the sun and warm air, with her face
raised and her arms outstretched. And run and run and run. She
was brimming with energy desperate to be spent.

After walking Bill she tied him up and ran some laps of the
oval and did some push-ups and other exercises on the equipment
in the park. But she still felt the need to keep moving. And be
around people. She took Bill home and collected her swimming
things and a clean set of clothes.

A serious workout at the pool finally helped her to feel more
settled and clear headed. She was thrilled when Lauren returned
her text saying yes to brunch at Alice and David's favourite café
near the market.

'Hiya,' Lauren said, closing her notebook and moving her bag so
Alice could sit down. She half-stood and they hugged before sitting
down again. 'Has David gone away on a work trip again already?'

'No, we've had a fight and he's off sulking at the office.'

'Uh-oh, because of quitting the job, right?'

'Yup. But we're not going to talk about it. Everything's always about me when you and I get together lately.'

'I must say, you're very chipper for someone whose partner has …'

'Uh-uh,' Alice said, waggling her finger in the air between them. 'I'm not ruining this beautiful day talking about it. It will be fine. The sun is shining and soon it will be winter, so we need to make the most of it.'

'Okay then. Got it,' Lauren said, grinning, as she picked up the menu.

'You seem cheery too, more so than usual. Have you had a writing breakthrough? When do I get to read something – it's been ages.'

'Do you want to?'

'Of course.'

'Well, I'm a little chuffed with what I've just done, actually,' Lauren said shyly. 'It just came out.'

Alice admired the serene look on Lauren's face, the complete and utter contentment.

'Here you are,' she said, opening her notebook and pushing it across the table to Alice. 'It's not very long.'

'Please don't feel you have to show me.'

'I'm cool. But don't feel you have to read it.'

Alice let out a laugh. 'Listen to us dancing around. Lauren, I would absolutely love to read your piece. It would be a privilege, especially because I just know that one day you're going to be famous.'

'You're too sweet. Well, I'm working on it. Tell you what, I'll go and order and you read. I can't bear to sit and watch you.'

'That's a good plan. I'm not keen on you hovering over me like a hawk, either. Here,' Alice said, fishing her wallet out and extracting some notes. 'I'll have the eggs and bacon on sourdough, an OJ and a latte.'

'Snap. Me too. Be back in a bit.'

Alice smiled as she watched Lauren practically skip her way to the counter, darting between the closely packed tables and other patrons. Then she started to read Lauren's story titled 'Day from Hell'.

From the first line Alice felt herself being drawn into the plot, and the activity and noise in the café seeped far away into the background. She was gripped by the story of Matilda, a young woman walking down an alley after a late night out, who had just heard footsteps behind her. Alice's heart raced along with Matilda's. She urged Matilda to get her mobile out of her bag, or better yet a can of pepper spray or mini-deodorant. Alice read on, a hand at her throat fiddling with her necklace, a habit she had when reading and engrossed. As she read she didn't even notice Lauren sit back down opposite her. Alice's heart almost stopped as Matilda turned the corner into a blind dead-end, a high brick wall in front of her leaving her nowhere to go. And then there were more footsteps, running.

Alice was hearing everything she was reading on the page as clearly as if it were a movie. Suddenly a voice shouted, 'Stop. Police. You're surrounded. Put the knife down.' There was a clatter of metal on cobblestone. 'Jason Parkes, you are under arrest for stalking.' Alice didn't realise she was holding her breath until she let it out along with Matilda as she slumped into the arms of a burly police officer. She was safe after two years of fear. 'You were really brave. It's over now,' the officer said, letting her sob into his chest before gently easing her away. Alice felt tears of relief and sympathy for Matilda gathering in her eyes, and quickly wiped them away.

She looked up from the page and took a few moments to get her bearings. She'd been there with Matilda in that alley. She blinked a few times and took a couple of deep breaths. She glanced across at Lauren who was clearly trying to not look at her.

'Wow, Lauren, that was incredible! I was right there with her – I heard and felt everything. I'd swear it was a much longer piece,' she said, flicking back the pages she hadn't remembered turning. 'In a good way. It was so intense.'

'Thanks so much. I really appreciate you saying that.'

'Thank you for letting me read it. It really is fantastic. Are you going to send it out to a competition or a magazine, or somewhere?'

'No, it was just a writing exercise about fear.'

'Well, you nailed it. Look at me, I'm a wreck. My heart was racing and I started to sweat,' Alice said, fanning her face with both hands. 'Lucky it wasn't a sex scene,' she said with a laugh, starting to feel a little self-conscious at how affected she'd become.

'Aww, bless.'

'I'm serious, Lauren, the whole world needs to experience your stories.'

'Well, I don't know about that.'

'Please don't hide your talent away and wait for an idea for a novel. You move people, Lauren. You're good. Really good.'

'Thanks. I'll think about it,' Lauren said, becoming visibly embarrassed.

After brunch they walked the aisles of the market and filled their shopping bags before saying goodbye.

Still feeling upbeat from her time out with Lauren, Alice was cooking a rich, creamy chicken, mushroom and garlic pasta sauce for dinner. She would use the meal to try to make amends, and she hoped David would be in a better mood when he arrived home.

'Fingers crossed the way to a man's heart really is through his stomach, Bill,' she said to the dog lying in his bed nearby.

'Hi, how was your day?' Alice said, half-turning from the stove with spatula in hand when she heard David's footsteps behind her.

There was silence. She turned back to the stove. She could hear him moving stuff around on the bench and then plugging his phone in to charge.

'Dinner won't be long. Can you set the table? And feed Bill?'

Again she was met with silence.

David walked around her to dish out dry food for Bill and then get placemats and cutlery out and set the table. After that he sat down, in silence.

Alice quietly dished up their meals and joined him. She stared at David as he started eating without looking at her and without uttering a word.

'David, are you seriously giving me the silent treatment? How bloody childish.'

'Well, I don't know what you want me to say,' he said indignantly.

'I don't know, how about, "Talk to me"?'

'There seems no point discussing your employment. You've made your decision, which I might add you chose not to discuss with me.'

'Jesus. David, would you listen to yourself. I told you I couldn't do it for another day. And before that I *did* discuss it. But you chose to be condescending or not hear me. Did you actually listen to me, David? I told you how I was feeling.'

'Come on, Alice, it was four weeks. It can't have been that bad. You were practically complaining from day one.'

'I was *discussing* how I was feeling from day one, David. I was trying to work through it – make it work. Seriously, do you *ever* listen to me?'

'Of course I listen to you. But, Alice, you didn't give the job or Carmel a chance.'

'You weren't there.' Tears filled her eyes. 'It would be nice if you cared enough to offer a little sympathy. You don't have to agree, but as my partner, you should at least care when I'm upset or hurting.'

'Of course I care, Alice. Don't be melodramatic. But let's get real here. You didn't really want the job. You don't want any job. You'd rather stay bludging at university. But you need to join the real world again. You've had your time to slack off and *find* yourself. I've carried you for long enough.'

I was genuinely excited about the job and the possibility of a career in real estate. Remember? But what was the point? David had clearly made up his mind about how he wanted to remember things.

'Not everything is about big money, David. I've always earned *something*. And what about all the emotional support I provide? All the housework and other stuff I do to keep things going while you do all your travelling, putting the almighty company first?'

'What do you think pays for this roof over your head – and the apartment before this? You can't live on air and dreams alone, Alice. Or *emotional support*,' he added with a sneer.

Alice was so flabbergasted and angry her tears stopped. *Who are you?* she thought. But of course she knew. She'd known all along. She'd just chosen to ignore that side of him and choose the path forward that looked so different from where she'd come from.

'What's really sad is that you'd have me stay in a job where I'm miserable,' Alice said sadly.

'Of course I wouldn't. Stop being ridiculous, Alice. I just think you need to be a bit realistic. Full-time employment isn't like being at university. It can be hard, not always enjoyable, and can take some getting used to.'

'Don't talk to me as if I'm a child, David. I have been employed full-time before, you know!'

'Well, your behaviour last night in announcing you'd quit was pretty immature from where I was sitting.'

'Yes, I'm sorry about that. I didn't mean to ...' But David wasn't listening.

'Intentionally trying to make me look bad – like I'm out of touch with what's going on in my own relationship – in front of my colleagues. Let's talk about who doesn't care. You don't seem to care about how much embarrassment you caused me.'

'Jesus, David, not everything is about you. And if you listened to me, really listened, then maybe I wouldn't have had to shock you into feeling something.'

'I feel something, Alice. Disappointment. In you and your petty behaviour. Actually, I'm going for a bike ride. I'll see you later.'

Alice stared, stunned, as he pushed himself back from the table and got up, tugged his phone away from the charging cable and strode down the hall.

Having moved her food around her bowl and only managed to eat about half her meal, Alice put the leftovers in the fridge and tidied the kitchen. She felt sick with how things had gone with David and worried about him being out on the road in the dark in an angry, distracted state. Why couldn't he understand? She picked up her phone from the top of the bench and tapped out a text: *I'm sorry. Please don't be angry with me♥Xx*

She sat nervously waiting, hoping, for a reply while aimlessly scrolling through her Facebook feed. When the reply came, she stared at it, her heart sinking even further: *Home later. Just remember, Alice, I'm not the enemy. D.*

Not the enemy? What was that supposed to mean? Alice shook her head. Oh well, at least he'd answered. Hopefully his rejection of her might be over soon. She should have known better than to hope for an olive branch. David never used terms of endearment or affection. And he never apologised. To the best of her knowledge, Alice hadn't ever heard the words 'I'm sorry' pass David's lips.

Chapter Nineteen

On Sunday David took himself off to play golf. Alice briefly considered going with him in an effort to placate his still frosty mood. But she'd decided she'd apologised enough for something she didn't think she should even have to apologise for. Okay, sure, she really shouldn't have announced her news in the way she had, and she'd apologised for that, but if he listened to her, really listened and actually heard and understood – had some compassion – then she wouldn't have had to. Alice found herself trying to work out if David had always been so self-centred. Perhaps the gloss was just wearing off and they were settling into more of a companionship type relationship. *God, it's been four years. We're in our thirties, not our sixties.*

How would it be when they had kids? David definitely wanted kids. Alice knew that. Though she wondered if it was more about appearing successful in another area of life – great job, big house, nice car, and a couple of kids. Alice thought she could take or leave having a family, but if she was going to do it, she wanted to be married first. And David had said he didn't believe in marriage because he was an atheist. Alice wasn't religious, but she liked and respected tradition. So they'd been at a stalemate and hadn't discussed it for the last year or so. She didn't mind not having to make a decision about having children – she'd been focussed on her studies. Perhaps if she re-considered her stance, she wouldn't have to look for a job … Alice felt a little ashamed. She bit her lip. So much for being a feminist and a strong, independent woman.

Her phone rang and she was pleased to see Lauren's name on the screen. She sometimes still felt her heart contract ever so briefly at the thought it might be Carmel, before realising it wouldn't be.

'Hi, Lauren, how's things?'

'Hey, Alice. I just wanted to check everything was okay now with David. I sensed it was maybe worse than you were making out. Can you talk or should I call back another time?'

'No, now's good. Oh, Lauren, I'm so glad to hear your voice. David's still furious with me. Though, I can't entirely blame him. I was an idiot, blurting out in public that I'd quit. I didn't mean to, it just happened. He's still barely speaking to me.'

'Oh no, that's not good. You'd better start from the beginning.'

'Are you sure you can be bothered listening to my woes?'

'Of course. I rang because I was worried about you.'

'That's so lovely of you,' Alice said. 'So …' she began.

'Wow,' Lauren said when she'd finished, 'I can see why David reacted the way he did.'

'I know. I was completely out of line in the restaurant. And I've put my hand up to that. But, seriously, he just won't let it go.'

'I'm sorry I put you in that position by leaving the cupcakes.'

'Don't be silly. It's not your fault. And I shouldn't have left them out on the bench, anyway. I'm still annoyed that he seems more interested in me having a job than actually being happy.

And of course that I dared not to discuss it with him first, before I left my job. But I did – well, not in so many words. Well, not in any words,' Alice conceded with a sigh. 'But I did discuss being unhappy there and why. And he did say if I wasn't happy to leave, which I now know was reverse psychology or passive-aggression, or whatever. Anyway, enough of all that. So here I am job hunting online. Did you know that even to wash dishes in a pub kitchen you have to have experience? Same with a job in a factory. I'm doomed.'

'Why would you be looking at those sorts of jobs?'

'Well, there's still nothing remotely related to my History degree.'

'So? You're also a highly prized admin whizz.'

'Yeah, right. Thanks for the vote of confidence, but we both know the truth about my situation.'

'You can't rearrange your whole life based on your experience with Carmel bloody Gold. I think it's safe to say that was unusual. And you'll find a way around the reference problem.'

'What I didn't tell you about Friday, Lauren, was that I was scared to go too close to the building where I worked and I hid from my old colleagues. I'm not joking. I was shaking and sweating. Properly terrified. Thank goodness they didn't see me. How bloody embarrassing. It was completely irrational behaviour.'

'Not from where I'm sitting. Alice, you're probably suffering from mild PTSD.'

'Don't be ridiculous! It's not like I've been to war, or in an accident, or watched someone die, or anything.'

'I'm being serious. To your well-educated, academic mind, it might seem a relatively minor and short-term ordeal, but it's really hit you hard and deep – you've said that. Remember how you said you felt your world had been turned upside down and you couldn't think straight. And the nightmares … Alice, benign experiences don't give you nightmares.'

'But isn't that just the brain or subconscious, or whatever, processing things, feelings, what went on that day?'

'That's dreams. I'm sure nightmares aren't normal and certainly aren't good.'

'I had another one last night. I was trapped in the corner of a room with Carmel standing over me, yelling. I couldn't make out what I was in trouble for and I couldn't get away from her. It was so real. I woke up sweating and wondering where I was.'

'Oh, Alice. Where was David? What did he say?'

'He was still up watching TV in the lounge. I didn't tell him. I'm sure the experience is just working its way through my system and I'll be fine in a few days.'

'I hope you're right. If it continues, it might be a good idea to see someone about it.'

'What, like a shrink?'

'A professional counsellor of some sort. Yes.'

'Then David really will call me a drama queen. Oh god, can you imagine?'

'Alice, don't dismiss it too quickly. If it's going to interfere with your life going forward, then it would be a good idea to talk to someone and work through it. You'll always have me, of course, but a different, neutral perspective might be useful too.'

'Hmm. Lauren?'

'Yes?'

'I'm sensing you knew how David would react. That's why you called, isn't it? You said you were worried about me.'

'I had a feeling.'

'Don't tell me you're psychic, Lauren, you've never even met him, have you?'

'I'm not psychic, but I'd had my suspicions that he's a bit of a control freak. Just things you've said along the way. And, remember, he's been to all three of our Christmas dinners, so I've actually met him a few times and seen you two interact.'

'Oh. That's right, of course you have. Yeah, I guess that's a fair description of him.'

'And seeing your house on Friday sort of confirmed it.'

'Because he's a neatnik bordering on obsessive? I can see how you came to that conclusion,' Alice said.

'It wasn't just that.'

'Oh, what else?'

'Alice, have you ever noticed that in all the photos of the two of you on display in your place he is always standing behind you with his hands on your shoulders.'

Really? 'That's because he's slightly taller,' Alice said, making her way out into the hall and down towards the living area.

'Fair enough. But he doesn't ever have his arms around you and he's never kissing you, or showing any affection. I just noticed it, that's all. I might be reading too much into it.'

Oh my god, she's right. Alice stared at the framed photos lined up along the pale timber sideboard and felt a cold sensation snake through her – not quite, but sort of, fear.

'Sorry, I didn't mean to pry. Just all me being a nosy writer.'

'Now you've pointed it out, it does seem a little bizarre. I've always thought it nice to feel his strength, his steadying influence behind me,' Alice said, truthfully, unable to drag her gaze away from the photos.

'Well, there you go. We all read things differently. Forget I said anything. This is me just overthinking things and blowing them out of proportion. I was just worried about you. I hope everything will be okay soon.'

'Honestly, I'm not sure it will be. The atmosphere here is pretty arctic and probably will be until I get another job, and stick with it. Speaking of which, I'd better get back to my job search.' But while her voice was strong, Alice felt the unnerving sense that the ground was shifting under her and that she'd discovered something that had, or would, irrevocably change things.

'It's Sunday, Alice. Give yourself a break. And you only quit on Friday.'

'I know, but …'

'Sometimes the best thing you can do is nothing at all. Take a deep breath, let the universe catch up and allow it to do its work.'

'Hmm.'

'Well, it's up to you, not me. You do what you've got to do. Let me know if you want to catch up sometime. And, remember, I'm only a phone call or text away.'

'Thanks so much. It really means a lot that you called to check on me.'

'Ah, what are friends for? There's no need for thanks. You'd do the same for me. Okay. Gotta go. Catch ya.'

'Yep. Speak soon.'

Alice hung up feeling grateful, but at the same time unsettled. Lauren's call had brought back into focus her frustration at David's lack of support. She also still couldn't drag her eyes away from the photos. Lauren was right: every single one of them was the same. And she started to feel a bit annoyed that she hadn't seen it before herself. Now that she thought about it, David did seem controlling. Even his smile in the photos seemed a little intense – barely a smile at all. He'd said from the start he had a problem with showing his teeth because he was embarrassed about them not being perfectly straight. Apparently his parents had run out of money and had to have his braces taken off early. David was still mortified. At both his crooked teeth – which Alice hadn't even noticed until he'd pointed them out – and not coming from a particularly well-off family. It was one of the first things he'd confided in Alice soon after they'd met. She hadn't seen why it was an issue – her parents certainly hadn't had lots of cash to splash about. She'd thought it great that David had used his upbringing as a reason to strive so hard. But perhaps he'd let it go to his head. There was a fine line with so many things in life. Oh well, he'd been, was being, very good to her. Everyone had their foibles.

'Lauren's right, Bill, job hunting can wait. All the new ones will probably go online on Monday anyway.' What David didn't know wouldn't hurt him, she thought, a little guiltily. Also, how would she sell herself – even in her cover letter – if she didn't get her head straight?

Chapter Twenty

By Thursday Alice was so frustrated and despondent about the job hunt that she spent most of her time in tears. She'd wanted to call Lauren – if only to hear a friendly, sympathetic voice – but didn't want to be the sort of friend who only ever called to moan. That had never been Alice's way before, but it was now. The thought of how different she was from the cheerful, optimistic person at uni made her feel downright depressed. Would she ever be like that again? She couldn't see how she could drag herself back, other than getting and keeping a good job, and right now that seemed as likely as finding a box full of hen's teeth. At least David didn't seem angry with her anymore. Though he'd as good as given up asking about her day in a way that elicited any discussion of feelings. Instead he asked for a rundown of what she'd done, as if she were answerable to him and needed to account for her time, which, she thought morosely, she pretty much was. She wasn't bringing in any money and she knew all too well money was power.

When a text from Lauren arrived Alice almost leapt with joy.

> *I'm in the area. Are you home? If so, can I get the Tupperware*
> *container? Xx*
> *I'm here! Would love to see you! (Be warned, though, there are*
> *tears.) Xx*
> *Oh no. What's happened?*
> *I'll tell you when you get here. (I'm okay. Just feeling sorry for*
> *myself.) Xx*

'You've no idea how good it is to see you, Lauren,' Alice said as she opened the door and then pulled her friend to her. She wasn't surprised to find herself sobbing into Lauren's shoulder. There seemed an almost constant flow of tears down Alice's face these days.

'Alice, what's going on?' Lauren said when they'd parted. 'I'm not in a rush. How about I come in and you tell me all about it. Unless you're busy?'

'Busy? You're kidding, right? I'm unemployed, remember?' Alice said as she led the way through to the kitchen.

'So, anything promising?'

'No. And it's worse than I thought. I relented about going back to an office and rang all the main temp agencies. Can you believe every one of them said not to bother coming in if I don't have a reference from my last direct report.'

'Why would you tell them you didn't have one?'

'I'm no good at lying, Lauren. And I thought if I was honest and up-front they'd find a way around it. So much for honesty being the best policy. I'm a damned good proposition. Why wouldn't they bloody well want to help me? It's as much their gain as mine.'

'At least you're starting to believe in yourself. That's a step forward.'

'More resigned to the fact that admin is all I know, and admin jobs are with people and in offices, so I don't really have a choice.'

'I'm sure you have plenty of transferable skills, Alice, you just need to be in the right frame of mind to think of them.'

'Exactly. At the moment I feel like I'm teetering on the top of a slippery slope. I'm angry with Carmel for doing this to me, making me like this. I'm still a basket case and a bloody mess most of the time. And I'm angry at myself for allowing her to do this to me. And I hate the world for making life so damned hard at the moment. There, listen to me feeling sorry for myself.'

'I think you're allowed to feel crushed and sad, and whatever else, Alice. You can't help your emotions,' Lauren said gently. 'Is David being more supportive now?'

'Yes. No. I don't know, to be honest. I have a horrible feeling this is as good as it gets with him. And, even worse, I think this is how he's always been and now I'm seeing it because life's not all going perfectly to plan. Sorry, I'm not really making sense. That seems to be me these days. I'm still all over the bloody place. I think David's always been the same – unemotional and only supportive in his own black and white way. He's not being unkind. He's being David. Oh, I don't know, I can't explain it, but I don't think it's personal – towards me, that is.'

'So, you think perhaps he had everything mapped out and because he's so ordered he's not responding well to things not working out as planned?'

'Yes, that might be part of it. But he's always saying that if something doesn't work, you find a way around it. He's always going on about solutions and thinking outside the box.'

'Maybe that's what he wants to believe, but it isn't working like that.'

'Sorry? I'm not following.'

'You know how people often have mantras? Well, sometimes I think those mantras are for things they *want* to achieve, be, not where they *currently* are.'

'Oh. I see. I think. Kind of like wishful thinking?'

'Exactly. Insecure people project feelings onto other people. Sorry if I'm overstepping, but in my mind he's showing some insecurity in the way he's reacted to you quitting. And there's a need to control you, to a certain extent. What I'm saying is that while you think he seems disappointed in you, I think he's more likely to be disappointed in himself for some reason. It's called projection.'

'He's probably annoyed with himself for choosing a partner who's not driven to be successful in the corporate world like he is. Don't get me wrong. I'd love to be rich, not have to worry about money, but I see what it does to him, and some of our friends and, honestly, I'm not sure that's what I want for myself. I thought I did, but with the big salaries you seem to lose your soul, too, a bit, don't you?'

'Maybe. I'm sure there are good companies out there. Alice, don't let one experience change your whole perspective.'

'Honestly, I don't know what to think anymore. But I'm sure I'm not living up to David's expectations.'

'I don't like that you're giving him so much power over you. You're your own person. You're the only one whose expectations you have to meet.'

'I'm not sure being in a committed partnership works quite like that. Lauren, I'm so confused and lost.'

At that moment Alice's mobile phone began to ring. 'Oh,' she said, picking it up and seeing *Mum – mobile* on the screen. 'That's odd, why is she ringing me when I should be at work?' she said. 'Hi, Mum, what's up?'

'I thought you weren't meant to answer your phone to personal calls at work. I was going to leave a voicemail message.' Alice cringed. She was being far too sensitive, but everything her mother said sounded like a rebuke.

'Well, I don't have long. What's up?' she repeated.

'I just thought you should know Ruth Stanley died. A sudden heart attack, apparently.'

'Oh no.' Alice's heart clenched painfully. Her chin wobbled and tears began to stream down her face. 'When's the funeral?'

'Tuesday.'

'What time?'

'Two o'clock. But you won't be able to make it if you're working. Surely not.'

'I can see if they'll give me time off,' Alice said, cursing the utterance of yet another lie – and in front of Lauren.

'Oh. I'd have thought you wouldn't have been there long enough.'

'Well, it *is* a funeral.'

'Yes, but Ruth wasn't family, was she?'

Maybe not to you. Suddenly Alice was desperate to get off the phone and give in to the sobbing that was lodged tight in her throat.

'Look, Mum, I need to go. I'll talk to you later.'

'Well, let me know if you decide to come and need picking up from the plane.'

'Okay. Thanks for ringing and letting me know.'

Alice hung up and sat staring at the phone in her hand. *Oh my god, Ruth. No.*

'What? What's happened?' Lauren asked.

Alice looked at Lauren, her brow furrowed and her bottom lip quivering.

'God, Alice, what's happened? You're scaring me.'

'One of my really special friends back at home had a heart attack. She died.'

'Oh no. I'm so sorry,' Lauren said, holding out her arms.

'Oh god,' Alice said, crumpling into Lauren's embrace.

'She was there for me when my marriage ended when my family wasn't. You know, I probably would never have had the courage to leave Hope Springs if it hadn't been for Ruth. I feel so bad that I haven't kept in touch more these past couple of years, especially in recent months.'

'Well, it's hard, with distance.'

'I meant to call her the other day.'

'Was she a friend from school? That's young to have a heart attack.'

'Oh no. No, Ruth and her family were close friends with my parents for as long as I can remember. She was like a second mother to me. Where Mum was always cold and unemotional, Ruth was warm and loving. She was always there for me. God, Lauren, I can't believe she's gone.'

'Was your mother upset? From what I was listening to, she didn't seem it.'

'No, Dawn doesn't do emotion. Ever.'

'It's good that she rang to tell you.'

'That'll be so I didn't hear from anyone else first. And also as a *So there*, a punishment.' Alice coloured. The words were out without her thinking. 'Sorry, I shouldn't have said that. You must think I'm awful.'

'Not at all. I am so lucky to have great parents I adore and who adore me, but I know it's not the same for everyone. And Brett certainly opened my eyes the other week,' Lauren said.

'Brett's really opened my eyes too …'

Once Alice had taken on board what Brett had said about Carmel, she'd dug deeper, going from website to website. Part of her was hoping to prove him wrong while another part was intrigued. She felt like jigsaw puzzle pieces in her life were finally falling into place. The internet was full of the subject. She wished she'd been surprised or horrified to discover she might have been born to a narcissist, but thought deep down she'd probably always known. She'd just never had the name for it. She'd always known that in her mother's eyes, her sister Olivia was the golden child, but it seemed Alice might be what was called a scapegoat within the narcissistic family dynamic. Coming to this realisation made so much about her and her upbringing make sense. It was both comforting and disconcerting.

She still didn't want to believe it, especially how damaged she might be. She didn't want to believe that she'd been as good as programmed to choose the wrong men thanks to her mother. But look what had happened with Rick. David was so different and their relationship was nothing like what she and Rick had had. Was it? She mentally shook her thoughts aside.

'What he said about his family rings so true for me, too, the more I think about it,' Alice said. 'I've also been doing a heap of digging online and stumbled on this great site about the daughters of narcissistic mothers. I didn't want it to be true. I just thought Mum didn't like me, not that she might actually have some sort of disorder. I've never felt that I could do anything right in her eyes, no matter what I did or how hard I tried. She's always been a bully, but of course no one else ever saw it. She was like Carmel – bullying and competitive.' Alice shuddered at the memory of her time with Carmel and how similar her own mother was in personality to the horrible woman. 'Anyway, Mum always had a problem with my friendship with Ruth. You reckon David's insecure,' Alice said. 'He's got nothing on my mother. For years Ruth and I had to pretend we didn't speak to each other quite so often because Mum would get all miffed about it.'

'I'm sure Ruth would have understood if you were so close for years and she knew your mum well. So, don't be too hard on yourself. Are you going to go to the funeral?'

'Yes. I really want to be there. But, god, I'm not very good at spontaneity. It's only on Tuesday.' Alice's head began to spin with trying to start making plans. 'Do you mind if I call David?'

'Of course not. Actually, I'll go so you can focus on the arrangements,' she said, picking up her bag and the plastic container.

'No, don't, he probably won't even answer. Actually, I'll email him.' Alice quickly tapped out her message.

> *Hi David,*
>
> *Mum just rang to say Ruth Stanley died this morning. You remember Ruth, it was Ruth and Thomas's house where we had Mum's birthday last year. Anyway, the funeral is in Hope Springs at 2 pm on Tuesday and I really want to be there. Can I please book flights using FF points?*
>
> *Thanks, Alice. Xx*

Alice cringed a little at the bluntness and presumptuousness of her message. But, maybe Lauren was right and she had been letting David have too much power. And she really did want to be there to say goodbye to Ruth, as hard and as horrible as it will be.

'David will go with you, won't he?'

'I wish. No. He won't want to be away from work.'

'Oh. Wow.'

'I'm used to it. It doesn't mean I like it, but I'm used to it.'

'But what about giving you some emotional support? Funerals are horrible. I couldn't imagine going all that way to a funeral on my own. But at least, I guess you'll be with your family. Though, if your mum's ... Hey, do you want me to go with you?'

'I couldn't ask you to do that.'

'You're not. I'm offering. I'm your friend, I want to help.'

'It's really kind of you, but I couldn't expect you to stump up for flights and David would have a fit if I asked him to use more frequent flyer points. Not that I think he's allowed to use them for anyone other than immediate family. Thanks, but I'll be fine.'

'If you're sure ...'

'I'll have to be.'

'Okay, I'll go now and let you sort this out. Call if you need me. I'll speak to you soon.'

'I'm so sorry I'm being such a bad friend, Lauren, and making everything about me all the time.'

'Alice, you've got a lot going on and nothing to apologise for. Let me know once you've made your plans. I'll call you later when you've had a chance to get your head around it.'

*

'Did you get my email?' Alice asked David that evening as he came into the kitchen where she was putting the finishing touches on a warm chicken salad for dinner. She was feeling antsy about the tickets and sad about Ruth and struggling to hold back the tears, which had finally eased after flowing on and off all afternoon.

'Yep. Here you go,' he said, extracting a printout of the tickets from his briefcase and laying it on the table.

'You could have at least replied and told me. Discussed it with me. I almost booked them on my credit card.'

'Sorry, I just thought it best to get them booked. And discussed what? You told me when you needed to be there and I've booked the flights, Alice. Here they are,' he said, pointing at the A4 page.

'Thanks. I really appreciate it.' *But oh how I wish you weren't quite so unfeeling. I'm really hurting here*, she thought, her eyes full again. 'Did you allow plenty of time for me to get to and from Port Lincoln?'

'Of course I did. I'm not stupid, Alice. And it's not my fault you're from beyond the back of Woop Woop where there are no direct flights.'

Alice put the plates on the table and picked up the printed page.

'Are you coming with me?' she asked quietly. After Lauren had planted the idea in her head, she'd started to hope he'd surprise her.

'No. Why would I be going? I can't leave the project now.' He stared at her, frowning, a truly mystified look plastered across his face.

Alice looked away.

'Anyway, someone has to look after Bill.'

Alice nodded as she wiped her damp nose and eyes.

'You're a big girl. You'll be fine. Your mother will be going, won't she? You don't need me there as the fifth wheel. I'd just be in the way.'

It's not a date, David.

Alice nodded again. She was too scared to speak – the lump stuck in her throat was threatening to explode and cause her to cry uncontrollably.

'What's wrong?' David said.

'I've just lost one of my oldest friends in the entire world and you don't seem to even care.'

'Of course I care. I've booked you flights, haven't I? They've cost me a heap of frequent flyer points. It's lucky I'm on silver.'

'It's not something I want to do on my own.'

'You won't be on your own. I'm sure you'll know practically everyone there. Don't you South Australians only ever have one degree of separation?' he said with a chuckle as he picked up his knife.

'That wasn't what I meant,' Alice said quietly, picking up her own cutlery.

'I don't know why you'd even think there's a chance I'd be able to go. You know how busy I am at work. And you wanted a dog, remember? Someone has to stay and look after him.'

'There are kennels and people who can come in and walk him.'

'Alice, I'm not going and that's that. She was your friend. I barely knew her. Maybe it will be good for you to get away on your own and think about things.' The words *and get your act together* seemed to hang unspoken between them.

While they hadn't been spoken aloud, Alice thought David was sounding just like her mother who had often said things like *Go off and brighten your ideas up* and *I'll give you something to cry about if you don't stop that snivelling.* But he hadn't said any of those things, had he? She was being overly sensitive – something else her mother had told her a million times growing up. But where was her hug? Why hadn't he come in, wrapped his arms around her and said something like, *Darling, you must be devastated. I'm so sorry for your loss, so sorry you have to go through all this on top of everything else. What can I do to make you feel better?* Alice sighed.

It's been nearly four years. As if he's going to magically change and suddenly become a romantic, touchy-feely, sensitive guy, Alice. You knew what he was when you met. And he was everything you wanted, remember?

She took a deep breath in an effort to steady herself and swallow back the tears. Maybe getting away and the distraction of travelling and being alone for a couple of days would be good for her. If only she wasn't staying with her mother …

'Alice, I don't know what else you want from me. I'm sorry you're sad, but …'

'It's okay, David. I know. I get it. Thanks very much for the flights. I'm just sad. I'm going to miss Ruth.'

'But you hardly ever spoke to her. When did you last call her? How can you miss someone you …'

Maybe if David had lost someone close to him he'd understand how she was feeling – like her soul was being slowly torn out in one long piece, her entire insides being seared as it went. Alice really did feel as if she'd lost a chunk of herself from deep within. She hadn't spoken to Ruth in about six weeks – and she felt terribly sad and guilty about that – but she already felt a gaping hole within her life where Ruth had been. She realised she felt as if she'd actually just lost her mother, and stifled a gasp. Ruth had taken her to buy her first bra, because Dawn had been working and didn't think it was important to find the time to go with her. And Ruth had asked her how she felt about things – and listened to her answers. Really listened.

It was Ruth, not Dawn, who had hugged her the night her dad had died, and at the funeral. Dawn had been too busy being stoic. It had been Ruth who'd held Alice's hand after her marriage ended and said, 'It will be okay. *You* will be okay.' And she'd actually tried to do something constructive to help her recover when Alice's own mother had just stood with her hands on her hips, glaring at her and as good as said the words, *You are a disgrace to this family.* Utterly bereft and devastated by the abandonment, Alice had tried hard to not let the memory settle within her, but it had – her mother's look of disgust and displeasure. That was when Alice had decided she would never rely on or truly confide in her mother again. And she hadn't. Why couldn't Ruth have been her mum instead? How many times had she silently asked that question?

'I'd better ring Mum and tell her the details of my flights before it gets too late, and check she can pick me up from Port Lincoln,' Alice said, getting up and taking her half-empty plate to the sink.

'I hope so, because I really don't want to pay for a hire car as well.'

And I really don't want to drive while I'm feeling like this. But Alice kept the words to herself. The truth was, she yearned for David to go with her, stand beside her. Just be there for her. She thought about what Lauren had said about the photos and his hands on her shoulders being a sign he was controlling. Well, right now she'd give almost anything for him to provide her some support of any kind.

Chapter Twenty-one

Alice wasn't surprised when David said he couldn't drive her to the airport, but she was disappointed. He still showed no sign of grasping just how hard this trip would be for her. Or he didn't care. She tried not to dwell on that thought. He had already left for work when Alice did a quick mental inventory before wheeling her case outside. Seeing Bill lying down in the passage with the please-don't-leave-me look he'd perfected almost made Alice fall apart completely. She was barely holding herself together as it was. For the first time she wished there hadn't been any flights available. Thankfully she'd only be away for a night and two days. Alice reminded herself she was always anxious when she travelled. Ordinarily she was stressed, but today she was completely frazzled.

At the airport she printed out her boarding pass and made it through security without any dramas, and relaxed. She let out a sigh of relief and paused to gather her thoughts and figure out if the Qantas Club lounge was to her left or right. She couldn't remember; in the past she'd always just followed David.

Uh-oh. Without him I don't have access. Damn. She'd been counting on sitting in a quiet place to settle her nerves.

Alice checked her gate number and its whereabouts before browsing the books in the newsagency. When she couldn't settle on a title, she moved on to the coffee stand and bought a latte. She had plenty of time for aimless wandering. In her current state she'd never settle enough to read anyway. She'd been like this practically since she'd started at Gold, Taylor and Murphy. When would she be normal again?

Alice told herself that even without the Carmel experience, she'd be a nervous, distressed mess today. After all, she was heading back to the place she'd practically fled from four years ago. Added to that was the fact she would not be having a fortifying cuppa with Ruth when she got there, but had to adjust to never seeing her friend again.

She sat down and thought of how Lauren always said she loved airports, especially wondering where the other travellers had come from, where they were going and making up stories about them in her head.

Ten minutes later Alice had finished her coffee and was restless and bored with waiting and looking for something to do with her hands other than scrolling through Facebook on her phone. She kept going back to the websites on narcissism she'd found, too, which probably wasn't healthy. Or maybe it was – she was learning a lot … So back to the bookstore she went, if only to kill some more time and find a prop to keep her hands busy.

After standing in front of the shelves deliberating for longer than seemed normal, Alice picked up a novel with a pretty floral cover, figuring it must be by a good author – or at least popular – if the store was expecting to sell as many as the large pile suggested. The book felt nice in her hands when she brought it up to the counter, and when she sat down again she turned it over and over, but had no inclination to open it up and start reading. Her phone pinged with a text message from Lauren:

How are you doing?
Okay. Thanks. So far so good. Xx
You've got this. Will be thinking of you and sending lots of positive energy. ♥

She knew Lauren would be heading into a lecture soon so she couldn't phone her. But suddenly Alice wanted to hear a friendly voice and be reassured she would be fine, was doing the right thing, and wouldn't regret this. What she really wanted to do was go back home and see Bill and pretend Ruth wasn't dead and her life, generally, wasn't a complete mess, wasn't unravelling around her.

Stop it, Alice, she told herself as tears sprang into her eyes. It didn't help that she hadn't slept much. She never did sleep well when she had an alarm set. Her body hated being jolted awake so she tended to wake on her own accord long before the alarm went off.

Alice hadn't read any fiction for years, having had to make her way through so many history texts and non-fiction books for uni. She hadn't read much at all since finishing her degree. Maybe this book would be her way back into what had been one of her favourite things to do since childhood. She turned the paperback over to read the back cover blurb. She had to read it four times to fully ascertain that the book was about a young woman who had gained a surprise and very generous inheritance from an unknown relative and had to decide whether to leave her life and friends behind and move to some small, far-off town, or stay and carry on with life as she knew it. Alice was sufficiently intrigued. She was a little surprised to feel slightly comforted by the book, almost as if she had a friend beside her. She could now see what Lauren meant about making friends with the characters in novels and being sad to say goodbye when the story ended. Lauren had also said that reading was the best way to forget about your troubles for a few hours.

She looked up at hearing a muffled announcement about her flight to Adelaide. Alice checked around her to make sure she had everything, and joined the milling passengers.

On board she had to jump up and let another passenger into the window seat. She cursed being in the middle. At least her neighbour didn't seem chatty. Upon settling into his seat, he'd instantly opened his book and buried his nose in it. Alice didn't think it would be safe to talk to anyone. If they asked her where she was going and why, she might just dissolve into tears.

She went back to Hope Springs for the obligatory occasions, like Christmas – well, as few of them as she could get away with. She hadn't been back for at least a year. The last Christmas had been their turn to go to David's family in Sydney. This year they were having a parent-free Christmas and staying home and catching up with friends who didn't have family in Melbourne or Australia, or for whatever reason were staying put and alone. Alice hadn't broached that with her mother yet. Dawn would show her disapproval – either with loud verbal scorn or quiet tut tutting and sighs, tightly pursed lips and icy looks. Alice would leave it as close to the event as possible to break the news. Then she wouldn't have to endure too many passive-aggressive phone conversations and attempts at guilt-tripping and, even worse, Dawn deciding to attend and Alice having to explain the concept of family-free. More than likely she'd give in and let her mother attend, as she'd done so many times over the years.

Let's just get through this visit, Alice told herself as she opened her book to the first page and proceeded to read the first three lines seven times before giving up and leaning back into her seat and closing her eyes. Perhaps a catnap would help.

Chapter Twenty-two

Alice carefully negotiated the rickety fold-down steps of the small plane at Port Lincoln, her legs wonky from the constant vibration under her feet for the past hour. At least the noisy plane had meant she didn't have to speak to the passenger next to her.

Alice glanced around her while trying to take an inventory of her feelings. Usually when she came 'home' as her mum put it, she felt the warmth of nostalgia and the disappointment of regret when remembering how it had all gone so wrong. There was also some sadness that she'd left somewhere she'd loved and knew so well. And then there was always the anxiety and pain over how let down she felt by her mother and sister, and feeling on-edge wondering how they would be this time around. It was a strange sensation to both belong and be an outsider all at once – a very uncomfortable feeling.

While Alice loved the quaintness and familiarity of the area and the small town she'd once been a big part of, she also bemoaned her family's lack of will to stretch their beliefs and ways of doing things. When she'd first come back to visit she'd brought with her so many ideas for the family's corner shop, but had been met with scorn and even horror.

'Why would you want to change things? People come here because we represent familiarity,' her mother had said.

'Yeah, don't come back here to throw your high and mighty ideas around,' her sister, Olivia, had said.

She and Olivia had never been best friends, but the animosity had reached new heights over the last few years. Alice's feelings towards Olivia hadn't changed and she'd tried hard to find some common ground with her. But while her sister seemed interested in hearing about Alice's life, she would often put it down by saying things like, 'Well, we can't all drink cafe lattes and sit and listen to lectures. Some of us have to work.' Olivia made it sound like she'd been given a life sentence, but she could leave any time she chose to – just like Alice had.

Alice would have given her left arm to have had the opportunity to take over the family business that her father had run for so long. That was another thing Olivia – and her mother, for that matter – had resented in Alice: her close relationship with their father. It was almost as if they somehow blamed Alice for his death, too. She had never felt anything but sympathy and understanding for him in the wake of his suicide. But Olivia and Dawn seemed to take his death and Alice's lack of anger surrounding it as an embarrassing affront and a personal attack. She thought that someone who decided to take their own life most likely didn't do it to punish those around them – they did it to end the pain after having exhausted what they considered to be all other avenues. Alice's mother and sister weren't able to see it that way even now, all these years on – evidenced by the fact Les Hamilton was never referred to. Ever.

Alice could see that Dawn's constant control and criticism of her father, as well as trying to run a small business that was struggling to survive because of a transport crisis, had pushed him into desperation, depression and beyond. As far as she could see, her dad had been doing his best, and it didn't help that shopkeeping wasn't in his blood. He came from a long line of farmers and graziers. But when he'd married into the Proctor clan, Alice supposed his gentle nature had been crushed by their domineering ways. He was never one to go against the grain, so he tried to do as his wife wished. Alice knew he wouldn't have left them unless he felt he didn't have a choice. She and her father had always been close, shared a special bond. Only later did she realise just how much this bond between father and daughter annoyed Olivia and angered their mother. Jealousy was such a nasty, destructive, sad emotion.

So, it was with mixed feelings that Alice raised her hand in greeting to Olivia as she made her way across the tarmac to the small terminal. They hugged briefly and awkwardly and then Alice followed Olivia out to the carpark and over to where her white sedan was parked. Oh, how she wished her kind, gentle stepfather Frank had come to collect her.

'God, I can't believe you came all this way,' Olivia said as she pulled her seatbelt on and snapped it shut.

'Ruth was a dear friend; she was very special to me,' Alice said quietly.

'Yes, but still … God, I wish there was a plane direct to Hope Springs,' she said with a loud sigh as she turned the key. 'It's a lot of mucking about.'

'I told Mum I could hire a car and drive myself up. But she wouldn't have it. I'm sorry if I've put you out, Olivia,' Alice said, folding her arms tight across her chest in an effort to physically hold herself together. Oh how she ached to give in to the sobbing simmering in her throat.

'Well, I hope we make it in time,' Olivia said, reversing out of the parking spot. 'So, how's David?'

'Good. How's Trevor?'

'Good. Just had man flu, though, so of course it was like he almost died,' she said theatrically. 'You know how it is,' she said, rolling her eyes. Alice smiled at the glimpse of the Olivia that could be quite amusing. 'Bloody big baby. How's the big new house?'

'Good,' Alice said. 'Oh, we got a dog. Did I tell you on the phone?' Alice knew she hadn't – she tried to avoid telling them anything personal these days, if she could.

'No.'

'His name's Bill. He's a Jack Russell. A little over two years old. We got him from the RSPCA.'

'Ooh, I bet he's got problems, then.'

Alice forced herself to not sigh at Olivia's negativity.

'He's great, actually. Very well behaved and a real character. I miss him already,' she added wistfully.

'It's only a dog, Alice. Wait until you have kids.'

They drove in silence for a while, then Olivia pointed out her window. 'Look at all this new development,' she said. 'Lots of farmers are retiring down here but they don't want neighbours nearby, so everything's being carved up into five or ten acre strips,' she added with clear disapproval.

Alice turned and looked, but remained silent. She didn't want to say anything that could lead to any criticism.

'So, tell me about your new job,' Olivia said.

'Not much to tell. It's just admin. Bit more challenging than I've had, though. It's nice not to be a poor uni student,' she said, cursing the stream of lies that were slipping so easily off her tongue.

'I bet. Though, uni *was* your choice. Is David travelling a lot?'

'Quite a bit. And he thinks there'll be even more soon, too.'

'You must miss him when he's gone. I wouldn't like it.'

'Yeah. But it's always been that way. I guess I'm just used to it,' Alice said. 'How's Mum? I certainly wouldn't be able to work with her. I'm not sure how you do *that*.'

'Ah, she's okay. Like you say, it's what you get used to. Oh. I saw your Rick the other week.'

'Olivia, he's hardly *my* Rick, considering we've been divorced for years.' Alice didn't want to ask, but she was a little curious to know about her ex-husband.

'He's good, in case you're wondering. Got a new lady friend.'

'God, you sound like Mum. Lady friend! Who? Someone local?'

'Nah. An out-of-towner – Yorke Peninsula, I think. He seemed happy enough.'

'That's nice.'

Alice had never quite got over her mother's disloyalty when she invited Rick for Easter lunch the year after they'd split up, just after Alice had left for Melbourne. She couldn't really explain her objection without sounding mean-spirited, but considering how much pain he'd caused her, Alice thought her mother might have shown more consideration for her feelings. It was almost as if he'd been kept in the family and she'd been exiled – even if it had been her decision to leave the town. If she'd tried to explain it, her mother would have most likely said something idiotic like, 'Well, he was hungry, Alice, I wasn't going to turn him away.'

To be fair, Alice hadn't actually told her mother or Olivia the finer details of her marriage problems and subsequent separation – although she'd figured someone else would have. Doing so wouldn't have garnered any more sympathy. Her mother would have somehow found a way to use the information to ridicule Alice further about her failure.

'So are Mum and Frank helping to cater for the wake?'

'Yes, but we'll see them at the cemetery first. Thank god for the Stanleys not being religious so we're spared the church bit.'

Alice couldn't remember the church part of her father's funeral – apart from just staring at the shiny dark wooden box, with flowers on top, sitting out alone up the front. The whole day was a bit of a blur. But she did remember standing beside her mother and Olivia at the graveside and hearing the clicking of what she thought was a camera. She'd been shocked to turn around and see that someone was in fact taking photos. Apparently her grandmother, her father's mother, had enlisted one of the cousins to do the honours of digitally capturing the proceedings for posterity.

Alice had been horrified. How was that not purely vile and distasteful? And why would you want to? Was it a common thing to do? She had never been able to look at the photos, despite being sent a USB stick with them on. Who wanted pictures of crying people – people standing around looking bereft? Her grandmother had been a strange woman, that was for sure, and Alice had never really liked her.

Now that she thought about it, Alice couldn't remember if they'd had a wake for her father. They must have. But where? It suddenly seemed terribly important to know. And the more she racked her brain to remember, the harder her heart pounded. She began to struggle for breath. If she didn't pull herself together she might start hyperventilating. She searched her memories and came up empty. She hated not knowing. *It doesn't matter*, she told herself, *let it go.* Gradually she calmed. Olivia drove on, seemingly unaware of Alice's torment beside her.

The rest of the journey was made largely in silence, punctuated by Olivia providing snippets of gossip about people Alice no longer knew or really cared to hear about. Alice tried not to check her watch every three seconds, but she was getting a little anxious that they would run late.

'It's okay, we're cutting it fine, but I think we'll get there in time,' Olivia said.

Their mother and Frank were waiting at the gate when they arrived, panting slightly. They'd had to run from where they'd parked the car back in a farmer's empty paddock that had been opened up for extra parking. They would have been right on time otherwise.

Alice was pleased to see so many had come to pay their respects to Ruth and her family.

'You're late,' their mother hissed, looking Alice up and down before giving her a quick hug. Sometimes over the years Alice had wished they'd just dispense with trying to hug and give a wave or nod of the head instead. Her father had been the only one in the family who'd given a big, warm, soft hug. Alice's mum and Olivia gave hugs that were cold and stiff, and very abrupt. Thankfully Frank was better at it, Alice thought as she sank into his welcoming embrace and leant her cheek against his shoulder. He kissed her head.

'We're a little stressed,' he whispered, 'but she is glad you're here. It's so good to see you, Alice.'

'Thanks, Frank. It's good to see you, too.' Alice smiled weakly.

'Come on. Come on. We're late,' Dawn said, tottering off at almost a run to catch up with the other mourners. Alice knew her mother would ease her way through to get as close to the front as she could. Dawn was competitive in everything she did and had to be the centre of attention. Oh, if only she had a dollar for all the times she'd wanted to say, 'Mum, it's not all about you.' At least now she had a name for it and her mother's behaviour made a lot more sense. Alice had an explanation, but not an excuse, for the many awful ways in which her mother had treated her over the years.

'I'd better keep up,' Frank said with an apologetic grimace, patted Alice on the arm, and hurried to catch up.

'Come on,' Olivia urged.

'You go on. I'll catch up.' Now she was here, Alice was really struggling to keep herself together. All the memories and feelings of loss for those she'd farewelled here before swamped her and her composure was slipping dangerously. *Oh, Ruth*, she thought sadly. She found a tissue in her bag and dabbed at the tears streaming down her face from under her sunglasses. Her legs were weak and she was fighting for breath against her fitted suit that suddenly felt unbearably tight. At the back of the throng the funeral director handed her an order of service. He'd officiated at her dad's service, and both of her maternal grandparents, and most other send-offs in the district. He smiled warmly then moved on to hand out more of the folded pages. It seemed the service hadn't started yet and she wasn't late after all. Alice let out the slightest sigh of relief.

She stared through her tears at the smiling picture of her darling friend Ruth on the cover of the folded sheet, and a pang of sadness gripped her stomach so hard it took all her will not to double over. She straightened up and turned to her left and then her right to acknowledge the people beside her. Then the music started. Alice couldn't sing, she could barely breathe, and so she stood gulping air and trying not to hyperventilate through the tears. Why did people have to play nice music at funerals and ruin the tunes for whenever you heard them in the future? Like 'Morning Has Broken', which Alice suddenly remembered had been played at her father's funeral. Or had it? Perhaps it was at one of the services they'd held for her grandparents. Regardless, she hated that song now. Just hearing the tune made her well up.

Alice estimated she knew ninety percent of the mourners around her. Here she was amongst friends, people she'd grown up with, had known all of her life until leaving. People she loved, she thought, smiling warmly and nodding to an old favourite aunt.

But with a shock, Alice realised she'd never felt so lonely. She was fine on her own – she was used to David travelling and rarely pined for him. But this was different. This was a feeling that threatened to tear out her soul and further shatter her already broken heart. There was an emptiness within her that she'd never experienced before – not when her dad had died or her marriage had ended. She realised with a slight start that this feeling had nothing to do with losing Ruth. And as the funeral director now standing up front said, 'Ashes to ashes, dust to dust,' and Alice was drawn along with everyone as they began shuffling forward in a line to accept a flower from the basket to toss onto the casket, a question arose in her: *What is the point of having a life partner if I have to be here alone doing this?* The question stayed, settling in her stomach like a stone – cold, hard and uncomfortable.

She accepted a pale pink carnation and tossed it in, her heart pounding. She sniffled and smiled through hugs and utterances with Ruth's husband, their two adult sons and three adult daughters, and moved on quickly to keep the queue moving.

After milling about and exchanging greetings with dozens of people, when the throng started to slowly disperse, Alice made her way over to her father's grave. She knew she'd get some time alone there. While Alice was sad and disappointed her dad, whom she'd loved so much, was gone, her mother and Olivia were downright angry about it – still, eight years on. They wouldn't be coming over to visit his grave.

Oh, Dad, what am I going to do? My life's an absolute mess. She put her hand on the tombstone that had been warmed by the sun. She longed to sit on the granite edge, but knew if she did she'd never want to move again.

With a shock she wondered if this hopelessness, this lost desperation, was anywhere near how her father had felt when he'd decided to end it all.

No. She had options. She just had to figure them out. She couldn't give in to feeling sorry for herself. What hurt was that she was here with the people who were meant to matter the most to her, support her the most – unconditionally – and she couldn't talk to them about it without fear of being put down and ridiculed. *Yep, so much for family being everything,* she thought, recalling Brett's words from that day in the pub. Right then she felt more supported by a man who was dead and buried beneath six feet of dirt. That thought sank her lower than she thought possible. She looked up, sensing movement nearby. *Time to go and put on a brave face at the wake, I suppose,* she decided and reluctantly turned to move away. But she stopped, startled to see her ex-husband standing a few steps away.

'Hey, Rick,' she said.

'Hey, Alice. How're you doing?'

'Pretty shit, actually,' she said.

'Yeah. Understandable.'

And then she was being drawn into a tight, lingering hug – the hug she'd been yearning for for goodness knew how long. From David. She sank into him, breathed in his scent that after so many years still smelt familiar. And comforting. As she felt herself relax for the first time that day – probably the first time in weeks – she also felt the dam holding back her tears break. She sobbed and sobbed and sobbed.

'Oh god. I'm so sorry,' she said when she'd finally managed to pull herself together enough to ease out of his grasp. 'You're all wet now,' she said, wiping at the big wet patch on his pale blue shirt.

'It's okay, Alice. Really. We've swapped more bodily fluids than that over the years.'

Alice shook her head and gave his chest a gentle thump. But she smiled too. And she was so grateful for him at least attempting to lighten the mood. So grateful for him being there, full stop.

'I'd better find Frank, Mum and Olivia,' Alice said, looking around.

'It's good you could make it,' Rick said, as they started to stroll slowly back towards the gate where people were streaming out and making their way to their cars – a few others were dotted about the small cemetery paying their respects to loved ones they'd lost as they went.

'Yeah.'

'A hard trip to make, huh? Hang on, where's your bloke? What's his name?'

'David. He couldn't make it.'

'I can't believe he'd let you come on your own – for the funeral of one of your best friends,' Rick said.

'So, how come you're here? You weren't really close to Ruth's family, other than through me, were you?' Alice said, desperate to move the conversation away from her and David before she accidentally confided in Rick. That wouldn't be good for anyone.

'No, Alice, I came for you. Funerals are also about paying respect to those who've lost, not just those who've gone. And I know your mum can be, well, um ...'

'Mean?' Alice offered quietly.

'Yeah, that'd be it, if we're using understatements. It might not have worked out for us, I might have been a shit husband, but, Alice, I'll always care about you.'

'Thanks, Rick, that's lovely. But don't be too hard on yourself.'

'I've actually been going to counselling,' he said quietly, the most embarrassed and uncomfortable Alice had ever seen him. 'I'm learning to love myself. God, doesn't that make me sound like a complete wanker?'

'Not at all. I'm glad you're getting help.' That was what had been the problem with them – Rick didn't know how to love someone else properly because he didn't love himself enough. She'd wanted to help him, fix him, give him the love he felt was missing from his own family, while clinging to him as a crutch for her grief and her own need to be loved after losing her dad. By the time she realised just how damaged he was, they were married and it was too late. If only they'd just stayed friends and she hadn't ignored all the signs.

'Please don't tell anyone about the counselling,' he said, 'you know what this place is like.'

'Yep, I sure do.' Alice thought of the rumours that she'd run away from when she'd left to go to Adelaide and then Melbourne.

'I really am sorry, Alice, for everything. The way I treated you ...'

'Thanks, Rick, but it wasn't just you. And it's all water under the bridge now.'

'We were too young. And did it for the wrong reasons.'

'Hmm.'

Alice turned and looked at him, frowning slightly as she marvelled at how he was the same yet also seemed so very different.

Rick, I'll always be grateful to you for trying to ease my pain over losing Dad. And trying to rescue me from my mother, she thought. But Alice couldn't bring herself to say these words aloud. She also couldn't say that she'd discovered the truth – that she didn't know how to love, either, because she hadn't been shown unconditional love by her cold mother and was predisposed to try to make it work with the wrong men.

'God, don't think I'm trying to crack onto you or anything. I'm not. I'm …'

'I know. I heard you're seeing someone, have a *lady friend*, Olivia said.'

'Not anymore.'

'Oh. I'm sorry. I really am. I care about you too, Rick. I do. I want you to be happy.'

'Thanks. So, things have worked out for you. Rich bloke, uni degree, big new house, I hear. And a new job.'

'Yep, all those things,' Alice said without enthusiasm. 'You know your secret about having counselling?'

'Yeah,' Rick said dubiously.

'Well, I'll keep your secret if you'll keep mine.'

'Sure.'

'I quit my new job and I'm too scared to tell Mum.'

'Why?'

'Why did I quit or why can't I tell Mum?'

'Both. And, or,' he said with a shrug. 'I'm listening. I'm sensing you need to tell someone.'

'I lasted four weeks.'

'Oh. I'm sure you had your reasons.'

'Mum'll gloat about what a failure I am and how my fancy education hasn't got me anywhere, blah, blah, blah.'

'You're probably going to have to tell her, you know. Sometime.'

'I was hoping to find another job before I did,' Alice said, looking down and shifting the dirt with her feet. 'Christ, my life's an absolute mess! David thinks I'm a failure too.'

'Oh come on. I'm sure that's not the case.'

'It was a really good job – well, on paper. In real estate.'

'Real estate!'

'Yeah. What's wrong with that?'

'Alice, you're too nice for selling real estate. Isn't it cutthroat, all about money and sales – especially in a place like Melbourne?'

Why can everyone see this and not me? Alice thought. 'I wanted to help people,' she said.

'Oh, Alice.' And Alice was slightly taken aback to hear him actually laugh. She glared at him. 'Sorry, but that's funny. Real estate helping people? I don't think so.'

'Thanks a lot,' Alice said, miffed, but smiled despite herself. 'Yeah, well, live and learn.'

'So, what went wrong? Why did you leave?'

'My boss was mean. A real bitch, which I probably could have handled if she didn't completely mess with my head as well.'

'She sounds lovely. Was she a bully?'

'Yeah, that too.' Alice didn't want to go too far into it.

'Well, good on you for having the guts to leave, I say.'

'Thanks, Rick. That means a lot. As I said, David is less than impressed with me.'

'But you wouldn't have left without giving it a damned good shot. I know you, Alice, you give things a decent crack.'

'I know four weeks doesn't sound long but I was miserable. I tried, but in just that short a time she managed to make me completely question who I was with her mental games.'

'Jesus, sounds like a psycho. So why would David want you staying in a job like that?'

'Mortgage. Money. You know, the usual?'

'Nope. I don't. No job is worth losing your mind over or being truly unhappy. Money isn't everything. It's nice to have, but it's not everything. I've learnt that. I reckon health's more important,' he said sagely. 'If David loved you, he wouldn't ... Shit. Sorry. I shouldn't have said that. I'll butt out.'

'You're right, though,' Alice said sadly. *You were seriously cruel to me at times, but here you are being so sensitive and kind. Who would have thought?*

'It'll work out. You'll see,' Rick said, putting an arm around Alice and giving her a squeeze.

'I hope so.'

'We'd better get going before they send out a search party,' he said.

'Yeah, you're probably right.' Though the last thing Alice wanted was to leave this little sanctuary she'd found.

'Do you think we could be friends, Alice, and kind of stay in touch a bit?' Rick asked as they walked. 'Not talking on the phone and stuff, but like on Facebook ...?'

'I don't see why not.'

They continued in silence until they got to the gate where Frank, her mum and Olivia were waiting. The approving look on her mother's face told her she was practically starting to prepare the guest list for Rick and Alice's second wedding. As if it would somehow erase the shame and embarrassment of the first one imploding. *No way, Mum. It's never going to happen.*

'Isn't it nice of Alice to grace us with her presence? All the way from Melbourne,' Dawn said in her nasty, sing-song voice. And there was the sneer that Alice now knew was practically a trademark of the narcissist.

'Yes. It's great to see her,' Rick said.

'Did Alice tell you about her new job? In real estate,' Dawn said with some evident pride. And any calmness Alice had achieved suddenly evaporated. She felt the blood draining from her face, her insides freeze, the bile rise.

'She did,' Rick said. 'And about her uni course. She's done so well to get a degree; that's a great achievement in itself. You should be very proud.'

Alice's heart surged towards him and she wished she could have said thanks or offered him a grateful smile without anyone noticing.

'Well, come on, we'll miss the wake at the rate we're going,' Dawn said.

Alice suddenly really didn't want to go. She'd finally got her tears to stop. And she was feeling anxious about all the lies she was telling. No doubt her mother had told the whole district about her new job in real estate, and she would be asked about it by at least a hundred people. *Oh god*. Right then she almost blurted, 'Mum, I've quit my job. There. Get your lecture over with.' Or maybe she'd say that as she left to walk across the tarmac at the airport tomorrow. She'd be out of contact for the next few hours while Dawn processed it.

'Rick, come to dinner tonight,' Alice's mother said suddenly. 'Unless you have other plans.'

'Oh. Um.' He looked stricken, like a rabbit caught in the middle of the road in the headlights. Alice was about to save him by saying he was seeing someone, but stopped herself. He's a big boy. Anyway, it would be good to have him as a distraction – take the headlights off her.

'Alice is heading back tomorrow. Of course she came for Ruth and not to see us,' Dawn said huffily.

Oh my god. Did you just say that? You're competing with a dead woman for my attention. You can't be serious! She shot Rick a stricken look.

'I'd love to come, Dawn,' he said, offering Alice's mother a dazzling smile. 'So, Alice, you may as well drive to the wake with me, then.'

Right then Alice could have kissed him. She couldn't bear the thought of getting into the car with them. Dinner would be bad enough.

'Well, you could have said,' Olivia said, and stomped off.

'Yes, Alice, we've been waiting here for you,' her mother said.

'It's fine, Alice, we'll see you there,' Frank said. 'Dawn, darling, we wouldn't have got out of here yet with all the cars anyway.'

As she walked with Rick to his car, taking a little satisfaction in seeing the stunned expressions of people around her, Alice thought she would be forever grateful to him for being here for her today.

Chapter Twenty-three

'I'm over this way,' Rick said, nodding his head to the right. Alice had to hurry to keep up with his long stride, regretting, not for the first time, wearing heels. They weren't high, but probably anything might have felt high and uncomfortable today – anything beyond slippers.

'Thanks so much for this,' Alice said. 'I would've thought spending less time with Mum and co would make me more tolerant, but oh no. The longer and further away I am, the more I'm realising how toxic they are and how much I really don't like them. Not Frank, he's lovely. Though I don't know how he copes. Sorry to go on.'

'Your mum sure was being a bit full on. Maybe it's her response to the funeral.'

'Maybe. But she doesn't seem at all upset about Ruth – stoic through and through. She's barely even mentioned her name.'

'Weren't they best friends once?'

'Yep. Hey, thanks for agreeing to tonight, too.'

'I wasn't sure if it was the right thing to do or not. Tongues will start wagging.'

'Like I care. Let them. It won't be any worse than when we split up.'

'No …'

'Anyway, wait until they see us turn up at the wake and then leave together. There'll be an uproar. God, I both love and loathe this place,' Alice said wearily.

'You don't come back very often these days, do you?'

'Nope. Only when necessary – weddings, funerals, Christmas. Seriously, Mum does my head in. And it's getting worse now I'm away from it and it's all becoming so much clearer. As I said. I don't know if that's a good or bad thing,' she added with a tight laugh.

'Today wouldn't be so bad if your bloke could have come too.'

'Hmm.' *Then he could have endured the inquisition as well.*

'I never realised how bad your mum was. I'm sorry. I'm sure there were lots of times I didn't support you enough on that score,' he said, turning and looking at her before getting into the car.

There certainly were. 'Yeah, but I understand. She's very good at subtle manipulation, bullying by stealth, so no one realises. I'm only just seeing a lot of it myself. Anyway, you've got to stop apologising. It's all in the past. I'm so exhausted, I'm not going to want to get out of this car ever again,' she said, getting in and trying to ignore the weird sensation that this had been their car and this had often been her seat before so much had changed. It even smelt the same as it used to. How was that possible after more than four years? It was quite unsettling to be sitting beside him, but still it was better than being badgered by her sister or mother. Or enduring their silent, icy treatment that came and went without warning or any logical reason.

'I might have come back more often if there was a way I could sneak into town and out again without having to see them,' Alice said. *But Ruth's gone now ...?*

'Wow. Really. You feel *that* strongly?' He looked as shocked as she had been when Brett had mentioned he was estranged from his family.

'Yep. Sounds awful, huh? I'm just really beginning to see the damage they've done to me and I guess I'm scared of being pulled back into that toxic world again. I think I'm the one who owes you an apology on that front.'

'Huh?'

'I was a bully and bossy and picked on you, too, just like you said when we were splitting up. I can see that now. I'm really sorry, Rick.'

'Ah, as you've said – it's all in the past. A lot of not very nice things were said by both of us. I think we're even on that score. Hey, if you ever do want to sneak into town, you'd always be welcome to stay at the house.'

'Thanks, but I think that would be taking us being friends a little too far, not to mention weird and creepy.'

'I guess offering to pick you up from the plane would be a bit OTT, too, huh?'

'Yes. As much as I'd love to avoid my mother and sister, it's probably easier to just go along with it. You'd think moving to Melbourne would be far enough away ...' she said heavily.

'Oh, I think Dawn would manage to infiltrate your life and try to tell you how to run it no matter where you were. You wouldn't even be safe in Siberia, I reckon.'

'No. You're probably right,' Alice said with a laugh. She liked feeling that Rick understood her, had her back, could see the truth, even if he was probably humouring her, trying too hard. If she put aside all the pain he'd caused her she might relax even more. But her tiredness was keeping her on edge, which was probably a good thing. That and all she'd been through with Carmel. Alice felt as if she couldn't trust anyone these days, except Lauren. Okay, she could trust David but he just didn't seem to understand her. He was good to her, wasn't he? Everything would be better when she got back and life returned to normal. Whatever normal was, really. Right now she had to concentrate on keeping it together through the wake and then trying not to snap at her mother or sister over dinner. After that she could go to sleep and then there was only breakfast and the trip back to the airport to deal with. It didn't sound like much, but Alice felt as if she were embarking on a mountain climb or some other extreme endurance event.

'Well, I'll leave you to mingle and catch you later,' Rick said as they entered the local golf club. 'I'm going to get a beer.'

'Okay,' Alice said.

'Alice, it's so good of you to come,' Ruth's husband, Thomas, said, gathering her to him.

'I'm so sorry for your loss, Thomas,' she said with a gulp as her tears started again.

'Thank you. It means so much that you're here,' he said, holding her by the shoulders and looking into her face. 'Ruth thought of you as another daughter, as well as a dear friend. We both did, do. Oh, okay, yes, sorry, Alice, I'd better keep moving,' he said as someone touched his arm to get his attention. 'Thanks again for coming all this way, Alice, it means a lot,' he said. And then he was gone.

Alice was left standing there, wondering if she could somehow escape now. Suddenly she felt the presence of someone close beside her, and her arm was gripped firmly.

'Come on, Alice,' her mother said, tugging at her.

Alice spent the next – she wasn't sure how long – being dragged around, paraded around, really, by her mother, from person to person, and introduced as if she didn't know this woman or that man, despite having known them all her life. Practically the whole district had been at her eighteenth, twenty-first, engagement, and wedding celebrations. If she didn't know better, she might suspect her mother was suffering memory problems.

Thankfully Dawn didn't give her daughter any opportunity to speak or answer questions for herself, and Alice managed to keep all her lies intact. A few times she cringed at her mother replying, 'Well, of course someone has to *die* for her to actually come home,' in response to someone saying how nice it was that Alice had made the trip. She wondered if anyone else noticed the barbs Dawn tossed about at her expense, or the hypocrisy that on the one hand Alice's mother seemed thrilled to have her daughter here to parade around proudly, yet at the same time was telling her off and putting her down. Why did everyone think her mother was oh so lovely?

Alice wished she could find a witty, sarcastic retort to throw into the mix, but even if she could think that quickly on her feet, she wouldn't want to lower herself to her mother's level and give her more ammunition. Deep down, Alice knew she'd never win when it came to her mother. Damned if she did, damned if she didn't. She tried not to wonder if she'd treated Rick like this. Oh well, it didn't matter now.

'Right, ready to go,' Rick said, appearing beside her. *Speak of the devil.*

'Yes. That would be good. Thanks.' Alice thought she'd managed to get around to most people she'd wanted to see.

As she followed Rick out to the car she released a long sigh of relief. She was halfway through this ordeal. Just dinner, breakfast and the trip to the plane to get through. Right at that moment Alice thought it might almost be worth the gossip to stay at Rick's place rather than with her mother, and nearly laughed aloud at the sad thought of Rick being preferable to her immediate family. The truth hurts, she concluded sadly and settled into the passenger's seat.

They arrived at the family shop, where Dawn and Frank lived on the top floor, moments before Frank and Olivia's cars pulled up.

'Don't worry, *I'll* carry your bag, *Alice*,' Olivia said pointedly, holding up Alice's carry-on case.

'Thanks, Liv,' Alice said, refusing to take the bait. She'd actually completely forgotten about it.

'Olivia, you do the greens. Alice, you set the table,' Dawn said. 'Frank, sort out the drinks. Rick, go and see if Trevor needs a hand closing up.'

Alice and Rick shared a knowing look, but both were wise enough to remain silent and do as they were told. As Alice took out the cutlery she marvelled at how amazing it was that while her life had completely changed – *she'd* changed so much – in the last few years, for the better until recent events, everything here and with her family apparently hadn't. Oh, except the placemats, she suddenly realised as her mother cried out, 'Come on, not those – the blue ones. Next drawer across.' While Alice wanted to defend herself and point out that she didn't actually live here anymore, so shouldn't be expected to know these things, she didn't want to provide another opportunity for her mother to deride her for not visiting more often.

Finally they were all seated around the table, including Olivia's husband Trevor, who Alice had never particularly liked but had never managed to put her finger on quite why. Most likely he was too much like Olivia and their mother and simply pushed all her hot buttons too. Or perhaps it was because he was a weak 'yes' man and she couldn't muster enough respect for him because of it. Frank was too, and it bothered Alice, but Trevor was missing the gentle kindness that Frank possessed.

She cringed when Trevor said, 'Nice to see you, Alice,' in the same derisive, drawling voice that her mother and Olivia used. *And there it is. Case in point*, she thought, sipping her wine. The last thing Alice felt like was alcohol, but she didn't want to prompt the question of whether she was pregnant, which would then see her mother making comments about marriage and David's lack of commitment, blah, blah, blah. They were big drinkers, so anyone abstaining caused a ruckus. She'd have to keep her wits about her. While it might be nice to block out the evening with an alcohol haze, potentially letting her guard down was the problem. And the last thing she needed was a hangover.

Alice looked at her plate wondering what they were about to eat.

Thankfully her mother suddenly proudly declared, 'Chilli con carne, eat up.'

She now remembered how unappetising her mother's meals had been when she was growing up. Dawn had always been on some health kick or other – eliminating this or that, overdosing them on something else.

That was one of the things Alice had loved about spending time with Ruth and her family, she thought sadly. Ruth hadn't cooked – and made no apology for it. Often when it was dinner-time they'd all trot off to the roadhouse, the only takeaway place in town, for a quarter-chicken-chips-peas-and-gravy hot pack – an absolute no-no in Alice's house. The Stanley kids were occa-sionally also allowed the wonderful sugary cereal that Alice had craved. One of her favourite memories was going to Ruth's place and watching PG movies – without parental supervision – when they'd been thirteen, clutching small bowls of dry Froot Loops and Coco Pops to munch on. She knew it wasn't the differences in food that she had loved so much, but the calm, gentle, easy-going atmosphere that permeated the whole Stanley house – a far cry from the tension and shouting within the Hamiltons' walls.

'So, while we're all here, it's a good time to discuss what we're doing for Christmas,' Dawn said when there was a pause in the conversation, halfway through the meal.

Out of the corner of her eye Alice noticed Rick shift on his chair as if trying to disappear or at least distance himself. *How inappropriate, Mum. And how awkward can you make things?*

'Alice?' Dawn prompted.

'Oh. David and I haven't discussed it yet,' she lied, hoping those around the table would attribute the extra colour in her cheeks to the glass of red wine she'd consumed.

'Good. That's settled, then. We'll have it here,' Dawn said.

'Well, actually, we might be going away,' Alice said quickly, knowing it was easier to pave the way now than trying to back out later.

'I thought you said you haven't discussed it yet. What is it, Alice, you *have* or you *haven't* discussed it?' her mother demanded.

Oh god. 'Um. Well …'

'Dear, it's months away,' Frank said, putting a hand on his wife's arm.

Thank god for Frank, Alice thought.

'Christmas is a time for family, Alice. Where are you thinking of going? Perhaps we can all go?' Dawn said.

Jesus, no!

'Rick, you're having Christmas with your family, aren't you?'

'You know, Dawn, I might just go somewhere else this year, too. I haven't really thought about it.'

'Ooh, well I wouldn't mind going to Melbourne – Alice and David have got plenty of space now. It'd be a cheap trip,' Trevor said.

Alice had to bite her lip to stop herself from telling him to shut up.

'Let's table the discussion for another day,' Frank said wearily. 'Who's for a refill?' he added, holding up the bottle of wine. Alice held up her glass, as much for a distraction as want of more wine. *Bless you, Frank. But, if you're aware enough to intervene, how is it you're still here at all? That is the question.*

Suddenly Rick pushed his chair back. 'Thanks for dinner, Dawn, Frank. I'd better be going. See you all,' he said with a wave. 'Have a safe trip back, Alice.'

'Thanks. And thanks for today,' she said.

Taking that as a sign dinner was over, she stood up and started clearing the table when Frank said, 'You go to bed, love. You've had a long day of travelling. We'll look after the washing up.'

Alice thought she heard her mother scoff, but hoped she'd been mistaken.

'Yes, all right, go,' her mother said with clear exasperation – most likely at Frank for intervening and taking away some of her control.

Chapter Twenty-four

Alice stepped into the shower and let the tears flow freely. She felt racked with grief over Ruth, a yearning for the unconditional love and affection of Bill and the steadfastness and predictability of David, and sadness at how little love there was for her here. And then the jagged edge of self-pity and anger stabbed at her. *Why would I expect it to get any better, be any different? Why do I keep seeking approval and love when I know I will never get it?* How was it that as a well-educated, thirty-year-old woman, she could feel like an angst-ridden child of around ten all over again just with one icy glare, one cutting remark, one sneering, crooked smile from her mother? That was the age she had been when she first noticed how cold and distant her mother was, and when Alice had made her first conscious efforts to get her mother to notice her, praise her, love her. Now after having read the articles about narcissism, Alice knew the truth – that she'd never had warmth and love from her mother. *So why the hell do I still try so hard? Why do I even come back here?*

Well, of course this trip was different. Would she one day have the guts to completely cut them off, like Brett apparently had his family?

She went to bed, ignored David's phone message and sent him a text instead. She'd call him in the morning, when perhaps she'd feel less exhausted.

Despite her wretched tiredness, Alice tossed and turned, unable to slip into sleep. Eventually she must have though, because she woke with a start to the sound of her phone's alarm going off. She had a quick shower and got ready before her mother could tell her she was running late. Then she took her bag out to the front door and placed her handbag on top. In the kitchen Frank was at the stove, a pan sizzling in front of him.

'It's just us. Your mum and Olivia have gone walking,' he said. 'Did you sleep okay?'

'No, not really,' Alice said after letting out a long sigh of relief. She liked that she could be honest with Frank and not receive an interrogation or any criticism.

'Completely understandable. With another big day of travelling ahead, I thought you might like a decent breakfast. Shh. Our little secret,' he added with a warm smile.

'Thanks, Frank, that's lovely of you.' She didn't have the heart to tell him just the smell of the bacon was making her feel queasy.

'I don't care what your mother says, sometimes one needs a hearty dose of carbs and animal fat,' Frank said kindly, placing a plate laden with fried food in front of Alice. 'Coffee?' Her appetite returned instantly and her mouth began to water.

'Yes, please. This looks great. I really appreciate it.'

'It's my pleasure. And of course you can't eat alone. So, thanks for being my excuse to indulge.'

'I suppose I'll be in trouble for not getting up early enough to go for a walk with them.'

'Ah, don't worry about that. Right now you need to take care of yourself, deal with your grief any way you see fit.'

Alice smiled at him, and she longed to lay her head on his shoulder and sob. 'I really miss her, even though … Oh, Frank, I feel so bad that we weren't in touch much lately.'

'Ruth knew you had your life to get on with. You can't be beating yourself up. I'm sure she was happy to know you didn't need her quite so much.'

'Hmm.'

'Don't worry, we've got plenty of time,' Frank said, clearly noticing Alice anxiously checking her watch. 'I'm taking you and we'll leave nice and early – as soon as we've had breakfast and cleaned up the evidence.'

Alice let out another sigh – relieved that she wouldn't have to share the car with her mum or sister, as well as knowing that she'd make the plane in time. For some reason her mother, and Olivia was the same, despite all her hurrying up and cajoling of everyone else, seemed to have no concept of time. She was always a few minutes late or took things right to the wire. Getting to school had always been stressful for Alice, and all too often she would find herself sitting in the car minutes after they should have left, honking the horn. Back then it seemed like her mother's annoying habit. Now, since she'd read about the traits of narcissism, Alice could see it was both a deliberate way for her mother to cause drama and draw attention to herself and a demonstration of a rules-don't-apply-to-me attitude.

As they washed and dried the dishes side by side, Alice wondered how Dawn treated Frank behind closed doors. Hopefully better than in public. Otherwise she'd lose all respect for him for allowing himself to be downtrodden and bullied. Perhaps Alice *was* just overly sensitive and intolerant, as her mother had so often told her.

'Righto, let's get on the road,' Frank said, wiping his hands and hanging up the tea towel.

Alice felt a little guilty at being relieved she wouldn't have an encounter with her mother or sister to ruin her morning, which had been better than expected so far. But two streets from the house there they were, power walking towards the car, their hips swinging at the same angles and rate. Alice almost giggled at wondering who was trying to outdo whom. She imagined them walking faster and faster, each trying to keep in front but not make the competition obvious by breaking into a run. God, it was too much, Alice thought, shaking her head. They were so bloody alike. *Thank Christ I got out of this place. And that I'm more like Dad, bless him.*

'Good morning, ladies,' Frank said, as he brought the car to a halt in the middle of the road.

'A walk would have been good for you, Alice,' her mother said, resting her hands on the passenger window. 'Fresh country air.'

'Yeah, it would have been fun to have you along,' Olivia said.

So you could try and beat me too? No thanks. Alice smiled to herself at remembering their last walk together – it was so much easier to get up and go with them than endure the jibes about her laziness for the rest of the day. 'I'm on holidays, I'm allowed to sleep in,' didn't wash with them. Having made a half-hearted effort to keep up but given up, Alice had deliberately lagged behind and walked at a more enjoyable pace. She wasn't unfit, just didn't want to play their silly game.

'Well, have a safe trip back,' Dawn said. Both she and Olivia were now stepping up and down on the spot, looking as ridiculous as someone in a 1980s or '90s exercise class. All they were missing was a fluoro pink dumbbell in each hand and matching leg warmers. 'We'd better keep moving before we catch a chill.'

'Yes, we don't want to cramp up. Bon voyage,' Olivia said.

Alice almost laughed out loud. *You're not bloody elite athletes, you've been for an hour's walk! Oh, too funny.*

'Thanks. Enjoy the rest of your walk,' Alice said. Olivia strode off with a wave.

'Perhaps next time, Alice, you might actually come and visit us. *And* stay for longer than twenty-four hours,' her mother said.

'Okay, then, we'd better get cracking. See you later,' Frank said.

Thanks a bloody lot. And why do you think I don't bother? How could someone be so stupid as to not see that such comments just drove people away, or kept them away? Not stupidity, Alice corrected herself, it was self-centredness. It was quite sad really when you looked at it through analytical, enlightened eyes. Of course she still felt wounded, but it helped Alice to know so much more about the psychology behind these people.

'She doesn't mean to upset you, Alice,' Frank said as they drove off.

Oh yes she does. It's textbook narcissism, from what I've read. She longed to fill Frank in on what she'd learnt, but didn't want to hurt him. God only knew why, but this was the woman he loved and had chosen to spend his later years of life with.

'I know,' she lied in an effort to mollify him.

'Is everything okay, Alice?' Frank asked after they'd been driving in silence for a while. 'Other than the obvious, I mean … Losing Ruth and tiredness from travelling.'

'I'm fine, Frank.' She could tell him the truth, but she didn't think he was the sort of man to keep secrets from his wife – a greasy breakfast now and then hardly counted. And she couldn't very well ask him to. That wouldn't be fair.

Alice was relieved when the ping of a message sounded on her phone and she was able to concentrate on that. It was from David: *Sorry. Probably won't be able to make it to the airport. You'll have to catch a cab.*

Alice let out a sigh and tucked the phone back into her handbag.

'Bad news?' Frank asked.

'Not really. Just David saying he probably can't pick me up from the airport.'

'Oh, that is disappointing.'

'But not at all surprising. Work. It's always work.'

'Is everything okay with you – you and David, that is?'

'Yeah, we're fine.'

The silence stretched on until Frank said, 'Oh, I love this song. Do you mind if I turn it up?'

'Sure.'

Alice was a little puzzled, she hadn't even realised the radio was on it was turned so low. She was even more intrigued to hear ABBA filling the car. And then Frank was singing along. A few moments later he stopped.

'Sorry. Can't help myself. I'm a huge ABBA fan from way back,' he said, blushing a little and shrugging his shoulders.

'Hey, don't mind me. Carry on,' Alice said.

'Only if you join in.'

And she did. By the time they pulled into the carpark at the airport an hour later, Alice's chest was aching – not from the pain inside her, but from singing a string of songs that had come on that she and Frank knew the words to. She felt so much better than she had in weeks.

'Thanks for that, Alice, your mum doesn't indulge me. She hates me singing.'

'I don't know why, Frank, you're very good.'

'Thanks, Alice. I had dreams of being on Broadway once,' he said shyly.

Oh you dark horse! 'Well, I think you would have been great.' She was about to ask him more but as they got out of the car the moment was lost.

Frank took her bag out of the boot, and as he walked her to the terminal he put his arm around her, his kindness causing all of Alice's painful emotions to come flooding back.

They each bought a newspaper and sat in silence flicking through them, as if embarrassed by their earlier shenanigans or not wanting anything to change the happier mood. Though for Alice it had already subsided. She hated goodbyes. It was strange, but while she loathed the way her mother treated her and no longer felt much of a direct emotional connection to the town she'd once lived in, she always felt a certain sadness when she left after a visit. She didn't know why. Perhaps it was because her mother, yet again, hadn't treated her as she'd hoped or that such a beautiful little town held so much pain for her. According to most films and folklore, small towns were generally supposed to be wonderful places full of generous people. But Alice knew only too well the toxicity hidden within Hope Springs' neat streets and carefully tended gardens. Just like her own family, really. Did everyone and everything put on a fake façade?

'Frank?' she said quietly, almost hoping he wouldn't hear her.

'Hmm?' he said, head down still reading his paper.

'I lasted four weeks in my real estate job. The woman I worked for was horrible and I hated it, so I quit. I was too scared to tell Mum.' Her voice was almost that of a little girl.

He looked up, returned a gentle smile and put an arm around her. 'I'm sorry you had an awful experience, Alice, and there's no shame in changing your mind, for whatever reason. But I do understand why you felt you couldn't tell your mother,' he said, giving her shoulder a squeeze before removing his arm. 'Would you like me to tell her, or would you like me to keep it a secret?'

'Could you tell her, please?'

'If that's what you want.'

Alice bit her lip and nodded.

'Okay then.'

'Thanks, Frank. I really appreciate it.'

'You're welcome, Alice,' he said, and returned to reading his newspaper.

When she hugged Frank just before heading out to her plane, she didn't want to let go. She felt the urge to tell him her woes about David and their relationship, even ask his advice. But it was too late now, anyway, and confiding in him might put Frank in a difficult position.

'It's been really lovely to see you, Alice. Travel safe,' he said, giving her a quick peck. And then, putting a hand gently to her cheek, he said, 'Sweetheart, everything always works out for the best, eventually, you'll see. Just be strong and kind to yourself.'

'Thanks, Frank. I will,' she said, choking on the words before turning and walking out the door. Tears began to fall as she made her way across the tarmac with the other passengers. Thankfully no one asked her what was wrong or if she needed a tissue, and she was able to settle into her seat and snuggle up to the side of the plane. She looked out the small plastic window up to the sky. Big black clouds were forming. *Oh, Ruth*, she thought. Suddenly a beam of bright sunshine shot through a gap between the clouds, causing Alice to almost completely lose what was left of her composure. *Goodbye.*

Chapter Twenty-five

Alice looked around when she heard her name called. Her heart leapt at seeing David standing there waving. She rushed over and hugged him. Suddenly everything felt so much better.

'Phew, I thought I wasn't going to make it,' he said a little breathlessly as he took her carry-on bag in one hand and clasped Alice's hand in the other. The heaviness within her shifted slightly and became a duller ache than the sharp pain that had been plaguing her for the past few days. But her heart sank again and then knotted as David began to speak – almost as quickly as he walked. Alice struggled to keep up.

'So, how was it?' *Have you forgotten the reason for my trip?*

'Pretty horrible.'

'Oh. Yeah. Of course. But at least you had your family around you.'

'I guess.'

There was never going to be much more discussion about her family. Alice knew David found them unsophisticated and not at all interesting. How fascinating was the current wholesale price of potatoes or the thrill of achieving a significant discount with a notoriously tight-fisted supplier when you mixed with the likes of those David mixed with? It was all a little quaint to him, Alice thought. She loved David's family, but didn't have anything in common with them, either. His parents were both public servants in Sydney.

'How's Bill?'

'He's good.'

'Have you been walking him?'

'Of course I've been walking him, Alice. I can take care of a dog, you know. And you did leave very detailed instructions.'

'I just thought you might have been too busy with work. Sorry. I didn't mean to criticise you. I'm tired.'

They made their way across the walkway to the carpark and David paid for the parking.

'So, did you see lots of people you know?' he asked.

'Yes. I think Ruth would have been pleased that so many turned out. And the sun was shining, so that was nice.' Alice had to give him points for trying. It wasn't David's fault he didn't know anything about grief – that he'd never lost anyone, didn't know what it felt like. How nice to still be in that position at his age.

Alice thought she'd probably been through more in her relatively short life so far than a lot of other people, though when she thought about her journey it was more with a sense of wonder than self-pity. When it came to her father's death she never allowed herself to think *Why me?*, because Alice felt that would bring it back to her. She didn't believe his suicide was about her at all. He'd believed his life was intolerable, and he'd decided to do something about it. That was his decision and his decision alone. Alice's mother might choose to make it about her – of course the effect and not the cause – but Alice wouldn't diminish her dad in that way.

She shuddered at wondering if Frank would get to that point someday too. But no, he didn't appear to be as deep a thinker as Alice's father had been – no doubt where she got it from – and he seemed to let things wash right on over. Although no one had realised where her dad's head had been at until his deed was done. Oh well, Frank knew her number if he ever needed to talk.

'I've got us some chicken schnitzels for dinner. And I'm going to do oven chips and homemade coleslaw. How does that sound?' David said as he unlocked the car and put her bag in the boot.

'Perfect. Just what I need. Thank you,' Alice said, her aching heart swelling a little.

'You can have a bath while I cook, if you like. Then how about an early night?' he said, once they were in the car. He patted her leg and then left his hand there. Alice looked at his hand. She knew what he was angling towards. Sex. And it was the last thing she felt like. The thought sent her to a whole new level of weariness. But she'd better pull herself together and participate if she wasn't to lose him, them, altogether.

'Any news on the job front?' he asked as he carefully drove out of the carpark.

'David, I've only been gone two days.'

'Well, how do I know if you've had any emails or not? You've got applications out there, haven't you?'

'Can you please stop nagging me? I'm doing my best.'

They drove in tense silence and Alice stared out the window to avoid looking at him and feeling even worse for appearing so unappreciative of him coming out to pick her up. The trip to the airport and back home was not inconsequential. And it saved her a taxi fare of around eighty to ninety dollars, she estimated.

Looking at the passing scenery, Alice marvelled at how built-up the area around the airport had become in the years since she'd moved to Melbourne. So much farming land had been swallowed up by big warehouses and semi-industrial developments, housing and shopping centres. What would it be like in twenty years?

Where would she be? It was both a scary and comforting question, Alice thought. On the one hand she had practically her whole life ahead of her. But on the other she didn't want to waste it. What if ten years from now she was still looking for the perfect job?

Don't be silly, she heard a voice in her head say, *you'll be the mother of David's children by then*. But would she? She turned to look at him and somehow saw a flash of what their life might be like in the years ahead. She was at home with a couple of kids, trying to get them fed and bathed while tearing her hair out because, of course, David was hardly ever there to help. He was off travelling or working late at the office. She frowned and chewed on her bottom lip in concentration.

'What?' David said, catching Alice staring at him.

'Are we ever going to get married, David?'

'What?'

'Are we ever going to get married?'

'What would be the point?'

Seriously? 'Um, how about as a sign of commitment?'

'I don't think you can get much more committed than living together, Alice. Where's this coming from?'

'So, you *really* don't believe in marriage, is that what you're saying?'

'Alice, you know my views – we've discussed it before.'

'But, I thought ...'

'What, that I'd change my mind?'

Alice burnt with shame. That was exactly what she'd thought. If she were being honest, she'd say she had wondered last time if he'd just used the first excuse that had come to him in order to deflect from the subject. She knew he wanted kids in the next five years; marriage was closely related to that topic, wasn't it? It was for her.

'So, to reiterate – no. No, I *really* don't believe in marriage.'

'Why not?'

'Why do you believe in it? I would have thought with your track record you'd have been sufficiently cured – having a failed marriage, that is.'

How bloody patronising! But, sadly, true. Alice coloured under his rebuke. 'I told you,' she said, 'commitment, love. Do you love me, David?'

'Of course I do. Where is all this coming from, Alice? I wouldn't have thought your mother would have been encouraging you to take another walk down the aisle.'

'But why don't you believe in marriage, David? I want to know,' Alice persisted, despite knowing full well she was sailing very close to the edge of his level of tolerance.

'I've told you often enough, I'm an atheist. Organised religion is a load of shit. Marriage is tied up in religion, end of story.'

'It doesn't have to be. We could have a civil service – say, in a park or something.'

'Alice, I don't see why I need to further prove my commitment to you – we live together, share the same bed and the bills. Frankly, it's a bit offensive having my commitment under question. Look where you were when we met. You're overthinking it. What you need is to get a job to sink your teeth into and stop you being so damned insecure. You're unsettled because of your friend's funeral. You need to just calm down.'

Alice wanted to slap him. It was lucky he was driving and she wasn't ready to die or she might just have done so. He took his hand off her leg and placed it on the steering wheel and concentrated on the road ahead.

'Well, I don't want to have kids without being married,' she said, folding her arms tightly across her chest.

'So now you're going to hold that over me as some sort of blackmail? Seriously, Alice?' He shook his head, which infuriated her even more. 'I don't see why marriage is so important to you.'

'And I don't see why it's not to you. So we have a problem.'

'Why are you making so much out of it?'

'Because I've just been halfway across the country to a funeral on my own and I'm really upset and you don't seem to care.' Tears filled her eyes.

'Of course I care, Alice. Stop being so melodramatic,' he said with a sigh.

'Not enough to go with me.'

'Come on, Alice, I couldn't, you know that. I had ...'

'I hate that you care more about your job, your fucking project, than you do about me. Money isn't everything, David!'

'Alice, don't raise your voice to me. We're ...'

'I know. I know. You've said it often enough. We're adults, we'll discuss it civilly like adults,' she said, mimicking him. 'Well, you don't seem to be hearing me. I'm telling you, David, it's not working!'

'Fine, rant and rave like a child throwing a tantrum if you want, if you think it will help.'

'All I want is your support, your love, your kindness, David – for you to actually show it,' Alice said quietly, the tears streaming down her face. She felt defeated. What was the point?

'How can you say that? Who's the one paying *all* the bills now you don't have a job?'

'Emotionally, David,' she said with a deep sigh.

'And, anyway, I'd like to see you live without money. They can all go on about how money doesn't buy you happiness, but try getting by without it.'

'Maybe I will,' Alice said in barely more than a whisper.

'Sorry? What?'

'David, this isn't working. Us, *we're* not working.'

'How do you think you'll survive out in the big wide world without me propping you up? You can't be serious.' Suddenly he seemed to deflate, lose his arrogant bravado. 'Don't be silly, Alice. You're just tired and upset. It's been a tough few months with moving house and the job and everything. Don't make rash decisions you'll regret.'

'I'm serious, David. I love you, but I don't think we share the same fundamental values.'

'What do you mean? We're both honest, kind, hardworking people. What other fundamental values are there?'

Alice stayed silent. She stared out of the window, her vision blurred from the wash of tears covering her eyes.

The minutes ticked by; the only sound was the quiet hum of tyres on the dry asphalt beneath them.

'Can I ask you a favour?' David asked quietly a few minutes later, his hand settling back on her leg gently. She looked at him. 'If you're serious about leaving me – and for the record I don't want you to, I think we're good together and a good team – please don't do it until the project is finished. The upheaval would put my whole career in jeopardy. Please, Alice, if you care about me at all …'

'Okay, David, fine. I won't make any decisions until then.' It was a half-hearted commitment. Alice was stuck on the fact that he still hadn't said the L word. Right now all he probably had to do was profess his love for her and she'd be putty in his hands.

They travelled on in silence, moving slowly in unusually heavy traffic, trapped in the car together in heavy tension.

'I didn't realise marriage meant that much to you,' David said a bit later.

Well, maybe it wouldn't if you showed your love and emotional commitment and support in other ways. She kept the words to herself. What was so obvious and important to her were things he would never comprehend. That was clear now. And she was so, so tired. She could barely muster the energy to utter another word.

'If it really means that much to you, I guess we could,' he said.

Alice looked at him. 'Is this you proposing, David?'

'Oh. Well, I guess …'

'Seriously? No. Not like this.'

'But I want kids, I want *you* to have my kids. And if …' he pleaded.

'You really just don't get it, do you? Any of it? I want you to *want* to marry me, David, and you don't. Let's just leave it. I don't want to talk about it anymore.'

She was no longer angry. But she felt as if her insides had been ripped out and she was completely empty. She was disappointed. In him, but also in herself. How had she been so stupid to buy into the happily-ever-after, love-will-conquer-all, he'll-change bullshit again? How had she spent more than four years with this person?

At the house they silently went inside, the mood between them a tense truce. Alice rushed in ahead to see Bill. She felt a few pieces of her soul glue back together at his cheerful greeting.

'I'll get started on dinner,' David called as he made his way through to the kitchen.

'I'm going to take Bill for a quick walk,' she said.

'Oh, well …'

'It's okay, I won't be long. Twenty minutes tops.'

Alice picked Bill up and ran to the park, keen to release the excess energy and stretch her limbs after being cooped up in planes and trying to hold herself together in front of her mother and sister and now David, and then sat cross-legged on a bench holding the dog on her lap. It was quiet, with not a soul around. With Bill held close, his heart beating against her own, she gave in to the sobbing she'd been desperately trying to hold in. After a few moments she heard footsteps and saw a jogger approaching. She wiped at her eyes and sniffed back the tears, and tried to pull herself together.

'Are you okay?'

Alice looked up in surprise at seeing a slightly older woman in running gear standing in front of her with a concerned look on her face.

'Yes, thanks. I'm just having a moment,' Alice said.

'I'm happy to stop and chat if it would help,' the woman said.

'Honestly, I'm fine, but I really appreciate you stopping and asking.'

'Okay then. It's good for the soul to have a good cry – and physiologically. So, let it out. All the best.'

'Thanks very much. And same to you.'

Alice sat and waited until there were no more tears to shed and then with her whole body aching, she made her way home. She was almost back when she realised she'd left without her keys. She cursed her lapse as she rang the doorbell and stood there trying to not look as sheepish as she felt.

David opened the door and before she could get inside he enveloped her in a hug.

'Please don't be angry with me. I don't want us to fight,' he said.

Alice held David tight, using that as her answer while thinking, *I'm not angry. I'm sad.*

Chapter Twenty-six

'Hey, Lauren,' Alice said, opening the door to her friend and embracing her. 'Do you need coffee or would you like to go for a walk?'

'I've just had a coffee, thanks, and how could I say no to that face?' Lauren said, pointing to Bill who was standing in the hallway behind Alice.

'Tell me about it,' Alice said. 'He does pleading-dog pose so well. Hang on, I'll just grab his lead and my phone and keys.'

'He's very good on the lead,' Lauren said while they waited at the lights to cross the busy road.

'Either his previous owners – who I don't want to think about – or the RSPCA did all the hard work with obedience training. He's a dream all round.'

'So, how are you doing?' Lauren asked when they were at the park and had started walking along the path. 'Did you tell your mum about chucking in the job?'

'No, I chickened out. I left that particular grenade with Frank, her husband. He told her, so now I'm dodging her calls.'

'Oh dear. How was the trip back there, other than the funeral, which I imagine was pretty horrendous?'

'The funeral was sad, as you'd expect. I'm glad I went, though.'

'You know you probably wouldn't have been able to if you hadn't quit.'

'Exactly. So that's one good thing to come out of it.'

'So, did you know everyone – it's one of those types of places, isn't it?'

'Yep. Oh, you'll never guess who turned up, that I wasn't expecting to see.'

'Who?'

'My ex-husband, Rick.'

'Oh, wow, awkward.'

'Actually, no, it wasn't at all.'

'Ooh, tell me more.'

'He was my saviour.'

'I think you'd better tell me everything.'

'Well ...' Alice started and told Lauren everything. 'And then Mum invited him for dinner. It was like we were right back there when we were married.'

'Jesus, that's some weird shit right there.'

'Yup, it sure is.'

'Doesn't she realise you're in a committed relationship, or doesn't she like David?'

'I have no idea what goes through that woman's head. Seriously, reading all I have on narcissism and toxic families and the like, after Brett told us about his family, has put some things into perspective. I really don't like my family, Lauren. Except Frank, god only knows why he sticks around.'

'And that's okay.'

'I know. In some ways I envy Brett his decision to cut ties with his.'

'Yes, but it's been hard for him. Really hard.'

Something in Lauren's wistful tone caught Alice's attention. 'Hang on. Are you two an item?' she said, glancing at Lauren who was blushing slightly and looking a little shy.

'Yep.'

'Since when?'

'We had a long deep and meaningful on the phone after that lunch and another over coffee, and then another. As you know, we've been mates for years, but I think him being so open and honest with his feelings flicked a switch in me. It's early days. We're taking it slow. He's still working through a lot of stuff, including the fact he's chosen the wrong partners in the past because of the whole narcissism thing.'

'Have you kissed?'

'Yup,' Lauren said, dipping her head coyly.

'And …?'

'Lovely. Really lovely,' Lauren said with a long, contented sigh. 'Just a bit of a snog, no more. As I said, he needs to feel his way a bit.'

'I bet,' Alice said, shooting Lauren a cheeky grin.

'Oh, ha-ha,' Lauren said, rolling her eyes and slapping Alice's arm.

'I'm only teasing. I think it's wonderful. He's definitely one of the good ones.'

'I think so. I like that we're already such good friends. Though, I can't believe I've never considered him as anything more.'

'Well, we did all wonder if he was gay there for a while in the early days, remember?'

'That's right. Isn't it amazing that just because a guy is kind and gentle and talks about his feelings we immediately think he's gay? Talk about putting people into categories.'

'It was an honest mistake. He does also have a fabulous dress sense and his hair is always immaculately done.'

'That is true,' Lauren said with a laugh. 'Oh, Alice, I don't want to rush things or jinx it, but I think I'm falling in love,' Lauren said with another long drawn-out sigh.

'Aww, that's lovely. I'm so happy for you. You would make a good-looking couple.'

'Mmm.'

They walked on at a pace barely more than an amble. Lauren's relaxed state and dreamy smile were contagious and Alice remained silent, soaking it in as she watched her friend, who was clearly lost in thoughts of her blossoming love.

'God, look at me, I'm losing chunks of time all over the place. You'd think I was a silly teenager,' Lauren said suddenly, as if snapping back to the present. She picked up the pace a little.

'I don't mind at all. It's a beautiful thing.'

'Yes, but I don't want to go losing my head and my perspective. We're taking things slow,' she said in a firm tone. 'So, back to you. How are you feeling about the whole Carmel thing – any more nightmares?'

'Just the odd one, but it's not so bad now. I still cry all the time. But speaking of sharing their emotions. Or not. I'm beginning to think David doesn't actually have any, isn't capable of anything deep.'

'Oh dear. What's happened?'

'Oh god, Lauren, I think I've blown it.'

'How?'

'My whole life is completely in tatters, and I don't know what to do to fix it. Well, other than get a new job, which is proving impossible. And, see,' Alice said, pointing to her face, 'I'm bloody well crying again. I'm a freaking mess.'

'I think we'd better sit down on this bench before Bill collapses from exhaustion.'

'Oh shit. Poor thing.' Alice stopped and sat down. They'd done two quick laps of the park without realising he was panting heavily. She looked at Bill who had flopped down on his belly on the cool grass with his legs stretched out, and offered a silent apology for her neglect.

'Right. Now, what's happened with David?'

'I didn't mean to say it; the words just came tumbling out.'

'What words, Alice? Take a deep breath and tell me – slowly.'

'He picked me up from the airport, which was brilliant of him, especially when I wasn't expecting it. And we were in the car and suddenly I'm like, "Are we ever going to get married?" And it turns out he's serious about not believing in marriage – I really hoped he was dodging the conversation or that he'd change his mind. Anyway, and then I ...'

'Right,' Lauren said when Alice had finished.

'So, what do I do?' Alice said, looking at Lauren. She was feeling a little breathless, but was relieved to have it out in the open. 'I don't know if I believe in marriage anymore, either, anyway. What was I thinking?'

'I think we probably all crave belonging – someone *choosing* us – to a certain extent. Maybe it's in our DNA, or it's societal, or something. But I reckon it's there. We just have to make sure it's with the right person and for the right reason. That's what Brett's working through,' Lauren said. 'He says he's discovered his view of love is skewed because he was never shown what true love is as a child.'

'I think I'm in the same boat. What do I do?'

'What do you want to do? Make up, which it sounds like you sort of have, anyway, or leave?'

'Oh, I don't think I could leave. Look, that idea has literally given me goosebumps,' Alice said, holding out her arm for Lauren to see.

'Because you're afraid of being alone?'

'I guess. And where would I go? I've got Bill to think of too. Most landlords and body corporates don't like dogs. That's why we never had one before. I don't have any money. I don't have a job or any means to support myself. See, it's all such a mess.'

'You do know everything works itself out, regardless of our angst and hair pulling, don't you?'

'I really don't feel like it right now.'

'You're going through a lot of emotions. Maybe it's best you've said you won't make a decision until David's project ends. Maybe you'll change your mind and be happy with him again by then, when all this other stuff settles and you're feeling better within yourself.'

'Honestly, I don't think I've ever been truly happy with him. I'm beginning to see that he was an escape route – a way out for me from my family, my circumstances and Hope Springs. God, can you imagine my mother at hearing I've had another failed relationship. She's already having apoplexy about the job, judging by the voicemail messages she's leaving.'

'That's no reason to stay, Alice,' Lauren said gently.

'I know, but, god, facing her – and my smug, perfect sister – makes staying feel like the lesser of the two evils.'

'That's sad. I'm so sorry you don't have a kind, loving family. I can't imagine how hard that must be. So, I guess asking them for some financial assistance wouldn't be an option?'

'Definitely not. An absolute last resort.'

They sat in silence for a few moments before Alice spoke again. 'Thank you for being my friend, Lauren.'

'Well, I'm not sure I'm very helpful.'

'You're being the voice of reason, and you care. And right now that's what I need.'

'Everything will work out for the best, you'll see.'

'Promise?'

'I promise. In not too long you'll be in a much better place and you'll look back on this time and laugh at how hopeless it all seemed. Meanwhile, I think you need to relax, ease up on yourself, not expect to have all the answers – that's the universe's job. Put it out there and ask for help. That's what I do. Make a list of the things you need to deal with to achieve your goal and whatever is bothering you, and then assess whether whatever it is is in your control. If it is, then work out what you need to do – the steps, actions, et cetera, to achieve it. If it's not in your control, then put a line through it and assign it to the "not my problem" bin. Write notes if that's easier than trying to keep it all in your head – that might just add to you feeling overwhelmed. Anyway, you know all this. Remember how you knew what you needed to do with all the uni essays and assignments. You were good at that.'

'But that was all so straightforward.'

'Approach life, all the stuff that's bothering you, the same way – methodically. Turn it all into bite-sized pieces. Everything can be broken down and managed bit by bit. But please don't settle for less than you deserve in life because it's too hard or overwhelming to change. I bet you felt exactly the same when you and your husband split up. And look where you've ended up and how much stronger you are now than you were then.'

'I don't feel it.'

'Ah, that's just because your confidence has taken a knock thanks to that bitch Carmel, and you're grieving the loss of your dear friend Ruth. Do you know they say divorce, moving house and losing a loved one are the hardest things you'll ever do in life? You've been through a lot recently. Cut yourself some slack. Breathe.'

'God, what would I do without you?' Alice said, leaning over and hugging her friend.

'I'm here for you, Alice. There's nothing wrong with asking for help or leaning on a friend. Just remember that. Come on, let's go back and have that lovely machine of yours make us a coffee.'

'Yeah, and then I'd better get back to the job hunt.'

'Still nothing?'

'Nope. Not even an interview. And that's before the matter of no-reference-from-last-direct-report comes up. Though no doubt my reluctance is coming across loud and clear. I so don't want to go back to an office, but that's really all I know.'

'What about customer service? Doesn't your family run a shop?'

'Yes, but there's no way I'm going to ask them for a reference. And, anyway, that might be a little iffy on the ethics, wouldn't you say?'

'Probably. But sometimes you have to do things you don't want to for the greater good. Sorry, that sounded condescending. What I meant is don't discount actions that are a means to an end.'

'I don't think you'd be a true friend with my best interests at heart if you didn't offer some tough love occasionally, Lauren, as much as I mightn't like to hear it.'

'Okay, well, speaking of that ...'

'Uh-oh,' Alice said.

'I think that's your phone ringing.'

'Yeah, it might just be my dream job that I don't know I want and haven't applied for,' Alice said, pulling her phone out of her pocket. She stared at the number. It was vaguely familiar, but it wasn't in her contacts. 'They can leave a message,' she said as she let the call go to voicemail. 'So, what were you going to say? You were about to dish out some tough love.'

'I've been thinking it might be a good idea for you to desensitise yourself with Carmel by going to one of her auctions or inspections. She wouldn't have to know you were there and I think it would help your anxiety – by facing up to your fear.'

'Oh. Just the thought of it makes my heart race,' Alice said, putting a hand to her chest.

'Seriously, Alice, you can't keep letting her have this sort of control over you. I know you've been through something traumatic because of her, but you're letting her win, letting her determine the course of your life, to some extent.'

'I know. You're right. It's completely irrational.'

'It's not completely irrational, Alice. That's not what I'm saying. I think you're having a perfectly reasonable reaction given the circumstances, what she put you through.'

'I can't believe I'm like this after working for her for only four weeks or so …'

'Alice, if someone was a mess after being locked up by a psycho-path for just one day – held captive – you'd be sympathetic. I don't think time is a factor. You can't help it if you're super sensitive. Now you just have to try to limit the damage and lasting effects.'

'I feel like such a fool for being so affected by it.'

'You need to stop that, Alice. You feel what you feel, end of story. Everyone's reaction to anything is different, their own. I'm not judging you. I'm trying to help.'

'I know, and I really appreciate it. It's just hard,' Alice said.

'I know it's hard. But, remember, nothing worthwhile is ever easy.'

'That sucks,' Alice said.

'Yes, it does.'

'But you're right. I need to get a grip on it. My whole life feels pretty screwed up right now, so maybe this is one little part I can try to fix.'

'That's the spirit. And, for the record, it might be playing a bigger part in your whole life than you realise.'

'Yeah, that's probably true. You're so wise.'

'Well, I'm not so sure about that. So, will you go with me – to one of Carmel's auctions or opens?'

'Okay. When do you have in mind?'

'Sooner the better. How about Saturday? Here,' she said after fossicking in her bag and drawing out a folded sheet of paper. She smoothed it out on her lap before handing it to Alice. 'You'd be doing me a favour, too, actually,' she said, 'by keeping me company. Dad wants me to go and bid for him and I'm bloody terrified. So, some moral support would be very welcome.'

'Okay, it's a date.'

'Great. Thanks.'

'No, thank *you*. As scared as I am, I would like to get over my Carmel phobia.'

'You do know there's always counselling and hypnosis, too?' Lauren said.

'I know, but I kind of feel I'd like to try to deal with it myself.'

'It's up to you. You have to do what's right for you. It's your journey, your life. So, should you check your message to see who called before we head off? I'm keen to know – call it the nosy writer in me.'

'Oh, yes, good idea. Maybe I've won lotto.'

'Do you buy tickets?'

'No.'

'Well, that's unlikely then, isn't it? But I do like your optimism,' Lauren said, with a laugh.

Alice was smiling as she dialled the number to access her voice-mail. And then she felt her face fall and her blood drain as she listened. Her heart began heaving again and her chest started to tighten. She began to sweat and suddenly the phone slipped from her clammy hand.

'What? What's wrong?' Lauren asked.

Alice barely heard her friend's question as she tried to tell herself to breathe, but her breaths became ragged gulps, getting faster and faster.

Then suddenly, as if a switch had been flicked, she was aware of where she was and what she was doing. Lauren had put a hand on her shoulder and shaken her gently and then Bill leapt up onto her lap and began scratching at her clothes. She blinked several times and finally managed a few deep breaths.

'It's okay. It's okay. Slow breaths, in and out, in and out,' Lauren said, rubbing Alice's shoulder in a gentle circular motion.

'Jesus, I feel like I'm having a heart attack or something. God, it hurts,' Alice said, wincing against her tight and painfully pulsing chest.

'It's a panic attack. Concentrate on your breathing. And pat Bill slowly – that might help too. Focus on right here and right now.'

Alice found Lauren's voice hypnotic and soothing, and slowly she returned to nearly normal. The only outward sign remaining were damp patches on her t-shirt under her armpits. 'Jesus, that was scary,' she finally said, letting a breath out loudly.

'Tell me about it,' Lauren said.

'Sorry.'

'There's no need to apologise.'

'Thank god you were here.'

'So, what happened? What was in the message? No one else has died, have they?'

'No, Gold, Taylor and Murphy Real Estate need me to go in and sign something before they can process my final pay.'

'Oh. Right.' The words *Is that all* hung unspoken.

'See what they do to me. You can't say what just happened isn't a completely irrational reaction,' she said, lifting her hands up and dropping them in a gesture of helplessness.

'We're not having that discussion again, which is why you need to deal with it – why you *are* dealing with it. When do you have to go in?'

'By close of business next Tuesday. I think that's what they said. I kind of tuned out after hearing who it was. Here, can you listen?' she said, bringing up the message again and passing the phone to Lauren.

'Yep, you're right, and the form is with the receptionist,' she said, handing the phone back to Alice. 'Get it over with. Don't hold off until after the weekend.'

'A part of me would rather forfeit the money.'

'I won't let you do that. And could you imagine the connip- tions David would have? We've been through all this. You're going to face your fear – just a little sooner than we'd anticipated. Why don't we go in and have lunch at a café nearby – the one you did your original interview with Carmel in. Then I'll wait while you go up and do your signing.'

'Couldn't you come up with me?'

'Of course I could, but I don't think that'll help you to get over your hoodoo.'

'You're probably right.'

'It'll have to be tomorrow, if you're not going to have it hanging over your head and worrying about it all weekend.'

'Okay, it's a date. I don't have to ring them back, do I? It just said the form is there and to come in sometime, right?'

'Yep. That's how I heard it.'

'God, I badly need that coffee now. I feel like I've been run over by one of those road rollers.'

Chapter Twenty-seven

As Alice made her way towards her former workplace she quivered with nerves, but concentrated on her breathing and convincing herself it was okay and that she wouldn't see Carmel. She tried to tell herself it was only Carmel who was the devil in this situation, not the others who worked there, but the truth was, Alice didn't want to be here doing this, full stop. No amount of telling herself it was gutless to be so anxious helped, either. She only hoped Lauren would be at the café already. Alice had briefly toyed with asking Lauren to meet her a couple of streets over and they could walk there together. But she had given herself a stern reminder that she had to face up to this if she was going to stop the anxiety over Carmel from ruining her life any further. *Enough is enough!*

At the door of the café Alice spied a table tucked near the back and made a beeline towards it while casting her eyes around to see if her friend was already there. No, not yet. She picked up the menu. *I'm here to enjoy a nice lunch out with a dear friend*, she told herself.

'Hiya, sorry I'm a wee bit late,' Lauren said, appearing moments later.

'Hey. You're okay. I've only just arrived,' Alice said.

Lauren pulled out a chair, sat down and dumped her large handbag on a spare one beside the table, seemingly all in one fluid movement.

'So, how are you doing?' Lauren asked as she settled back into her chair and unwound her scarf.

'Okay. I'm okay.'

'Great. That's the spirit. Nothing to worry about. Let's enjoy a long, indulgent lunch. I'm dying to see the menu,' she said, picking it up. 'I've seen some excellent write-ups about this place online.'

'I'm thinking carbs are definitely in order – I just need to decide between the gnocchi, pasta or risotto,' Alice said.

'Hmm. It all sounds fabulous. What about dessert, shall we be totally decadent? Have you checked what's on offer there? That might have a bearing for me, especially as to whether I have an entree or main size.'

'No, I think I'm pushing it thinking of a creamy dish as it is,' Alice said a little ruefully.

'We could always do dessert after you've been up to the office – it could be your reward. You can't go wrong with tiramisu or cheesecake.'

'Sounds like a plan,' Alice said.

'So, you seem calmer.'

'Like a duck on water,' Alice said. 'Seriously, though, I'm just keen to get that bitch and all she represents out of my mind and get over it.'

'So, ladies, are we doing lunch or just coffees?' a young waiter asked, materialising beside them, pad and pen in hand.

'Definitely lunch,' Lauren said.

'Great. What can I get you?'

'I'll have the chicken and mushroom risotto,' Lauren said.

'And I'll have the pumpkin ravioli with sage and burnt butter sauce. Yum,' Alice said.

'Main or entree size?'

'An entree for me,' Lauren said.

'Same for me,' Alice said.

'Perfect. Something to drink?'

'Just tap water is fine with me, thanks,' Lauren said, looking to Alice for confirmation.

'Perfectly fine with me.'

'Anything else. Some bread or perhaps a salad to share?'

'Oh, salad, that's a good idea,' Lauren said. 'Which one?' she said, picking up the menu again.

'I think the garden or Greek would go best with what you've chosen,' the young man said.

'Alice?'

'You choose,' Alice said.

'Greek, thank you,' Lauren said, looking up at the waiter.

'Done. Greek it is,' he said, smiling warmly.

'Maybe some coffee and cake later, but for now that's us,' Lauren said, shooting him a dazzling smile.

'Perfect. Won't be long,' he said, gathering up their menus.

'We're not in any rush,' Alice said.

'Even more perfect,' the waiter said.

'God, it's nice to have friendly, attentive service,' Lauren said, leaning back again in her chair.

'I love that about Melbourne,' Alice said.

'You know, I can forgive a not-so-tasty meal before I can forgive surly service,' Lauren said.

'Yeah, me too.'

'Here we go, ladies,' the waiter said, appearing again, this time with a bottle of water and two glasses.

'Thanks so much,' they each said as he placed a glass in front of them and poured the water.

'God, I hope he didn't hear us and think we meant he was surly,' Lauren whispered when he'd walked off.

'Oops. Yes.'

'Right, to sorting stuff out, and the future,' Lauren said, raising her glass.

'Yes, here's to Alice getting her shit together and stopping being such a great big wuss,' Alice said, clinking her glass against Lauren's. 'Now, please distract me from you know what for a bit. How's the lovely Brett?'

'Dreamy – at the risk of sounding like a loved-up teenager. He's attentive without being too gushy or clingy. Oh, Alice, it's just perfect.'

'That's awesome.'

'It's early days. I keep telling myself that so I won't get too carried away. Love being blind and all,' she said with a dismissive wave of her hand. 'And distracting, damn it.'

'Well, they do say all experiences are good for a writer.'

'Yes, fingers crossed my Great Australian Novel doesn't decide it wants to be a romance! You know how I despise that stuff.'

'Ha-ha, you're too funny.'

'I'm a literary snob, is what I am.'

'You've always said you want your female characters to be deeper, their journeys more meaningful than just a search for Mister Right. That's not being a snob.'

'Maybe. I want my characters to know they don't *need* a man and probably shouldn't want one too badly.'

'She says as she goes all glassy-eyed over Brett,' Alice said, grinning.

'God, please, change the subject. I don't want my subconscious getting any ideas! Hey, has your mother caught up with you yet?'

'Yep. Unfortunately David handed me the phone while refusing to tell me who was on the other end.'

'That's not very nice.'

'No, he thinks I'm being silly when it comes to how I feel about my mother.'

'But of course he only gets nice-as-pie Dawn, I suppose?' Lauren said.

'Exactly. I just wish people would be real and honest, and stop playing mind games. It's so bloody annoying.'

'Hear, hear,' Lauren said. 'So, how was it, what did she say?'

'Fine. You know, sometimes it's not as bad as I think it'll be.'

'Most things rarely are when it really comes down to it.'

'But there are the times – and, oh there have been plenty of them – when there's a situation where I think she couldn't possibly say anything to put me down or make me feel uncomfortable, but she still somehow manages to.'

'Which is why you're best to stay on your guard.'

'Hmm. But it's exhausting.'

'What did she say about the job?'

'"Oh, Alice, that *is* disappointing,"' Alice said, mimicking her mother, which Olivia had said, during one of their friendlier conversations, she was a whiz at. 'It's the disapproval in the tone. It can be barely distinguishable to the uninitiated, but to me it's as subtle as a blunt knife slicing right through me.'

'What did you say to that?'

'I said, and I quote, "Oh well, Mum, shit happens, it's not the end of the world."'

'Ha-ha, did you really?'

'Yep. All in the name of growing a backbone. I was annoyed she got me at the wrong moment – when I wasn't prepared. Anyway, enough about me. What other news do you bring?'

'Nothing, really, just plodding on and hoping decent inspiration will strike at some point and before I buy into the thought I might be completely kidding myself about being able to write or one day making a career out of it.'

'You will, I have full faith in you.'

'Hey, I don't want to alarm you, but isn't that Carmel over there – to our left,' Lauren said quietly as she leant across the table. 'I recognise her from the photo on her brochures.'

Alice took a covert glance. Instantly her heart began to pound against her ribs and her hands started to shake. She nodded, unable to speak with the sudden dryness in her mouth and throat. She looked around, feeling trapped. There was no way out but to pass right beside Carmel's table and Carmel herself. She began to sweat.

'Calm down, she can't hurt you,' Lauren whispered, and placed a cool hand over one of Alice's. Alice stared at her hands and nodded. She tried to swallow and when she still couldn't she took a large sip of water.

'Breathe, Alice,' Lauren said, 'I'm right here. You're not alone. Look at her. Desensitise yourself.'

'I can't.'

'Make yourself. Just a quick look. You're here to face your fear. Well, there it is.'

'Not like this. It wasn't meant to be like this,' Alice hissed quietly.

'Maybe this is even better. And the universe has clearly decided this is the way it's meant to be. Just go with it. There is no right or wrong.'

Alice forced herself to look at Carmel. Then she noticed that a young man with what looked like a display folder in front of him was sitting opposite her ex-boss.

'Oh my god, I bet she's doing an interview. That looks like a résumé folder,' Alice said.

Lauren looked. 'Poor kid,' she said. 'He looks a wreck.'

'Just how she likes them. Remember this day, mate, because it's all downhill from here if you take a job working for that bitch.'

'I really hope he's a journalist, or copywriter, or something else, and not a prospective PA.'

'God, I've got shivers just looking at them,' Alice said, shaking her head and shoulders.

'Here we are, ladies.' The waiter placed the salad on the table and then their meals in front of them.

'Thank you,' they both said together.

'Pleasure. Enjoy.'

'It looks amazing,' Alice said, while thinking she'd completely lost her appetite and wasn't sure how she could eat anything now. But she had to, she really didn't want to offend the waiter, or the chef, by returning a plate of untouched food. That would be insulting to all concerned. The steam wafted off the plate, bringing with it an incredible aroma. Alice's mouth watered despite her frazzled state of mind. She picked up her fork and then tasted the ravioli.

'Oh. My. God. This is incredible,' she said. All thoughts of Carmel momentarily vanished as the nutty flavour of the delicately burnt butter swam around her tongue and lingered in her mouth. It was astonishing that something so simple as cooking with good, basic ingredients could make such an impact on the palate. Alice had never tried making sage and burnt butter before, but made a mental note to do so very soon.

'Yes, this is fabulous,' Lauren said. 'I'm going to eat slowly to savour it.'

'Good idea,' Alice said, putting her fork down and taking a sip of water.

'How is it, ladies?' the waiter asked a few minutes later. 'All good here?'

'Great,' Alice said.

'Amazing,' Lauren said.

'Wonderful,' he said, and put his hands together in front of him in a gesture Alice took as gratitude, and left.

She stole another glance at Carmel, testing her fortitude. *I'm okay. Calm even.*

'And this, kids, is why you don't ever give up carbs,' Lauren said.

'Amen to that. I'd put money on that being a job interview,' Alice added quietly, nodding in Carmel's direction.

'You know, someone should warn him.'

Alice looked up quickly at Lauren, her chest suddenly in a vice-like grip.

'Calm down, I wasn't being serious, Alice. We're here to face your fears and help you, not send you into the depths of hell. He's a big boy. And, anyway, for all we know they might click and have a completely wonderful working relationship.'

'Maybe it was just me – a clash of personalities – the wrong match,' Alice said.

'You don't think that for a second.'

'No, no I don't. Narcissists aren't capable of being kind, or keeping up their façade indefinitely. God, I'd love to go over there and tell him a few home truths about her,' Alice said. 'If only I wasn't so gutless.'

'In this instance, it's nothing about having guts and everything about having manners.'

'Anyway, she'd probably threaten libel, or defamation, or something like that.'

'Would she have a case if what you said was true? We had a lecture on defamation in publishing the other year, but I can't remember all the details,' Lauren said. 'Just keep enjoying your lunch and let karma take care of her.'

'Why does karma never come around quickly enough?' Alice said. 'Or never appears at all, in most cases?'

'No idea. One of life's great mysteries. But I know it exists, or perhaps that's just my wishful thinking.'

'Better to be an optimist than negative, I guess,' Alice said.

'Looks like their meeting is over,' Lauren said.

Alice turned to see Carmel and the young man standing up and shaking hands. Then the man left and Carmel sat back down alone. As their plates were being collected, Alice noticed Carmel standing up and walking over to the counter to pay. And in the next moment she was gone and Alice was letting out a breath she didn't realise she'd been holding.

'See, you survived,' Lauren said. 'And you didn't even need to breathe into a paper bag!' she added.

'Thank god for that!' Alice said. 'Seriously, though, I'm actually okay. I feel all right.'

'Well, I reckon now would be a good time for you to head upstairs and get this over with,' Lauren said.

'Do I have to?' Alice said. 'It's a shame to ruin such a lovely lunch.'

'Yes, no chickening out. Go on. It will take you all of five minutes. Then we can have dessert. And, no, I'm not going with you. You've got this, Alice, you really do. Now, go do it. I'll be right here.'

'Okay. Wish me luck.'

'You don't need luck.'

Alice cursed her shaking legs as she stood up. Damn it. She was feeling calm over lunch and now the anxiety was coursing through her again. *Perhaps I shouldn't have had such a rich, heavy meal after all,* she thought as she felt her lower stomach contract painfully.

'Just one foot in front of the other. Slowly if you need to,' Lauren said. 'Focus on keeping yourself in the here and now, and slow down your breathing, so it can't run away from you.'

'I'm fine,' Alice said, as much in an effort to buoy herself as anything else.

'Yes, you are. Now off you go. I want cheesecake!'

Alice stepped into the lift. Thankfully she was alone and could work on some deep breathing to steady her nerves. Her heart was strangely slow and steady, but beating hard within her.

'I'm okay,' she said as she stretched out a tingly finger to select the twenty-fourth floor. 'In, sign the paper at reception, and then out,' she whispered to herself as she passed each floor with no stops.

She gingerly stepped out into the reception area and took a look around before making her way over to the desk. She didn't recognise the young man sitting behind the expanse of marble.

'Hi, um, I'm Alice Hamilton. I understand payroll has left a form here I need to sign.'

'Yep. It's right here,' he said, swivelling around to retrieve a clipboard from a shelf behind him and placing it on the counter top.

'Thanks,' Alice said, and tried to detach the pen, but it was somehow caught under the clip. As she tried to work it free, she heard voices to her right – muffled at first and then becoming clearer. Some of them were familiar, and she turned around. There was the guy she'd seen with Carmel in the café. He was shaking hands with Paul, Mary and Rose. Alice was shocked to hear the same people say exactly the same words that they had said to her after her own interview. She found herself staring, unable to drag her gaze away. Paul caught her eye and nodded and smiled. Or was it more of a wince? She nodded back, struggling to raise a genuine smile. Their looks could easily be the bland, friendly expressions they'd offer to anyone – to people who might be unimportant, or might turn out to be somebody worth smiling at, somebody worth keeping on-side. Did Paul even remember who she was? He'd seemed such a reasonable man when they'd met, but he'd handled her situation so badly. They all had, really, but Paul especially, given he was the CEO and clearly the leader of the group, she thought as the trio disappeared through the glass doors. She watched the young man – whose name she hadn't caught – make his way to the lift, and she bit her lip.

'Sorry, I've just realised I've forgotten to feed the meter. I'll be back in a minute,' Alice said to the receptionist, seeming to startle him slightly.

'Er, okay.'

She raced towards the lift just as the doors were closing on the young man.

'Excuse me, can you please hold the lift?' she called. She cringed and held her breath as she thrust her arm into the gap between the doors. 'Thanks,' she said. 'God, I hate doing that, you never quite know if you're going to get your arm crushed or the door will actually stay open,' she added with a laugh.

'Yes, it's a scary thing to do,' the guy said. 'Ground floor?'

'Yes, please. I'm Alice,' she said, holding her hand out to the now slightly startled looking man.

'Er, hello. Rhys,' he said, as he tentatively accepted her hand for a brief shake. Speaking to strangers in a lift was frowned upon; introducing oneself was a definite no-no. The way he looked at her Alice could tell he thought her a little deranged and he was being polite so as not to offend her or incite a nasty incident.

'I'm sorry to barge in on you and I know it's none of my business,' she rushed on, fully aware of their limited time together and the possibility that they could be interrupted at any moment by someone stepping into the lift at another floor. 'I saw you meeting with Carmel Gold in the café earlier.'

'Yes?'

'I know it's not my place, but I need to tell you because no one told me and it became a real mess and …' Alice cursed her blundering. They were at the tenth floor already. 'I was Carmel's last PA. She was a monster. Possibly a narcissist and a psychopath – I'm no expert. It might be different for you. I don't know. I hope it is. But I just wanted you to be aware. And there'll be no point going to management if you have a problem with her. Carmel's a partner with her name on the wall and she brings in too much money. Paul and Rose and Mary were really nice as people, but not at all helpful.'

'What did she do?'

'Made me run around doing errands for her instead of the work I was meant to be doing – so I got into trouble with others in the company. And you can't win – she said she wants you to take the initiative, but when you do she loses it at you. It makes you second-guess yourself and feel as if no matter what you do, you'll never win her approval. I know it sounds ridiculous and petty and you have every right to think I'm just after revenge or simply some random nutcase bailing you up in a lift. I'm not. Well, I kind of am. I wasn't before I worked in this place. I lasted four weeks and almost lost my mind. I wasn't always this anxious and scatty, either. I promise. I was damned good at my job until she completely messed with my head. And now I don't have a reference to get another job. I know I'm not making any sense, and I'm babbling like a freak, but as I said, I just felt the need to warn you. Google "narcissist", "bullies in the workplace" and "gaslighting" and you'll have a pretty clear idea of what she did to me. Oh, and I wasn't her first PA to leave – I think I was number seven in two years, or something.'

'Oh. Wow. Right.'

The light above them was on the G. The lift doors opened and they stepped out.

'I really hope it's different for you, Rhys,' Alice said.

'Thanks, Alice, it was, um, nice to meet you. I have to admit, I did have a weird sense that she was a little off – sort of too good to be true.'

'Well, go with that. Believe me, it's not just the shiny façade of the seasoned sales person.'

'That's exactly what I told myself it was. It was a great job offer. They agreed to what I asked for without batting an eyelid.'

'Yep. Me too. I was so excited. I thought I'd found my dream job. I'd better go. Oh, shit, I've got to go back up. I have to sign my exit papers. Well, I'll leave it with you. Maybe she just didn't like me – a personality clash, or something,' Alice said with a shrug, as she pushed the button to call a lift.

'Well, thanks very much for the heads-up. You've given me a lot to think about.' He started to walk away.

A lift arrived and Alice stepped in.

'Um, Alice?' Rhys called. He was hurrying back towards her.

She put her hand against the edge of one of the doors to keep them from closing. 'Yes?'

'Could I get your number, um, in case I need to compare notes? If I take the job – I really need to, it was hard enough to get the interview.'

'Er, well, um, I ...' Alice stammered.

'Seriously, I'm not creepy or anything. I promise.'

Alice felt it would be rude to say no. After all, she'd bailed him up in the lift. And, anyway, if he called or texted she could always ignore him if she wanted to. It wasn't as if he had her full name or knew where she lived.

'Okay, sure.' He handed over his phone. She could hear a little voice in her head telling her to just change a digit around. But Alice was sick of telling lies. And Rhys seemed all right. He hadn't told her to bugger off and mind her own business, or called security. And she felt really good that she'd said her piece. It was entirely up to him what he did with the information now.

'Thanks,' he said when she handed the phone back. 'I'll just send you a text so you have my number too,' he said, tapping on his phone. Alice's phone pinged. She glanced at it and smiled at his message: *Hi Alice, It's Rhys, the guy from the lift.*

'Got it. Okay. I'd better go,' she said.

'Well, thanks again, Alice. I appreciate the warning. I'll let you know what I decide to do. Probably go back on the job hunt.'

'Yeah, me too. Sorry to burst your bubble.'

'Better that now than losing my mind later,' he said. 'Take care of yourself, Alice.'

'You too, Rhys. All the best.' She let go of the door and it began to close. Rhys was still standing there watching her.

As the lift rose, Alice took stock of how she felt. Good. Really good. This was her. Being helpful was what gave her the biggest buzz of all. She was smiling and couldn't wipe it off her face. Her anxiety was all but gone.

She stepped back up to the reception desk, the smile still planted on her face. 'Sorry about that,' she said.

'No worries, the parking inspectors around here are pretty ruthless. Here's your form.'

This time Alice had no trouble sliding the pen out from under the clip. She quickly scanned the document. Yes, it was just a confirmation of the termination of her employment – and she signed it.

'Thanks very much,' she said, handing the board and pen back. As she turned away she took a look around. She was calm. She let out her breath.

'See you later, Alice,' the receptionist called.

'Bye,' she said. *No, you will certainly not see me later – well not here, anyway. I'm done.*

Alice watched the numbers of the floors ticking off as she headed down again. She was smiling. At almost every floor the lift stopped and people stepped in and out. She didn't mind. There was no urgency, no frantically beating heart urging her forward with nervous energy. She smiled a little at each person who entered and shuffled aside to make room.

By the time they got to the first floor the lift had become more crowded than was comfortable, and Alice was squashed into a back corner. Thank goodness she was calm now, otherwise she might have lost the plot over this invasion of her personal space.

On the ground floor she waited patiently for the passengers standing at the front to go first.

And then, just as Alice walked out, she saw Carmel Gold rushing across the foyer – racing, clack, clack, clack on her high heels – to catch the lift before the doors closed. Alice concentrated on keeping the slight smile on her face and giving the appearance of being nonchalant, which she almost was, and avoided looking directly at Carmel. Her pulse quickened slightly, but there was no significant flight sensation coursing through her. Phew. Alice kept walking. She could see Rhys in a corner of the foyer talking on his phone and looking her way. Alice waved to him. He smiled back and mimed that he'd call her – well, that's what she assumed he meant. She responded with a single thumbs-up gesture.

'Hi, Carmel,' Alice called brightly as they passed. As she strode towards the sliding glass doors at the front of the building, Alice hoicked her shoulders up a notch.

'There you are!' Lauren said, hurrying up to Alice, who turned towards her friend's voice.

'What are you doing here?'

'You were gone for ages. I was worried you'd had a panic attack and you were hiding, crumpled on the floor of the loo upstairs or something,' Lauren said.

'Sorry. I'm fine. It just took longer than I thought. Boy, do I have a story to tell you. And I just saw Carmel, literally could have bumped into her.'

'Yes, I saw. You should have seen the look on her face. Shock mixed with, I don't know, it looked like fear to me, but I don't imagine she'd ever be afraid of anything, let alone show it.'

'I didn't notice, I was too busy shooting her a winning smile and keeping my voice steady while I said hi.'

'Good for you.'

'Have we lost our table?'

'No. I left my credit card with our lovely waiter and assured him we'd definitely be back for dessert. Thank god you're okay. Was that the guy from the café you were waving to?'

'Yep. That's Rhys. We met in the lift.'

'Oh. Right.'

'I told him the truth about Carmel – well, my experience. And, Lauren, it feels so good to have warned him. I'm not sure what he'll do with the information, but that doesn't matter.'

'Wow, that was brave.'

'God, I feel great!'

'I can tell.'

'Sorry, I'm being a little OTT. But it's like I've shed a massive layer of pain, or something. I feel free – completely free of Carmel and bloody Gold, Taylor and Murphy and the hold they had over me.'

'Alice, you're practically skipping.'

'I have no idea what I'm going to do with my life, but hey, one step at a time, right?'

'Yep. Now you've got all that negativity out of the way, you'll give your dreams a chance to find you.'

'Ladies, you came back!' their waiter said as they walked through the busy café to the table and he handed them the menus again.

'Thanks so much for holding the table,' Alice said. 'We really appreciate it.'

'Ah,' he said, waving a hand.

'Don't go,' Lauren said, 'we won't be a moment. Right, Alice?'

Alice nodded. 'Yep. Two secs. You go first, Lauren.'

'Okay. I'll have the passionfruit cheesecake and a cappuccino, thank you,' she said, handing her menu back.

'And I'll have the tiramisu and a peppermint tea, please.'

'Ooh, you're a lot more cheerful than when you left,' the waiter said. 'I hope you don't mind me saying, but it suits you. You're glowing!'

'Thank you.' Alice blushed. 'I feel like I just turned my life around with one short conversation.'

'Good for you. That's what we like to hear. I'd say dessert is a great reward. I'll be back soon.'

'Look at you, blushing like a teenager after that compliment,' Lauren teased gently.

'Don't be silly. He's probably gay. I still can't believe it. I did it, Lauren. I faced Carmel.'

'You did. Well done. Be proud of yourself.'

Alice took a few deep breaths. 'My heart's racing a bit, but I'll get over that.'

'Here we are, dessert for two lovely ladies,' their waiter said, placing their plates down. 'Coffee and peppermint tea are on the way.'

'Thanks,' they both said, flashing him smiles worthy of a tooth-paste commercial.

'Right, so tell me what you said to Rhys about Carmel?' Lauren said, digging her fork into her cheesecake.

'Pretty much everything. I didn't hold back.'

'I hope you haven't left yourself open to a lawsuit. If Rhys tells Carmel what you said, she might ...'

'Oh, I didn't think of that.'

'You could get into serious trouble, Alice, depending on what you said and if she finds out.'

'The way I'm feeling right now, I don't care. I'd say, do your worst, bitch, bring it on.'

'Well, okay, then. Good for you. I think,' Lauren said.

'I don't think Rhys would say anything. But if he does, that's up to him. I spoke the truth. He seemed really grateful. That's what I'm going to focus on. No negativity. If there's some fallout, I'll deal with it then.'

'Fair enough.'

'Hey,' Lauren said, when they'd been making their way through their desserts for a few minutes, 'are you still keen to come along to the auction with me for my dad?'

'Yep. No problem at all. David will be out of town, yet again, anyway.'

'How are things there?'

'Okay. Tense. Awkward.'

'Hmm. It's hard to make a relationship work if one person stays the same and the other has a fundamental shift in perspective,' Lauren said.

'Yeah. I don't see how we can get back to where we were, or if I even want to. I feel like I've changed too much, learnt too much, maybe. But, I've said I'll stay, so that's where we're at for now. It is what it is.'

Chapter Twenty-eight

Alice found the café where Rhys had suggested they meet and went inside, wondering if she'd recognise him again. But he'd clearly recognised her, because there he was, waving to her. She smiled and made her way over to the table under the window. He leapt up and they shook hands.

'Thanks so much for coming,' he said, 'I really appreciate it.'

'No problem. Thanks for inviting me. I was glad to get out and away from the depressing job websites.' She was completely taken by surprise when she found herself being pulled into a hug, and stumbled a little, '*Oh.*'

'Sorry, but I needed to do that. I'm so grateful to you,' he said, releasing her seconds later. They sat down and reached for the small wooden clipboard menus in front of them.

Soon a waitress appeared and deposited a bottle of water and two glasses in front of them.

'Thank you,' Alice said, smiling up at her.

'I'll be back in a bit to take your order,' the waitress said, and left.

'I hope this isn't too weird for you – I mean, meeting a strange man for lunch,' Rhys said.

'Not at all.' Alice had told David about her encounter with Rhys and his invitation to lunch. She figured it might be important for Rhys to get something off his chest. David had been busy on his laptop and had only mumbled, 'That's nice.'

For not the first time recently, Alice had wondered if he'd always been so distant and self-absorbed. Though, she couldn't talk, she'd stopped showing more than a passing interest in his work ages ago. Was the current project a rollout of a new IT system through Australia and New Zealand for one of the major banks, or was that the one before? God, was she like him too, had they become the same since living together? She'd initially found David's drive to get on in his career and his passion and focus for every project attractive. Now she was feeling so different about it all, about him. As much as she wanted to blame the project, she suspected this might actually be another part of his character she'd somehow managed to ignore or overlook. Or perhaps there'd always been a project that had taken precedence over her, and over *them*. Where would any kids come in the pecking order? Would he change his priorities when they had children? As she'd watched him packing his bags to go away again, Alice had been a little shocked at how much she was looking forward to having the house to herself again.

'So, no joy on the job front, then?' Rhys said.

'No. It's proving impossible without a reference from my last direct report.'

'Oh, shit. Yeah, of course.'

'Anyway, until the other day I really wasn't sure I could face going back to office work.'

'Fair enough. So what changed?'

'Meeting you, actually. Warning you. Saying it all out loud to a stranger somehow took the fear away. So, I should be the one taking *you* to lunch to say thank you,' she said, smiling.

'Okay, it's your treat next time.'

'So, I take it you turned down the job with Carmel, then?'

'Yep.'

'I'm so sorry it didn't work out. I know how hard it is just to get an interview.'

'Yeah. But don't worry. It was entirely my decision. And I'm so grateful for your warning. I'm probably still a bit too fragile to be changing careers, anyway, let alone opening myself up for the sort of treatment you described.'

'Oh?'

'I lost my gran to cancer a month ago and it seems to have hit me harder than it should have.'

'Oh, I'm so sorry to hear that.'

'I was her main carer. She was in her eighties and hadn't been well, so …' he said with a shrug.

'That's a big loss. Clearly you were very close. And just because she was old doesn't mean you're not allowed to be upset by it, Rhys. Grief is grief. It's a hard process that you have to work through at your own pace. It's debilitating and all-consuming. You're never exactly the same person once you've lost someone close.'

'It's really hard to find the will to go on, to be honest. Not that I've thought of – well, you know. I haven't got quite that bad.'

'But you find it disheartening and exasperating that life just goes on, right?'

'Yes. Exactly. You've been through it too?'

'Several times. And, recently, too.'

'Gran's the first for me.'

Alice would have liked to warn him that it doesn't get easier. Time does *not* heal all wounds. In her experience grief compounded with all the pain and heartbreak doubled the second time around, and so on. People who say you get over losing someone – ever – are full of shit. Once you get through the crippling sadness, the reality is it leaves a residue that settles on you like a heavy cloak and informs who you are and what you do going forward. Well, that's how it had been for her. It was probably different for everyone. But of course, she couldn't say any of this to Rhys. It wouldn't help. Thankfully he continued before she figured out what to say.

'It's all just so awful. There's such a bloody big hole that feels like it actually physically hurts.'

'I know what you mean. Tell me about your gran.'

'Well, she was mentally as sharp as a tack right to the end and was one of my best friends in the entire world. She was wise and so ahead of her time. And really brave. I never heard her complain once during the chemo, when she must have been in so much pain.' Tears streamed down his face. He wiped them away with his sleeve. 'Sorry, I just miss her so much,' he said. 'How about you? Who did you lose recently? Do you want to talk about it?'

'I don't know. Ruth. Ruth was my mum's age and the warm loving mother figure I never had. Oh, I have a mother, but she's, well … That's a long story for another day,' Alice said with a sigh. 'Anyway, because of my move to Melbourne a few years ago – I'm from country South Australia – and study and getting my life back in order, I wasn't in touch with her recently as much as I had been. So I'm feeling a bit guilty about that.'

'I'm sure she would have understood.'

'I know she would have, she was pretty awesome, but I think punishing ourselves is part of what those of us left behind have to deal with. It must be part of the grief process.'

'Hmm. I keep replaying all the times I didn't call Gran when I should have, blew off meals to hang out with my mates. Grief is shit.'

'Yes, it is,' Alice agreed.

'Come on, let's change the subject. I didn't bring you here to make you depressed. We'd better order,' he said, picking up his menu again. 'The waitress keeps coming over and hovering nearby. I got completely distracted.'

'Me too. Oops, I didn't notice her. Yes, we'd better order.'

'Do you fancy sharing a pizza?' Rhys asked.

'Sounds good. What about the BBQ chicken one.'

'Great. Would it bother you if I have garlic breath?'

I'm not planning on getting that *close to you.* 'Not at all. We can't have pizza without garlic bread, if that's what you mean. It just wouldn't be right.'

'I agree. Do you need a salad?'

'No, I've never felt the need to ruin my pizza-eating experience with salad.'

'Perfect. Would you like a drink – of anything other than water?' he asked, turning to look for the waitress and catch her eye.

'No, water is good for me, thanks.'

'So, tell me, Alice,' Rhys said, once their order had been taken and they were alone again. 'Why real estate? I remember you saying in the lift you thought you'd found your dream job.'

'It sounded like a great opportunity to start an interesting career. And I thought I could help people make a good sale and a good purchase.'

'Fair enough.'

'How about you?'

'The money. I can't lie. Sorry, I sound like a bit of a wanker. I don't mean I want to be one of those BMW four-by-four driving types. I just want to earn a decent living from something I enjoy. I love the built environment. I was actually studying architecture.'

'What happened?'

'Gran got really sick.'

'You know, I'm sure she wouldn't want to be responsible for you giving up on your dreams.'

'I know. For a while I was too busy taking care of her. Then I couldn't concentrate or force myself to go to class, and now I'm not sure it's what I want anymore. Gran suggested I do a typing and data entry course while I was looking after her. I turned out to be good at them. Admin seems a good fallback. I like order.'

'Me too.'

'I'm sorry you had to go through all you did with Carmel.'

'Thanks. I'll be okay. If I can find another job. My partner is getting exasperated with me.'

'But it's not your fault the job market's tough.'

'He's annoyed I didn't stick it out – thinks I should have sucked it up.'

'Nothing is worth making yourself miserable over.'

'No. The good thing about the Carmel situation – or, well, leaving it – was that I got to go to my friend Ruth's funeral. Silver linings, and all that. Listen to us. Two lost souls,' Alice said with a laugh in an attempt to lighten the mood.

'You said you want to help people. What about medicine or nursing?'

'I'm not academically smart enough in the right areas and I'm pretty sure I couldn't cope with the blood involved with hands-on medicine.'

'What about counselling or psychology? You've helped me and you're a great listener.'

'Thanks. I'm not sure I could face going back to uni.' *David certainly couldn't.*

'I think if you enjoyed it, if you were really passionate about it, you'd be fine with it.'

'I've just done an Arts degree. Now I need to start pulling my weight financially.'

'Says who?'

'My partner.'

'Oh. Right.'

'It's okay. I can see how it looks.` But we've just bought into the great Australian dream and have a whopping big mortgage to prove it, so …'

'Hmm, well, my gran always said a marriage, or any partnership, should be about two people supporting each other to be the best they can be and the best for society as a whole.'

'I like the sound of your gran,' Alice said.

'Yeah, she was amazing. She also said, at least a million times, where there's a will there's a way. I think you can achieve anything if you want it badly enough.'

'It's hard when life gets in the way though.'

'I know. I'm struggling to clearly see ahead one day at a time at the moment, let alone plan my future,' Rhys said.

'Maybe it's just too soon for you to make any big decisions,' Alice said.

'Yeah, perhaps. But how long does it take – before the fog lifts and you feel normal again?'

'As long as it takes. And be prepared for it to not be the normal that you remember. Too much will have changed. *You* might have changed too much for things to truly be as they were.'

'Grief really ages you, doesn't it? Sorry, I don't mean you look old, I meant … Oh, I don't know what I was trying to say. I'm tired. It's exhausting being sad and trying to keep it together all the time when you just want to curl up in the corner and wait for it all to be over.'

'I think what you're describing is wisdom – that grief ages us at a soul level. We're wiser because of what we've been through,' Alice said.

'Yes, maybe that's it. I think you'd be a really good grief counsellor. You seem to know how to explain it all so it makes sense. You're also a really calming and comforting presence to be around.'

Alice was shocked to find herself blushing slightly.

'Sorry, please don't think I was coming on to you. I'm not, honestly.'

'Thank you. That might be one of the loveliest things anyone has said to me in a long time.'

'I only speak the truth.'

'With counselling I'd be worried about taking on other people's problems or emotions.'

'Maybe the course would teach you how to deal with that.'

'Maybe. It's certainly something to think about.'

'I can't believe a counselling course wouldn't have been right on your radar – I think you'd be a natural.'

'Thanks, but where I'm from, we never had any psychologists or a counselling service beyond the local GP, and it was nearly impossible to get an appointment with him. Also, I was raised that you don't discuss your problems with strangers – well, you didn't complain full stop. Keep it all safely bottled up.'

'Why was that?'

'I think it's a small country town thing.'

'Not a very healthy long-term strategy, though, is it?'

'No, probably not.'

'Just think, you could get qualified and go back there and clean up all their problems.'

'That's the last place on earth I'd live permanently. There's so much narrow-mindedness and bigotry. I didn't see it when I lived there, and I only realised how damaging it is when I left.'

'It's funny how we crave what we haven't had. I'm city through and through,' Rhys said, 'but I've thought about giving friendly country life a go.'

'It's great if you love gossip and everyone knowing your business – or thinking they know. Oh, don't get me wrong, in times of need – like floods and bushfires – small towns are the best. Everyone comes together and gets things done and helps people back onto their feet.'

'But they aren't always like that?'

'Oooh nooo, definitely not. Well, not in my experience, anyway.'

Their food arrived and they tucked in, chatting between mouthfuls about where they'd grown up and other random topics.

Every time there was a lull in the conversation Alice's mind went back to Rhys's suggestion of her becoming a counsellor.

'I'm so glad to have met you, Alice. You've given me lots to think about. And cured me of my country squire yearnings,' Rhys added with a grin, after the waitress cleared their table.

'Happy to be of service,' Alice said, grinning back. 'But, seriously, it's been really nice, Rhys.'

'Let's catch up again sometime?'

'Definitely,' Alice said. 'Right. Well, I'd better get home,' she added, standing up.

'Yes, I have to go and get some stuff done for Centrelink before they cut me off.'

They walked out into the sunshine together and hovered on the footpath for a moment.

'Well, thanks again, Alice – for everything,' he said.

'Thank you, Rhys,' Alice said. 'You take good care of yourself. And if you need someone to talk to, you have my number.'

'Thanks, but be careful what you offer. I'm a bit of a mess, remember.'

'You're okay. And you'll *be* okay.'

'I'm a phone call away, too, if I can help you with anything. I feel like I nearly owe you my life, or first-born child, for warning me about Carmel. I think I really dodged a bullet there.'

'Right time, right place, I guess,' Alice said, feeling a little overwhelmed at his praise.

As she walked down the street towards the tram stop, she had the strange thought that perhaps she'd had to go through all she had with Carmel in order to protect Rhys. Ruth had always said things happened for a reason, and that people came into your life for a reason too, and also at the right time. And Alice was okay with that. She felt strangely exhilarated and peaceful all at once.

Chapter Twenty-nine

After enjoying an exuberant reunion with Bill, Alice sat down in the lounge and kicked her shoes off onto the floor and then sat staring at them. She really should take them to the bedroom or at least line them up neatly at the end of the couch. She moved to do so – on autopilot – before stopping herself. *Jesus, I've become a robot, David's robot. Come on, he's not that bad*, was her next thought. *There's nothing wrong with being tidy.*

She shook the thoughts aside and opened the laptop on the coffee table and typed *how to become a counsellor* into the search box and pressed *Enter*. There was a vague memory lurking far back in her mind. It had been with her all the way home since leaving Rhys. What was it? She tried to ignore it – it would reveal itself when and if it was meant to. Instead, she concentrated on the results on the screen in front of her. She clicked on the first one, which started by listing the tasks a counsellor would be required to do during an ordinary work day. She read on through the personal attributes required, the different areas of specialisation and then the necessary training. There were no great surprises in anything she read. Was this a path she wanted to pursue? She didn't feel the same level of excitement she'd had about the job in real estate, but perhaps that was because she was now so much more realistic thanks to the spectacular letdown.

Her phone rang and she cursed not putting it on silent or turning it off completely. She nearly didn't answer it because she was enjoying her peace and tranquillity so much. *David – mobile* was on the screen. She toyed with letting it go to voicemail, but knew he'd just call back later or she'd feel compelled to call him, so she may as well get it over with now.

'Hey, how was your flight?' she said, having mustered a cheerful tone.

'Good. This hotel is nice. I wouldn't mind coming back here again sometime.'

'Sounds good.'

'How was your lunch? Did he offer you a job?'

'Sorry? A what?'

'A job. Isn't that why you were meeting?'

'No. Why would he offer me a job? He's unemployed too.'

'Oh.' Alice could hear the confusion in David's tone. He clearly hadn't listened when she'd told him about having lunch with Rhys. Ordinarily she'd just put it down to David's mind being on his project or upcoming travel, or one of the multitude of other more important things he juggled. Recently, however, she'd begun to realise it went deeper and that he perhaps didn't really respect her. These discoveries were settling heavily and uncomfortably on her, like a blanket left out overnight that soaks up the dew. Oh how she longed to be wrong and toss aside this oppressive, disappointed feeling …

'Rhys is the one I warned about working for Carmel,' Alice prompted. 'He wanted to have lunch to thank me and tell me what he decided to do.'

'Oh. Right. Do you think that was wise?'

'What do you mean?'

'Warning him off working for Carmel. You can't condemn her because you were too sensitive.'

It was a little more than that, David. But Alice wasn't going there. 'Um, David, what do you think of psychology, counselling?' she asked, before the pause stretched on for too long.

'As in you and me going to couples' counselling? No. I'm not remotely interested in discussing any petty issues you might have with a stranger and being asked "how do you feel about that?" over and over.' Alice was taken aback at how much like her mother his words sounded, how instantly defensive he became.

And then she remembered the thought that had been tugging at her. In high school Alice had once briefly considered counselling or psychology as a career, but her mother had dissuaded her, saying that it was improper to air one's dirty linen to others, and equally so to encourage such behaviour. Also, they couldn't afford to fund Alice studying in Adelaide, six hundred kilometres away, and anyway, she would find studying at tertiary level far too hard. Alice couldn't curse the limitations placed on her because she'd chosen to abide by them. That was then, now was now … She forced her attention back to the current conversation.

'No, I meant me becoming a psychologist or counsellor. What do you think?'

'You can't be serious, Alice. Where is this coming from?'

'Rhys said I'm good to talk to, and you know how I like to help people.'

'Alice, I think there's a little more to it than that.'

'I think I'd be a good counsellor, actually. I've had plenty of life experience. I'm thoughtful and empathetic. I've been looking into it.'

'What, so now you want to start another three-year degree? Absolutely not.'

'Well, I could start with a shorter course – there's plenty online to choose from.'

'And, anyway, would you really want to listen to stupid people going on and on about how bad they feel and how crap their life is? You'd have to sit there and be sympathetic when all you'd really want to tell them was that they needed to stop feeling sorry for themselves and to get their shit together.'

'Wow, David, have you thought of becoming a counsellor. You'd be great,' she said, faking a laugh. 'Not everyone has had the same smooth ride in life that you've had. And just because someone has a problem they're working through doesn't mean they're stupid.'

'Well, if you want to listen to that day in day out, then that's up to you. But I won't be funding another degree.'

'Maybe I'll find a scholarship. And, anyway, you didn't fund my last one – I paid my fees up-front myself.'

'You know what I mean. It wouldn't exactly be a highly paid career, either, would it? Why don't you do an MBA and get into business? That's where the money is. I still can't believe you turned down Outercover – there was your opportunity.'

'David, I'm not you. We don't have the same interests or ambitions. I don't think I want to work for big business.'

'Your problem is you don't seem to be ambitious at all these days. I thought you were when we met. Quite frankly, it's exasperating. I let you do a run of the mill, non-vocational Arts degree in the hope you'd sort yourself out, figure out what you wanted by the end.'

'I did figure it out, David. It's not my fault there's nothing going in History at the moment.'

'But it's not really a serious career, is it?'

No, it probably isn't without honours or masters, or at least an area of specialisation. And you were against that too. Alice knew she should pick her battles so she kept the words to herself.

'And now you're saying you want to turn around and start all over,' David continued. She could practically feel him rolling his eyes at her, like she was at him.

'Lucky for you that you knew you wanted to be in the IT industry and knew the path you needed to take to get there, but not everyone is so focussed. David, you're not me. I want to do something I love, something I'm passionate about,' Alice said.

'Well, you can't be too passionate about psychology or counselling, or whatever, because this is the first time you've mentioned it. What will it be next week? Seriously, Alice.'

'It was just an idea.'

'My point exactly, Alice,' he said.

'If psychology or counselling aren't highly paid enough for you, David, why are you okay with me being a lowly admin drudge?'

'Because that's at least a way up the ladder, highlighted by the fact Todd offered you a way into being national marketing manager of a decent sized business. And you could have become a successful real estate agent if you'd stuck it out with Carmel. Why couldn't you look at other firms, anyway – why quit the whole industry after one bad experience?'

'What about having kids?'

'What about it?'

'Well, I'd be out of the workforce for several years. Perhaps I should be doing that now. Maybe I'm meant to be a mother.'

'That's a convenient way out, isn't it?'

'Well, you've made it clear you want kids before too long.'

'Yes, but you're not going to be a stay-at-home mother.'

'What? But what about taking care of the kids?'

'That's what childcare's for.'

'You can't send tiny babies to childcare. That's cruel. They need to be with their mother or father.' Alice felt an icy chill run right through her.

'Plenty of studies have shown that children in care from a young age develop superior social skills and increased independence, Alice.'

'You can't be serious, David.'

'I'm very serious,' he said, clearly missing the disgust in her voice.

'I'm sure you'd find plenty of studies saying otherwise, too, if you looked.'

'Alice, I'm not interested in arguing with you. I really don't have the headspace for it right now. But you do raise a good point. Perhaps now is the perfect time for us to be having kids. Perhaps you should stop taking the pill. It'll probably take a while for you to be fertile after being on it for years, anyway.'

'Oh. Right. Okay. Oh, shit, I'd better go. I've just realised I have soup on the stove and it's about to boil over,' she lied.

'Okay. I don't know why you didn't just use the microwave, but anyway. Speak to you again soon. Take care.'

'You too. Enjoy your hotel.' Alice hung up and sat staring at the phone. Who was this man? Not only were they not on the same page, they were clearly not even in the same library when it came to raising children. Four years. Again she wondered how they'd come to this point. What other serious issues were they diametrically opposed on? It didn't matter really, did it? There was no way Alice was letting a baby of hers go to childcare when she could be raising the child at home. She wasn't going to back down on this. No way. And David was unlikely to. So, there was only one course of action. She had to leave him. She would not have children with this man. She pulled Bill close, buried her face in his fur, and allowed a burst of tears of self-pity.

Chapter Thirty

'Oh my god, you're never going to guess what happened,' Lauren cried as soon as Alice opened the door.

'What?'

'I won a short story competition.'

'Wow! That's fantastic. Is it with the one about the girl in the alley? I loved that one.'

'That's the one.'

'Well done. I'm so excited for you,' Alice said, pulling Lauren into a hug. She was glad Lauren was too distracted to comment on her tired, haggard appearance. She was well dressed in jeans and a crisp, oversized white shirt, but she knew her eyes were red from tears and lack of sleep. If she didn't know Lauren needed her moral support at the auction today, she might have cancelled. She hadn't wanted to leave Bill, as she was feeling particularly clingy about him since her conversation with David and the realisation that they were over. She really did feel it was now herself and Bill alone against the world, and she didn't want to let him out of her sight.

Lauren shuffled her feet on the path.

'Look at you, you're a ball of energy,' Alice said with a laugh.

'Sorry, can't help myself. I'm so bloody excited, I'm jumping out of my skin.'

'It's brilliant news. I hope it's inspired you to send off some others – you must have practically a drawer full of stories by now. The one about the girl who found the precious brooch at the op shop was awesome too. Oh, and the one about the guy who falls asleep on the tram and wakes ... well you know what happens. I've loved them all.'

'Thanks. I have, actually, sent both of those off. I'm finally being brave and putting myself out there. Eek,' Lauren said, cringing.

'That's great. As I've said a million times, I think the world needs to read Lauren Finmore. And I am not saying that just because I'm your friend and clearly biased.'

'Well, fingers crossed. I hate the waiting game. It's excruciating.'

'Just think of it as waiting for an assignment to be graded.'

'Yeah. You're right. And no news is good news, isn't it?'

'Exactly.'

'Okay, I'd better get my brain around bidding now. Come on, we don't want to be late.'

'So how come you're only telling me about your win now? It's Saturday,' Alice said when they were in Lauren's car and snapping on their seatbelts. 'Why weren't we out celebrating with bubbles last night?'

'I only just found out. This morning. I guess it's the time difference – it's in the UK.'

'Trust you to have your debut success on the international stage. That's even better. Wow. How bloody awesome are you!'

'Well, it's thanks to you. And Brett. He's been fantastic too – so encouraging. I wouldn't have had the guts to pull my finger out and actually send my work anywhere if it weren't for you guys.'

'You're the one with the talent. You write beautifully and you've had distinctions or high distinctions for all your writing assignments. But I get that it might be scary to put your work into the big wide world.'

'Maybe doing so well at uni is a double-edged sword. I think I'm terrified of rejection.'

'That's pretty normal, isn't it? But, sadly, isn't being rejected a big part of the journey for a writer?'

'I guess. I need to toughen up, don't I?' said Lauren.

'I didn't say that. But hiding your wonderful work away isn't going to get you to where you want to be. And anyway, how will you be able to really appreciate the magnificent highs that I'm sure are on their way if you haven't had any lows?'

'I guess. That's wise. Thanks.'

'Ah, what sort of friend would I be if I didn't try to give you a gentle nudge out of your comfort zone?'

'Well, I appreciate it. Now, speaking of leaving one's comfort zone – I'm terrified about bidding.'

'You'll be fine. And I'll be right beside you for moral support.'

'As long as I remember Dad's limit and don't go over it, I'll be okay. But, god, I hate the thought of sticking a paddle up and shouting out a number or whatever you do and attracting everyone's attention.'

'It might be good practice for when you become an internationally famous literary figure and in high demand on your book tours.'

'Ha, ha, let's not get too ahead of ourselves. But I do appreciate your enthusiasm,' Lauren said. 'I don't think it's a very widely known competition.'

'It's widely known enough for you to have heard about it here in Australia, so don't downplay it! A win's a win. It's not an honourable mention or highly commended, it's an actual win. First place. Okay?'

'I'm pretty chuffed, to be honest,' Lauren said. 'Now, how are you about seeing Carmel?'

'Perfectly fine.'

'Really?'

'Yep. All good. I told you, I'm cured.' *I have so many other, more important, worries today, but we won't go into that ...* 'Don't you worry about me. You stay focussed on not going over your budget.'

'Yes, god. Oh, look, some people have brought their dogs along,' Lauren said as they walked towards the property. 'We should have brought Bill.'

'He would have loved it, but I don't think the owners would want dogs trotting through their pristine home – and I want to have a stickybeak.'

'Okay, brace yourself,' Lauren said in a whisper. 'Here's Carmel.'

Alice plastered on a beaming smile as they joined the end of the line to register to take a look through the house before the auction got underway. 'Hi, Carmel,' she said brightly when it was her turn to give her name and mobile number before going inside.

'Alice. Well, hello. Buying another house, are we?'

'No, my friend Lauren is here to bid today,' Alice said, indicating Lauren.

'Lauren Finmore,' Lauren said.

'Finmore. Now why is that name familiar? Have you bought from me before?'

'No, but you might have come across my father, Charles Finmore. He's invested in a few properties, so it wouldn't surprise me if you know of him. I'm here on his behalf today.'

'Ooh. I hope you'll be successful. Welcome, welcome.'

'Thank you.'

'You've chosen a great property. It's five bedroom, four bathroom with a ...'

'Yes, I'm fully aware of its many attributes, thank you,' Lauren said, cutting Carmel off.

Alice marvelled at Lauren's professional tone.

'Excellent. Well, good luck with the bidding,' Carmel said. 'Alice,' she added in a dismissive tone bordering on disgust.

'Actually, Carmel, could I please have a word? In private?' Alice found herself saying.

'As you can see, Alice, Talia and I are very busy. Aren't we, Talia?' Carmel said, placing a hand on her assistant's shoulder. The young woman seemed to cringe and purse her lips. Suddenly Alice realised Talia was actually Paul's executive assistant. The poor woman looked to be there under sufferance, too. Alice hoped she was being paid for giving up her Saturday.

'It will only take a moment.'

'Right. Anything you want to say can be said right here. I don't have time for silly covert discussions. Hurry up.'

'Okay, then.' Alice tried to look as if she wasn't taking a deep breath before continuing. 'I'd like a reference from you, please, Carmel,' she said boldly.

'You'd like a what?' Carmel let out a laugh that was more like a sneer.

'A reference, please.'

'After only four weeks or so, and leaving me in the lurch like that. You can't be serious?'

'I am, Carmel. Very.'

'Why would I give you a reference? You weren't made of tough enough stuff, Alice. You were useless. What would you expect me to say in this reference – I take it you want a *good* reference?' And there was another smirk.

'Obviously,' Alice said, her hand by her side itching to slap the smug bitch – something she'd never felt before about anyone. She was barely holding her anger in, but she was determined to.

'Well, you've got some nerve, I'll give you that, Alice.'

'And you're a bully, Carmel. You were dreadful to work for,' Alice said calmly.

'Oh come on, Alice, just because you couldn't handle the fast pace of real estate.'

'That had nothing to do with it, and you know it. I was damned good at my job. So, you won't give me a reference – a good reference?'

'I don't see why I should.'

'Perhaps because if you don't you might hear from my solicitor about a lawsuit. I know I was the latest in a long line of PAs who left you. It wasn't just me. I was good at my job, but you sabotaged me. Why, I have no idea.' Alice was now really struggling to keep her voice even and both hands by her side.

'Oh, Alice, you poor deluded thing. And I suppose you thought you were clever warning that Rhys fellow about working for me, too. It makes no difference. There's an ocean full of people wanting to learn from the great Carmel Gold. In fact, you'll want to watch yourself. You're in public. I might instigate a lawsuit of my own – for defamation.'

'The truth always wins, Carmel, and always comes out in the end. Anyway, what harm would it do to you to give me a reference and help me get another job?'

'My reputation, Alice. I can't put my name to a reference recommending sub-standard employees.'

'Which you know damned well I certainly am not. So, the answer is no, is it, Carmel? Is that your final word, just to be clear?'

'Yes, Alice, that's my final word. Now go away and let me get on with what I do best. And I warn you,' she added in a hiss, with her mouth now very close to Alice's ear, 'don't you mess with me.'

'Oh, Carmel, you really are a piece of work. You might think you're somebody because you're rich and drive a flash car, but it's all a façade. You think you can look down on people, put them down. I hope, for your sake, when karma bites you it's less than what you deserve, because you're a nasty piece of work.'

'Are you quite finished, Alice?' Carmel said, pleasantly. But underneath the thick layer of makeup and false smile, Alice could see she was unsettled. It was barely noticeable, but it seemed the impeccably presented woman was struggling as much as Alice was to hold it together.

'Yes, Carmel, I'm quite finished, thank you. I hope you get a good price for the property today and I wish you all the very best.' And with that, Alice turned on her heel and stepped away with Lauren following.

'Oh my god, that was awesome!' Lauren said when they were out of Carmel's hearing and heading into the house.

'I'm shaking,' Alice said.

'Well, on the outside you look very composed.'

'That's good, because I feel queasy.'

'Seriously? Because we can go if you need to.'

'No way, you've got a property to view and then bid on. I'll be okay. I'm sorry I …'

'Don't you dare apologise. It needed saying.'

'But it won't help. She won't give me a reference.'

'No, but at least you asked, and told her what you thought of her. I'm so impressed, Alice. That took some serious guts.'

'I'd feel better if I thought I'd achieved something other than humiliating myself. She'll be royally pissed off with me saying all that in public. Did you see how many people were lined up behind us?'

'Well, you did give her the option of speaking in private. Come on, I need to have a good look at this place.'

'It's beautiful. Will your parents live here if you get it?'

'No. It'll be just another investment for Dad's portfolio.'

Just another investment. Wow, Alice thought.

*

'Well, that was an anticlimax,' Lauren said as they made their way back to her car when the auction was over. 'I'm glad I got to bid at least. It'll make it easier for next time.'

'God, how about Carmel trying so desperately to get you to up your limit,' Alice said. 'She really wasn't happy you wouldn't budge.'

'Yeah. It was satisfying to say no to her, anyway. I bet she doesn't hear that word very often. I'm also glad I didn't add to her coffers.'

'I wonder if putting the reserve so high was arrogance on her part or the vendor's.'

'No idea, but they'll be pissed off that it was passed-in. It was way over-priced.'

'Why would they do that?'

'Probably it's an investment property that they didn't need to offload, but would if the price was right,' Lauren said. 'Greed.

That's my guess. Still, it seems an awful lot of expense to go through if you're not serious ...'

'It didn't look to me like the last bidder was keen to negotiate, either, so it might have been a waste all round.'

'Oh well, there are plenty more properties out there,' said Lauren. 'I pity that woman with Carmel who had to give up her Saturday. She didn't look best pleased. With that look on her face I doubt she'll last long. Her latest PA, do you think?'

'Oh no, she's Paul, the CEO's PA – bribed handsomely, no doubt.'

'Well, I hope she's smart enough to figure out Carmel and report back to the other managers.'

'Here's hoping.'

'Thanks for coming to keep me company.'

'No worries. Any time.'

'I need ice-cream now, to commiserate, and then you're going to tell me why you're so glum,' Lauren said.

'What? I ...'

'I know you think you've done a very good job of putting on a brave face, but you were decidedly sad and tired when I picked you up, or hungover. And as you didn't demand we drive through Maccas on the way, I'm guessing you haven't been over-indulging on the alcohol.'

'You know me too well,' Alice said with a sigh.

'Right, hold that thought until we have fortifying ice-cream,' Lauren said, getting into the car.

As they drove away, Alice thought how lucky she was to have Lauren. Talking to her wise, level-headed friend, who always knew the right thing to say and when, seemed to make whatever her current problem was just that little bit more manageable. Though today's was the biggest problem she'd ever discussed with her.

After buying their ice-cream at a little café on Toorak Road, they found a parking spot alongside the Botanic Gardens and then a bench overlooking the lake. It was a magical place to sit with the sun on their backs with the ducks gliding peacefully in front of them.

'Mmm,' Lauren said, closing her eyes and sucking on her small plastic spoon. 'Best ice-cream in the world.'

'Yep. I concur,' Alice said. 'Did your dad mind too much missing out on the house?' Alice knew Lauren had texted him and that she'd had a reply.

'No, he's a go-with-the-flow kind of guy. If it's meant to be it's meant to be, and all that,' she said with a shrug.

'Ah, so that's where you get it?'

'Yeah, but I'm more highly strung than him. I blame the streak of creativity – the passion,' she added theatrically, and waved her spoon about.

'I'm so thrilled for you about your short story. That's huge. I can't believe you're so calm about it.'

'Well, I guess it's a bit anticlimactic as well. It's like, right, okay, that's great, but now what? I don't know. Weird, huh?'

'No idea. I've never won anything.'

'Yes you did, you were asked to join that honour society because you got such high marks at uni, remember?'

'Oh, yeah. Right, I see. It's a fleeting feeling of accomplishment and then almost instantly back to business as usual. Is that what you're feeling?'

'I guess. Maybe it's shock, and it's still to hit me. Perhaps it's relief – no, that's not the right way to put it. But I feel like, well, bloody hell *finally* someone's taking my writing seriously. Thank you very much!'

'Yes, I can see that. But, really, you've only just started sending them out.'

'I know. But it doesn't stop me wanting more – and now! It's like a door has opened a crack and I desperately need to see what's on the other side. I'm so annoyed with myself for being such a wimp and not putting myself, my work, out there sooner.'

'You've done it now and that's brilliant.'

'Well, I'm determined to make the most of this little success. Thank Christ I've got Mum and Dad funding me!'

'It must be nice to have a family who encourages your dreams … That sounded woe-is-me. I didn't mean to.'

'I know. I wish you had a generous family too. I'm blessed. And you're allowed to be a little envious, but just don't hate me.'

'Oh no, I'm not. I'm …'

'I was kidding, Alice. Chill. Okay, so speaking of lack of support, I'm guessing something else has happened with David.'

'I don't want to talk about it. We're always on about my stupid problems.'

'Alice, your problems are never stupid, or trivial. And you're not getting out of it. Unless you really don't want to talk about it.'

Alice didn't reply and they silently finished their ice-creams. Runners jogged past not far behind them, their feet making rhythmic scratching sounds on the gravel path. Nearby, birds squawked in delight. Alice detected the fresh scent of pine and the earthiness of freshly laid mulch as a gust of wind swept around them while she tried to form her opening words.

'I need to find somewhere for Bill and me to live. I have to leave David,' she finally said.

'Oh, Alice, I'm so sorry. Did something else happen or have you just decided?'

'Both. I realised he doesn't get me and he never will. Hell, I don't think he gets humans, full stop. I can't believe I've wasted all these years on him,' she said, swiping at a lone tear rolling slowly down her cheek.

'It's never a waste if you learn something and use what you've learnt.'

'But I seem to keep making the same mistakes. This is the second relationship that hasn't worked.'

'Don't you dare say you're a failure. A relationship takes two, and some people change while others stay the same – some grow and some stagnate,' Lauren said. 'Are you sure it's not just a phase? Could it be your grief over losing Ruth and all the emotional stuff around Carmel? Don't forget having too much time for thinking while you're unemployed won't be helping, either.'

'You know, I think all that's helped, actually. It's highlighted just how different our priorities are. And, yes, I'm sure – sure I need to leave David, that is.'

'Okay. Definite is good. David's away, isn't he? So now we need to find you and Bill somewhere to live – preferably before he gets back. Come on, let's go and do some investigating and make some calls.'

'Thanks, Lauren, you're the best.'

Chapter Thirty-one

Alice had to hurry to the pub so she wasn't late for lunch with her friends from uni. She had lost track of time at the park with Bill. She'd been ambling along, chewing over her decision and the ramifications. Of course it would be easier to stay with David, but the more she thought about her situation, the more she felt stifled. Sure, she'd be poor – hopefully not for too long – but she could pursue whatever occupation and enrol in any courses she wanted to without question. Would she go back and do honours or masters in History? She wasn't sure. First she had to find somewhere to live and a way to pay the bills. When she started to think about how hard it all was she reminded herself that plenty of people had done this very thing and survived just fine. As she had done after she'd split up with Rick. That thought didn't help, though. Picking herself up and dusting herself off after her marriage break-up had been hard, and she wished she didn't have that experience to tell her what was ahead.

The reality was, if she didn't do this she was selling herself short. And she was young – well, young-ish. Deep down Alice knew if she didn't leave now then she'd have this same dilemma in a few years' time anyway. Because if she'd learnt anything from this year, it was that she couldn't let herself be unhappy. She would not stay in a miserable situation long-term again. She had stayed so long with Rick because her mother and sister had brainwashed her to believe that a failed marriage equalled failure as a person, and that it would be a disgrace to the family. The jibes, pursed lips and spoken and unspoken criticism and put-downs had only just been bearable when she compared them with the alterative of staying with Rick for the next fifty years – or taking an even more drastic way out, as her father had done. At least this time she wouldn't be around the gossipmongers or her family.

Brett had been right when he'd said the notion that family is everything could be so wrong. Alice was now seeing how her life had been influenced by her family and their insecurities. Thank goodness she'd left Hope Springs when she had. Imagine where she'd be if she'd stayed … She shuddered at the thought. Although perhaps ignorance really was bliss. Olivia didn't seem to have a clue about what she'd become and what she was surrounded by – she lived life blissfully unaware.

Perhaps that's my problem, Alice thought as she pushed open the pub door. *I've seen too much out beyond Hope Springs. I'm just too big for my boots, as my mother would say.*

She suddenly had the thought, *I wonder if Olivia hates me because she's her mother's puppet or because I escaped.* Too heavy for today, she decided and took a deep breath.

Alice stopped short at seeing Helen sitting at their table in the corner with Rhys. *Oh god. Not her.* Alice's heart sank. She really wasn't up to dealing with Helen's holier-than-thou smugness or blunt comments, or hearing about her perfect life today. Nonetheless, she waved and smiled.

'Hello,' she called and sat down next to Rhys. 'Hi, Rhys, you've obviously met Helen. I'm so glad you could come,' she said. 'I'm really sorry, I was hoping to be a bit earlier so you wouldn't be here alone.'

'It's okay. I haven't been here long. And the barman pointed me to the right table.'

'I think I arrived only a minute or two later,' Helen said. 'We've been here just long enough for about three sips of beer,' she said cheerfully. 'We decided on a jug and I have enough glasses for everyone. Can I pour you one?'

'Yes, please, that would be lovely,' Alice said, accepting the beer and taking a long sip. 'Thanks, Helen, just what I needed.'

'Thanks very much for including me, Alice,' Rhys said.

'Ah, no worries – the more the merrier. How are you?'

'I'm getting serious about going back to uni. I went and saw the admissions people the other day.'

'That's great. Well done.'

'How about you, Alice? Any news?' Rhys asked.

'Hang on. Hold that thought,' Alice said as Brett and Lauren arrived hand in hand. *They really do make a lovely couple*, she thought, smiling warmly at them. Before she realised what she was doing, she'd leapt up and was hugging them both.

'Helen's here,' she whispered into Lauren's ear.

'Yes, I can see that. It'll be fine. You'll be fine. Safety in numbers,' Lauren whispered back, before releasing Alice from their friendly embrace.

'How's your house hunting going, Alice?' Lauren asked after Rhys had been introduced to her and Brett and they'd all sat down. 'Any news?'

'Nope. And you'll be the first to know.'

'Didn't you just buy a house?' Helen asked. 'Or did that fall through?'

'Yes, we did. But I'm moving – on my own. I'm leaving David.'
She tried to keep the defensiveness in check. 'So, if you know of
any rooms going cheap – and any well-paid admin jobs, too, for
that matter – let me know.'

'Oh dear, you sound like you're going through a rough time,'
Helen said.

'You could say that.'

'I've put a notice up on each of the boards at our faculty,' Brett
said, jumping in.

'Thanks, Brett. Though the idea of a share house gives me the
shivers.'

'Yes, I would have thought you'd be a little past that,' Helen said.

'Not all share houses are parties every night and lounge rooms
full of overflowing ashtrays and empties rolling around,' Rhys
said. 'Mine happens to be tidy and clean. We are also a very well-
mannered bunch.'

'Is there room for one more?' Alice enquired.

'Sorry, I'm afraid not, but I'll ask around. What did you decide
about the career change we discussed?'

'Ooh, what's this?' Helen said.

'Rhys thought I'd make a good counsellor or psychologist, but
I'm not sure I want to start over with a new degree, and I'm pretty
sure I don't want to listen to people's problems day in day out.'

'Pity. I think you'd be great. You're very kind and level-headed,'
Helen said before putting her glass to her lips again.

'Oh. Thanks, Helen.'

'But I do agree it could become exasperating and draining.
I don't think you're really free to give your *actual* opinion a lot
of the time,' Helen said. 'You're meant to simply guide people
into figuring things out for themselves, which could take aeons,

and if you're like me you'd lose patience and want to jump in and help.'

'Yep, I'd be exactly like that,' Alice said, feeling a warmth towards Helen that she hadn't experienced before.

'How about physiotherapy? That's a helpful occupation,' Brett said.

'I think you have to be a certain type of person to push people through the pain barrier, especially when doing serious rehabilitation,' Rhys said with a shrug. 'It could be a really hard job until you had a few years' experience.'

'What about History? I thought you loved it when you studied History at uni,' Helen said.

'I think I was kidding myself. There aren't any related jobs that I can get into at my level.'

'What else interests you?' she asked. 'What did you think about doing when you were a child or a teenager?'

'I had my heart set on running the family business – it's a corner shop, a small supermarket really – with Dad. But after he died my mother decided to hand it over to my younger sister, so … It was all I'd ever thought about and wanted.'

'That must have felt like an awful betrayal,' Helen said.

'Yes, and it didn't help that my mother never actually encouraged me to do anything else beyond getting married and having kids, well, not that I recall, anyway.'

'Wow, I thought you young things had escaped such antiquated notions. It's sad that it hasn't really changed,' Helen said.

'Well, it probably has elsewhere, but the small country town I'm from is a bit behind the times.'

'*Society* is behind the times when it comes to women's rights and equality. But don't get me started,' Helen said.

'Did you all know what you wanted to do early on?' Alice asked. 'I know Lauren's always wanted to be a writer.'

'Yup, since I was about seven,' Lauren said. 'Though I'm beginning to think being clear about what you want isn't much of a help either. It doesn't always mean you'll get there.'

'I knew I wanted to nut things out from the age of about twelve, and engineering seemed to be the logical path,' Brett said. 'But my parents didn't really encourage me to do anything, either. I was just lucky I had the right teachers – people who were passionate and committed. That's the curse of being the child of a narcissistic parent. They sabotage you or ignore you in case you show them up – well, that's my interpretation from what I've read, anyway.'

'Hmm. Helen, what about you?'

'I always wanted to be a teacher. And I did teach. Briefly.' Alice looked at her with surprise. She'd assumed Helen had always been a professional student. 'I loved it, but couldn't stand the politics and not being able to properly discipline the kids. The parents seemed to think we were there to teach their darlings manners, actually do the job of raising them. Not my responsibility. Fortunately I have a wonderfully supportive husband who has done well and we can afford for me to do as I wish. Don't worry, I know how blessed I am.'

'Rhys is thinking about going back to architecture after a break, aren't you?' Alice said.

'Yes, after a bit of a wobble. It's what I've wanted to do since I was ten, but life sort of got in the way for a while.'

'Good for you,' Helen said.

'Why can't I figure out what to do now?' Alice said, her frustration bubbling to the surface. 'It's driving me nuts.'

'It sounds to me as if you're trying too hard to figure it out – overthinking it,' Helen said.

'But how else do I find it?'

'Sometimes the best thing you can do is nothing at all. I know it can be hard to sit back and wait, but often the best ideas come when we least expect them, and when we're at our calmest and our brains are still,' Brett said. 'Like in the shower, walking, or sitting on the train staring out the window. Right, Lauren?'

'Absolutely.'

'Hang on, why all this talk about finding a new career? Didn't you just start a job in real estate? What happened to that?' Helen said.

'It didn't work out.' *Oh god. Please don't make me go through it all again.*

'Ah, well that explains why you can be here on a Friday again. I just realised what day it is.'

'Alice was subjected to workplace bullying,' Lauren explained.

'Yes, by a narcissistic psychopath, by the sounds of it,' Brett added.

'Really? Wow, I didn't think tall, beautiful creatures like you got picked on – I thought that was left for short, dumpy, plain Janes like me.'

'Um, well, I …' Alice stammered, blushing.

'Oh, don't get me wrong, it's not that I don't believe you, it's just a bit surprising. All the pretty girls – the *cool* group – were the ones doing the bullying when I was at school. Just thinking about high school gives me the horrors. For it to happen to you in a workplace … No wonder you're feeling out of sorts. Bullies might not leave bruises for the world to see your pain, but they certainly can mess with your mind,' Helen said.

'Yup. That's right. I'm pretty much a mess all round,' Alice said. She tried to be light, but was shocked to find tears suddenly springing from her eyes. She gulped them back and wiped her face with her paper serviette from the table. 'Sorry, I'm fine, well, other than my life being a disaster, obviously,' she said with a weak smile.

'It sounds to me as if you need a holiday, a break away, so you can get yourself back to feeling positive and excited about the future,' Helen said. 'That's the only way you'll attract good things into your life. It's about the law of attraction.'

'The what?' Alice asked.

'Look it up – the law of attraction. I swear by it. Also, feng shui. Even if you don't believe positioning things in certain places can make any real difference to your life, I don't think you can go wrong with being tidy and clutter-free – tidy life, tidy mind and all that. Here,' she said, writing some notes on a beer coaster and handing it to Alice.

'Thanks.'

'Things will turn around, you'll see. But you have to do your best to give them the opportunity.'

'God, do you know how frustrating it is to keep hearing that!' Alice said, her emotions boiling over again. 'Sorry, but at the moment it really doesn't feel like anything is all right or ever will be again.'

'You have to believe in yourself and put your faith in the universe – it has your back. It might not seem like it at times, but it does. Always. Just don't let yourself sink too far into self-pity for too long,' Helen said.

Thank Christ she didn't say, 'Have faith in God.' I might have actually hit her, Alice thought.

'You just need a glimmer of positivity and to then focus on that. But you need to be open to seeing that glimmer,' Helen added.

'I don't think we should be afraid of change, or of changing, but afraid of being the same person in the same place fifty years from now,' Brett said. 'It's hard when it feels like the whole world is against you, but believe me, things do end and make space for better things. You just need to try to keep an open mind. I've been there.'

'Don't forget, you're also grieving, Alice,' Lauren said. 'You need to be kind to yourself and just *be* for a bit.'

'Pretty bloody hard when your partner is an unemotional prick who thinks you should buck up and suck up a job you hate just for the money.'

'Oh, well, I'd be getting a new one of those. That's not on,' Helen said. 'You're much better being on your own without that sort of pressure. Seriously, Alice, and I hope this doesn't sound too harsh, but you need to start making decisions for yourself. The sooner you realise you can only truly rely on yourself for your wellbeing and happiness and that knights in shining armour, that doesn't eventually tarnish, are rare, if not non-existent, the better off you'll be.'

'Yes,' Brett said, 'if what you say is true about your mother possibly being a narcissist and your sister being the golden child, then as the scapegoat you most likely grew up feeling unloved.'

'*Actually* unloved,' Helen added. 'Narcissists are incapable of true love. And you've most likely felt pressured into conforming – in all sorts of areas. And I'll bet no matter what you achieve in life you'll never feel quite good enough. You'll spend your life seeking your mother's approval despite knowing you'll never get it, and going through the hurt of her rejection and disapproval over and over. Also, there's a high chance until you heal you'll always choose a man who will never love you properly – because you've never had the chance to learn what proper love is, thanks to your cold, unemotional mother.'

Alice looked up, unable to hide her astonished expression.

'Oh, yes, I know all about having a narcissistic mother. Once you figure it out and how it's affected you, you can start to heal and really sort yourself out. It's about breaking free and truly becoming your own person.'

'At least limit your contact and don't tell your family anything about your life, because then they have nothing to criticise,' Brett said.

'Yes, turn conversations back to them,' Helen said. 'Narcissists love nothing more than talking about themselves and how good they are.'

Alice looked at Brett then Helen and quietly said, 'I'm tired.'

'I'm not surprised. You're constantly navigating a minefield,' Helen said.

'Oh god, tell me about it,' Brett said. 'And, Alice, you shouldn't have anything to do with anyone your family is in contact with either. Just the other day my uncle told me I couldn't cut my father completely out of my life because it was hurtful – *to my father*. What about all the hurt he's caused me over my lifetime? But, as you said, Helen, I didn't have the bruises. Sticks and stones will break my bones, but names will never hurt me – what a crock of shit that is! And then he got affronted when I said I wanted nothing more to do with him for being one of my father's flying monkeys. Didn't get it. I wasn't going to waste my breath and energy explaining that by approaching me he was clearly doing my father's bidding – whether intentionally or because he'd been cleverly manipulated. Sorry, here I go getting on my soapbox. It's all just so incredibly awful.'

'Yes, and as I said earlier, there are a lot of narcissists and manipulators,' Helen said.

Lauren leant forward, about to say something when her phone rang. 'Excuse me, I need to take this,' she said, looking down at the name on the screen.

'I need the loo,' Alice said, getting up. *And a good weep.*

She'd hoped to come out for a friendly meal and time away from her problems and the reality of the sad state of her life. And look where she was. She stood staring into the mirror. Her thoughts were spinning underneath a growing headache. Hopefully their meals would arrive soon and the mood would become lighter. But it was nice to have the support of the others and not feel so alone.

She returned to the table just as Lauren came back and sat down.

'That was Dad,' she said to Alice. 'Um,' she continued. 'I have a proposition for you – and, well, a favour, actually.'

'Oh?'

'Mum and Dad have decided to stay on overseas – spend a couple of weeks looking around Asia. But if they don't have someone in the house by Tuesday their home and contents insurance will be null and void. Dad's a real stickler for doing the right thing and not taking risks with those sorts of things. Anyway, I really don't want to go back to Ballarat. Would you be interested in housesitting for us for a couple of weeks? And of course Bill is more than welcome ...'

'My dog,' Alice said as Helen's mouth dropped open in slight surprise.

'You wouldn't have to move out after the two weeks are up. Dad said he and Mum would be happy for you to stay on as long as you like when they get back. There's plenty of room in the main house and there's a self-contained cottage, too, if you'd prefer to stay there.'

'Oh. Right. Wow. Um.'

'You don't have to decide this very second,' Lauren said. 'And, no pressure, but you would be doing me a huge favour. I really don't want to leave Brett,' she said, clasping his hand on top of the table. Brett squeezed her hand back and for a few seconds they gazed adoringly into each other's eyes, seemingly oblivious of everyone else around them.

'I don't want you to, either, but we'd cope,' Brett said. 'I could come and visit on weekends.'

'No, it's fine. I'd love to go to Ballarat,' said Alice.

'Would you? Really?'

'Of course. You've been such a good friend to me, of course I'd be happy to help you out. And it's not exactly an imposition – it's a win for me, too.'

'Thank you,' Lauren said, smiling.

'Oh, wow. No, Thank *you*,' Alice said, the magnitude of what had happened starting to sink in.

'I'll come with you and help get you settled, though, so don't worry about that.'

'I don't want to put you out – I could just catch the train, couldn't I?'

'Not really. We're rural – a little way out of the city, so it would be a bit tricky.'

'Oh, but I don't have a car for getting groceries and stuff.'

'That's okay. Dad said you're welcome to use one of their cars – he's going to get you listed on the insurance.'

'That's very generous of him. Are you sure he'll really be okay about it? I'd be very careful and only do the minimum driving.'

'Alice, seriously, it's cool. They're cool. And, remember, you're doing us a favour too.'

'Well, I really appreciate it.'

'I know you do.'

'I'd say that's just what you need, Alice – a proper break away with a complete change of scenery,' Helen said.

'Apparently "Ballarat" is an Aboriginal word for "resting place", so it's practically an order to take it easy, which is clearly what you need right now,' Rhys said.

'Oh, how perfect is that? See, things are looking up already, Alice,' Helen said. 'The universe is starting to listen and show you signs that it is.'

'Wow. Thanks again *so* much, Lauren – and to your mum and dad.' Alice felt a little light-headed. 'Now, can we please stop talking about me? We need to celebrate Lauren's short story winning an award and her first publication,' Alice said.

'That's fantastic, Lauren. Well done,' Helen said.

'Yes, brilliant,' said Rhys.

There were hugs and cheers all round, which died down when their meals were delivered.

After lunch they all leant back in their chairs feeling satisfied. Conversation had slowed as they allowed their food to digest. During a moment of silence a ding from a phone rang out, causing them all to cock their heads as each tried to detect if it had come from their device. They'd often joked about how they were glued to their phones, and how hard it was to ignore a notification and how long they lasted trying – not very. They chuckled when there was a burst of several different tones.

'Oh, go on, kids, check your phones. I know you want to,' Helen said with a laugh. She was the only non-millennial in the group. 'I don't mind, honestly. It's not like we're engrossed in deep and meaningful conversation now. I'm just deliberating over whether I need to undo the button on my jeans or not.'

'Apologies for my rudeness, but I need to keep an eye on my email. I'll be two secs,' Brett said, turning over his phone, which was sitting on the table.

'Yeah, I need to keep an eye out, too,' Lauren said, 'in case Dad needs to tell me anything else.'

Alice turned her phone over as well, and was staring at her screen where notification details of an incoming email were visible: *Carmel – subject: reference …*

Her eyes were wide and her lips were frozen around a silent 'O'.

'What?' Lauren said, nudging Alice.

'Sorry?' Alice said, jolted from her trance.

'You look like you've seen a ghost.'

Alice turned the phone around so Lauren could clearly see what was on the screen.

'Oh! Well, come on, open it.'

'What? What is it?' Helen and Brett said in unison.

Lauren read out the name and subject on the screen, and Rhys gave a low whistle.

'I'm too scared to. What if it's her telling me to fuck off or giving me a serve about how dare I even ask for a reference after everything, blah, blah, blah – having the last word. What if she's actually sent me a virus or something?'

'You won't know unless you look,' Helen said. 'Who are we talking about, anyway? Who's Carmel?'

'The bully boss we were talking about earlier,' Lauren said.

'Oh! Right! Go on then.'

'I think Carmel Gold would value her reputation far too much to be bothered with anything sinister. Well, you'd hope so,' Lauren said. 'Though, I understand your paranoia after everything she's put you through. How about you just open it?'

'Okay,' Alice said. 'Right.' She read the email to herself quickly and then aloud. '"Dear Alice, Please find attached a reference, as requested. I still don't think you deserve it, but I don't wish to stand in the way of you getting another job thanks to a personality clash. I'm not one to hold grudges. I wish you all the best with your future employment. Regards, Carmel." And now for the attachment.' Alice blinked several times and read it through twice to herself before fully comprehending the words and the enormity of them.

'Here we go. "To Whom It May Concern, Alice Hamilton worked for me as executive personal assistant at Gold, Taylor and Murphy Real Estate for a period of four weeks, having agreed at short notice to fill in an urgent vacancy due to illness. We remain extremely grateful to Alice for jumping into what was a demanding role in a new industry for her. She performed admirably and exceeded all our expectations here at Gold, Taylor and Murphy. Alice showed great attention to detail, exceptional organisational skills and sound initiative. It's unfortunate that we didn't have a full-time role to offer her at the end of her brief time here, but commend her to any future employer looking for a highly skilled, top-level administrative employee. Alice has a bright future ahead of her and we believe she will excel in whatever path or industry she chooses and be a great asset to whichever organisation she partners with. Regards, Carmel Gold (Partner) and Paul Taylor (CEO)." And they've both signed it.'

'I thought it was a permanent role and you left abruptly,' Brett said.

'I did. "Temporary position to fill" is stretching the truth. A lot.'

'But at least it solves the gap in your résumé,' Lauren said.

'Why wouldn't you just leave it out – make it just look like you were still looking for work? What's four weeks in the scheme of things?' Helen said.

'I know it seems like nothing, but I can't lie, not when it could come back to seriously bite me, which I think something like this definitely could.' *Especially now I'm back to being the straight-down-the-line Alice I was before Carmel.*

'Okay. Fair enough, I guess,' Helen said with a shrug and picked up her refilled glass of beer.

'Did you know she was going to send you a reference?' Rhys said.

'Well, I'd hoped. I bailed her up at an auction the other day.'

'You should have seen how gutsy she was,' Lauren said. 'She all but roared at Carmel, but remained very professional. It was. awesome.'

'See, something else good has happened, Alice. Your life is really starting to turn around now you're taking control and making some changes and decisions for yourself,' Helen said.

'Who would have thought,' Alice said. 'She's clearly done it under sufferance, though.'

'Perhaps Paul or his PA wrote it and made her sign it,' Lauren said.

'Oh well, it doesn't matter – it's bankable, as they say. Though, it won't really help since I can't even seem to get any responses from my job applications, let alone requests for referee details.'

'Don't wait for that; send this reference with any applications,' Helen said.

'Oh, is that the right thing to do, if they don't ask?'

'Sure, why not. Unless they won't accept attachments. And even then you should be able to insert it into the body of the email.

It's supporting evidence. It would be so rare these days to have a written reference – beyond a basic statement of employment – it would probably give you an edge.'

'Just follow your instincts in all situations and you can't go wrong, Alice,' Lauren said.

'Maybe having this will make you feel more confident about your applications and you'll come across better, and that'll help you get noticed,' Helen said. 'Seriously, it's all about picturing and *feeling* the desired outcome. It's not silly, well, to some it probably is, but *I* say you can't go wrong with being positive. When you smile, others around you smile – it's catching. It's the same with what you want. What you put out you get back.'

'God, it's actually a huge relief to get it and I do feel more confident about applying for jobs. Admin is all I really know, so I'll keep looking for something there. Well, I guess in Ballarat. Okay. I wonder what the work situation is there.'

'No idea, but it won't be hard to find out,' Lauren said.

'It's been lovely, but I really need to get going,' Helen said when they'd finished their second jug of beer. She got up and put a hand on Alice's shoulder. 'I believe everything happens for a reason, Alice. I wonder if the answers for your future can be found in your recent experience of having a bully for a boss and discovering the truth about your mother. It's one thing to learn and overcome, another to use the experience for the good of others,' she said thoughtfully.

'Um. Yes. Thanks, Helen,' Alice said, trying to take in the words amidst the flurry of everyone getting up and gathering their things ready to leave.

'Yes, I'd better be off, too,' Rhys said.

'It was great to meet you, Rhys. I hope next time we see you you'll be settled back into uni life,' Helen said.

'Yes, good luck, Rhys. It was lovely to meet you. Stay in touch,' Lauren said.

'Good to meet you. Don't be a stranger,' Brett said. They all shook hands with Rhys, except Alice who drew him into a hug.

'I'm so pleased you're going back to study. You take good care. And feel free to call or message if you need a chat,' she said before releasing him.

'You too, Alice. I'm sure everything will work out fine. Thanks so much, everyone – I really appreciate it,' Rhys said. 'This has been great. Just what I needed.' And with a wave he left.

'All the very best, Alice. I mean that. I'll be thinking of you and sending lots of positive energy your way,' Helen said, giving her a tight hug.

'Thanks, Helen,' Alice said.

'I'll call or text you to finalise the details, but let's aim to leave around nine-thirty on Monday morning,' Lauren said when they were standing outside the pub on the footpath.

'Sounds good. The sooner the better for me. God, I'm excited, but I'm terrified about telling David.'

'Well, whatever you do, don't do it by phone or email,' Lauren said.

'No, I'd never do that,' Alice said, 'but my heart is hammering just at the thought.'

'When is he home?'

'Sunday night.'

'It's good that you're leaving the next morning and won't have to drag it out, and have the tension and awkward silence when you're passing each other in the hallway. What are you going to do with all your stuff – put it in storage here in Melbourne or bring it to Ballarat? There are plenty of outbuildings at the house, so you're welcome to bring it there and save on storage costs.'

'I don't really have anything besides my clothes and a few trea-sured knickknacks and Bill and his stuff,' Alice said.

'Oh. Really? Your house is full of nice things.'

'It's mostly David's taste.' Alice tried to rack her brain for what else she might want.

'Well, have a good look around and see. And you can always decide later, once your mind is clear and the emotional pain has subsided and you can think straight,' Lauren said.

'Alice, I don't want to be negative or scare-mongering, but it would also be a good idea to print out, scan or take photos of any paperwork relating to any assets and debts and any other financial matters, just in case you ever need to negotiate,' Brett said. 'David might let you take the odd bit of furniture later, but I bet he wouldn't be keen on giving you access to his superannua-tion statements or share records if it means suffering any financial loss – no matter how fair it is legally.'

'I'm pretty sure I'm just going to walk away,' Alice said.

'Honestly, Alice, that's not a decision you can really make right now. There's a two-year time limit to sort it out, so you don't have to decide yet,' Brett said.

'Well, then I can see later.'

'Yes, but what I'm saying is that *later* you might not have access to all the paperwork you might need. And don't think you can rely on honesty when it comes down to it. This is one time when I really think you need to be on the front foot. Just get the information. I'm not saying you have to use it – now or ever. I've just seen too many breakups that seemed perfectly amicable until it came to the money.'

'Okay. Thanks for the advice, Brett.'

'It's a good point, Alice. You need to get your fair share. Don't forget you told me that your divorce settlement paid for your uni fees.'

'Yeah, and part of the deposit for the house that's in David's name,' Alice mused.

'Exactly. So, don't try to be a martyr – that'll never get you anywhere,' Lauren said.

'Definitely get some evidence of your contributions, Alice,' Brett said. 'And don't forget, if it's not a joint account, the second you tell him you're leaving David might change the passwords and you'll lose all access. He could be fine, but he might also be pretty pissed off. I've met him a couple of times at the Christmas dinners, remember? He was okay, but I have to be honest, he did also seem very materialistic. He was completely obsessed with his BMW and kept bragging about the five-star hotels he'd stayed in. Those types of people tend to only really fight over one thing – money. I hope your situation is different, but you need to be prepared. Sorry to harp on, but I care about you.'

'And I really do appreciate it, Brett, it's just that it's a lot to think about. I need to go before my head bursts,' Alice said wearily.

'Hang in there, I'll be in touch,' Lauren said, hugging her. 'Call if you need anything.'

'Yes, and call me anytime too, especially if you need any heavy lifting done,' Brett said.

'There shouldn't be, but thanks,' Alice said.

As she made her way to the train station she started making a mental list of documents to print out or scan. On the train she put that list into her phone as a memo. While it was a task she didn't really want to do, she had to admit she felt good about having a focus and taking control of things – of her life. Her ex-husband Rick had deliberately held off being paid for assets he'd sold not long before ending their marriage so there was less money to divide between them. At the time Alice had just wanted to be free of him. She had the same feeling now, too, but she could see that was a little gutless. Lauren and Brett were right. At the moment it was hard to see past the blinding stupor of hurt, disappointment and heartbreak, but once the emotional fog cleared, who knew how she'd feel. Alice understood that she had to stand up and defend herself financially, at least get back what she'd put in.

Once home, she started making her way methodically through their filing system, which she'd set up. They had a drawer each. She felt deceitful going through David's, but it wasn't locked. She was shocked to find statements showing she'd paid two semesters of David's MBA course fees. God, she'd completely forgotten about that. And they wouldn't have this house if she hadn't added ten thousand dollars to the deposit to get them to the twenty percent threshold and avoid costly mortgage insurance. It wasn't a whole lot of money in David's world, but still …

Chapter Thirty-two

In between taking Bill for two long walks, Alice spent Saturday going through the paperwork and putting together a file of printed information to take with her. She really hoped she'd never need any of it, but Brett was right – it was a good idea to have it. She could see that now. While she liked to think David would be fair, the thought of the quote 'Money doesn't change anyone, it reveals them' kept her going. The reality was that while once she would have been sure David would be reasonable when it came to dealing with the financial aspects of a split, he was actually an unknown quantity when she thought about it now.

Sunday dawned and Alice felt completely wrecked. Constantly running through what she'd say to David and pre-empting responses to any questions or comments he might have had kept her awake all night. She hated conflict of any kind and she could just imagine his calm interrogation, which would be decidedly more unnerving than when Rick had yelled and screamed at her during their time together. But she told herself, as she lay in bed with Bill peering at her, waiting for the signal they might be off for a walk, it didn't matter. She was done. Perhaps the saddest thing was that it was so obvious why people stayed in a relationship and over time became like robots, without feelings or reactions, and just went through the motions. It was easier and less fraught than going it alone. And perhaps it was easier than telling one's narcissistic mother and enduring the criticism. Just the thought of that made Alice quiver all over like a scolded teenager.

Here we go again … At least they can't pierce you with their withering gazes this time around. You'll be about eleven hundred kilometres away.

Alice could almost imagine her mother trying to talk her into going back before anyone found out – just like she had when her marriage to Rick had imploded. She'd been so hurt by how little her mother had appeared to care about her feelings. Now she knew her mother better she realised that she most likely saw Alice as an extension of herself and really didn't care what her daughter was going through. Dawn was only concerned with the perceived humiliation she faced as Alice's mother; that she had raised a daughter who was incapable of abiding by the vows of 'until death do us part'.

Alice hoped this knowledge about her mother's personality might spare her some pain, and that she wouldn't take Dawn's cold comments to heart. But deep down she wasn't entirely optimistic. She'd spent far too many years seeking her mother's love and approval, only to be rejected, to truly believe it could be different now. Also, she knew that narcissists didn't change. They might be capable of temporarily appearing to be a different colour to blend in with their surroundings – like a chameleon or a Thorny Devil – but it wasn't permanent. Their true colours always returned.

Suddenly Alice realised that this time around she wouldn't have Ruth to smooth the waters of emotion, to encourage her, and to reassure her. Tears started streaming down her face. And then Bill was beside her, trying to snuggle between her and the pillow she was holding close like a teddy bear for comfort. *Yes, I'll have you, Bill. But how can I do this without Ruth?*

Would it be easier to stay with David? Yes, of course it would be. But that's not fair on you. You have a life to live, joy to be had. This is not the life you want, deserve. The words came from within her, but the sound was very much Ruth's gentle voice.

'I miss you,' Alice whispered.

'I'm right here,' she thought she heard back. But she couldn't have. Her mind was playing tricks. She was emotionally wrung-out.

I know my dad's with me, so why not Ruth?

So many times at university Alice had thought she couldn't do this essay or that exam until she reminded herself she was partly doing the degree for her father, who hadn't had the opportunity. And somehow she'd always find her way through. This was a little different, but she knew Ruth had a very special place deep in her heart. She'd just have to try to channel Ruth's wisdom as she had done with her father's strength and determination.

Alice knew a lot of people thought those who took their own lives were weak. But she could see her father's situation so clearly now and couldn't blame him for choosing such a drastic option. She didn't like it and it had changed the whole direction of her life, but she understood and was empathetic, especially knowing what she knew now.

Enough! she told herself. She was getting too morose. She threw back the covers and got up, causing Bill to get excited and spin around on the spot. That made her smile – the complete and utter joy about something that to her was so mundane. Oh to be like that!

Alice didn't feel it was right to finish packing before she told David she was leaving so, after taking Bill for a walk, she cleaned the already spotless house from top to bottom. She then headed out and did a larger than usual grocery shop, buying extra to take to Ballarat to get her started, before setting about filling the remainder of the day with cooking meals she could store in the freezer. If David was sad when she left – and a part of her really hoped he would be – or busy with work, he might appreciate having a stash of home-cooked meals that just needed defrosting and reheating. Alice felt bad for going back on her word about not leaving until his project was finished, and this was the only way she could make it up to him a little now.

By mid-afternoon batches of pumpkin soup, rissoles and lasagne had been divvied up and were cooling on the bench ready to go into the freezer. Lamb shanks would then go into the slow cooker for their dinner, to be accompanied by creamy mash and fresh, crisp asparagus. She'd got a bit carried away at the butcher's. The last supper, she thought at one point, cringing. Perhaps it was a bit heavy when she doubted she'd be able to eat anything, either before or after telling him. Too late now.

After the slow cooker had been filled and set going, all the dishes done and the kitchen tidied, Alice sat down to watch TV. She was worn out, but was also itching to keep moving. She looked at Bill sprawled out beside her.

'Do you fancy another walk, Bill?' she asked. The dog looked up briefly and flapped his tail once before settling back down again. If she wasn't so strung-out she would have laughed. The word 'walk' usually acted like a switch, instantly sending him into a ball of wiggling energy that she had to struggle to contain.

Alice flicked through the channels and then looked at the selections saved on the hard drive. Nothing took her fancy. She tapped her feet and picked at her nails. Bill looked up at her before giving a groan and settling back down, as if to say, 'Would you just sit still!'

By four o'clock she could no longer ignore the pile of striped PVC zip bags favoured by students and backpackers the world over that were in a pile just within sight. It was too bad if David was affronted even more by her having already packed. She needed to do something.

When she'd finished and looked at the large suitcase, carry-on bag and two huge striped bags lined up inside the spare room, she felt gloomy and sad. All she had left in the built-in wardrobe was a change of clothes for tomorrow. She had a spare bag ready for Bill's things. Then she just had to add her toothbrush and everyday toiletries to her sponge bag, put that in the top of her carry-on and she'd be set.

Fear gripped her, adding to the sadness. All she owned was right there in front of her. She swallowed back the lump pushing at her throat, determined not to give in to self-pity. She had to hold it together. David would be home soon.

Alice forced herself instead to be grateful for not being a follower of fashion or a shopaholic with piles of clothes. She also had to acknowledge her gratitude to David for insisting on a clutter-free house and their habit of going through their clothes every twelve months to discard any they didn't wear. Of course having just moved house had helped to declutter and throw out any unnecessary possessions too. It was both surprising and a little sad for Alice to see how light she would be travelling. It should take her and Lauren only a few trips to the car to pack it all in on Monday morning.

Alice heard a car pull up out the front. Her chest clenched and her heart skipped a beat and then began to race. *Well, this is it, wish me luck*, she thought as she went to meet David.

Chapter Thirty-three

Right, game face on, Alice told herself as she heard David's key in the door.

'Hi, how was it?' she asked as he put his bags down.

'Good. Okay. Same old.' He gave her the lightest and briefest of hugs, barely a hug actually, she noted – hands on the shoulders to bring her to within a few inches, peck on the cheek and then release. It was done out of habit – he said he felt icky after travelling and didn't want to subject her to any body odour. But Alice always longed for a decent hug, to breathe in his worn aroma. She loved the scent of him several hours old, as well as the fresh scent when he was just out of the shower having washed with milk and honey body wash. She watched him take off his heavy woollen coat and carefully place it on a hanger and then onto a hook on the brushed aluminium rack that looked to Alice like a deciduous tree in the middle of winter.

'How was your weekend?' he asked as he unwound his scarf and carefully tucked it over the bar of the same hanger as his coat and straightened it out neatly.

'Not much to report. I cleaned, did a heap of cooking, managed to wear Bill out with several long walks,' she said, hoping her voice didn't sound as shaky as she feared it might.

'Sounds good.'

Their interactions were sparse lately. It was as if David didn't want to hear how many jobs she hadn't been called up for. And Alice knew he was deliberately keeping the conversation away from anything personal because he didn't want tears. And she was still prone to bursting into floods of them when Ruth's name came up, or when Alice thought about all that had gone on this year and how unloving David was being. He wasn't cruel – well, she hoped he wasn't being deliberately uncaring – but he didn't seem able to cope with tears and didn't seem capable of doing anything beyond saying, 'Don't cry' and 'Please stop crying,' and looking perplexed. When they'd met he had been able to react appropriately and utter the right words. Otherwise they wouldn't be here now.

Alice closed her mouth and held her breath so she couldn't fill the empty air with the words sitting just behind her tongue: 'David, I'm leaving you. I can't do this anymore.' Oh how she wanted to get it over with. But there wasn't an easy way, was there?

'Ooh, something smells good,' he said, sniffing at the cooking smells drifting down the hall from the kitchen.

'Braised lamb shanks, mash and asparagus,' Alice said. 'You're right on time.'

'Ah, you're too good to me,' he said, following her through to the kitchen. 'Wine?' he asked, sitting down at the table.

'Yes, thanks,' she said from the kitchen bench where she was poking unnecessarily at the meat in the slow cooker so she didn't have to look at him.

'The hotel was lovely. We must go there sometime.'

'Yes, you mentioned that on the phone the other night,' she said as she dished up their meals.

She placed their plates on the table and sat down, hoping her cheeks weren't flaming quite as obviously as they felt.

'Ahh, nothing beats a home-cooked meal after travelling,' he said, picking up his cutlery. 'Thank you.'

'Good. You're welcome,' she said, attempting to smile warmly but instead thought her expression was probably more of a grimace. Her face was tight and her whole body was taut with the anticipation, the anxiety. She was beginning to get a headache – could practically feel the tension in every muscle, tendon and sinew from her shoulders, up each side of her neck to behind her ears, where a pulse twinged. She looked at her plate of food – suddenly the portion she'd served herself seemed enormous. How the hell was she to get through this? What had she been thinking? She sighed and then picked up her knife and fork.

'You sound tired. And you're quiet,' David said. 'Is everything okay?'

No. David, we need to talk. I'm leaving you. 'Just tired.' Alice cursed being too gutless and letting the perfect opportunity slip by.

'So, Tom and William say hi.'

'Oh, that's nice. How are they?'

'Hungover last time I saw them,' he said with a laugh. 'We had a bit of a big night Friday,' he added, tucking into his meal with gusto.

Alice was halfway through her meal when she realised if she held this in anymore she might just vomit. She was so tense she was having trouble swallowing and what she had managed to eat felt lodged just below her throat. She put down her knife and fork slowly and then took a deep breath, taking extra care to do it silently.

'David. I've decided to leave,' she said.

'Leave?' Confusion was etched across his face. 'Leave *me*?'

'Yes. I'm sorry, but I can't do this anymore. It's not working.'

'But you promised you wouldn't make a decision before the project has finished.' His confusion fell away and what was left was the face of a stricken, crestfallen little boy. Alice felt like reaching out to him. Until she reminded herself that he wasn't saying, 'No, don't leave me, I love you, I need you,' and was still going on about his damn project.

'I can't have this sort of upheaval at the moment. It's at a critical stage and needs all my attention and me at my best,' he said, confirming her worst thoughts.

Anger welled up, clambering over the uncomfortable mound of food in her stomach. She told herself to remain calm, and even took the time to count quickly to five before speaking. 'You and I both know there'll always be a project, David. You'll finish this one and start a new one, probably get a promotion, so I will mean even less to you than I do now.'

'Oh, come on, Alice. I'm doing this for us.'

'No, you're not. I can see that now. I just wish I'd seen it sooner.'

'Look around, Alice, I work hard so you can live in a nice house in a nice suburb.'

'It's not the house of my choice,' Alice said quietly.

'Oh come on, now you're being petty. Just because you can't get your act together and find a job you like – find *any* job for that matter – there's no need to try to bring me down.'

'That has nothing to do with it.'

'Okay,' he said, making an elaborate show of carefully placing his cutlery down on his plate and then folding his arms across his chest. 'Tell me what I've done that makes me so bad.'

'Our values are different. We clearly don't want the same things,' she said.

'Alice, you can't have everything – money without hard work. Unless you win the lottery of course ...'

'It's not about that.' *Well, it kind of is, but ...* 'You don't believe in marriage.'

'You're leaving me because I won't marry you, is that it?'

Alice gave him a look she hoped was withering.

'We'll get married, then. I didn't realise it meant so much to you,' he said, lifting his hands up and dropping them onto the table in a gesture of surrender. 'Haven't we been through this? What else?' he demanded.

Alice was seriously rattled. She felt unnerved by his calm but forceful words. But she had to say her piece. Plough on. 'You want to send our kids to childcare. As babies!'

'So? It's a good idea.'

'Well, that's where we differ. It's a clear difference in funda-mental values, David. And the fact you're all *It's my way or the highway and not up for discussion* tells me a lot, too.'

'Okay, fine, so you're leaving. Where do you think you're going to go, how do you think you're going to survive?'

Alice's anger was now dangerously close to the surface and threatening to spill over. Again she counted to five before speaking. 'I'm going to Ballarat with Lauren. She's picking me up tomorrow morning.'

Alice almost smiled with triumph at seeing the shock and unease on David's face, his sneer of you-can't-survive-without-me confidence slip away. He was so taken aback he even let out an '*Oh.*' He'd clearly thought she was throwing another spur of the moment hissy fit.

'Yes, you might think you're god's gift and tick every box, David, and maybe for someone else you will. But I can't live with how unemotional and unsupportive you are.' Alice cursed that her choice of words essentially played right into his hands. She sighed at knowing exactly what was coming next.

'Unsupportive? You're kidding, right? Who's just spent three years having you lolling about the house as a student and only working part-time? Exactly who's been paying most of the bills?'

I meant emotionally *unsupportive.* 'I've paid my fair share, David. And you just don't get it,' she said. 'Not everything is about money!' She could feel the blood burning behind her eyes as if fuelling her anger.

'Don't raise your voice to me.'

'I'll fucking well speak how I want. You don't control me anymore, David,' she said, and stood up.

'Control you? Oh dear, you really are deluded, Alice. Look, I know you've been through some stuff this year and maybe I have been working hard and haven't been quite as sensitive as you'd have hoped, but, come on, don't throw away four years.' He raised his hands, motioning for her to sit down. 'Take some time out, sure, if that's what you need.'

'You're still not hearing me, David. You never listen to me!' she said. She was holding on so tightly to the back of the chair her knuckles were white and painful. 'I'm leaving you. I'm not taking some time out. I'm not coming back. Ever. It's over.' She noticed out of the corner of her eye Bill snuggle deeper in his basket, and she felt terrible. Her raised voice must be terrifying to the dog – for all she knew he'd come out of an environment where there was domestic violence. She swallowed and forcibly regained her composure.

'Oh, Alice, don't be so melodramatic.'

'David, you can patronise me all you want, call me every name under the sun, put me down as simply being a hysterical woman, whatever makes you feel better, but the truth is, this relationship isn't working and I'm not doing it anymore. I can't be any plainer than that,' she said, picking her plate up from the table and taking it to the sink where she resisted the urge to smash it on the floor.

'Great, so I've just wasted four years of my life on you, on us? I thought we were the real deal, that we'd have kids together, be together forever.'

Well, we might have if you weren't such a self-centred arsehole. 'You want someone who won't question you, David. Who will idolise and adore you while getting little emotionally in return,' she said, turning back from the sink. 'Well, that's not me. I'm done. You'll have to find someone else to tick that particular box on your list of accomplishments going forward, or your five-year plan, or whatever it is. Because, seriously, David, that's how being with you feels – that I'm just an accessory, an accomplishment.'

'And if you were, don't you think I'd have chosen someone who'd actually accomplished something?'

'Wow. Really, David, you're going to stoop that low? Well, here's your chance to have someone who better fits your needs in that department.'

'I didn't mean …'

'I think you did. And it doesn't matter, David, all it tells me is that I've made the right decision. You're a pathetic excuse for a man and I'm actually disgusted in you right now. I never quite realised how shallow you are, but wow! There it is. I'm going to bed,' she said, wiping her hands on the tea towel. 'I'll sleep in the spare room. Come on, Bill.'

'Just where do you think you'll find somewhere to rent with a dog? And with no job?'

'Well, that's not something you need to bother yourself with, David. And I've already told you, if you were listening.'

'Do I get a say about the dog?'

'Surely you don't want him when you're barely ever here? Hell, come on, don't be stupid. You're a lot of things, but I'm hoping you're not that too.' Alice cursed her manners and almost apologised for her putdown. But she was suddenly feeling ferociously protective of Bill. David got up and picked up his own plate, just like after any meal.

'Do what you want,' he said with a weary sigh. 'I'm just really disappointed you couldn't at least keep your word and wait until the project was finished, as we agreed.'

Alice was shocked to realise she had to stop herself from rushing back to the table and picking up a wine glass and throwing it at him. Her fingers itched. *He still doesn't get it. Oh my god!* She picked up Bill's bed and started walking towards the hall, the dog by her side.

'You go. But don't think I'll be taking you back when you realise it's tough out there going it alone, Alice.'

She stopped and turned to look at him. 'I've done it before, David,' she said, and instantly regretted engaging again.

'Yes, perhaps you should be wondering what's wrong with you that you can't keep a man – or a job – instead of blaming everything on me.'

Alice continued walking, the gathering tears and the truth behind his words stinging painfully.

★

She was curled up in the bed in the spare room, which was comfortable enough but felt foreign to her. She was wide awake and tuned in to every sound in the house. Would David come knocking? She heard the door from the hall into the garage open and then the main lift-up door grind into action. She held her breath, listening. Was he leaving – taking the car out? No, she heard the large door humming closed again and no engine starting. He must have taken his bike out. God, she hoped he'd be careful in the dark. At least there might be less traffic at that time of night. She relaxed a little knowing he was gone and wouldn't be disturbing her. *But what a mess*, she thought, stretching out and putting her hands behind her head. Bill hopped up beside her and snuggled into her armpit, making Alice smile.

'We'll be okay as long as we have each other, huh, Billy boy?' she said, and reached over to ruffle his ears and then leant over further and kissed him on the head.

Chapter Thirty-four

Alice didn't think she'd ever get to sleep, but she must have because she didn't hear David return. She thought she remembered Bill stirring at some point and sitting up to attention. He must have woken when David came back into the house.

The light was only just peeping around the edges of the shutters when Bill scratched at the quilt in order to gain her attention.

'Time to get up, huh?' she said, rubbing her gritty eyes and resisting the urge to roll over. Bill whined. 'Okay, okay, you win,' she said, throwing back the covers and climbing out of bed. Her whole being ached and she felt as heavy as a lead block. It took her an age to drag on her clothes. Sitting on the edge of the bed pulling on her socks, Alice considered how she was feeling. *Okay. Just.* There was a dull pain lodged deep within her where the ache of grief resided, even more painful now than when she'd learnt of Ruth's passing. It was strange, but in one way she didn't mind the pain. It was a reminder that at least she felt *something* and wasn't cold and calculating like her mother. Even David, with all his faults, wasn't as bad as Dawn in that department, she admitted to herself. Discovering differences between herself and her mother always came as a great relief to Alice.

While working out how she was feeling, Alice realised she didn't have a fear of being alone. When she'd split from Rick, well, rather, after he had forced her from the farm, she had felt scared to be on her own, but this time it was different. She didn't think it had anything to do with Lauren taking her under her wing. Rather, she was not afraid because she was taking a stand and choosing to be happy.

Alice began to feel quite excited, just as she had leading up to moving to Melbourne with David and then starting university.

I'm good at change, she told herself.

'Who's a good boy?' she said as Bill hopped up beside her. 'You are. We're going on a little adventure with Auntie Lauren,' she said, and buried her face in his neck just behind his silky ears. He smelt a little of freshly cut grass, a smell Alice loved because it reminded her of her dad cutting the lawn every Saturday afternoon. It had been one of their special times together, keeping each other company. Her father did the mowing while Alice had sat and watched.

She checked the time. *Lauren should be here in an hour*, she thought with a little jolt of nervousness mixed with excited anticipation. Just long enough to take Bill out for a short walk, shower, have breakfast and do a quick check she hadn't forgotten anything.

Thankfully there was no sign of David when she returned to the house. She checked the garage and relaxed when she saw his car wasn't there.

In the kitchen she stared at the coffee machine over her bowl of popping rice bubbles. Dare she take it with her? She looked around and thought about all the items – the best of the best – hidden behind the gloss-white cupboard doors. No, she had enough to load into Lauren's car as it was. And, anyway, if she started going through the cupboards, where would it end? She'd want all the Le Creuset, which weighed a tonne, but it wouldn't be right for either her or David to have certain pieces and not all of them. Each piece had been carefully selected. They'd spent a fortune, but only on what they needed. Perhaps it would be different if she were going straight into a rental. She wondered how long she'd be able to stay at the house near Ballarat. Could she really keep living there for a while when Mr and Mrs Finmore returned?

Just take it one day at a time, she reminded herself. It was the same advice Ruth had given her when she'd left Hope Springs and had been feeling so overwhelmed.

She watched Bill eat. She still had to pack up his bits and pieces – she'd made a list, which was in her handbag. *Oh*, she thought, *the contact on his microchip will need updating. Where was that info?* Alice found her heart starting to race. Until she reminded herself she'd actually packed the whole file she'd set up for Bill and it was in the bottom of one of the striped bags.

Okay. What else have I forgotten? Alice was suddenly concerned she'd missed something major. She didn't want to have to ask David anything. It wasn't that she would avoid talking to him, but she didn't want him to think that she needed him or wasn't perfectly capable on her own.

Alice rinsed her bowl, spoon and mug and placed them into the dishwasher alongside David's breakfast things, feeling a pang as she thought that this would be the last time. *God, I'm being so silly*, she thought, swiping at the single tear tingling at the corner of her right eye. *They're just bowls and cutlery.*

She and David had enjoyed some good times together, of course. They had been together for four years, after all. Alice was feeling a little jittery and found herself thinking, *I'm doing the right thing, aren't I?* Then a picture of her standing alone at Ruth's funeral came into her mind. *Yes, I am.* There was really no point having a partner if they didn't provide emotional support. *Hell, Bill's more emotionally supportive than David, and he can't even speak English!* she thought, looking down at the dog who was gazing up at her adoringly, his little tail swaying gently back and forth. *Right. Enough.*

'Let's pack your things, Billy boy.'

As she shook the PVC bag out of its tight folds, Alice thought about how grateful she was for being methodical and organised. It was her default position and held her in good stead during these upheavals life seemed to send her. She must have inherited these traits from her father because neither her mother nor Olivia could organise themselves out of a paper bag even if their lives depended on it. Alice didn't know how they were still in business. She couldn't even go into the storeroom in the family shop without feeling anxious at the haphazard arrangement of stock and other goods. Speaking of which, and in the interests of dealing with things head-on, Alice sat down at the kitchen bench and took a deep breath and picked up her phone. *Right, here goes.*

'Hi, Mum.'

'Alice. What are you doing calling on a Monday? Is everything all right?'

'Well, not quite.'

'What now? What's happened?'

'I've left David.'

'What do you mean you've left David?'

Alice rolled her eyes and then closed them briefly. 'Separated, Mum, left him.' It was a huge effort to keep her tone neutral and not give in to her exasperation.

'Oh, Alice, whatever did you do something so silly for? He's a lovely young man. And so well-off.'

'I wasn't happy, Mum.'

'Oh, come on, Alice, you can't be happy all the time. Life isn't like that. You had a roof over your head and a good man with a good job. What else can you expect?'

'Honestly, Mum, I'd rather be on my own than be with someone who isn't supportive.'

'Isn't supportive? Alice, how can you possibly say such a thing after all he's done for you?'

'Emotionally supportive, Mum, he's not emotionally support-ive,' Alice said, her shoulders slumping.

'I suppose this is all about him wanting you to get a job and stick at it after wasting three years studying. Come on, Alice. What could you possibly be expecting?' she said. 'Where do you think you're going to live, anyway? You don't have a job.'

'I'm going to house sit near Ballarat for a friend.'

'Oh, Alice, don't tell me you've left David for another man.'

'No, Mum, I haven't. House sit, not move in with, Mum.'

'What friend?'

'Lauren. From uni.'

'But we don't know anything about her.'

'*You* don't need to, Mum. She's *my* friend. And she's good enough to be kind to me – unlike you.' Alice cursed the leaking of her fury.

'Now, there's no need to be contrary, Alice. Just because you can't stick at anything doesn't mean it's my fault. I hope you're not going to regret this. Poor David. Whatever must he be thinking? And we were starting to plan our trip over for Christmas. Where will you be now – Ballarat? Perhaps we should ...'

'Mum, I have no idea. That's months away. I really need to go now. And for the record, I wasn't phoning for your advice or your opinion. I just wanted to advise you of the situation and where I'll be. It wasn't an easy decision for me to leave David and this is a really difficult time. So thanks very much for your understanding.'

'But *where* will you be, exactly – what does *near Ballarat* mean? How will I contact you?'

'You have my mobile number and there's always email, Mum, that's all you need.'

'I'll need an actual address, too, Alice. Just in case.'

Alice tried to stifle her sigh. 'Get a pen, then, Mum.'

'Okay. I have a pen, Alice.'

Alice read out the address from the note she'd written for David and placed on the kitchen bench. She really hoped Dawn wouldn't decide to turn up unannounced.

'Thank you, Alice,' her mother said in a haughty tone when she'd finished. 'Now what about David?'

'What about him?'

'Well, I assume he'll be devastated.'

'He's fine, Mum, and he will continue to be fine. I have to go.'

'All right. You'd better call if you need anything,' Dawn said with all the warmth of a marble bust.

'Okay. Thanks.'

'And, Alice?'

'Yes?'

'I hope you know what you're doing and aren't going to regret this.'

'I'll be fine, Mum. And, really, it's nothing to do with you. It's my decision.'

Alice hung up and sat staring at the stone bench top, assessing how she felt. Annoyed, but otherwise all right. The conversation had gone perhaps a little better than she'd expected. Now she knew what made her mother tick she had the bar set low. Dawn might have reeled her in and kept her talking longer than she'd intended, but Alice had had the final word – and she'd been firm and kept her emotions largely in check. And now Alice refused to feel like a chastised child all over again, as she had so many other times when she and her mother had talked on the phone. She wished she'd managed to refrain from giving her mother the address, but at least she'd made the call and it was over and done with.

Alice had lined up all her bags against the wall in the hallway and had just finished a final check of the house when she heard a car pull up out the front. She opened the door and went to greet Lauren.

'Hey, how are you doing?' Lauren asked, looking into Alice's eyes after they'd hugged and said hello. 'Really?'

'A little frazzled. But, seriously, I really am okay. Come in. I'm all ready to go.'

'Look at you all organised. I would expect nothing less.'

'I hope you've got plenty of room,' Alice said.

'Hello, Bill, are you excited about going on a holiday?' Lauren said, bending down to give him a pat. 'Is this all you've got?' she said when she stood back up.

'Yep. Just my clothes, a few treasures I had from before, my computer, some files of paperwork – as Brett suggested – and Bill's stuff.'

'You don't want to take anything else?' Lauren said, making her way through the house and looking around.

Alice followed her. 'I just thought if I started I might never stop,' she said with a shrug. 'I've got copies of all the photos.'

'Well, it's not like you can't ask for something later, I suppose,' Lauren said. 'And maybe it's good to make a fresh start.'

'Hey, do you think I need sheets, pillow and a quilt? They're a bit bulky.'

'Do you want to take them? We're not short on room in the car.'

'I don't know.'

'I'd say yes if you've got a favourite pillow you won't want to live without, but other than that we've got heaps of bedding at home. Seriously.'

'I don't want to be scabbing off your parents too much.'

'If you'll be uncomfortable, Alice, then take them.'

'I think I will, actually. I've got one spare bag. See, I'm getting dithery and starting to question everything,' she said with a sigh.

'As long as you're sure about leaving, then you're fine,' Lauren said, helping Alice strip the spare bed and then fold up the sheets.

'No, *that* I am sure of.'

'Good. I don't want you having any regrets.'

'No, there'll be none of those. I'm determined.'

'Excellent.'

Soon Lauren's old Volvo station wagon was loaded, Bill buckled into his harness in his bed on the back seat, and Alice was standing at the open front door to the house wondering if she'd missed anything. She was struggling with actually pulling the door shut, closing that chapter of her life completely. Then she heard Bill whining and snapped back to attention. She looked to where Lauren was leaning against the car waiting for her, and felt a strange sense of being torn.

'What do you want to do about the house keys?' Lauren said quietly, coming back up the path towards her.

'I'll deadlock the house and then put them in the letterbox. It's locked, so they'll be safe. I just can't make myself pull the door shut and actually leave. And I don't even really like this house,' she said with a tight laugh. 'I'm certainly not going to miss living here – well, the house, that is. The suburb is nice.'

'Of course it's hard, Alice, it's literally locking yourself out of your old life and starting over. There's no going back when you do. Well, perhaps there is …'

'It's just fear of the unknown, isn't it?'

'Yep. Probably. Are you sure you have everything you think you'll need – everything?'

'Yes, I think so. I don't think that's what's stopping me.'

'Passport, bank details, passwords, Bill's vaccination and micro-chip details. Though, you could always phone the vet for that – get him scanned again to get the number. Really, all you need are your clothes, passport and bank cards.'

'Yes, you're right. I just have to do this.'

With her heart hammering against her ribs, Alice held her breath as she pulled the front door closed.

'Good on you. Come on, let's get out of here,' Lauren said, gently tugging at Alice's arm. 'Keys in the mailbox, and then we're off to start you on a new and wonderful life as a strong and independent woman,' Lauren said, linking arms with Alice.

Alice pushed the keys through the slot in the letterbox and got into Lauren's car.

'I'm not sure being given a ride and somewhere to live counts as being strong and independent,' she said as she snapped on her seatbelt.

'Ah, mere details, darling,' Lauren said as she put the car into gear, checked her mirrors and pulled slowly away from the kerb.

Goodbye house, goodbye David, Alice thought. *It was good while it lasted.*

'Why do all good things come to an end?' she asked Lauren after they'd been negotiating the traffic for a few minutes.

'Well, there's no such thing as fairy-tale happy endings,' Lauren said without missing a beat.

'Do you think I'm being unappreciative, should have stuck it out?' Alice said.

'No. What is tolerable or intolerable to you might not be to me, or vice versa. I won't judge you, Alice, I'm not your mother or your sister. Speaking of which, have you broken the news to them yet?'

'I have, actually. I rang Mum earlier.'

'How did it go?'

'As expected. A lot of "Oh Alice" and "poor David", et cetera,' Alice said, giving a fine impersonation of her mother. 'I wish you'd heard it. She really is something else.'

'It's okay, Alice, I believe you. It's like Brett said – that one of the biggest problems for victims is being believed, because they're the only ones who see what the narcissist is really like. Otherwise, most people get the charismatic, nice-as-pie façade. I get it.'

'You know, I'm not even sure I hate Mum. I think maybe I pity her. But I do hate the fact I've spent so long wanting and needing her approval, or at least not her disappointment. It's like some form of self-inflicted torture,' Alice said.

'It's good that you're starting to see things so objectively. That must help.'

'Oh, does it ever. Once you delve into it, it's actually a really fascinating subject.'

'That's the spirit. I'm so glad you're feeling okay – about everything.'

'Better than okay. Free. I gave her the address, and left it for David, but there shouldn't be any need for either of them to contact me, not for a while anyway.'

'Go, you.'

Alice stayed silent while Lauren navigated the suburban streets and got into the flow of traffic.

'Thank Christ you got away from her and left Hope Springs,' Lauren said when they were on the main road.

'That's thanks to Ruth. I wouldn't have moved to Adelaide and then met David if it weren't for her encouragement,' Alice said quietly.

'Oh god, I'm sorry, I didn't want to make you feel worse.'

'I'm fine. Really. I just miss her. And my dad. God, I can see now how hard it must have been for him to cope with Mum, especially knowing what I've learnt recently. He also had the pressure of never living up to her parents' lofty views. I don't know why, but it always felt like they thought Dad wasn't good enough for their family, their daughter. But they were only shopkeepers, for god's sake – nothing special. Not that it matters what anyone does. I miss him terribly and for years I was disappointed he didn't leave instead – and take me with him – but at last I get it. I don't see him as a coward. He was just a man who realised he'd never win and couldn't live with that uncertainty anymore. Some think people commit suicide to punish those left behind, but as I see it, they are simply doing what they believe is the only way to escape an intolerable situation. And there's no way a decision like that is the *easy* way out. Well, that's my opinion, anyway.'

Alice had had to grieve in private because of her mother's reaction to the suicide. Now she didn't tend to think about it much at all, and didn't talk about it, if she could help it – not because her mother had successfully shut her down, but because she'd come to terms with it.

'Oh, Alice, I'm so sorry.'

'No, no. I didn't mean to depress you.'

'I'm fine, it's you I'm worried about.'

'Don't be. I've had quite a while to come to terms with it. And I have.'

Alice heard a text message arrive on her phone, and she fidgeted in her seat as she tried to ignore it.

'Check it; it might be important. I don't mind,' Lauren said.

'No doubt it'll be my mother trying to have the last word,' she said as she pulled her phone from her handbag at her feet. 'It's from Frank – my step-dad. Oh, that's nice. He says, "So sorry to hear your news, Alice. I hope you're okay. Here if you need me. Lots of hugs, Frank." He's even managed to include heart and sad face emoticons. Aww, that's so nice of him,' she said, hugging her phone to her chest. She tapped out a quick thank you, added a heart and pressed *Send*.

'At least someone from over there is on your side. What about your sister? Olivia, is it?'

'Yes. Mum's little shadow and puppet.'

'Oh. Okay. Enough said.'

'Yes,' Alice said with a laugh and put her phone back into her bag.

Gradually the view from the car had changed from established suburbs to light industrial, and then to pockets of new housing developments. Now they were finally getting out into the country where the houses were further and further apart and there were swathes of green paddocks dotted with large, graceful trees.

'Bill travels well,' Lauren said, looking into the rear-vision mirror.

'Yeah, not a peep. I wasn't quite sure what to expect,' Alice said, turning to sneak a look at the dog who was fast asleep in his bed. 'But he seems fine.'

'It's not much more than an hour's drive and we're over halfway there. Not too much further.'

'I'm surprised at how quick the drive is from Melbourne. You know, I've got a sense of déjà vu,' Alice said. 'I drove with David in my car from Adelaide to Melbourne when I moved here. I sold my car soon after because we only had the one parking space with the apartment and David had a car. Actually, it feels a little odd, unsettling, not to have my own car now. It's the first time I haven't had one or access to one since I was sixteen.'

'Well, feel free to use one of Mum and Dad's whenever you want. Honestly. But I know what you mean. It's not the same. You'll feel like you've had your wings clipped. Living rural means I've always needed a car. I guess it was the same for you growing up in a small country town. We're not too far off the beaten track, but still there are no trains, taxis or buses going past the driveway every five minutes like in the city or like it was when I grew up in the English countryside.'

'I reckon city people probably take getting around easily for granted.'

'Yep. Probably. Okay, not far now,' Lauren said, slowing, indicating and taking a left-hand turn off the main highway onto a bitumen road with a single lane going in each direction.

'I caught the train out once to meet David. He was at some rah-rah, team building session for his work. I remember how Ballarat seemed to be the best of both worlds. It has the friendliness and charm of a big country town with its wide streets, but with the sophistication of the city thanks to the gorgeous shops and cafés and restaurants. And galleries full of beautiful art, and with so many stunning ornate old buildings. I loved being surrounded by all that history ... We had a ball. The Gold Museum was awesome, but a highlight for both of us was panning for gold at Sovereign Hill. I know it's a bit childish, but I loved it,' Alice said, wistfully. It was one of their best weekends together and seemed so long ago.

'I loved Sovereign Hill too. I'll bring Brett here for a weekend and we can all go. I'm sure he'd be up for it. We have pans at the house, too, and a stream, though you probably won't find any gold. I spent a whole summer panning for gold once and only found a few specs. Just enough to keep me coming back to try again.'

'Oh wow. I might give it a go. I can feel my luck changing.'

Chapter Thirty-five

'Welcome to Toilichte House. "Toilichte" is a Scots Gaelic word meaning "happy". It was already named when Mum and Dad bought it,' Lauren said as she turned off the road into the driveway beside a large white mail box with red lettering that read 'Toilichte House, C.R. & M.T. Finmore, 968 Bower Road via Ballarat' on a black wrought-iron stand with matching decorative ironwork curling around and above it.

'Wow, that's an incredible mail box. I've never seen anything like it,' Alice said. 'Are they butterflies coming out of the top?'

'They are. Isn't it stunning?' Lauren said. 'A real work of art. Apparently it was made by a local artist who's no longer around. Again, before our time.'

'And this is lovely, too,' Alice said, as they drove between two neat rows of huge pine trees. Flashes of light and dark and all shades in between struck the car like a flickering black-and-white movie. Suddenly they drove out from under the canopy into the muted, late morning light. At the same time Alice's eyes locked onto the enormous old stone house in front of them and widened in awe and slight disbelief. She forced her mouth closed, only just then realising it had dropped open. She turned to Lauren. 'You didn't tell me you lived in an historic mansion!'

'You didn't ask,' Lauren said, grinning.

'Oh my god, it's like a film set from a Jane Austen movie, or *Poldark*,' Alice said, bringing her hands to her face. 'Stop the car. I need to take a photo,' she said, rummaging in her handbag at her feet looking for her phone.

'You'll have plenty of time for that. You're going to be living here, remember,' Lauren said with a laugh. But she brought the car to a halt anyway. Alice leapt out and snapped a heap of pictures with her phone. Then she stood staring at the house, barely feeling the icy breeze racing around her. Instead she felt warmth and harmony settle within her heart. *I feel at home here already. Oh how I love old architecture*, she thought. She let out a long, contented sigh before getting back into the car.

'Lauren,' she said, staring at her friend. 'Why the hell would you ever have trouble finding inspiration for your writing? I feel inspired just looking at the place – even though I have no idea what I'm inspired about ...'

'Listen to you, you old romantic.'

'Yes, I am, and that's probably the problem,' Alice said wistfully. She could feel the weight of the last few months slipping off her shoulders.

Lauren drove around the side to the back of the large house, which looked almost as lovely as the front. 'The only mod-con we don't have is a garage attached to the house. The groceries you brought with you will be fine for a little while longer. Let's do a quick tour of the house before we unpack the car – you'll get a good idea of your bearings from upstairs.'

'Okay, sounds like a good plan,' Alice said as she got out of the car and stretched. 'Do you mind if Bill wees on the lawn?' she said, pointing to a large expanse of neat grass.

'Of course not. Where else is he to go? What else is lawn for, huh, Bill?' Lauren said, walking around to the passenger side.

'I promise I'll pick up all the poo.'

'I know you will. Hey, Alice, chill. Make yourself at home. Please.'

'How come the lawn doesn't need mowing or the roses pruning if your parents have been away for ages?' Alice said, looking around and taking in the immaculate garden of compact, bare roses near the clean edges of the lawn. 'Do you have someone do it?'

'Of course.'

'Of course,' Alice mimicked with a laugh. 'Listen to you.'

'God, that sounded arrogant, didn't it?' Lauren said. 'I didn't mean to. But Mum and Dad travel a lot and I'm usually in Melbourne, remember, so they have someone go through the mail and take care of the place. It's our neighbour, Blair. He manages the farm for Dad.'

'How much land do you have?'

'Four hundred acres, give or take.'

'Wow. That's huge.'

'Well, Dad didn't want to carve the place up, and you wouldn't believe the concessions the Australian government gives to primary producers. So, it made sense to keep it running as a farm. Come on, leave all that for now and I'll show you around,' Lauren said. 'Better, Bill?' she said to the dog, who had just trotted across the lawn and cocked his little leg against the base of a rose bush. 'Here, I'll block the door open so he can have a look around and come and find us when he's ready.'

Alice looked at the dog and hesitated. She really didn't want to let Bill out of her sight.

'Don't worry, he won't be able to go far enough to get himself into any trouble,' Lauren said, punching numbers into the keypad just inside the back door. 'The alarm code is 9-6-8-1 and then the hash key – both for arming and disarming. It's our road number plus one on the end. For now. We do change it regularly – mainly just the last digit. Okay?'

'Got it.'

'So, this is the mudroom, as we Poms call them – the back room in Aussie lingo, I guess,' Lauren said, putting her handbag on a chair beside the table. 'There's a spare loo and shower room just through there.'

As they moved through the house, Alice started to lose her bearings. The place was enormous. Her bewilderment must have shown because Lauren said, 'You won't get lost – it's not *that* big. Downstairs is the kitchen, dining room, lounge room, vestibule and Dad's office. Upstairs is pretty much the bedrooms and bathrooms. Oh, and a more casual sitting room that's used as the library.'

'How come it's toasty warm? I was expecting it to be cold inside when I saw the size of it,' Alice said.

'We don't do cold, so we certainly wouldn't expect you to. Dad asked Blair to turn the central heating and hot water service on yesterday for us.'

'Oh, thank you. I could get used to this. It's incredible,' Alice said. 'Sorry I keep going on, but it's just magnificent.'

'I know. And don't think I take it for granted. Or maybe I do, actually. It is lovely. I wasn't totally sure when we bought it. I thought Mum and Dad were mad to take it on, to be honest. It was a bit of a tip. Had been unloved and unlived in for over a decade. But they had it restored and added all the bells and whistles and creature comforts. It's the best of both worlds – old-world charm but without rattling pipes or freezing your arse off. Mum had dreams of running it as a guesthouse or wedding venue in her retirement, but she couldn't really decide. And then she got sick.'

'When we last talked about it you said she's all right now, though, didn't you?'

'Yes. Thankfully she caught the cancer early enough and has been in the clear for a couple of years. But it reminded them of how short life can be so they decided to do some travelling.'

Lauren opened a heavy wooden door and Alice stared in awe at the vast dining room full of dark antique timber furniture with curved-backed chairs upholstered in striped navy, red and white silk to match the curtains.

'What did they do before they retired? I don't think you've ever told me,' Alice said.

'Dad was in finance. Actually they both were when they met, but Mum decided to be a stay-at-home mother and then lost the corporate urge. Dad managed to time things right and we left London just before the global financial crisis. Then he had a university teaching gig – he still does a bit of teaching. Mum went back and studied sociology and still occasionally does some teaching too, just because she loves it.'

'They sound perfect,' Alice said, a little wistfully.

'Well, they're far from that, but they've always let me know they love and support me, so you can't ask for more from parents, really. Okay, so this is the front hall, or vestibule. That's the front door,' Lauren said, pointing. 'Know where you are?'

'Yep. Ooh, I can just imagine this space filled with wedding guests, photos being taken of the bride and groom and everyone up there,' Alice said, walking over to the sweeping staircase made of a dark timber with a shiny curved balustrade. The stairs were covered with a stunning navy blue runner held down by shiny brass rails.

'That's exactly what Mum said when she saw it. She fell in love with the staircase before anything else.'

'I'm not surprised,' said Alice.

'Okay, let's go upstairs.'

'I think I'd better carry you, Bill,' Alice said, looking down at the dog beside her, who seemed to be staring up at the long staircase and finding it all too much to tackle. 'Come on,' she said, picking him up.

'So this is Mum and Dad's room,' Lauren said, opening a door at the end of the landing. 'It's not the biggest, but Mum likes the view.'

'Oh, wow,' Alice said, looking around the room.

'You're really going to have to stop saying that, you sound like a broken record,' Lauren said with a laugh.

'Sorry. But, oh my. Your mum has gorgeous taste,' Alice said, taking in the antique timber suite complete with canopy. The bed was draped with mid-blue floral silk fabric and covered with an assortment of cushions.

'Mum does things the wrong way round – she chooses furnishings and then the paint colour. Dad's not into all the tizz – nor am I, really – but he'd do anything for Mum.'

'That's nice.'

'Yeah, but it's probably ruined me. Poor Brett! Mum's chosen a colour theme for each room. This is the blue room. Obviously,' Lauren said.

'I love the colour – it's almost a Wedgwood blue,' Alice said before going to the window and looking out. Just like the house, the view – of mainly trees and farmland, and blue hills far off in the distance – was breathtaking.

'We're down at the end of the hall,' Lauren said, heading out of the room and waiting with her hand on the door handle for Alice to walk out before pulling the door closed behind them.

'I'm in here,' Lauren said, opening a door to another tastefully decorated room, with walls painted in a deep aubergine. 'I give you, the purple room,' she said dramatically.

'Do you have your own en suite?' Alice asked.

'Of course. I did say Mum and Dad did a full update, didn't I? Every room has its own bathroom and walk-in robe.'

'Even mine?'

'Yes, even yours. They're small, but perfectly adequate. You're too funny, Alice. You're like a kid at Christmas.'

'I feel it.'

'You're in the green room,' Lauren said. '*Voila.*' She opened the door and stepped aside.

Alice walked inside, her mouth gaping again. The furniture was white lime washed, and the quilt and matching curtains were covered with a delicate floral pattern. Alice went and sat on the bed before her legs, which were suddenly jelly-like, let her down. She couldn't take her eyes off the wall in front of her. It was a mid-green with a slight blue-grey tinge. Eucalyptus was the best way to describe it. Suddenly her throat constricted and her eyes filled with tears.

'What is it?' Lauren said, coming over and sitting beside her. 'Are you okay? What's wrong?'

Alice shook her head, wiped the tears away and sniffed. She tried to speak, but couldn't. Lauren put her arm around her and gave her shoulder a squeeze. 'You're probably going to get sad and homesick – if only for a *feeling* of home, being settled. You're going through a major upheaval.'

Alice shook her head again and lifted her hand to point to the wall in front of her. 'That. That was my Ruth's favourite colour in the whole world,' she finally managed, tears starting to stream again.

'Oh, Alice. I'm so sorry. Let it out. Cry,' Lauren said, pulling her friend towards her.

'I miss her so much, Lauren.'

'I know you do.'

Slowly Alice pulled herself together. 'Sorry,' she said as she straightened up.

'You don't have to have this room – there are plenty more to choose from. And there's the cottage.'

'No, I like it. I think it's comforting, actually. Now I've got over the initial shock. It's such an unusual colour, I think it's meant to be. Almost like Ruth is here watching over me. As naff as that sounds.'

'It doesn't sound naff at all. You should hold onto whatever gives you comfort. And you can always change rooms later if you want.'

'Oh, Lauren, thank you for bringing me here.'

'You're going to have to stop saying that, too. It's getting embarrassing.'

'Sorry.'

'And that, Alice. You are worthy, you need to get that through your head. And, as I keep saying, you're doing us a favour agreeing to house sit for us. Come on, I want to show you the view from the end of the hall. Then you'll really get the lay of the land.'

Alice stared out at the yard dotted with a collection of large and small brick and stone outbuildings.

'Stables, random building, self-contained cottage – where we lived while doing up the house – well, paying others to do up the house – barn-now-garage, old engine room-now-general storage,' Lauren said, pointing to each building.

Alice sighed contentedly. Everything was beautiful, neat and orderly and not at all cold and minimalist. *Wow, wow, wow. How lucky am I to be here?* she thought, keeping the words to herself. She also didn't tell Lauren that she could feel her broken heart and soul slowly starting to knit back together. This place not only looked beautiful, but it *felt* beautiful too – calm and welcoming, even on a cold, grey wintry day. If there were any ghosts residing here, they were definitely at peace. Not that Alice thought she believed in ghosts. *It truly is a happy resting place*, she thought, remembering the name of the house and Rhys's comment about the meaning of Ballarat.

'Okay?' Lauren said.

'Perfect,' Alice said.

'Come on then, let's bring in your gear. Then I'm doing us a roast lamb with all the trimmings to celebrate your arrival. It's a bit of a welcome home family tradition for us.'

'That sounds wonderful.' *Could things get any better?* Alice tried not to let a stray thought of David, how he was spending his day and what he'd be eating for dinner, take hold and ruin her mood. While Lauren had her back to her, Alice literally shrugged and shook him away.

Chapter Thirty-six

Alice looked around the room, taking a moment to snuggle in under the luxurious quilt and to adjust to the soft light filtering in. She smiled at hearing Bill groan in his bed nearby, and while she couldn't see him she could picture him having a good stretch. She was pleased with how settled he seemed here. She lay on her back and stretched her arms up above her before linking her hands and putting them behind her head. It had been less than twenty-four hours, but she felt really settled here too. She'd slept the best she had in months and was completely refreshed. While she'd assured Lauren she'd make the most of her time here to get some rest, Alice felt energised – exhilarated even. Mainly about sorting out her life. And there was no better time than today to get started. She threw the covers off and got out of bed.

'No wonder you don't want to get up, Bill,' she said, marvelling yet again at how warm the thick oriental floor rug was under her feet. She pulled on the pile of warm clothes she'd left draped over the upholstered wingback chair the night before.

'No you don't, lazy bones,' she said to Bill as the dog stretched again and curled up with a front paw over his eyes. 'Yes, you're very cute,' she said, laughing at him. 'But up you get. Surely you need a wee by now,' she said as she left the room. There was a sigh behind her as Bill got up and then the click of claws as he crossed the timber between the bedroom rug and hall runner.

'Good morning,' Lauren said when Alice appeared in the kitchen. She was putting the lid on a travel mug.

'Good morning.'

'Did you sleep okay?'

'Oh my god, did I ever. I had an incredible night's sleep,' Alice said as she held the door open for Bill.

'That's fantastic.'

'I tell you, this place has the best energy. Not only a resting place, but restful too. And definitely happy!'

'That's so good to hear. So you think you'll be okay on your own? Even at night?'

'Absolutely.'

'So, no qualms?'

'Nope. Not a one.'

'I'm so relieved. I'm a bit jittery about leaving you here on your own.'

'Why, is there something you're not telling me?'

'No, of course not. But night time in a big old house can get a bit scary.'

'I'll be perfectly fine. Honest. I'll make sure all the doors are locked. And there are about a million security lights around, which will light up like a stadium if anything sets them off.'

'Are you sure you won't be lonely?'

'Honestly, Lauren, I don't think I could ever be as lonely as I've been in bad relationships,' Alice said thoughtfully and truthfully.

'I really appreciate your concern, but I am perfectly fine – better than fine, great – so, you get back to your lovely Brett and stop worrying about me.'

'So, you wouldn't mind if I left, like, now-ish?'

'Of course not. I really appreciate you driving me out and settling me in, but please don't feel you need to stay. We're all good, aren't we, Bill?' she said to the dog as he trotted in, followed by an icy blast of fresh air. 'You, mister, need to learn to use the doggy door. That's one of our tasks for today. I think we'll wait to see if the rain stops and the sun comes out before going for a walk. Say goodbye to Auntie Lauren,' Alice said.

'Bye, Bill, see you soon. Have fun,' Lauren said, squatting down and patting the dog.

'Okay, so you've got Blair's number. He won't bother you, but he'll come if you need him to – he's only a couple of miles away. You've got the keys to the cars and to the house, and you know the alarm code,' Lauren said as they walked out to the car.

'Yep. Just go, Lauren, we're perfectly fine. You've done a great job of showing me everything,' Alice said, holding the driver's door open.

'Well, I'm only a phone call or text away, too,' Lauren said, hovering.

'Got it.'

'And I can always drive back if you need me to.'

'Lauren, just get in the car and go and be with Brett,' Alice said with a laugh. 'Bill and I have got this.'

'Okay. Cool. Brett and I will see you Sunday week when we bring Mum and Dad home,' Lauren said, and gave Alice a quick hug before getting into the car.

'Yes, you will. I can't wait to meet them. And, please, double-check they're okay for me to do a welcome home roast dinner for them. I don't want them feeling jetlagged and wanting to go to sleep but having to be sociable. There'd be nothing worse than that in your own home.'

'I'm sure it'll be fine. They'll only be coming from Singapore. But I will certainly check and let you know.'

'Great. Thanks. Now, off you go,' Alice said, checking Lauren had all her limbs inside the car before closing the driver's door.

'Have fun. See you soon,' Lauren said from the open window as she drove off with a wave.

'We will. Drive safe,' Alice said, waving. She watched Lauren's car make its way down the long driveway for a few moments before the cold wind hit her.

'Right, Bill, shall we give the doggy door a go?' Alice said, leading the way into the mudroom. 'Oh, right. Well, that was easy,' she said, as Bill disappeared through the flap before she'd even had a chance to bend down to show him how it worked.

Back inside, Alice set about getting breakfast for herself and Bill. As she sat at the kitchen bench eating her bowl of muesli with Bill munching on his dry food nearby, she paused to take stock of how she felt. She'd been telling Lauren the truth. She did feel great. And inspired. As clichéd as it was, Alice really did feel that today was the first day of the rest of her life. *And I'm going to make the most of it – the day and my life!*

Having tidied the kitchen, she took her laptop and a mug of coffee and went and sat in Mr Finmore's office. Settling back into his plush, high-backed leather chair behind his antique desk, she let out a deep sigh of contentment as she looked around. *God, what a magnificent space. How lucky am I?* She gazed at the floor-to-ceiling timber bookshelves spanning an entire wall of the huge room, and could practically feel the books releasing their wisdom. She didn't feel at all sad or anxious. She felt safe, exhilarated about the future, and grateful for the opportunity to have the freedom to think and sort her head out. And for the first time in months she really felt she was close to doing just that.

She was on the cusp, standing on the edge of a fabulous new life, and shedding her old one along with all the insecurities she now knew she had within her because of her upbringing. She would fight the crippling self-doubt that was the most profound legacy from her family life, and win. Just as Lauren had said, Alice had every right to feel worthy. She'd done well at uni. That was down to her hard work and discipline, and no one could take that away from her. She'd absolutely loved studying and had proven she was good at it. She wasn't above herself, had never looked down on her mother or sister or been critical of them in her mind for anything other than their mean-spiritedness and bullying of her. Going to university had been her choice just as much as her sister had chosen not to go. Alice would not wear their insecurities any longer, now she understood them and knew their origin.

She'd tried so hard her whole life to be what her mother wanted, but she could now see how impossible that really was. No more being a square peg trying to fit herself into their perceived round hole – a space that kept changing. She'd recently realised that is what her life had been. But now she was free. She felt enormous gratitude to Brett, and in a strange way Carmel, for giving her the box of truth and taking off its lid. The world was finally hearing about the sexual abuse that perpetrators, particularly offenders who were rich, famous and powerful, had got away with for many years. Obviously Alice's experience wasn't in that league but, still, there must also be a stack of people who were in or had been in situations like she had at Gold, Taylor and Murphy …

More and more organisations will start being held to account for the trauma inflicted and the fallout … Won't they? Well, one can hope …

Alice found herself thinking about how Helen had surprised her with her kind words the other day at lunch, and smiled. They had a lot more in common than Alice had ever realised. Helen had also said everything happened for a reason. Alice was certainly starting to feel it, believe it – because here she was. But then something else Helen had said and Alice had forgotten about came back to her clearly. She'd said, 'It's one thing to learn and overcome, another to use the experience for the good of others.' *And those people wanting to hold those organisations to account will need some help … Won't they?*

The feeling inside Alice that she was really close to knowing what she wanted to do next with her life grew like an inflating balloon – bigger, bigger, bigger.

Oh. My. God. I've got it. I know what I'm going to do. Alice's heart slowed and seemed almost to stop for a second. And then it began to thud hard and fast against her ribs. *Oh wow. I am. I'm really going to do this.* Her whole being inside fluttered with excitement.

But then a twinge of apprehension seeped in. *No, go away. I can do whatever I put my mind to. There are no limits. I have nothing to prove to anyone but myself, and I'm not answerable to anyone but myself. And I can always change my mind if I choose to. But I won't. This feels right, so right.*

Alice flipped open her laptop and almost held her breath as it fired up. *If it's meant to be it will be. Show me a sign, Dad, Ruth, the universe, whatever. Am I right about this?* She tapped her fingers on the desk and then brought up the search engine and keyed in her query – *Online Law degrees Australia* – and then waited for the answers to come up. If possible, she would study online so she could work around it and not have to leave Bill alone any more than necessary.

Of the list of answers that came up, one caught her attention. The course was called Juris Doctor and the short paragraph about it told her it was designed for students who already had an undergraduate degree that wasn't Law. Perfect. She put *Juris Doctor online Australia* into the search engine.

It seemed most universities ran the course. Going through the options, Alice decided she liked the sound of the one that was offered completely online and also on-campus. The university ran a summer semester, which she could take to accelerate her progress through the three-year course. But, eek, the fees! No, she wasn't going to think about them – she'd find a way. *I'm doing this!* Thank goodness for government student loans. Maybe she could get a scholarship to help, too.

Alice trawled through page after page of information, including articles related to the questions she'd typed in: *Is a career in Law for me?* and *What students and graduates wish they'd been told before they'd embarked.* Instead of being put off, the more she read, the more she felt she'd be very well suited to the course and later a career in Law. Applications had just opened, so Alice went ahead and filled out the online form. There was no point in holding off.

So, where would she live? Would she stay in Ballarat? Why not? There was no reason not to. It was a lovely city and the surrounding area was beautiful. Returning to Melbourne would almost feel like a backwards step. Starting completely fresh appealed to her much more. She'd miss Lauren and Brett, but they'd surely visit regularly.

Perhaps Jared and Pip would visit sometime too. The three of them had kept in touch via Facebook Messenger and swapped the occasional text – mainly about office goings-on. The latest was that Carmel Gold now had two PAs catering to her every whim.

Alice would miss her occasional shopping day with Liz, Sarah and Claire, too. She hadn't heard from them and doubted she would again. She knew all too well the way friends stayed with one person or another when a couple split. The close friendship group she and Rick had shared comprised mainly of couples who were also farmers. Alice had been devastated to discover they'd all chosen to side with Rick – but not entirely shocked. The division between townies and those who worked the land was well known. She had tried to reach out to her old friends, but had been unsuccessful. This time she wouldn't make the same humiliating mistake. She'd leave it up to Liz, Sarah and Claire to decide if they wanted to stay friends with her. If so, great, and she'd welcome it, but Alice understood that their loyalties most likely remained firmly with David. After all, they were the wives of his colleagues.

Alice had never lived alone before. Now she wanted to. No, she *needed* to. The force of the realisation was intense. And then she started to feel really excited about it. Accommodation should be more affordable in Ballarat than in Melbourne, too.

She fired up one of the main real estate sites. There was a fully furnished one-bedroom unit within the budget she'd quickly done in her head. Just the one, but she refused to feel dejected. One was all she needed. And while the decor looked a little dated in the photos, it also looked clean and tidy inside and out. Again, that was all she needed. Nothing flashy. And, it had a note that pets would be considered upon request. The unit was available for signing now, and for all she knew it had been on the market for rent for ages. If she didn't get it, there would be other options – like decking out an unfurnished apartment. *There's always more than one way to skin a rabbit*, she thought, her father's well-used phrase coming to her as she clicked the link to book an appointment to view the unit. Thank goodness she still had a couple of thousand dollars tucked away, which meant she could easily pay the bond – thanks to Ruth.

Just before Alice's marriage to Rick, Ruth had made Alice promise she would always keep a small stash of money in a separate, secret, account in case she ever needed to leave in a hurry. Alice had initially been quite taken aback by her friend's negative attitude, but Ruth had hastened to add that far too many women got trapped in abusive marriages because they didn't have their own funds to provide an escape route. Having always valued Ruth's wisdom, Alice had complied. Over the years it had been hard not to give in and dip into it. But what had stopped her was the thought that to do so would be a huge betrayal to her dear friend. Feeling so secure with David, she'd almost weakened and added it to their house deposit. *Oh, Ruth, bless you …*

While nothing was set in concrete yet, Alice believed that all the pieces of the puzzle were falling into place, and everything felt right.

Next she needed a job. Full-time would be good but part-time would give her more time to study. *Okay, part-time it is. Oh, here we go,* Alice thought and almost laughed out loud at seeing a listing for an admin job in a real estate office. David was right, though, she shouldn't judge the whole industry based on one experience. Anyway, it was different now – she was only looking for a job, not a career, she thought as she filled in the details and clicked *Send.* Alice's heart slowed again and almost stopped when she scrolled further down the employment site and an admin role at a law firm came up. It was almost too perfect. *No, there's no such thing. It's my time. Everything is going to work in my favour.*

She was exhausted but felt a great sense of achievement a few hours later when she closed the laptop, pushed the chair away from the desk and leant back into it. She'd applied for the university course, a place to live, and two jobs. Now she had to wait and somehow quell the excitement raging within her. It was so strong she could barely sit still. She'd been planning a long walk, though now she felt the need to run. Hard. Thank goodness the sun had finally come out.

Chapter Thirty-seven

Alice was stunned at just how quickly and well everything had come together for her. She'd borrowed Mrs Finmore's Audi sedan, which was a little smaller than Mr Finmore's Mercedes, and had driven into Ballarat and interviewed for the real estate and law firm admin jobs, and been offered both on the spot. It had reminded her of the experience with Gold, Taylor and Murphy when she was offered the job at the end of the interview, but instead of letting it worry her, Alice had chosen to see it as a further sign that she was definitely on the right path. Obviously she'd chosen the law firm.

Her new employers were thrilled she'd applied to study Law and planned to eventually join the profession, and assured her they would be as accommodating as they possibly could when her course began. Being a small family firm, she'd met everyone at the interview – Lyn and Peter, the senior partners, their daughter Ashley, who hadn't been long out of university herself, though she was younger than Alice, and Kylie, who was the other admin assistant and also the receptionist. They all seemed down-to-earth, which Alice liked, and she felt an instant rapport with them. Ashley had even offered to mentor her. Knowing it would be a big help to have the partners' support and wisdom, and access to the office library, Alice had immediately accepted the job. She was genuinely excited about starting with them.

Even the furnished flat had turned out to be perfect – small but cosy and filled with light, and it was in a quiet street. She discovered it was a comfortable ten-minute walk from the office of Baker and Associates, and the agent agreed that because Bill was so small Alice could bring him with her. Her guess had been right; the apartment had been listed for a while. She'd snapped it up and could collect the keys and move in on Tuesday.

Alice and Frank had had a few short text conversations, but her mother and sister hadn't contacted her. They probably thought they were punishing her with their silent treatment, Alice decided. But in fact, not having to listen to their criticisms or be quizzed by them was blissful for her.

The only frustrating thing for Alice at the moment was waiting to hear if she'd been accepted into her course. It would probably be another month or so before the university sent out its offers. She wasn't really concerned – her high distinction average surely put her in good standing and everything felt too right for her not to get in. There was nothing she could do about it but wait. Thankfully she could put it out of her mind and focus on planning the welcome home dinner for Lauren's parents instead.

The day had dawned bright and sunny and Alice had jumped out of bed ready to get to work. She'd been to the farmers market the day before and bought everything she needed, and then dusted, vacuumed and cleaned the house. So, all she had to do today was cook and set the table. They would be eating at eight o'clock, which gave them plenty of time to drive to Ballarat from the airport. There would be six people for dinner. Lauren had texted a few days ago to ask if it was okay if she invited Blair, the farm manager, as well. It was fine with Alice and she liked that there would now be an even number of people around the table. She still hadn't met Blair, or even seen any sign of him around the place. Far from bothering her, she'd found she'd really enjoyed being there just with Bill. As each day had passed she'd felt more and more ready and eager to live on her own.

It was early afternoon and Alice, way ahead of schedule, was cutting up the vegetables for roasting when she thought she heard car tyres on gravel. Perhaps she'd finally meet the apparently lovely Blair before dinner after all. When she heard the front door knocker, she wiped her hands on a tea towel and went out to answer it.

'Stay,' she told Bill.

'Oh! David,' she said.

He had his hands thrust deep into the pockets of his heavy black woollen coat and seemed to be hunched against the cold wind, which hit Alice in the face.

'Alice.'

She hadn't had any contact with him since she'd left, and was both a little relieved and surprised that seeing him didn't fill her with a wave of anxiety. She felt no regret, no surge of love, no anger – strangely, no emotion whatsoever.

She walked out and pulled the door closed behind her. 'What can I do for you?'

'Wow, this is nice,' he said, giving the house an approving glance.

'It is. What do you want, David?'

'Come home, Alice,' he said. 'Enough is enough. You've made your point.'

'No, David. I wasn't making a point, as you put it. I left you. I thought I made that clear.'

'Alice, I've learnt my lesson. I'll appreciate you more, *show* my appreciation more. Come on, get your things.'

Alice remained silent, standing on the step above him with her arms folded. As she looked at him she realised how unsettled he seemed. David did not like not being in control. Alice liked seeing him that way.

'Look, I've found you a plum role at the office,' he said, reaching into his coat and bringing out a folded business-sized envelope, which he held out to her.

Alice remained motionless.

'I pulled a lot of strings to get this on the table.'

'Well, that's on you, David, because I didn't ask you to.'

'I'm not sure what else you want me to do,' he said.

'Nothing, David. I don't want you to do anything. I don't regret my decision. I know you're trying to help and you think you're doing the right thing, but we're just too different. I'm sorry.' Alice cursed the apology slipping out. Damn that habit – it was something she was determined to stop. She had nothing to apologise for.

'So you've made your decision? You're not coming back?'

'No. I'm staying right here, David.'

'Okay. Well, sign this, then. He tucked the envelope back inside his coat and pulled out another, identical, one. He pushed the unsealed flap up and extracted some printed A4 pages. He then produced his flashy stainless-steel pen and held it and the pages out to Alice.

'What's this?' she asked, nodding at the document, but otherwise remaining still. Her hands were now tucked under her armpits against the cold.

'The financial settlement – to dissolve our relationship, since you say you've made your decision.'

Alice was aghast. 'So you came here with an each-way bet? Wow, David, you really are too much. And you wonder why I left. I hope you don't, because there it is right there, in your actions today. You always want to be in control.'

'Come on, Alice,' David said. 'I've driven a long way. And it's cold. Are you at least going to ask me in? We can go through the figures.'

'No. It's not my home to invite you into. Leave the papers and I'll look at them in due course and get back to you,' she said, stretching out her hand.

He was clearly deflated as he gave them to her.

'Goodbye, David. I take it that is all. Now I really must go. I've got a lot to do.'

*

'Hi, honey, we're home,' Lauren cried, coming through the back door into the kitchen and racing over to hug Alice. 'Charles and Melissa Finmore, this is Alice,' she announced.

'Alice, it's wonderful to finally meet you,' Melissa said and Alice was surprised and pleased to be pulled into a warm hug.

'It's lovely to meet you too.'

'Hello,' Charles Finmore said, also hugging Alice. 'And this must be the handsome Bill we've heard so much about,' he said, patting the dog, who wiggled from head to wagging tail. 'Hello, there.'

'What a sweetheart,' Melissa said. 'Lauren told us how well behaved he is.'

'Yes, he's such a darling. How was the trip? I'm dying to hear all about it and see the photos,' Alice said.

'Wonderful,' Charles and Melissa said at once.

'But it's always so good to come home,' Melissa said.

'Yes, it certainly is,' said Charles. 'And you have no idea how good it is to return to a lovely home-cooked meal. Yum, roast pork. My favourite. Thank you so much, Alice. And for taking care of the house.'

'My pleasure. Thank *you* both so much.'

Alice waved to Brett, who was standing out of the way. He might have felt a bit on edge as it was his first time meeting Lauren's parents and visiting their home, but since he was smiling broadly she figured he was okay. The huge kitchen was suddenly starting to feel a little claustrophobic.

'Dinner is almost ready if you'd like to go through to the dining room,' Alice said.

'Is that code for get out of my way?' Lauren said. Alice smiled; Lauren was clearly enjoying having her parents back. Introducing them to Brett and the drive from the airport must have gone well because she was bursting with energy and her eyes were sparkling.

'Um, well …' Alice said. She felt a little uneasy being in charge of someone else's house now that the owners were here.

'We'll get out of your way, Alice. Come on, Brett, let's go and sort out the wine,' Charles said.

'Good idea. Yes, poor Alice. All this sudden commotion,' Melissa Finmore said. 'Is there anything I can do?'

'No, thank you. I'm all organised. We're just waiting on Blair.' She checked her watch. It was seven-forty.

'I told him a quarter to eight, as we agreed,' Lauren said. 'Don't worry, he's usually on time. See,' she said, as they heard the sound of the door knocker. Alice relaxed a little.

'I'll get it,' Lauren said to her mother, 'you go through and look after Brett and Dad.'

'You know, I still haven't met Blair,' Alice said. 'I was beginning to wonder if he actually exists,' she said with a laugh. She was feeling a little nervous and under pressure from the scrutiny and the bustle going on around her.

'Oh, he exists all right,' Lauren said, and practically bounced out of the room.

Alice was pleased to be on her own again, and she quickly got to grips with where she was up to. The roast pork needed to come out of the oven and rest before she brought it in to be carved at the table. She had to put the roast vegetables and steamed greens into the bowls that were warming in hot water in the sink, tip any liquid from the pork into the gravy, pour it into the jug, and she was good to go.

'Alice, this is Blair,' Lauren announced.

Alice looked up from having just finished tipping the steamed green beans into a white serving bowl. She forced her gaping mouth closed. Blair was hot! The clichéd tall, dark and handsome description didn't do him justice at all.

'Hi, Alice. Thanks so much for the invitation,' he said, stretching his hand across the bench for her to shake. *Hmm, smooth, firm grip, not too tight*, she thought, trying not to blush. 'These are for you,' he said a little shyly, holding out a small box. Alice recognised it at once – it contained handmade chocolates that she'd tasted at the Ballarat market the other day. She'd longed to buy some but had resisted. 'I brought a bigger box for everyone to share, so these are all yours,' he added, as if reading her mind. Oh god, and that deep, slightly raspy voice.

'Yes, yum. Thanks, Blair,' Lauren said, holding up another, larger box.

'That is so lovely of you. Thank you,' Alice said while thinking, *Wow, you're so lovely*. Her knees had gone weak and she was struggling to take her eyes off the dimple in his cheek. But then she reminded herself that he was most likely married. Oh well, but he was nice to look at ...

'Can I help with anything?' Blair asked, looking around.

'Um. No. I'm almost done. Oh, actually, you could take this bowl in. That would be good,' Alice said, desperate to get him away from her so she could concentrate. Everything had gone too well today for her to drop the ball now.

Around an hour later the dessert dishes had been stacked in the dishwasher and they were adjourning to the formal lounge room for coffee and sherry. They all gave Alice yet more compliments on the delicious meal, which made her glow with pleasure. She was thrilled with how well everything had gone. Not only was the meal great but the whole evening was amazing.

'Well, you can stay, Alice,' Lauren said, throwing herself onto the couch beside Brett. 'Can we keep her? Please, Mum and Dad,' she said, putting on a little-girl voice. 'You know I've always wanted a sister. And, like Brett, Alice needs a new family. Her own doesn't deserve her,' she added.

'Oh, Lauren, you really are the limit,' Charles said, but laughed. 'Seriously, though, Alice, you know you're welcome to stay as long as you like.'

'And given that we believe family doesn't necessarily need to be blood, you are welcome to become an honorary Finmore, just like Brett,' said Lauren.

'I'd love that. Thank you,' Alice said, smiling warmly. The Finmores, and Blair for that matter, seemed to be really lovely, upbeat people and she already felt part of the family. She loved the warm feeling it gave her. Her words in response seemed so banal considering what they were offering – the magnitude of which they would never really know. But what else could she say? Her heart swelled and suddenly tears were filling her eyes. She blinked them back and bit her lip to stop it quivering. Thankfully no one noticed and Alice quickly regained her composure.

'So, tell us, Alice, how have you enjoyed Ballarat?' Charles asked. 'I assume you went into town at least once in order to get everything for dinner.'

'Alice has been to Ballarat before, anyway, Dad,' Lauren cut in.

'Yes. I've had an amazing time. And, actually, about that. I have some news. I'm staying. I've got a job that I start on Monday and …'

'Good for you. What a great idea,' Charles said when Alice had finished telling them all about her course.

'I think you'll make a really good lawyer,' Brett said.

'Yes, absolutely,' said Lauren. 'I can't believe we never thought of it before.'

'It's going to be a long, slow slog. I know that, but I'm determined.'

'And that's half the battle,' Melissa said. 'You'll be fine. Do you need any furniture or anything for your new home?'

'No, thanks, the unit is fully furnished. I can't wait to show it to you. Oh, I almost forgot to tell you the best part. Bill can come to work with me if he gets along okay with the Bakers' dog, Max, who is a gorgeous black toy poodle. He's the sweetest thing. I just know Bill will love him, and vice versa. I'm going to take him in for a visit next week to see how they are together. It'll be a weight off my mind knowing he won't be sitting at home lonely all day. And the walk to and from the office will be ideal for him – for both of us. Though, he might need tiny shoes for dealing with the hot footpath during summer.'

'Aww, so cute,' Lauren said.

'Or you could be like those celebrities and put him in your handbag,' Brett said.

'True. What do you think about that, Bill?' Alice said, reaching down to pat the dog sitting on the floor beside the couch. 'It really is all just so perfect,' she added, letting out a sigh.

'We're really happy for you, Alice,' Melissa said. 'And you know where we are if you need anything.'

'Yes, anything at all,' Charles added. 'Though you seem to have thought everything through,' he said, smiling broadly.

'I hope so. But, um, I'll need a ride into Ballarat on Tuesday when I move into the unit, if that's okay.'

'Of course it is,' Melissa said.

'I need to go in, I can take you,' Blair said.

'Okay. Great. Thanks. Oh. I forgot to bring in your chocolates, Blair,' Alice said, getting up.

'I'll get them – I put them in a cupboard out of the way,' Lauren said, easing herself out of her seat. 'Can I get anyone anything else while I'm up?'

'Actually, darling, can you please bring in a jug of water and some glasses, too?' Melissa said.

There were murmurs from the others saying they were fine and nothing else was needed.

'I'll help carry,' Alice said, getting up and following Lauren out.

'I think you'll be a great lawyer, Alice, I really do. But, why? What made you decide?' Lauren asked as she leant against the bench waiting for the jug to fill from the small filter tap, which Alice had found during her stay to be very slow.

'It's because of all the stuff I've learnt about narcissism – it's bloody everywhere, and, as I know, can be very damaging! According to so many people on the online forums, the narcissists are still managing to pull the wool over the eyes of a lot of the judges and lawyers in custody battles and divorce settlements and so forth. And I keep thinking about all the people in offices working for the likes of Carmel and not getting any support from management. And then there's the online bullying and university hazing that's always in the news – don't get me started on that!' Alice was shaking a little and her heart was racing. She took a deep breath to steady herself. She probably wasn't even making sense.

'Wow, I love hearing you so fired up.'

'I am, Lauren, I really am – like I've never been before.'

'That's great. Keep going. You still haven't answered, why Law.'

'It's so hard to put succinctly. But it was remembering what Helen said that clinched it – that I should use my experience for the good of others. Narcissism's a big part of "metoo" and "timesup". Thanks to those movements, people who've been silent for years, decades, about their abuse – and about all sorts of abuse at that – are finally speaking out. The tide is turning and soon I reckon there's going to be a shitload of lawsuits. It makes sense. People are, rightfully, going to want public apologies, compensation for lost earnings and their careers being derailed, et cetera. And there's so much commentary about lawyers lacking in compassion and understanding at a human level – plenty of them are probably narcissists, too ... Anyway, I want to be one who gets it – really gets it – emotionally and mentally. Obviously, I have a long way to go, but I can see lawyers with genuine empathy becoming a crucial, and sought after, part of the healing journey for survivors. That's it, really, in a nutshell – a pretty big nutshell,' Alice concluded with a shrug.

'It makes perfect sense to me. You're going to be awesome. I'm so glad you've found your groove,' Lauren said, stacking the jug and glasses on a tray.

'Thanks. It feels right,' Alice said, carrying the box of chocolates and following Lauren back into the room.

'I still can't believe you didn't tell me about it all before now, though,' Lauren said. 'How could you have kept all that to yourself?'

'There's nothing wrong with a few secrets, Lauren,' Brett said.

Alice didn't feel the need to remind Lauren that they'd barely been in contact in the almost two weeks since she'd left Melbourne. No doubt her friend had been too distracted by Brett. She was happy for them. Everything is perfect, she thought, beaming. They were so kind and positive – there had been no negative comments, no sneers, no sarcasm, and not one huff when she had told them about her job, her new home and her course. Nothing but approval, encouragement and offers of unconditional support. It was new territory for Alice, and she liked it.

Epilogue

Around one month later.

'Alice, are you okay?' Ashley asked, sliding in the drawer of the filing cabinet.

'Sorry?' Alice said, looking up from checking her phone.

'You've been sitting there staring at your phone since I walked in.'

'Oh. Right. Sorry.'

'Don't be sorry. I'm just concerned. Has something happened? You look worried.'

'No. I've just received an email from the university and I'm too scared to look. Can you?'

'Sure,' Ashley said, holding her hand out.

Alice unlocked the phone and passed it over.

'You're in!'

'Really?'

'Yep, here, see for yourself.' She handed back the phone.

'Wow.' Alice let out a deep breath after she'd read the email through twice.

'Well done. That's great news,' Ashley said, hugging her.

She went out into the hall, leaving Alice feeling stunned. 'Dad, Mum, Kylie – Alice got into her course!' she called.

Soon everyone had crowded into the office, and they were hugging Alice and offering hearty congratulations. She'd stood up when they all came in but still hadn't said a word. *Oh my god, it's happening, it's really happening*, kept running through her head.

'You're probably a little shocked,' Lyn said.

'I am a bit, to be honest.'

'It's a big step. And after waiting so long and feeling like your whole future rests on it, finally finding out might feel a little unsettling at first,' Peter said.

Alice nodded and looked down at her phone again. 'Do you mind if I just send a couple of texts to let some friends know?'

'Of course not,' Lyn said. 'You must.'

'Yes, tell your people and shout it from the rooftops. I'm calling an early mark. It's a quarter to five, anyway,' Peter said, checking his watch.

'I'll get the champagne and glasses,' Kylie said, patting Alice on the shoulder and leaving the room.

Alice was so touched by everyone's enthusiasm she had to blink back tears as she tapped in her brief message to send to Lauren, Brett, Charles and Melissa. She felt a little knot of sadness about not texting Frank straight away, but she would not run the risk of her mother finding a way to ruin this moment.

She stared out the window where Bill and Max, now firm best friends, were pottering about the small garden together. Warmth and serenity flooded through her. At that moment Bill paused and looked up at her with his head cocked and tail wagging. Her heart surged. *I am so blessed to have you, Billy boy*, she thought.

Everything was coming together beautifully. This was the start of a whole new, exciting adventure, and she felt completely at peace about it. And strong. During the past month she'd had a few jitters about whether she was really on the right path, but there were no twinges of apprehension now. Not a one.

I'm doing this! And I'm going to be awesome!

Acknowledgements

Many thanks to:

James, Sue, Annabel, Adam, and everyone at Harlequin Australia/HarperCollins for turning my manuscripts into beautiful books and for continuing to make my dreams come true.

Editor Bernadette Foley for her kindness, generosity, valuable insights and guiding hand to bring out the best in my writing and Alice's story.

Amy Milne at AM Publicity for getting the word out, and the media outlets, bloggers, reviewers, librarians, booksellers and readers for all the amazing support. It really does mean so much to me to hear of people enjoying my stories and connecting with my characters.

And, finally, to my dear friends who provide so much love, support and encouragement – especially Mel Sabeeney, NEL, WTC and LMR. I am truly blessed to have you in my life.

Turn over for a sneak peek.

The Long Road Home

by

FIONA McCALLUM

Available April 2020

FICTION
HQ

Chapter One

It was a quarter to six when Alice's bosses closed and locked the door of the office of the law firm Baker and Associates behind her. They each gave her a hug.

'Are you sure you wouldn't like us to give you and Bill a ride or call a cab?' Peter Baker asked.

'Thank you, but we'll be perfectly fine, won't we, Billy boy?' she said, looking down to the Jack Russell sitting to attention at the end of his lead.

'Okay, if you're sure. Stay safe,' Peter said, surprising Alice with another hug. 'Congratulations again on getting into your course.'

'Yes, we're very proud of you. Walk carefully, now,' Lyn said, also hugging Alice again.

'See you tomorrow at ten at the end of the market, almost-birthday-girl,' Ashley Baker said. And Alice received another hug. She didn't think she'd enjoyed so many platonic hugs in her entire life as she had since moving to Ballarat. It was lovely.

'Yes, you will. Come on, Bill,' she said, and set off down the street with a wave of her hand. As she walked, she marvelled at having forgotten about her birthday amid the excitement.

The early evening sun and fine weather caused the Ballarat central business district streets to glow yellow around the long shadows of the old buildings. Even if it hadn't been a perfect spring evening, Alice would have still been smiling – she hadn't stopped since learning of her acceptance into the Juris Doctor postgraduate law course she'd applied for. Her smile and the warmth in her heart had been increased when her new employers, and now firm friends, had insisted on diverting the phones to message bank a few minutes early and celebrating with champagne. It was further confirmation she'd done the right thing moving to Ballarat from Melbourne when practically everything had gone wrong all at once, just a few months earlier. Now, outside in the fresh air, her legs, actually her whole being really, felt spongy, even heavy, but oddly light and buoyant all at once. She was happy. Though, a little tipsier than she'd realised.

As she walked, with Bill trotting alongside her, Alice tried not to think of the last job where she'd had after-work drinks. But there it was. At least she no longer shuddered at the thought of the awful weeks when she'd been bullied and manipulated almost to madness by the great Carmel Gold of Gold, Taylor and Murphy Real Estate.

A tiny part of Alice was angry that she'd only lasted four weeks and that Carmel had triumphed over her, but an even bigger part knew she had the nasty woman to thank for where she was now and where she was heading. *I'm going to be a lawyer, and a damned good one! I'm going to be one with heart and compassion – there for those who, like me, got bullied out of occupations because management wouldn't do the right thing and put dollars and profit and earning power ahead of common decency.* She hoped one day Carmel would get her come-uppance, though it was doubtful Alice would ever know about it. That was the frustrating thing with karma – it never quite seemed to happen right when you needed it to. Oh well. Alice wasn't a vindictive person.

Of course, that was one of the problems and how she'd come to be a survivor of Carmel at all – and the latest in a long line of executive personal assistants who had left abruptly. Well probably now maybe not even the latest – about two months had passed. For all Alice knew, more had bitten the dust. God, how much must they actually be losing in advertising, interviewing and retraining of staff ...?

The great Carmel Gold, indeed, she thought, and actually snorted aloud. And giggled, noticing the sideways look Bill gave her.

'Sorry, Billy boy, too much champagne,' she said.

Her legs were feeling heavier as she stood at the kerb waiting for the buzz and flash of green to tell her she could cross the street. She eased her scarf up and over her chin for more protection against the chilling air before bending down to give Bill a pat. He looked adoringly up at her. Alice's heart surged. He was such a darling, perfectly behaved dog and she was so lucky he'd been there at the RSPCA shelter when she and David decided they would now have a dog along with their new home and sizeable mortgage.

Oh dear. She so didn't want to think about David either. That was the champagne. A slight melancholy was laying itself over her and sapping her buoyancy and contentedness. She'd thought they'd be together forever. Well, she'd hoped.

It had taken her four years to realise how different they were and that they didn't share the same values – the import-ant ones. She'd thought he was everything her husband Rick hadn't been – driven, ambitious, city through-and-through. Alice had now realised she'd run to David from Rick and before that from her mother and family to Rick. Thankfully she'd stopped running now.

This was really the first time in her adult life Alice was truly living a life for her and really felt free at a deep, soul level. On the surface she was almost broke and living alone in a tiny one-bedroom flat in Ballarat, starting all over again at nearly thirty-one. Fear gripped her every now and then until she reminded herself that was just the lifelong conditioning of her mother – aided by her younger sister – poking through her newly acquired armour. No, she didn't need a man and there was so much more she could contribute to the world than as a wife and mother. Thank goodness she'd seen it in time. Thank goodness for Carmel Gold. *Oh dear, I must be more than a little tipsy!*

But it hadn't just been Carmel's illuminating behaviour. It had taken her dear friend from university, Brett – now her best friend Lauren's boyfriend – to open her eyes to what Carmel was doing, what she *was*, and that in turn had made Alice see the truth of her own past.

She still marvelled – more so cringed – at how similar her mother was to Carmel. Alice had spent her life seeking Dawn's love, acceptance, approval. And failed. She'd have settled for the occasional compliment and nod of approval, but even when she'd succeeded in graduating from university with stellar grades, she'd been warned not to get too above herself. Just daring to leave the tiny rural town of Hope Springs on South Australia's Eyre Penin-sula meant, they said, she thought herself 'too good for us' and 'all high and mighty'. Now she knew she really *had* spent her life striving and failing in the eyes of her family. Her father, who had been gone for around nine years, would never intentionally have made her feel like that.

She continued to miss him every single day, but she didn't blame him for resorting to suicide. She hadn't ever, but now, with what she'd learnt about narcissists, she had a new appreciation of how hard it would have been for him living with Dawn, who possessed most indicators of the personality disorder: someone who was obsessed with themselves and achieving dominance while disregarding everyone else's wellbeing. Someone who lied, cheated and manipulated in order to receive the adoration they craved. And, perhaps most difficult of all for Alice to come to grips with, was that they weren't capable of having empathy and because of this didn't care who they hurt or destroyed along the way.

Alice shuddered at wondering what gaslighting her dad might have undergone – the feeling that something felt 'off' but you weren't really sure why. Carmel Gold had managed to have Alice questioning her sanity in a matter of days and nearly sent her completely mad in just a few weeks – imagine living with it twenty-four/seven for years, decades … she was so grateful to her father for the neutralising effect he had provided for so long. If she hadn't had that she could quite easily have turned out to be the sort of person who didn't cope at all well with life – an addict or someone with other serious problems – which, apparently, was a common outcome for so many left feeling they'd never be good enough, no matter what, which was the ultimate indoctrination of a narcissist parent.

Goodness only knew what Dawn was doing to Frank – her husband of around seven years. Alice loved Frank to bits and she'd quite recently found an ally in her stepfather after tending to always hold herself back with him. She'd assumed that was because she'd already been an adult when he'd joined their family or because he hadn't had kids himself and she didn't feel he'd understand her. She'd also wondered if perhaps she'd kept him at arm's length as some sort of loyalty to her father. Now, with all she'd learnt this past year, she suspected she'd been subconsciously protecting him. If Dawn knew how much Alice liked and respected Frank, her mother might just turn on him too. Alice couldn't bear it if another kind, gentle man chose to leave her the same way her father had.

Though why did Frank stay with Dawn? She thought about it. For as long as she could remember she'd watched her mother be attentive and super friendly to guests at dinner parties and customers in the shop and then cold and critical to Alice out of sight. She'd thought for years her mother simply didn't like her. She probably didn't, but Alice now understood all too well how the narcissists could switch their charisma on and off at will. Sadly, only their victims saw the truth and were often not believed. Alice hated being referred to as a victim, but she was. But she was also a survivor. What about Frank?

Dear Frank, Alice thought, smiling, remembering how good he'd been to her when she'd made the difficult trip 'home' to her dear friend's funeral. It was probably the most time she'd ever spent alone with him – it was certainly the closest she'd ever felt to him. And she'd seen a glimmer that he too saw some of the truth of what Dawn was.

Alice shook it all aside as she pushed the button on the next pedestrian crossing and then began to cross.

But the thoughts refused to leave. She longed to tell Frank her news about being accepted into law but wasn't prepared to have her bubble burst by one of Dawn's cruel comments – one of her few certainties in life. Alice longed for the time to come when she could laugh off the things her mother and sister said and did. Better yet, shrug them off and not give them any more negative air.

But she wasn't there yet. Her mother's comments and unspoken criticisms, sneers and general lack of support still hurt Alice as much as a knife to her heart would. She knew she shouldn't seek Dawn's approval or love, but still she did to some extent. Sometimes it wasn't intentional – was just a passing comment here or there from the down-to-earth open-book Alice. But always she was swiftly reminded of her place – or lack of – in her mother's heart and affections.

Alice didn't hate her mother. Sometimes she hated what she did and how she treated her, but now with all she'd learnt about narcissism she just pitied Dawn. Apparently, the barbs and mannerisms of a narcissist were deliberate and by all accounts they weren't capable of changing because the ego was so strong that they saw nothing wrong in their behaviour. So it was those around them who had to adjust – usually by resorting to going 'no contact'. Alice wasn't there yet, either, but she felt close. She was currently avoiding her mother's calls as much as she could and keeping her responses confined to text messages. She'd been doing that for around a month. Alice wasn't sure how long she'd be able to keep it up. It was important for her healing. Unfortunately, Dawn had a knack of luring her in thanks, damn it, to all the years of conditioning, especially that family is everything! Brett was so right about *that* being a load of shit.

Alice turned into the small cul-de-sac of five updated and well-maintained single-storey brown brick units. She felt a little surge of something – she still did every time she came home after being away. Excitement? More like peace? Contentment? Maybe a mixture. Freedom? But was that really an emotion? Ah, it didn't matter. What mattered was she liked her little home.

Hello, house, she silently said as she put her key into the lock of the cream gloss painted door. As with the outside, the fully furnished inside was nothing special. It was all neutral tones, but clean and fresh. Alice longed to add some touches of her own colour to the space but was still keeping a tight rein on her spending. She probably always would – she was that sort of person. She was working full time for now, but next year she'd have to cut back her hours to fit in her study. Thank goodness she had employers keen to do everything they could to help her succeed. It would all sort itself out. It had already, she thought, as she stood at the small hall stand inside the front door.

She put her phone and keys in the wooden bowl on top and her handbag on the shelf underneath, and hung her coat and scarf on the hooks above. She'd always been tidy, but now had to be more so because the smallest thing out of place made the flat look cluttered. Bill's bed in the corner of the loungeroom was bad enough. She loved this little ritual of settling herself back in too.

Several times she'd marvelled at how, despite the whiteness around her, it didn't feel at all cold and sterile like the house she and David had bought in Melbourne had. She hadn't realised just how much she hadn't liked that place until she set foot in here for the first time. It was as if the tiny space wrapped itself around Alice in a comforting hug right when she'd needed it and had never let go. Even when she was out she often longed to be back here. For the first time in her life she was alone. Completely alone and free to make all her own decisions – not waiting for her husband Rick to come in from the paddock or the shed or David from a long day at the office or an overseas trip. If she wanted to eat a bowl of cereal for every meal for a week she could and there was no one to comment or scowl.

She knew there were times ahead when she would crave some company. And of course making all the decisions all the time might become stressful. But plenty of other people managed just fine. Alice felt a heady level of exhilaration and pride in herself that she'd finally set herself free.

Yes, I have so much to be thankful for, she thought as she took her phone over to the couch, where Bill was already in position. She smiled and gave him a pat. He loved their home too. He exuded gratitude from every pore. And every *paw*! Alice smiled and then concentrated on reading the well-wishing text messages that had come through in the last hour and a half. All the important people in her life were cheering her on: Lauren, Lauren's parents – Melissa and Charles Finmore – and Brett. Jared and Pip from Gold, Taylor and Murphy – though she felt she was losing touch with them a bit now she was living so far away.

Her heart sank a little. Frank. She brought up his name in her contacts. Her finger hovered over it for a moment. No. She'd update her online profiles instead. Put it off a little longer. Because as much as she wanted to share her news with Frank, she didn't want to with her mother. And she couldn't ask him to keep secrets from his wife. Thankfully, years ago, after complaining about how few people followed them or showed any interest at all in what they had to say on Facebook and Twitter, Dawn and Olivia had both flounced off social media for good. Alice had resisted pointing out they might have to show more of an interest in other people, but there was no telling either of them anything. Alice had blocked them both everywhere and kept an eye out in case they were still lurking about.

Alice updated her social media accounts to say she now lived in Ballarat, had been accepted to the course and worked at the law firm. It all felt good – like she really had stepped in the right direction of putting her life back together. Getting on with it. She felt a surge of pride ... until a little voice inside her said she was getting above herself. A little voice that sounded just like her mother's stern, condescending tone. *No.* What was wrong with feeling silently proud of one's achievement? She'd earnt her place fair and square – her transcript from her Arts Degree with Modern History major was full of high distinctions and distinctions. She'd worked hard to achieve them. She was not boasting. She was stating facts. If her family – or anyone else – felt uncomfortable with it, well that was their problem. Alice Hamilton was done with censoring herself to keep others happy or comfortable in their little boxes. She'd done that for most of her life and it had got her nowhere.

Nonetheless, she was pleased to see a heap of likes and comments appear. Seeing Frank's love heart emoji appear under her Facebook post twisted Alice's heart. She longed to pick up the phone and speak to him. But it must be almost dinner time in the once-Hamilton-now-Roberts household. No doubt he was being told off right then about having his head in his phone and not giving Dawn his undivided attention. Alice had actually forgotten he was on Facebook. She'd accepted his friend request years ago and had never seen him post anything, well, not that she could remember. Wary of becoming addicted and wasting too much time, she'd pulled back while at uni and not been a huge user of any social media for years. But recently she'd got more into it again in an effort to feel not quite so sad and lonely as she'd gone through the turmoil with her last job, leaving David and life in general. There were some things she absolutely loathed about it – the false façades people put up of how absolutely brilliant they and their lives were. And there were things she absolutely loved about it – posts of lost persons and pets being shared and hearing of good outcomes, people's milestones and humour and connections, and valuable information from reputable sources. Since discovering the subject of narcissism, she'd been sharing the posts of several good pages in an effort to help spread the message. She figured if everyone knew the tactics and what to look for in these horrible people, perhaps the predators might eventually be stamped out or at least neutralised. Of course, a certain level of narcissism was supposed to be useful in the world, though Alice didn't see why people couldn't be strong and assertive without being arrogant wankers, which was what she chose to call them – at least to herself.

Chapter Two

Alice's heart seemed to stop momentarily at seeing a notification of an email from David – the de facto partner she'd recently left – with the word 'Settlement' in the subject line. She held her breath as she opened it. She blinked, almost unable to believe what she was seeing. And then she let out a long sigh of relief. There was a bank receipt notification of transfer of payment – the full amount she'd asked for. She felt a pang of guilt. Not that she'd done anything wrong; she'd only asked to be compensated for what she'd actually put into the house deposit and his uni fees. She'd been fair. Ashley at work had told her she was entitled to a lot more. But Alice knew David would struggle as it was with what he had to pay her. He might even have to ask his parents – both civil servants in Sydney – to help, which would just about kill him. Money and reputation were everything to David Green. Alice had briefly thought about walking away without a cent and she might have if it hadn't been for the fact when she left she had no job and no home and very little left in her own bank account.

When she'd left, and was house-sitting for the Finmores, he'd turned up with his version of a settlement and pushed her to sign it on the spot, but she'd been rushed into signing paperwork when her marriage to Rick had ended, only realising later she'd been ripped off. She wasn't making that mistake again. The figure she'd calculated, which was almost twice David's, Ashley had put in a letter on the company letterhead and sent on Alice's behalf. This had prompted a nasty voicemail from David. The man who had always told Alice 'we don't raise our voices; we are adults and will discuss this like adults' was severely pissed off that she'd questioned him and that he might have to fork out more money. As much as Alice didn't want to hurt him – she held him no malice; they were just too different – she had herself and her future to think of. And her own pride, when it came to it. If she were to be a strong, independent woman she had to start standing up for herself to David as she had Carmel Gold. It obviously helped that she had free access to legal advice and correspondence.

She hadn't returned David's call or any of his emails, in turn pathetic and pleading, manipulative and threatening. And now, three weeks later, she'd been paid the full amount she, via Ashley, had asked for. No doubt he'd been to see his own lawyer in that time and told he was damned lucky it was only this amount. She could see it.

Alice took several deep breaths. She was now really free of David. There was no need for them ever to have contact again. How did she feel about that? Sad? Relieved? Both, but mainly sad. She'd been here a month, but suddenly felt for the first time she *was* really here. Really alone. For the rest of the time she'd been avoiding thinking too deeply about her situation, her new circumstances and the abrupt end to her life with David. The end of her Melbourne life, full stop. She'd been kept busy with getting to know Ballarat streets, learning her new job, waiting to hear about her uni application. Settling in. Now as the tears prickled painfully in her eyes, Alice realised she'd been outrunning her feelings or shoving them down inside her.

She was *scared*. Maybe David was right. How was she going to survive on her own financially? Emotionally? Physically? She'd felt abandoned by him in her time of need, when her dear friend Ruth had died suddenly and she'd had to venture back to Hope Springs alone to the funeral. Perhaps, as he'd said, she'd made a hasty decision, been too emotional at the time. Had over-thought it. Could you be both over-thinking and overly emotional at the same time? Wasn't that oxymoronic? Had she made the wrong decision after all? Tears streamed down her face and her insides felt both empty and painfully tight. Oh god. She pulled one of the cushions on the couch to her stomach and held on, hoping the lost, drowning feeling would pass. Maybe her mother was right: she shouldn't be on her own; she'd be lonely.

The tears stopped. Alice blinked. And as her vision became clear again, so did her mind. She would never forget how she'd felt that day standing in the Hope Springs cemetery, surrounded by people she knew but feeling so desolate – sadness the likes of which she hadn't felt since losing her father. She'd felt completely and utterly abandoned. No, she was just feeling sorry for herself. She was allowed such moments. But not too many or at least not for too long!

As her dear friend Lauren was always saying, she had to be kind to herself. She really had been through quite a bit recently and needed to process it in a gentle way. She wasn't selfish and calculating like her mother and sister. She was deeply emotional and super sensitive like she gathered her father must have been. If only men hadn't been raised to believe they couldn't be emotional or shed tears. Oh how she missed him. But she did also like to think she felt him with her – urging her on to find herself, find her way – and soon. Thank Christ she'd left Hope Springs and the narrow-minded family that remained there. She had David to thank, though if she hadn't had some courage of her own she would have said no.

Alice looked at the email from him again and wondered if she should respond. And say what? Thank you? On email it could sound abrupt – like she was being smug or victorious or something. She'd sleep on it.

Alice returned to the Instagram app and smiled at all the well-wishes from her friends and acquaintances. She wasn't alone.

She laughed aloud at Lauren's gif of people waving their arms and cheering. No, she wasn't alone. She might not have blood relatives she could count on, but the Finmores were amazing. If she had a car she could have driven out there for a hug. They would completely understand what she was feeling, even if she couldn't express it herself. They never said, 'Oh, Alice,' in that condescending, sneering tone her mother and Olivia used. And they certainly wouldn't tell her to pull herself together or that she was an embarrassment for being emotional. God, how had she got through her childhood and early adulthood? But at least she was tough and capable.

'Well, when I'm not blubbering like an idiot and feeling sorry for myself, huh, Bill?' she said, ruffling the ears of the dog lying beside her. He turned and licked her hand and flapped his tail. *How do people get through this stuff without a pet in their lives?* She turned back to her phone and felt both affection and apprehension – the latest comment was from Rick, her ex-husband: *Awesome news. Well done! Xx* ♥

She stared at the two Xs and the heart. Oh shit. Perhaps she shouldn't have agreed to connect again with him online after all. He'd asked after Ruth's funeral when she'd been so vulnerable, and she couldn't have said no after he'd been so good to her that day. But oh dear, maybe she'd opened up a connection better left closed. He was single again and vulnerable. So was she. Alice pressed the home key on her phone and turned it over.

As she clicked the TV on she wondered if she should, could, buy herself a house-warming-slash-celebratory gift. Nothing too expensive, but something for herself. Should she think about buying a cheap car too? She didn't like feeling she couldn't just go somewhere for a drive when she wanted to. But she reminded herself she liked the idea of an extra buffer in her bank account more. One of the Finmores was in Ballarat several times a week and their home was really the only place she couldn't easily get to in a cab. And they were only about half an hour away. Charles and Melissa had said plenty of times she was welcome to call them if she wanted to visit. They were both retired and could come and get her. And there was always their farm manager Blair.

Ah, the intriguing, very good-looking Blair … She'd met him at dinner at the Finmores' and he'd brought her in the day she moved into the flat. She'd also thought she'd seen him at the market the other day, but she could have been mistaken. She'd spent time sitting beside him in his ute and at the dinner table, but didn't know anything else about him beyond the fact he seemed friendly, was olive-skinned and muscular, judging by the bulges under the dress and polo shirts she'd so far seen him wearing. She'd had to forcibly avert her gaze from the huge brown eyes, the broad smile and the thick dark hair, which might be wavy but was kept trimmed a little too close to his head to really tell. She'd snuck more than a few covert glances at his rounded backside and long lean legs. Hmm, annoyingly, he'd piqued her curiosity and distracted her far too much, despite her telling herself he was most likely married and she was certainly not looking for a love interest anyway.

Alice brought up her favourite online homewares and gift store and clicked on throw rugs, taking the red sale signs plastered over the site as a good sign. Her mouth practically watered at seeing a magenta wool throw staring back at her. She went into her bedroom and tried to imagine it on her bed and decided it would look perfect on both the navy sofa and the grey waffle quilt cover. Did she even care if it worked or not? She almost pressed the add to cart button at thinking how much David would hate it. He was all about grey and white and everything minimal. It was still very expensive at half price, though … no, she'd sleep on that too. Your ex hating something was probably not a good enough reason to buy it.

She'd also have a look at the stores in the mall tomorrow morning while she was there with Ashley for the weekly market. After that she and Bill were being collected and going out to the Finmores' gorgeous historical home – Toilichte House, which apparently meant happy in Scots Gaelic. They were English and might or might not have Scottish heritage – she'd never asked – but the house had been already named when the Finmores bought it quite a few years back. Speaking of mouth-watering. She just loved being there. She couldn't wait to see Lauren and Brett, too. Then she'd really get stuck into her reading and get a jump on her course. She had a few months yet but figured she could never be too organised or well prepared. The challenge had her fired up. So what if she lived in a tiny rented flat? She had a wonderful life and exciting times ahead. She would make sure of it. She was in charge now. And it was going to be a great birthday.